Praise **Relentless Aaron**
and his smash-hit novels

"Relentless is VERY REAL."   —98.7 KISS FM

"A pure winner from cover to cover."
          —Courtney Carreras, *YRB* magazine on *The Last Kingpin*

"Gripping."   —*The New York Times* on *Push*

"Fascinating. Relentless has made the best out of a stretch of unpleasant time and adversity…a commendable effort."
          —Wayne Gilman, WBLS News Director on *Push*

"Relentless redefines the art of storytelling…while seamlessly capturing the truth and hard-core reality of Harlem's desperation and struggle."
          —Troy Johnson, Founder of
          the African American Literature Book Club

"Relentless is seriously getting his grind on."   —*Vibe*

"Relentless writes provocative stories that raise many questions but presents stories that everyone can relate to."
          —*Da Breakfuss Club*

"Relentless is on the forefront of a movement called street-lit."   —*Hollywood Reporter*

"One of the leaders of a 'hip hop literature' revolution."
          —*Daily News*

"Self-publishing street-lit phenomenon Aaron serves up a smoldering batch of raw erotica and criminality."
          —*Publishers Weekly*

Topless

An Urban Drama

Relentless Aaron

St. Martin's Paperbacks

This is a work of fiction. All of the characters, organizations, and events portrayed in this novel are either products of the author's imagination or are used fictitiously.

Relentless Aaron, Relentless, and *Topless* are trademarks of Relentless Content, Inc.

TOPLESS

For information address St. Martin's Press, 175 Fifth Avenue, New York, NY 10010.

ISBN: 978-0-312-94965-5

Printed in the United States of America

Relentless Content, Inc. trade paperback edition / July 2004
St. Martin's Paperbacks edition / October 2007

St. Martin's Paperbacks are published by St. Martin's Press, 175 Fifth Avenue, New York, NY 10010.

10 9 8 7 6 5 4 3 2 1

Special Dedications:

This book is inspired by all of the crazy, sexy, cool women in my life. No question: you all know who you are! To the many radio personalities throughout the country who have supported Relentless: Thank you for giving my words a voice. Bugsy, Champaign, Lenny Green, Chaila, Jeff Foxx, Talent & Bob Slade (Kiss FM/NY)...Thank you, Wendy Williams, for recognizing true talent. And a Good Morning to you, Ms. Jones & Ms. Info, New York's Dynamic Duo. Thank you to the homies in Philly; Glen Cooper, Golden Girl, Q-Deezy, Tiffany & S.O.L., Colby Cobe, Patty Jackson; in Louisiana (KVEE/) Eric.

Super Thanks to:
Southpole and Thinkking Media
Sponsors of the Relentless brand

As always:
To my friend & mentor: Johnny "Jay Dub" Williams;

Thank you to Tiny Wood: (My close friend & confidant)
To my friends at Allenwood FCI, Otisville FCI, Fort Dix FCI and other prisons throughout the country: Thank you for your support in my personal struggle to be me, to be free, and to be progressive. I hope I represent all you can be.

KEEP YOUR HEADS UP & HOLD ME DOWN!

To Julie & Family,
(I KNOW I CAN... BE WHAT I WANNA BE...
IF I WORK HARD AT IT... I'LL BE WHERE I WANNA BE!)

To Emory & Tekia Jones:
Can you believe this??? Spit in the wind, and you might create a thunderstorm! (D.B.D.) Thank you for your support.

To Michael Shapiro; to Karen & Eric @ **A&B Books**; to Nati @ **African World Books**; to Carol & Brenda (**C&B Books**)...Thank you, ladies. To my inner circle: Curt Southerland, Darryl, Adianna, DTG, Joanie, Lance, Lou, Rick, Demetrius, Angel, Renee Mc Rae... to Danica, thank you for helping with our street grind! You go, girl!

To Makeda Smith at **Jazzmyne Public Relations**, my publicist, banker, diva & therapist... thank you ever so much. And stay away from the matched! Special thanks to **Stephanie Renee**, the mogul from Philly... Naiim, Mr. Perkins, Mr. Reeves, Petee (thanks for the street hustle), Ruth, **Courtney Carreras/YRB Mag** (you wizard, you). And how could I ever forget you, Renee. You're on fire and I'm burning up! Thanks to Earl Cox.

Thank you all.

To the many bookstores and websites and others around the world who carry Relentless Content: Thank you for affording me space on your shelves. I intend to cause a major increase to your bottom line.

Vinny, Shetalia, A.J., T & Dez:
you're in the house now, girls.
Represent!

Thank you, Joanie & Lorna...
To A.J. I want to say thank you for letting me stalk you!

And, last but not least,
to my earth, moon and star:
Paulette, DeWitt & Fortune
Love you guys to death.

Foreword

On the Southern end of Mount Vernon there was a bar known as *Gilmore's*. It was a family-run hole in the wall that was addictive to both men and women for different as well as similar reasons. The club was an attraction that sucked in all walks of life through its doors; men who had discretionary income; men whose pastime and passion was to meet, gaze at, and even touch the young, sexy and sometimes desperate women who worked there; women who didn't mind taking off their clothes for a few bucks.

Something of a flesh-fest, this money machine continued to crank on for a few decades, trouble-free, from 12 noon, until 4 AM, rain or shine, weekday, weekend, or holiday. Put simply, Gilmore's had a supply and demand that seemed to have no apparent end.

Not until the investigation of a dancer's murder has the whole world of Gilmore's been exposed. Not until now has the story of this empire been brought to the surface for all the world to see in all of its colorful detail, by the **only** person who was there, both inside and out.

As much as this is a story of success, of greed and of lust, it is also a crisp, concise, tell-all memoir like none other. *Welcome to Gilmore's, the Leader in Adult Entertainment...*

PART ONE

CHAPTER ONE

Valerie's Pleasing Arrival

Air Canada's flight 204 glided in and down onto the runway of New York's LaGuardia Airport. The great white commercial bird was then taxied to a corridor that had been extended, awaiting the arrival. It was 8:05am, and the blur of passengers that scurried off of the plane assumed the role; intentionally forming a human chain that marched onward towards the baggage claim area.

Fine and curvaceous, Valerie could've been a stewardess, standing so erect and up close to the conveyor belt, except that the bright red leather outfit she had on was a dead give-away that she was more of a hot girl than a stewardess on the Air Canada payroll. Valerie was indeed a flight 204 passenger, and she carried herself confidently, as though she'd been through this sort of thing hundreds of times before. And although she traveled light, and she had little luggage to retrieve, you could never tell that this woman was burdened with a ocean's worth of concern. She was going through it, mentally replaying all of the drama of the days past. Yet in the meantime she was also inspired by a sort of soundtrack playing underneath all of her thoughts. This had to be her favorite song these days—she wasn't sure of the group; some name with the word *Soul* in it. That, and she knew they were from Europe somewhere.

"Keep on movin'
Keep on movin', don't stop, no . . .
Keep on movin'."

For the moment, these words and their melody inspired Valerie, and virtually *carried* her through these trying times. They even somehow escorted her into her new independence here in the United States.

For now there were two shoulder bags she was looking for, and although they had not yet weaved their way around the conveyor belt, Valerie could at least imagine them coming. So far, no luggage had appeared on the expansive maze of stainless steel and rubber. But, silly as it seemed, the damned thing still managed to entertain the 90-something idle travelers with its harmonious squeaks and hums, merely building their further anticipation. This even served as the appropriate time for ticket holders to conclude those conversations which the flight had encouraged. For Valerie, however, being back on solid ground hadn't yet settled her. She was still on the plane; still in the sky; still rushing through Toronto's Pearson Airport, or of course, still making that great escape from her obsessive ex-boyfriend.

A wall of limo drivers and cabbies stood behind 204's passengers, most of them holding signs and shouting last names. Meanwhile, there were those warm and hearty kisses, embraces amongst family and friends, and of course, who could do without the impersonal drone of announcements overhead, queuing the dozens of arrivals and departures. All of this organized confusion was just a reminder that one person's flight, or ticket, or luggage, was but one irrelevant, infinitesimal and unaccountable part of a much bigger picture; the wide, wide world of air travel.

With a heavy emphasis on the illusion of luggage on the conveyor belt, Valerie had no way of knowing how she unconsciously attracted a lion's share of attention. And those tiny beads of perspiration on her brow and temple were likely seen as her radiance. Her nervousness, such as her toe tapping the floor, was nothing more than the preliminary attempts at some dance. And, yes, there was no doubt that she even earned a fan or two with those authentic Caribbean attributes. However, the events of the past month were nothing to be romantic about. In fact they were nothing short of one big nightmare.

"It was *forged*," she told herself, determined to believe the naked truth. It was hard *enough* to love a white man, with all of the negative energy that accompanied the relationship. But now, Valerie had to do whatever she could just to erase him from her mind. It wasn't easy.

"Did I shack up with Richard to escape Barbados? Did I do it just to get off of the island and experience the states?" Valerie could almost hear her native dialect as she was questioning herself, providing her own brand of therapy. Valerie thought about how "all the other girls were doing it." That, in her mind, would sum up the colony of relationships that mixed black women and Canadian travelers. The presence of white, male Canadian travelers was suddenly more than just a fad. Or so it seemed. And Valerie was somewhat aware of the trend, where for more than five decades black women would be easily swept up and out of the naivety of their culture and heritage in Barbados. The movement created thousands of interracial relationships that perpetuated the red-leaf country. However, standing alone and unaccompanied in this mammoth New York airport, Valerie now felt a sense of accomplishment. As if she had weathered certain storms. First, she was able to escape from under the umbrella of her family, to whom she vowed to return as an established restaurant owner. Second, she cut away from the migration of interracial couples in Canada, and finally she was able to get away from Richard. Angry, obsessed Richard.

He expected Valerie to be the beginning and the end of his day, as well as every waking moment in between.

"You're not to leave the condo . . . "

"Stay off of the phone . . . " and then of course there was the statement that she hated to love, *"Here's some spending money. Buy something nice for yourself."* As if that alone would resolve all of their relationship issues. These were issues that, while they were ongoing, Valerie didn't really understand. She couldn't make two cents out of what was happening to her. Yet, her intuition had awakened her from that living coma. The aggravation and escalation of events had pushed her to leave. What

made her escape all the more eventful was how Richard didn't expect it. Valerie had been quietly stashing a few dollars here and there like a squirrel. She didn't ever guess that she'd have to use the money for a getaway, but when that incident . . . when he . . .

She just hated to think about what Richard did to her because she'd get mad. She wasn't a hateful person. But when Valerie was in the mood, on the flight at least, she found herself smiling to herself when envisioning his face. *Wow. When he finds my stuff missing? He's gonna blow his top.* And the thought made her smile even more.

Valerie was somewhat mumbling to herself as she said, *"At least I never . . ."* She snickered at the thought of him asking her to— *"The nerve of him!"* with a contemptuous heart and mind.

Still looking for her 2 purple shoulder bags, Valerie found herself lost in the gaps that separated so many bags and suitcases as they approached. And while passengers converged closer to the conveyor belts, awaiting their claims, Valerie's bags appeared from around the bend. She recognized them the moment she saw his face. *Richard!* He was lying across the top of the luggage, *with his head perched in his palm?* She figured that his obsession had driven him to hop into the baggage port of the plane and survive the flight just to emerge victorious . . . and what—*he's singing? What the—*

> *"It's sad. So sad.*
> *It's a sad, sad situation.*
> *And it's growing more and more absurd."*

Of course Richard's obsession with all-things-Elton John would also come to haunt her. But just as quickly as Valerie was jolted by the mirage, so too did she instantly shake it. Thank God it was a figment of her imagination! The encounter caught her off guard, like a sudden chill. And yet, as she stretched for her bags, she couldn't help but to look to her right and left to be certain that—who was she kidding? She only hoped that no one discovered her moment of imaginary turmoil.

In the meantime, one bag was a little bigger than the other, but she managed. With one at her side and one over her shoulder, she approached the exit. An elderly man waited guard, checking baggage claim slips to correspond with the tags that hung from luggage handles. The clerk didn't appear to be alert enough to stop everyone. He was merely a deterrent, Valerie was saavy enough to guess. But just the same, she didn't anticipate that she'd have much of a problem, even these days with how travelers who didn't appear to be American were scrutinized more than usual. Even when Murphy (of Murphy's Law fame) came along at various instances, things always managed to happen her way . . . *for* her, usually protecting her like a watchful guardian. When danger lurked, she came out ahead even if it was a long and painful victory. Perhaps this would always be the case.

Outside of LaGuardia's arrival terminal, two baggage handlers almost bumped heads trying to assist the gorgeous traveler. And since the threat in the eyes of the larger man was sharp enough to stab someone, the smaller skycap backed down with little apprehension.

With not a care in the world (or so it seemed), all 5 feet, 6 inches of Valerie stood there in the broad daylight, apparently unaffected by the brisk autumn chill. Her presence on the walkway was as obvious as a fashion billboard. And it might've been a bit much for the baggage handler since his eyes were bugging out, looking hard at the package, this Caribbean woman in the tight leather jacket and pantsuit. The jacket hugged her waist snug and pants were tapered smoothly against her shapely hips, legs and calves.

Screech!

A cab pulled to a sudden halt and just about frightened her to death just to win the fare. It took a few seconds, but Valerie caught her breath and exhaled. Her sharp eyes broadcasted a twinge of discomfort to the apologetic driver through his windshield. But then she found some compassion since this wasn't the first time guys acted the fool in her midst. If she gave any serious thought to it, she'd know these incidents to be frequent ones, from the moment she stepped out of the house. And yet, it was just as easy for Valerie to be naïve towards it all. She didn't see herself as a walking attraction who kept others spellbound.

And now the cabbie was trying not to stare at Valerie, still with some uneasiness in his expression as he strutted around the vehicle to unhand Valerie's luggage from the skycap. Into the trunk it went. In the meantime, the skycap nearly tripped as he assisted the passenger into the rear door of the cab.

As she got comfortable in her seat, Valerie noticed the driver adjusting his rearview mirror.

Valerie was forthright as she spoke.

"Take me to the Bronx, please."

"Address, ma'am?" asked the cabbie in a rich Nigerian accent.

"Yes . . . of course." Valerie's voice was just as rich with island flavor. She went into her purse and pulled out a note. "Dyre Avenue, please." The agreement in her eyes was direct, and still she was seductive as she urged the driver to move on.

There was an abrupt **knock, knock, knock** at the rear window, with a sound and vibration inches from Valerie's face.

The Nigerian stalled on the brake with his intentions only inches from the accelerator.

"Should I?" the cabbie asked, wanting to pull off.

"Wait. It's okay." Valerie recognized the man as her neighbor from an adjacent seat on the flight. She pressed the button to lower the window. The aroma of flowers breezed in. *For me?*

"Hi. I'm the guy in the next seat . . . I mean, from the flight." He was uncertain, as if he was asking for forgiveness and sympathy in the same breath. Sure enough, the passenger-next-door offered the quick bouquet through the 4-inch opening of the window. "These are . . . I got these from . . . for you."

Valerie could sense a number of eyes on this little interaction; the skycap, the cabbie.

"Oh. For me? Well, thank you . . . you're so *sweet*." Valerie calmed the guy within a matter of seconds with her generous Caribbean karma. It was an unpracticed resource that was once captivating to other men, but now that she was a free woman again she was determined to mold her 22 years of island-girl characteristics into a future undenied.

The fellow passenger blushed, and to save face, Valerie interjected, ready to put an end to any more unnecessary conversation. The guy was already beet-red and had that hunger in his eyes, like he was ready to talk her to death.

With a quaint smile she said, "Have a nice day." Up went

the window. The driver acted quickly on the cue, leaving the man frozen with awe and a few shades paler.

Not even so much as an over-the-shoulder peek, Valerie was now focused on the future. School. Money. A *real* life. No more obsessed boyfriends. No more coincidental relationships. Valerie was ready for life and destiny.

CHAPTER TWO

Mechelle's Bus Trip

Mechelle Ramirez spent 2 years studying at Tuskegee University in Alabama. Her major was Business Economics, but she also majored in socializing and earned her popularity as a cheerleader for the school's football team. Instead of finding comfort with one of the many team players that propositioned her, Mechelle went against the grain and found most of her comfort and serenity with a classmate far removed from the sports arena.

Denworth was soft. Except, he had nerve enough to tell Mechelle about his homosexual tendencies. It took Mechelle some time, but with those ass-swishing talents that she perfected on the 50 yard line, with some teasing and tickling in the right places, and not to mention one particular unsolicited kiss that she planted on his lips, Denworth was a changed man. He was putty in her hands, catering to her every whim. The chemistry between the two also made moving into his family-financed apartment a convenient reality, saving her both money and the headache of not having a trustworthy dick to sit on when she needed it. Sure, theirs was a shallow arrangement from the start—the couple survived two abortions (she already had 3 others in high school and again during her first year of college)—but now that school was over for Mechelle there was a do-or-die issue of the future to discuss. Eventually Mechelle and Denworth agreed to marriage. The plan was simple. In two more years, once Denworth completed his full 4-year degree, the two would move into their own house and live happily ever after. But of course if the world took a gamble on whimsical college dreams, then every member of Generation X would require their very own survival guide. Maybe even a subscription to *Reality Check Magazine*.

In the meantime, since Mechelle was done with school, she decided to visit her immediate family back in Brooklyn, New York. There were a couple months of shameless sex, and then in December she took off to help out her twin sister with the children. Maybe she'd even find a temporary job during the 2 years that Denworth needed to complete his master's in Political Science.

It was days before Christmas when Mechelle found herself in a daze, looking out of the smudge-ridden window at the middle of the New York-bound Greyhound bus. Mechelle thought about the engagement. It was real, but then again there wasn't a ring to bind the commitment. There was no date set for the wedding. And now (although she loved Denworth as far as she could see), *no sex for 24 long months?* Quiet as it was kept, Mechelle had been looking forward to the break from that good old southern hospitality of Alabama. She was born with a New York state of mind, and she was already savoring the taste of the city in the salted pretzel and ginger ale that she bought at the bus station.

The trip to New York would be tedious. But Mechelle had no alternative. To hop on a plane would be too expensive. So she purchased a ticket for $75.00 and counted ten stops before she fell asleep. It was sometime later when her journey took a turn for the worst. Deep into a dream which had her pregnant by Denworth, a noise under the bus woke Mechelle at a stop somewhere in North Carolina. She seized the opportunity and rushed up the aisle and into the bus station to use the ladies' room. What Mechelle didn't know was that the bus had already been stationary for 15 minutes. The stop was scheduled for a 20 minute wait. The driver was nowhere in sight and the few passengers who were on the bus were asleep. So nobody knew that Mechelle had stepped off. And that wasn't anyone's responsibility but hers anyhow.

Waiting to use the stall, Mechelle twisted her nose slightly to avoid the stench of cheap perfume and disinfectant. Finally, she slipped into the only stall, shed her shorts to her ankles and spelled relief. Mechelle didn't often have the opportunity to share this idiosyncrasy with others. Maybe Denworth noticed one or two times; or maybe not. However, nobody would understand what a joy Mechelle experienced when she urinated. Without perversion, squatting and discharging her steamy fluid was somehow liberating. It had always felt this way; orgasmic. And here in North Carolina, during her few minutes in the bus terminal, and even with the surroundings being somewhat rundown, the experience for Mechelle was no different. She could take this very activity anywhere and it would still feel very personal, and very intimate for her. It was even more of a thrill now, considering she had a couple of hours' worth of juice to discharge.

By the time Mechelle emerged from her very climactic encounter, the bus was pulling off.

"Shit! Shit! *Shit!!!* My stuff is on that bus!" Mechelle screamed at nobody in particular. The driver was apparently more concerned with his schedule than he was with counting his passengers.

At 8:55 the station's manager completed his duties and stood by the double glass doors with keys in hand. He watched as the woman raced past him in the direction of the bus, left amidst its exhaust fumes. He watched as she ran like a gazelle with arms waving frantically, and then as she cursed the world for her own shortcomings.

"Humph . . . ya lives and ya learns," said the older white man. And despite the woman's distress he still turned his key to lock the door. Not to mention the way his eyes cut with prejudice as he flipped the CLOSED sign and pulled the shade.

Abandoned

It was 9 PM when the bearded old fart turned on his heel, no less removing himself from the dilemma, content that the locked door and the "closed" sign would answer the young lady's inevitable questions. Mechelle was indeed that troubled woman returning to the entrance after a failed attempt to chase after "*that damned Greyhound.*" She even made a desperate, last minute attempt to climb up onto a trash can, hoping that someone on the bus would notice her, and she fell on her ass. Teary eyed, with no other options, she came to face the locked door of the ticket office, slash, convenience store.

Some convenience you are, thought Mechelle, swearing that the lights had just been switched off on her trek back toward the station entrance. The lights were dim now, but she knew for *sure* that the scruffy old man was still inside. Instead of becoming anal retentive (Mechelle's definition of her worst attitude) and smashing the glass, she counted to ten, settled herself, and indulged in a much needed sigh. The greater reality here was: it was cold, dark, and Mechelle was stranded at this unattended bus terminal in what seemed like the middle of nowhere. She was left to assume a fetal position on an old marked up, splintered bench, clenching her legs, and doing her best to maintain warmth. Other than the moon, the only light came from a modern Coke machine which seemed like such an artificial part of this deathly-isolated stretch of dirt road. So alone and feeling abandoned as hell, Mechelle finally let out some tears of frustration. She was thinking about her 4 heavy suitcases left on the bus. Worse than that, she reached in the pockets of her shorts only to find thirteen dollars and twelve cents. More tears. She still had her ticket stubs, praying that the next bus driver would understand.

And when was that damned bus coming anyway?

At 5'4", Mechelle Ramirez was considered short, as compared to the runway models that she so admired. However, she had everything else going for her. Everything else that a so-called fashion model might possess. She had her velvety-smooth amber skin and a set of alluring bedroom eyes. Besides, Mechelle's talent spoke so much louder than her appealing looks. She had a wizard's relentless wit and a chameleon's skill of adjusting to her environment. In one instance, while using proper etiquette and her best manners, Mechelle managed to have her English Literature professor fix her grade. According to his records, her attendance was lacking. And so he indicated that she'd receive a C for the semester. But Mechelle wasn't having that. Calling him all kinds of mother-fuckers on the way to his office, she somehow contained her anger and instead used her God-givens. Her persuasion was best seated in her intellect, humor, and that snappy tongue to match her sharp looks. All of those combined resources could be dangerous if she used them as weapons. But for the professor, she didn't have to lay it on heavy. Of course she could've fed into his advances and taken the easy way to the grade. However, Mechelle took the high road and simply "convinced" him that he was wrong.

Nevertheless, A+ grades, coupled with all the wit and shapeliness in the world, wouldn't be able to help Mechelle now. Nor would it keep her from weeping. Worse times had prepared her for situations like these. But feeling abandoned, stranded and alone was just a bit much for her to carry. For the moment it just seemed easier to cry than ever before.

Next to where Mechelle was curled up, there was a window with a bus schedule posted inside. The hue of light from the soda machine was enough for her to recognize the arrival and departure times for Greyhound. And according to the schedule there would not be another bus coming through for 11 hours. *Eleven hours!*

Nine AM. Just the thought of that caused Mechelle a great sigh. At least she knew when the next bus was coming. At least she could anticipate the next time that she'd see people, and she never thought there'd be such a need or desire to see them.

Growing drowsy, lonely, and already drained from crying, Mechelle made the best of the idle time by dreaming, reminiscing and planning. It had been easy to just lay at home while Denworth kissed her ass to the limit. Literally. After all, Den did love her more than life itself. But the distance, whether on the bus, or now at the bus station, had Mechelle thinking. She began to realize that she loved Den more for the security that he offered than for his love; she loved his servitude and financial support more than she liked his company. No, she didn't love just for the sake of loving him, or any of that unconditional banter that lovers claimed. No. Essentially, what Mechelle was doing was *playing* Denworth. She played him and was feeling quite proud about it, too. Mechelle recalled how Denworth was that class geek who knew it all. His pants were always too short. His eyeglasses were outlined by thick frames, and his hair was always glossy from so much curl activator. Perhaps his initial appearance was the aftermath of growing up in a female dominated, fatherless environment. But Mechelle loved Den in such a routine way. Always the missionary position. And the *first* time they did it? She laid in his bed while he serviced *her*. *He* was the bitch. Freshening up in the bathroom; changing into something comfortable, and then when he came out (checking first to see if the lights were out or if she was looking), he shot across the floor like a burning flame in a pair of black silk shorts that were at least one size too small. On top of that scared-shit move, he slid into the bed and underneath the covers as if to hide himself. After 5 or 10 minutes of his bullshit conversation, obviously nervous as a bowl of Rice Krispies, Mechelle thought up her own desperate humor.

"What are we gonna do? Watch TV or fuck?" She took a deep breath and released a wearied "oh *brother*." Then she reached for his hand and guided it to familiar areas of her body that aroused her most. If not for his excessive perspiration his erection wouldn't make it through her doors since, 1) Mechelle just wasn't excited enough to take him with natural juices, and 2) there was no way she was gonna suck his dick since she hardly knew him. As their encounter progressed, Mechelle began to find fun in teaching him. He began to catch on, despite an onslaught of amateur licking, kissing, touching and caressing, until the idea of teaching a virgin finally excited Mechelle to the point of climax. An infrequent event for her.

And now, nearly two years later, these thoughts somehow kept Mechelle warmer than she should have been. The tears had soaked away, now replaced with goose bumps on her arms and legs. In the meantime she was passing away the hours, consumed in her own tight embrace and trivial memories, with the night slowly drifting by.

CHAPTER THREE

Debbie's Chicago Tragedy

For 7 weeks, Debbie Rose was attached to her computer, as if it was her personal life support system. Her interactions with David, a virtual boyfriend over the Internet, had all of the elements of a long distance relationship. He lived in New York, and Debbie was from Chicago's south side where even the poverty-stricken still enjoyed the luxury of one and two-family houses. Debbie's mom was one of those home renters who would soon be able to purchase and retain equity in her home. Then she could finally begin to build a nest egg for her family. It was hard to accomplish average progress as a single mom, struggling up the workforce ladder. Sometimes an affair with a new boyfriend, or some new sugar daddy, would assist her with that extra push. But when those relationships faltered it felt as though she had taken one step forward in order to take two steps back.

The one blessing that Debbie's mom had going for her was her job as assistant to Mr. Felton, one of Chicago's most aspiring Black entrepreneurs. Thanks to his unconditional helping hand, Ms. Rose was secure even in her times of grief. On the days when Debbie or her brother Raymond were home sick from school, Ms. Rose was given the day off with pay. There were two or three instances when Ms. Rose's car broke down, to the point that Mr. Felton made it his obligation to talk to a friend who owned a dealership. By her boss's suggestion, Ms. Rose visited this same dealership and she was suddenly offered a deal that she couldn't refuse; a new car with a $3,000 discount, not to mention the monthly payments that didn't begin until 3 months after she drove the car off of the lot. Talk about a deal!

Just when it seemed that everything was going Mama's way, the Rose family experienced a big family tragedy. Debbie, Raymond and Mama Rose had been quietly enjoying the Jamie Foxx show when a crash sounded. It was so unexpected that it almost blended in with the television, like some sound effect. But in fact, broken glass littered the couch and Debbie's brother instantly fell over to the floor. Seconds later, it was clear that a bullet had ripped through the back of young Raymond's head. A stray bullet had shattered the living room window and took his life. Just like that. 13 years old.

This was extremely traumatic for the Rose family. Reducing the Rose family to a simple mother and daughter relationship.

Ms. Rose cried nightly for more than 2 months. And yet, again her boss supported her leave of absence. Paying her salary the whole way through, as well as Raymond's funeral arrangements. In a note that accompanied a huge boxed delivery, Mr. Felton wrote: *This could never replace the fond memories that you will always have for your son. But maybe this kind gesture will be accepted as a token of my condolences.*

The note was attached to a brand-new Pentium computer.

Thanks to Mr. Felton's generosity, Debbie began to learn more and more about the new technology, vowing to one day move her mother out of the urban decay that had caused their family so much heartache. In time, Debbie's favorite place to be was on the Internet. The salary from her part time job at McDonald's supplemented this extracurricular activity. As a cashier, Debbie would outlast all the other teenagers who worked various jobs. One after another they were fired because of stealing, giving extras to friends (an extra burger here, an extra shake there) or constant lateness. She wondered if this was only happening where *she* worked.

Debbie's take-home pay was usually about $190 a week after taxes. She'd pay $5 towards her $20 monthly internet service fee, $30 to the hairdresser for her Saturday afternoon ritual and she'd give $75 to her mom to help with the bills. She had already contributed what she considered her life savings to pay for the circumstances surrounding Raymond's funeral.

"WELCOME!"

Debbie's online service was easy to use and she caught on quickly to the routine sign-on. She clicked the icon that flashed on her monitor, signifying "No" that she didn't want what was being sold in the pop-up advertisement. Next, a mini news flash appeared in the screen.

"YOU'VE GOT MAIL!" The computer's voice bellowed audibly through the attached speakers. Debbie smiled since she was expecting an e-mail from David, her New York Internet love interest. She clicked the mailbox icon and waded through the junk mail until she hit pay dirt. She opened the mail that was titled "BOY WANTS GIRL". That was David's wit. And it made Debbie curious and anxious to always hurry to her e-mail. David was always saying something new and exciting. Everything he did seemed to make her day.

"HI DEBBIE! *I felt in the mood for some poetry today . . . Hope it hits your spot . . .* " As Debbie scrolled down the message, she focused her glossy eyes on David's beautiful words:

> *If love is a flower, then you are its seed*
> *If love is the power, you are its energy;*
> *Love will not perish, so long as you give*
> *Because your love I'll cherish, for as long as I live.*

The message ended with David's usual signature send-off . . .

> *"Stay Sweet, Black Queen."*

Debbie was awestruck by the words in the poem, but his signature always felt like a killjoy. Ever since she could remember, her Camay skin color had a negative stigma in the Black community. There was always the presumption that she thought herself above being Black, just because she liked to walk with her head up. But it was never that way. They quipped that she was "acting white," because she had proper dialect or that she spent so much time at the computer. Wrong again. Debbie was definitely from the mean streets of Chi-Town, with those mean streets even intruding into what she thought was her "safe" home. But why was it that when a girl wanted to better herself that folks from the hood (who could care less about bettering themselves) would try to bring her down? Why was it that her light skin scared folks with darker skin? After all, she wasn't prejudiced, so why should others be that way? That bullet that killed her brother didn't care if he was light or dark; so then, why would anyone else care? Why were people so damned miserable???

Although Debbie had these questions, she never voiced them. She didn't get up in people's faces and fight them over their ignorance. Instead, she simply recorded it all. *You high yellow, bitch. Wanna be Black.* Or worse: *"You bourgie heffa."*

Debbie hated these titles and found it increasingly hard to love herself for who she really was with all of the negative comments directed at her skin color. The hate began to let up a bit when Vanessa, Halle and Jada felt as if they were representin' her as they boldly challenged the adversities of light skinned folk with their raw talent. Still, Debbie was ashamed that her neighbors and classmates ignored her inner and outer beauty because of her lighter skin tone. Yet there was no disputing Debbie's beauty. She might have been the spitting image of a young Dorothy Dandridge, except that Debbie had a head of natural bronze hair.

As Debbie grew older and more aware, she aspired to be aggressive, to achieve, and to capitalize on her gifts one day. She didn't quite know how or when, but life would reveal its greatness to her. On that goal she was determined. And, as of lately, it was David's words that were reminding her of her great potential during their pen pal pursuits. As pen pals, the two were often online at the same time. They would constantly communicate with one another in words or pictures and still maintain the mystique that long distance relationships create. The networking could have carried over to telephone calls for more candid, more intimate conversation. However, the Internet made their inevitable intimacy seem more substantial; bigger than life. At the same time there was more mystique and, well, this interaction was just damned inexpensive and convenient.

David initially read Debbie's ad in the singles area of "NET NOIR", a community of like minded blacks on the Internet. The two became an item in the Ebony chat rooms. And although more than 78 others answered Debbie's ad, David was the first mover. Once he downloaded her photo with the help of his high-speed modem, he realized what a prize he lucked-up on. She was beautiful with big glassy eyes like the women in magazines. She had high cheekbones and alluring full lips, like the ones he admired in music videos. In the photos that David first received, he could see that she sported a hairstyle that was popular amongst girls today. So, for all he knew he had struck it rich. Debbie was everything he imagined. With no artificial flavorings. And to further protect his stake, so that he wouldn't miss out on his "sure thing," he persuaded Debbie to refrain from letting anyone else see her images on the Net.

"It's not really safe enough yet . . . plus, you don't want everybody and their mother to have your face on their computers. You never know what kind of grimy, slimy dudes are out there." David tried his best to thwart any other possibilities of someone finding this "dime" who resided somewhere in the middle of Chi-Town. And suddenly, paranoia hit.

There was a period of months when the AOL Internet service incurred a heavy burden; trapped in their own universe of trying to satisfy an overwhelming customer base. Customers were growing angry since they had grown so dependent on access; auxiliary numbers were exhausted and members were forced to either keep trying to get online or go elsewhere. These complications created a dilemma for David. He had been hot and heavy on Debbie's ass. More and more, day by day he had been working on his goal of earning her trust. His overall objective was to lure Debbie to New York. However, through all of their communications and chat room ventures, David never pushed for her phone number and she never offered. So the conflict forced him into a desperate search to find her. He worked his own process of elimination, first digging into a list of 35 McDonald's restaurants in Chicago. He eventually found the right franchise on his 11th attempt, and then he lied about an emergency of some sort.

"Mickey Dees," the young voice sang with a slight squelch.

"Hi. I'm looking for Debbie Rose?" David announced, trying to sound sure of himself.

"No sweat. Hold on." The response was promising and David felt relieved that this would be a cinch.

"Ahh . . . who's calling," the same voice returned and caught David off guard. Unprepared, he blurted a hasty response.

"Her brother—" he said without thinking, squeezing his face hard and cursing at himself once he realized what he'd said. The messenger on the other end of the line was unaware of the lie or the Rose family's tragedy.

"Yo baby, yo . . . he says he's your brother."

David could hear the muffled conversation through the receiver and cringed when he imagined Debbie's face.

*   *   *

For Debbie, on the other hand, the mere thought of her brother on the phone had stopped her heartbeat for a few strokes. It had been about 3 years since his murder and frankly, she had missed the last two visits that her mom made to the cemetery. Before anger could overcome her, guilt did. She took gloom with her to answer the call. The cashier next to her took a moment to whisper into another employee's ear—the big secret.

"Hello?" Debbie held her breath while her mind recalled a couple of still photos of her late brother, Ray Ray. And then the anticipation.

"Debbie, I'm sorry to disturb you at work, but I didn't know how else to reach you. I haven't been able to get online for weeks . . ." Debbie could hear David trying to explain his life away in hopes that she would not hang up. But, honestly, her mind was somewhere else.

Raymond.

"Oh . . ." said Debbie with a subtle sigh of emotion. It wasn't but a second or so later that she replaced her anguish and pain with that pleasure—the snapshot photo that David had emailed her. He was tall and tan, like she was. Plus, he was handsome. There was determination in his eyes. And he had the confident posture, wearing preppy clothing . . . all the stuff she liked.

"Hi." She felt awkward.

"Sorry again. Is there another time I can call you? At home, maybe?" She could tell that David relaxed some, less discomfort. And Debbie eventually became excited herself about David's call, figuring that he must have wanted her bad enough to call long distance; to call her place of work. Plus she had missed him too. And his voice! She had no idea how mellow and secure! She liked it. She liked him. And now she could put his face and name with a sound. Now, she was even curious to know his body.

The following weeks brought the two closer. David would intentionally schedule his phone calls in increments of 3 days, then 5 days and even a week apart. Debbie, in the meantime, melted into his mold like soft butter. She moaned when it was time to hang up and she cheered when he called again. Her nostrils flared and her folds moistened with desire.

Growing up with a single parent made it difficult to feel independence, so this was feeling just right. Ms. Rose became extra obsessive in the years following Ray Ray's death. She wanted to know where Debbie was throughout the day and she wanted her home in bed by 10 PM.

Meanwhile, Debbie's social life was a shambles. Girls her age were flaunting it all at the Big Skate Roller Rink, at the amusement park and at the school basketball games. The neighbors on the left and right of the Rose home had daughters. There were 5 girls altogether. They did all types of girl-things together. It was stressful for Debbie to see them all together for different outings like dates for concerts and parties. She felt left out and could do nothing about it. Part sympathy and part obedience kept her from arguing with her mother, but it also kept her on the computer.

And now Debbie was getting older. The madness had to stop. After all, she was practically a virgin.

Like a Virgin

One particular experience tested her chastity just two days before the big tragedy. Robert Bass, the former all-star from South Chicago High School's basketball team, visited Debbie while on spring break from the University of Illinois. He slipped in and out of the house with great ease (while her mom was at work) between 3 and 5 PM Monday through Wednesday. Debbie was off from work on these days and was entertained by the hulking college pro, with his soft kisses and his tender touch. Robert's last day at the Rose home was the most eventful.

The two had never consummated their relationship. They never fucked. But Debbie had recently turned 18 and Rob felt it was his sacred duty to break the ice. One more virgin on his belt wouldn't make him or break him. However, Debbie was different. She was so protected throughout his final high school years that he could never get close like he could with the school cheerleaders. And Lord knows he wanted to. Debbie was developing attractive breasts and they held up so tight that she was the underrated school gem. Even under a thick sweater she was shapely. Sometimes Rob would swear he could see her nipples through a winter bomber. Or maybe that was his imagination; but no matter. Intentionally, or not, this was the fantasy that Debbie sold daily. In the summertime all of the boys in her classes kept perfect attendance, if only to soak up the vision of Debbie in a t-shirt, halter top or skirt. All she could do was blush, unaware that she was the focus of many wet dreams in Chi-town.

On the day that Rob first touched Debbie, he felt as if he'd violated a heavenly angel. But it was indeed his goal to "break" this forbidden zone of hers. He absolutely lusted for the cameo bombshell. All of it building up to this one visit. The first two days of his spring break were cordial and sweet, with a subtle kiss to end his stay. But the 3rd day ended with both of them drenched in sweat after heavy necking and fondling. Rob licked her neck so good she stretched herself out on the couch like a feast. He took the cue and knelt down beside her to begin a head-to-toe review of her. Beginning at her forehead, he smoothed the back of his tongue down the slope of her nose to her upper lip. She wanted to return a kiss, but he held her down gently and then reversed the motion of his tongue to tease the edges of her nostrils. The eyelids, cheeks, earlobes and cleft in her neck kept him busy for 20 minutes more. He was beginning to drive her crazy. When Rob reached Debbie's cleavage, breasts and nipples, she experienced the pleasure long enough to feel a burst in her abdomen. It frightened her and she pulled away from Rob like the plague. Still, Debbie made arrangements to see him again on the following day. She could see he felt awkward and maybe he didn't expect to go as far as they had. But nevertheless, Debbie was apologetic and submissive, and she eventually surrendered.

They went up to Debbie's bedroom hand in hand. She advocated the heavy action by pulling the curtains and shades. She locked the door and then switched on her York stereo. The CD's that were positioned in the tray contained her all time favorites: Mint Condition, Brandy, R. Kelly, Aaliyah and, of course, Beyoncé was at the top of her list. And no need to play DJ, since her stereo was programmed to play songs at random.

After Debbie scurried to adjust their environment, she

turned to slowly approach Rob with her arms extended around his neck. She passionately shared her tongue with his. After a moment, she stepped back for him to get a full eyes' view and began a sort of strip tease to Brandy's *"Almost Doesn't Count"*. Somewhere during the song, Debbie even sang a line into Rob's ears, making it ever so clear that *"almost doesn't count."* It didn't take another song for Rob to shed his sweats and join her, curling his toes deep in the room's pink carpet.

"Are you sure you're ready for this?" Rob asked seriously.

In truth, Debbie was scared to death while she tried her best to imitate a scene that she once saw in a movie. But the excitement, coupled with her desire, pushed her to the edge. And, although she didn't say it in words, she was quite ready to jump. She couldn't answer Rob directly, so instead she reached for him. With her arms circling his head above her, she pulled his mouth to hers. Her tongue answered his question most definitively.

In the darkened room, Rob hovered over Debbie's nude body in his boxers. He held her back up off the carpet in an arch, while her upper body and arms stretched back. Mint Condition's *"Breaking my Heart (Pretty Brown Eyes)"* kept the pace as Rob reached into his sweats laying on the floor next to them. In his wallet he kept a single condom for emergency occasions. *This* was an emergency of the best kind. Debbie watched as he maneuvered the rubber onto his erection. His hands explored her own wetness. Controlling every moment, he quietly conjured a mouthful of saliva and let it fall from his lips into the folds between her legs. With his pelvis he caused the perfect amount of friction to work the moisture around. With the tip of his erection wet and slippery, Rob slowly entered Debbie. Very slowly. She winced at his first probe. When an inch had hidden inside of her she reached back as far as her body could stretch and grabbed fistfuls of her pink carpet. Now she whimpered along with an accompanying tear. Rob began to go for another inch when suddenly Debbie's door swung open. Young Ray Ray came home early from Little League practice and was now standing like a statue in shock with two hands covering his silent holler. Debbie did everything *but* drop-lock the latch on her door. And now the two surprised teens fell limp and disappointed, scrambling for their clothes. In the end, their private passions and unlived fantasies were left scattered amidst the room's musty aroma.

It was now 4 years later that Debbie found herself in a hopeless attraction to New York and David Morton. She evaded the possibility of having to face her mother to explain. Instead, she left a 3-page letter, complete with the phone number to her old classmate Jackie, who was staying in New York. Jackie and her mother managed to escape their unbecoming circumstances of an abusive husband and father for a final frontier in Queens, New York, which was where Debbie was headed.

So, Debbie cleared her bank account, booked a flight at a bargain price and headed for New York. With some laser pictures, a bag of letters, and memories of innumerable telephone calls, she flew blindly into this new adventure with her new Internet love interest. David's world was waiting for her.

CHAPTER FOUR

An Entrepreneur Is Born

The Gilmore empire was not realized without great struggle. In the early days, Douglass Gilmore was a local entrepreneur who built a string of small grocery stores that operated in the remote urban areas of Mount Vernon, New York. At the time, such an enterprise was known as a convenience store. And as the decade and his business affairs progressed, Gilmore added on a laundromat and then a liquor store to his achievements. By now, as the owner of more profit-producing undertakings than any other attempt in the community, Mr. Gilmore (most affectionately referred to as "Gil") was one of the area's most aggressive businessmen. As the business expanded further, Gil introduced his 8-year-old son Douglass Jr. to the tasks of stocking and pricing groceries, counting inventory and eventually, operating the cash register. The young boy was a fast learner. He was reliable and skilled at giving change precisely and quickly. He enjoyed challenging himself to complete sales faster and more efficiently than all of his dad's employees. More than just making a sport out of it, Jr. also wanted to gain his father's approval. He saw his father as a role model and an image towards which he could reach. Yet, the youngster never quite felt complete. There was never a time that his father stopped everything to say, "*Son, I want you to know that I'm really proud of you.*" And thus, the father-son relationship was never a rich one.

Years took their toll on the Gilmore enterprise. The city of Mt. Vernon was also a *victim* of that change, as opposed to growing with or preparing for the ever changing times. Crime and poverty, weakened property values and joblessness imposed a sense of helplessness upon the working class. As property values dropped, low income housing attracted hundreds and hundreds of families that were forced out of neighboring middle-class communities. The only choice for many of these families was the projects and housing developments; and the 70's still showed signs of segregation—as youngsters swallowed realities such as bussing and lingering racism.

Naturally, barber shops, laundromats, grocery and liquor stores would continue to prosper due to the growing need. But a few robberies by gunpoint and a burdensome work schedule pressured Gil into downsizing. He eventually consolidated all of his resources into a single property on the south side of Mt. Vernon. This was a corner property, and quite a property it was too. There was the convenience store, a liquor store, a bar and 5 apartments overhead. In addition to simplifying his business interests, Gil was also very innovative. To combat the crime that threatened his business, he had a permanent partition built in the liquor store. It was made with 1½-inch thick bullet-proof glass. The idea was such a success that Gil had a partition built for the convenience store to accommodate the after-hours crowd. It could be pushed up to the front entrance of the store and secured as a makeshift walk-up window. Clearly, Mr. Gilmore was adjusting with the ever changing times, preparing for the weathers of the world in order to protect his business and sole source of income. By the early 80's the grocery and liquor stores were rented to an Arab family. The new occupants converted both stores into one large supermarket. But Gil remained a staple in the neighborhood, eventually concentrating all of his attentions on the bar and lounge which anchored one end of his now subleased property.

The Evolution

The bar and lounge, formerly known as *Denny's Irish House*, was renamed as *Gil's Irish House*. The façade of the establishment was red brick with a section of thick block glass. Two windows, with exterior grills to prevent break-ins, were draped with dark red curtains hung on the inside of the bar. When the bar was open for business, orange neon signs for *Ballantine Ale* and *Miller* beer would shine brightly in both windows. The green canopy above the outside entrance was altered with a neat patch affixed over the old name.

Now that Gil had solely concentrated on the lounge business, new activities began to evolve. Previously a watering hole for local blue collar workers, the business now began to expand its attractions. First, porno videos were introduced on Wednesday nights. When that feature became boring and predictable, Gil brought in a topless dancer that performed at the same time the movie played. Soon enough the word spread, drawing new customers. Wednesday night attendance began to surpass all other days of the week combined. Popular demand cried out for more, until dancers were eventually showcased every night. The entertainment filled the club beyond its legal capacity of 150 persons. Now, instead of a local tavern, *Gilmore's* was the spot where pretty, young black women stripped down to their panties.

Things had taken a major shift. Englebert Humperdink's "*After the Lovin'*" was replaced by Madonna's "*Like a Virgin.*" The clientele that had consisted of white, Latino and black factory workers was now made up of white-collar workers, sports celebrities and all-night partygoers. The hours of *Gil's Irish House* were once 11am to 8pm. Now, the club opened at 12 noon and closed at 4 AM. Naturally, prostitution worked its way into the fold as Gil made a musty-smelling back room available to close friends and customers. To no one's surprise that was a big hit. Gil began to rent the room for $20 per half hour so that anyone (including police officers, firemen and sports stars) could take their pick of private dancers to the back room. The individual dancer charged a separate amount for her services. Depending upon the girl, and if she was good at what she did, a romp in the back room could cost $50 to $200. Gil also got a percentage of that from the dancers.

Essentially, Gilmore's had become the area's ultimate inner-city brothel—a money machine that featured live dancers, porn videos on the big screen and a back room for sex. Worth its weight in gold, the club attracted Army personnel who traveled from North Carolina; it attracted players of various New York sports teams after their various games; and, of course, the local patrons simply ate it up. It was an excitement that was ever-peaking and never ending.

As fate would have it, too much of a good thing became a problem. There were very few parking spaces available by the roadside, and cars were often parked recklessly along the sidewalks and in the driveways and on the lawns of nearby residents. After a long night men would also leave the club intoxicated and flagrant, loudly reviewing the evening's highlights at 2 and 3 am. Many customers made it a routine to urinate against trees, fences, hedges and other people's vehicles. Apparently, stepping out into the night air to relieve their bladders was sort of a signature to suit the animal in them. And the restroom inside the club was too good for that.

As a small bar, the Gilmore enterprise never really raised eyebrows. People grew up in the neighborhood to accept it as a landmark of sorts. If anything, locals were accepting of the operation just as they were the trees and street signs. But never did the neighborhood expect such a dramatic change in clientele, in traffic and the overall growth; how the business grew so fast. Nobody was prepared for this big fish in their small pond. The spill-over from Gilmore's affected homes for blocks, whether it was noise, urine odor, or empty beer cans tossed in the front yard. Things seemed to get that much worse on weekends and holidays.

All told, Gil could not keep those homeowners at bay. Customers who happened to live in the neighborhood accepted the excitement. But others merely dialed 911 when their tempers hit high. In response, police attacked wrongly parked cars with parking tickets. And because Mt. Vernon didn't have a towing or impounding routine like the big city did, the city's only alternative was high penalties. At the time, $30 and $40 tickets were considered high, and that was for double and triple parked cars.

However, customers continued to do as they pleased, parking however they wanted. The tickets were not a deterrent. No match for the pleasure customers experienced. So the police were forced to step it up. They raided the club. They did shakedowns and even arrested dancers once or twice for "inappropriate attire." But in Gilmore's to show as much skin as possible *was* the "attire." And yet, business was as strong as usual the next day. Customers weren't the least bit intimidated by the attempts. And since the club had local policemen who worked on staff, these scare tactics were all but disregarded. Besides, Mt. Vernon was only 4 square miles, and everybody knew everybody who was anybody. Truth be told, since half of the police force were backroom clients themselves, the city couldn't withstand the scandal that could surface. At the least, wives would find out where their husbands had been for all those long nights that were said to be spent doing overtime.

And yet, the club continued to bump and grind. A typical night inside of Gilmore's promoted the aura of sex. Dimmed lighting. Gyrating music. Musty air. Nicotine was built up on the wood paneling and ceilings as if it was intended varnish. But it added a particular element of authenticity. The chairs and stools that were either broken or breaking—more *authenticity*. The plywood stage with the cheesy linoleum surface was rickety and squeaky. Mirrors throughout the club (and especially behind the dancers on stage) were cracked and exposed enough for 2nd and 3rd degree cuts. Still, more authenticity. But this was all of what made Gilmore's the real thing. That raw, undeniable climate of smut and lust, with the young, shapely, sexy women at the center of it all. The whole picture was just one big adventure.

Since the local law enforcement was partly under the club's influence, and no significant penalty was in place, further action was pursued. The State Liquor Authority (S.L.A.) began to make visits. This was a subtle, quiet approach in addressing the lawlessness of Gilmore's; but effective and mighty for sure. It was the word on the streets that Gilmore's provided a nightly ritual of illicit activities. The hype that came with it all made for a great diversion for S.L.A. agents to go and visit the club to observe the outrageous claims of neighbors. Since S.L.A. was the authority which granted permission to sell alcoholic beverages, the investigators were essentially the rightful individuals to police such matters. And it just so happened that S.L.A. investigators were present on one of the many evenings when things at Gilmore's got a little out of hand; although it was perfectly normal for patrons in the busy venue to touch and fondle the dancers. Everything in this environment was okay, so long as it felt good. Yet while the risqué activities proceeded, they were also serving to build new standards for amendments to antique liquor laws. It was an untold history in the world of adult entertainment, but in those circles of thrill-seeking men, the art and the term of lap-dancing began right there in Mt. Vernon. This rough, full clothed version of simulated sex, (where dancers sat on the patron's lap gyrating until friction became fantasy; where a drought turned into a drip) was actually what S.L.A. reps came to witness. But to their surprise, there were events that were even more awakening.

A bachelor party of 12 was celebrating late into the night. Party animals all of them. The group and the groom occupied the whole front row of chairs. Loud. Frolic. Intense. The club was so busy that the stage seemed to extend into the immediate audience. Everyone, including the bachelor's friends and the club's regulars, were immersed in the anticipation of just how far all of the excitement would go. The group continuously tossed singles, fives and tens at the feet of different dancers who came to the stage for their 20-minute sets. The more lewd the dancers became, the more expressive her actions, the more provocative she was, the more money she got. The scene was a seduction for dancers to do whatever, however. Sometime around 1am, after Juicy was introduced to the stage to join 4 other dancers, the group hollered in excitement. The bachelor's entourage enticed Juicy to "put it on" the groom with a wave of their 20-dollar bills. Already sliding her bare feet through a modest pile of singles, Juicy agreed. She approached the blushing husband-to-be in a seductive wiggle, eventually swinging her body around until her back was facing him. With his chair and knees flush against the foot-high stage, the bachelor found his face in a unique position. Juicy backed up until her perfectly round, brown cheeks and the split of her ass hugged his face. A tremendous ROAR! followed as the club's standing-room-only crowd howled in appreciation. The thundering oneness of voices could be heard for blocks as the groom's nose and tongue disappeared between Juicy's cheeks for close to two minutes.

But that evening, and on through the ensuing months, that ROAR! proved to be the sound that rocked Gilmore's. Juicy and Gil were arrested that night. They spent the night in jail until the judge permitted them free on bail the next morning. Furthermore, the club's license was revoked. But Gilmore was relentless. He reopened the club the very next day and it was business as usual. Instead of liquor, he sold soda, water and "no-beer," a beer-flavored beverage that had less than 10% alcohol content. For the same $4-per-drink price, customers would unconsciously gulp down the alternative to booze and act just as intoxicated as if it were 80-proof vodka. After all, it was the main attraction that was intoxicating. Dancers now had liberty to perform all-nude, drawing even bigger crowds, despite the loss of liquor privileges. It was during the subsequent months that Gil realized that his club, his concept would survive virtually anywhere.

Expansion

The time had come for a location change. The pressure from the city of Mt. Vernon was mounting. The local paper maintained headlines that seemed to focus on the descent of the area's most successful black businessman. Gil was steadfast, however, keeping his long hours and routine unchanged. The face-between-the-cheeks incident resulted in a small fine and a suspended jail sentence for Gil and Juicy. But now, without the S.L.A. jurisdiction, without liquor sales, and with the rights and freedoms of speech to protect nude dancing, Gilmore's was now back to square one—under the laws and jurisdiction of the locals. The state had exhausted its every procedure in attempts to close the club, but Gilmore's was no longer an SLA problem.

"Redneck town—redneck laws." Gil would often complain while in the company of his close comrades. And the ill feelings were definitely reflected in the deficiency in the club's income. The difference in revenue was close to three or four thousand dollars a week. But again, this didn't stop the cash flow altogether. What was a problem most overlooked was the *future* of Gilmore's.

Mt. Vernon's officials were faced with a big question: *what was legal and what was not legal about the local tavern turned strip club?* There was no law that could prevent an all-nude, liquorless business. Not yet. But for Gil, there was an undercurrent of concern. *What would the city come up with next? How much longer would this type of entertainment prevail in the small residential town?* While Gilmore's went on to test the city and their continued police raids with his First Amendment right, he was nonetheless thinking of staying one step ahead of his adversities.

"Dad, we need to get out of this bullshit town," argued young Douglass, who was now 27, full of rebellion and energy. "The mayor is a hypocrite. Sneaking in here with sunglasses. Thinking we don't notice. He's probably Juicy's best customer! The neighbors smile in our face by day and press the panic button by night. And Dad, we need *more room*. There's always a line outside." On Friday and Saturday evenings especially, anyone on line would usually have to wait for a person to exit for there to be enough room for a new customer. It wasn't so much a legal capacity issue (because that number was always exceeded). There was simply nowhere to stand.

"Besides, Dad, this place is falling apart."

Douglass Jr. had been to many nightclubs by his mid 20's. Many more, in fact, than his father would ever care to visit. The elder Gilmore was focused on one thing; opening and closing his doors and making sure there were enough dancers and drinks. To him, nothing else mattered. But in the meantime, his son's vision was an expanded one. He was introduced to the club scene by his neighbor Steven Juliano, a veteran of the nightclub business. By watching Steve's hard-nosed business savvy, Douglass learned and experienced a lifetime of seasoning within a very short time. He'd witnessed first-hand what a successful clubowner did as a routine. He was behind the scenes to record the unmentionable, as well as on the outside looking in as a clubgoer. There were business decisions that made sense and there were losses that made sense too. As Steven's apprentice, Douglass Jr. absorbed it all. And it was that invaluable experience that led Douglass to make those suggestions to his dad. He was so persuasive about it that Gil agreed to consider moving the club. Both father and son knew that the business had grown into a monster. A big whale of an idea confined to a fish tank. To survive and grow, the club had to be relocated away from the suburbs and into the New York City jurisdiction where healthy competition was welcome. Most importantly, in New York City, with its red-light districts, accepted prostitution and infamous sex clubs, such a business was nothing but common.

With his dad's firm "go," Douglass hunted block by block, district by district, until he discovered a hot property just a mile away. It didn't matter that the location had 2 auto body shops, side-by-side, and that it was fully operational. Douglass Jr. saw past that. He had a vision and a dream to be fulfilled.

Conveniently, the proposed property was on the same truck route as the old location. Furthermore, since the new location was positioned just over the county line in the Bronx, the property was geographically a part of the New York City jurisdiction. So with all things considered, and armed with his father's blessing, Douglass Jr. approached the proprietors of 1440 Boston Road.

"Hi, I'm . . . I'm interested to know if you'd be selling this property anytime soon." Part inquiry, part suggestive, Douglass Jr. was focused and convinced as he addressed the body shop owners.

"Huh?" The twenty-something Italian man returned a twisted expression.

"Your garage. I'd like to know if you want to sell." Douglass's vision was straightforward as a matter of fact. Meanwhile, the shop owner was sarcastic. Reviewing the request as if it came from a panhandler. But young Gilmore overlooked the cold reception and because he was direct and intentional, the proprietor invited Douglass to return with an offer. Within two days Douglass typed up an offer to lease-option the property for $2,000 per month. The length of the lease was 2 years, time enough to re-invent the wheel. Renovations. Marketing and reestablishing market position. Time enough to get back a cash flow and to raise $800,000 for the full purchase price of the property. The price could've been one million dollars, or even a million five. Either extreme would have been kosher with the Gilmores. They knew what the potential of their idea was. They knew that the new location was equal to the largest pot of gold they'd ever know. And of course the sellers imagined that the offer was just as crazy as the people making it. But they didn't hesitate to go along with the deal.

Boston Post Road was a local truck route that ran parallel to Interstate 95, the multi-billion dollar throughway which stretched from New England to Florida. At any moment, day or night, cars and trucks would take an off ramp exit to fill up on gas, food or rest. The exit closest to the new club site was named Conner Street. Major franchises were already profiting from the traffic. Others were beginning to expand. McDonald's was the largest attraction along the throughway, with a 24-hour drive-thru and a newly added indoor playground. Directly across the street from the golden arches was a Dunkin' Donuts franchise. Naturally, where there are donuts, there are also police. So the area consequently projected some sense of security (even if only due to the high traffic) during the evening and early morning hours.

On another corner was an immense transmission franchise. And across the street, next door to the projected club, there was a 16-pump, 24-hour gas station. Altogether these elements meant one thing for certain and two things for sure: traffic and cash.

The Rocco family owned the property where the auto body work was done. They discussed the particulars and quickly agreed to Gilmore's terms. And as quickly as the key to the property changed hands, enterprising young Gilmore was an explosion of newfound energy, removing piles of debris left in the shop. Trunk covers, axles, grease. You name it. Douglass was gung-ho and highly motivated for the new challenge, building a nightclub. Meanwhile, Gil began to spread the word amongst his regulars. The Mt. Vernon location was still thriving. Even more so because of its forthcoming and encouraging move. The convenience store which Gil once operated was doing well for the family that took over. They upgraded and improved the business often. The business flourished enough for them to see promise in owning the entire Mt. Vernon property. Since there was already speculation of an interest in purchasing the lot, Gil didn't have to go looking for a buyer when it came time to relocate. So just like that, Gil sold the stores and the apartments above it, as well as the bar that started it all, for a lump sum of $100,000. It was enough money for the move and for the renovations of the new establishment: *Gilmore's Fool's Paradise*. This is what Gil labored years for. His equity. His enterprise. His future.

The transaction was expected to go smoothly. At most, once the property changed hands, the Gilmores anticipated that the business would digest a 2 to 3 week loss in revenue. But this was accepted as a rest period. A little time to breathe. A well-deserved but short vacation. However, as time would tell, nothing worth attaining . . . nothing so huge and powerful can be achieved without struggle or challenges. And those struggles and challenges were awaiting the Gilmores from the day they took over the Boston Road property.

Problems with licenses, permits, and variances were already difficult challenges. There were already so many other entrepreneurs who also sought licenses and permits for clubs throughout the Bronx. And furthermore, it seemed like every city service or department required some payoff or promise, whether over or under the counter. There wasn't one inspector who walked into the Boston Road property who didn't see a $100 bill folded in front of them. And Gil was warned ahead of time.

"After you put the money on the counter, the inspector will ask, '*Is that yours?*' And your answer should be, "*Is what mine?*" And then, turn your back. When you turn around, the money should be gone." This was the process, time after time, inspector after inspector, until it got to a point when Gil was never quite sure who would stop by next with a tie and a clipboard to inevitably ask *"Is that yours?"* Not to mention how much harder it was to brush off these inspectors, some of whom found reason to show up a second time. Who knew that opening a nightclub in the city would entail facing a loaded revolver of underpaid city-slick civil service workers. And yet, the *real* struggles were still ahead. Obtaining a certificate of occupancy from the Bronx Building Department, and coping with these old ways and means were nothing compared to the challenges ahead.

During a cold and snowy weekend in New York City, a two-story social club by the name of *Happy Land* was the place to be for many Latino partygoers. The establishment, one of hundreds that operated illegally throughout the city, was bustling when a man spotted his girlfriend in the club and turned into an instant pyromaniac. All he could envision was his woman in the arms of his friend as he charged mindlessly through the street to the nearest gas station. The attendant sold him a couple gallons of gasoline which he toted back to Happy Land's entrance. Inside the doorway, the angry man poured gas about the stairway and entrance. Spitting all kinds of profanities in Spanish, he shouted one last, boisterous farewell:

"Adios. Hasta la vista. *Y Valle con Dios!*"

After the farewell, the guy lit a match and tossed it inside the doorway. A bonfire raced up the stairway until the crowd was overcome by smoke and flames. Finally, because there was only one way in and one way out of the hot spot, the fire took the lives of everyone inside of Happy Land.

The Happy Land tragedy rocked the city of New York. The consciousness of everyone was driven, pulled and jerked by various forms of media for the next month, which was a lot of press for NY, where generally, a murder was here and gone by the next day—pushed aside by the next wave of current events. Increasingly, the public demanded action. David Dinkins, struggling to maintain his polls and acceptance as New York's first black mayor, was pressured to step to the plate in avenging those circumstances of the tragedy. In fact, the instigator of the disaster was not enough of a scapegoat for the public outcry. People wanted to see heads roll. So Dinkins organized a "Social Club Task Force." This was but a makeshift posse that did little more than raid legal and illegal social clubs alike. Making their presence known, the gang of auxiliary police padlocked many of the unlicensed establishments around the city. If that wasn't done, then the task force merely trounced through clubs checking that there were appropriate exits and clearances.

Gilmore's Fool's Paradise, the new establishment that was in development on Boston Post Road, was not forecasted as a social club. Instead, this enterprise was reaching to qualify for all of the requirements that any other legitimate nightclub or restaurant would need to adhere to. To operate legally, Fool's Paradise would need a Cabaret License as well as a Certificate of Occupancy. But, regardless of Gilmore's objectives, the Happy Land incident had an effect on most of New York City's night-life, as well as the city departments that governed these operations by day. Bottom line: Happy Land's heat made obtaining a C.O. nearly impossible.

The last thing that the Gilmores were familiar with was the world according to New York City policies and politics. But fortunately, his son had a friend that was not only familiar with the drama, but he was *indeed* in-the-know.

"Steve, I have a problem with the city. We've already sold the old club and moved out. I've been bustin' my ass down here at the new spot with the construction, the layout, and now this Happy Land stuff is killin' us. They're makin' it difficult for us to get opened."

Steve and his family owned, or had interest in, 6 or 7 of the city's top nightclubs. The Copa was considered the top night spot—with pink palm trees and 4 million dollar interior. Another club Steve had a hand in creating was Bentley's, with an attraction of heavyweight sports and entertainment celebrities who came out to mingle and dance with the tri-state area's "grown and sexy" crowd. So, needless to say, if there was anyone that the younger Gilmore could turn to for advice, it was Steve.

Douglass was 19 years of age when he met Steve. It was an indirect introduction—how the club owner was informed about this certain young man's entrepreneurial energy by a mutual friend. Steve relayed a message that he was interested in meeting Douglass. When the two finally met, the chemistry was classic: Steve was a little older, he was Italian, with experience and plenty of money. Douglass was a younger, black and hungry entrepreneur. For whatever reason, the two hit it off well. That meant getting into certain clubs for free. That meant being in Steve's presence weekend after weekend as he handled or delegated issues like a master at work. Once in a while, Steve would raise his voice, shouting at an employee with his favorite line: "YOU IDIOT!" And, inevitably, Steve and Douglass partnered on various concert promotions and other business ventures.

"Whatever you wanna do," Steve said when the two first met, "you bring it to me and I'll back it."

Of course, being a struggling businessman in his 20's, Douglass couldn't have lucked up any more if he had stumbled into an orchard of money trees. Not only was Steve a consistent investor in Douglass's business ventures, like the one with the chocolate roses, or the concerts and club promotions, but he was also philanthropic, often handing his young protegee a couple hundred dollars here and there.

"Yeah. I've been under the gun too . . ." Steve responded, during one of many phone calls about the new club and the Happy Land incident. "It doesn't make sense. This shit is supposed to be for social clubs. Not *legitimate* establishments. The mayor is going around like a puppet on a string, with his goon squad task force. It's the public pressure." Steve was passionate about the business and he knew about all elements that might threaten his environment. "Here. Take down this number for a lawyer I know. Our family deals with him. He's good and aggressive, and if there's anyone who can help you through this mess, he can."

"Thanks, Steve."

"Don't thank me. Just get that club opened."

CHAPTER FIVE

Bronx, New York

The $100,000 investment for the new club turned into a negative $40,000 within weeks. When it came down to the meat and potatoes of opening a nightclub, the Gilmores were just not built for it. There was no blueprint, no written plan and no accountant to watch the money. But, even in their ignorance, the effort was simple: *"We got this here hundred grand in our pockets and we're gonna turn these two garages into one big nightclub."* But, as they say, things aren't always as simple as they seem; and the effort to open Fool's Paradise was nothing but stress and frustration. It was like one desperate race for survival where the end always looked grim. Contractors for plumbing, electrical, masonry and general construction were on the job day and night. They all played it by ear, doing their best to convert the property into a fully operational topless bar. Most contractors extended credit and anticipated the huge outcome of wads of cash and plenty of dancers to spend it on. Meanwhile, the two-week downtime turned into a month-long attempt to salvage a businessman's dream. There was no cash flow. Some contractors grew frustrated and walked off the job. One plumber was so full of rage that he took his heaviest wrench and began destroying work that he'd done, including bathroom sinks, in-ground pipes and valves. There were plenty of other bills that also had to be negotiated. But creditors had no other choice but to wait. Meanwhile, Gil's lease payments at home were already 3 months in arrears and the fridge was bare. Gil's life savings were tied up in this new venture, causing life-threatening heart pressure that ultimately sent him to the hospital. But, as soon as he could, Gil was back on his feet, determined to make money by any means necessary. Even without all of the permits in place, on a shoestring of a liquor selection, the club was opened.

"The liquor license is approved, so why wait?" Gil argued to his son. But it was this by-any-means-necessary attitude that forged the doors of Gilmore's to open for good. Sure, it began as a weak effort to drum up some much-needed cash. However, even with a project that was nowhere close to finished, girls hurried to answer Gilmore's calling. Sure, the grand opening was imagined to be a show-stopping event, and wasn't even worthy of a street-corner announcement. But, even with its unfinished, cinderblock walls, a small bathroom and sparse lighting, contractors made the club slowly but surely come to life. They put up two-by-fours and insulated the walls of sheetrock. The walls were already 30 feet high, reaching to a heavy, stucco ceiling. And when the club wasn't open for business, Douglass did most of the painting. He went with his vision of red and black colors. He painted the walls crimson red and used an air pressured paint gun to cover the ceiling in black. Ten foot mirrors were tacked to various walls in the establishment, creating an illusion of infinite space. The floors were almost completed with a checkerboard design, more black and red. Still, the unfinished part of the floor was still bare cement. Also, there was a division between the pair of garages that was a solid cinderblock wall and a doorway. Once the contractors got to work on the wall, the doorway was widened to a giant underpass. There was a solid beam which was left alone as a building support, and closer to the front of the club, a huge portion of the same dividing wall was broken out into the shape of a 20-foot high oval arch. Directly under the arch, stretching from one side of the club to the other, was a big stage. An oval bar enclosed the stage on both sides of the club. Just like that, raw and without the trimmings, Fool's Paradise went into business. Instead of special effect lighting, a light bulb dangled in a corner of the club that was designated as the "stage area." The stages that would inevitably be used by the dancers were still undergoing construction. So, with a blanket thrown over the cold, cement floor, dancers wiggled and twisted to the hollow tunes played over an oversized boom box.

Yes! This was *cheeeeeeeeeeeeeees-y*! And still dancers tolerated the rugged atmosphere, while construction continued with those heavy plastic sheets hanging from high above, shielding customers and entertainment from sawdust and the loud, searing saws spinning throughout the day. Although the club opened at 4PM, construction was still progressing on the serving bars, bathrooms, dressing rooms and offices. Men would mule into the club, grieving as if they were in withdrawal of some kind. But the entertainment was here, leaving them no other choice. For some the re-opening was long awaited. And for those die-hard regulars, the closing of the old spot was like suffering through a deadly storm.

This all convinced Gilmore that he had a "special" brand of entertainment that was unobtainable anywhere else. And it wasn't just the customers and the ownership that were going through withdrawal during the closure. For instance, there was Disco Dave, the guy who generally cleaned the club once the night was over. "Disco Dave" was a nickname that Douglass gave to Dave because of his irritable, nervous bouncing in place. It seemed that Dave was always fidgeting and looking for some activity—dancing. The one good thing that he could do was clean the mirrors and take out the garbage at the end of the night. Because he sure couldn't dance a lick. Douglass also had his personal label for Bob, the club's manager. "Drunk-ass Bob" is what Douglass always whispered to himself. Now, Bob was handy as ever with fixing things and following directions. But leave that man alone with some liquor??? That would be a big mistake.

Now, there were two attractive bartenders. There was Katey who was working her way into Gil's pants, and there was Veronica, a woman who Douglass bumped into outside of Bentley's one night. She'd been turned away. There was already a "SOLD OUT" sign on the door. Douglass saw this, he waved his magic wand, and he grabbed her hand, muscling his way through the thick crowd of disappointment. Perhaps it was her southern drawl and good looks which attracted him, but he insisted that she join him, and the two slithered into the club. One thing led to another, and Veronica was working at Fool's Paradise. Finally, the Fool's Paradise staff was completed with Dan the cashier. Dan was no more than a damned loyal customer who gained Gil's trust and happened to be in the right place at the right time. A team of weightlifters doubled as club security, completing the Fool's Paradise family.

It was as diverse and colorful as the staff that, at least, projected their dedication, but most importantly, this was easy money to operate a club full of half-naked women. It was a service that paid salaries, and people needed the salaries to survive.

So, the organization behind Gilmore's: Fool's Paradise had now come back to life. It was a place where music bounced off of the walls, where black, Latino and white women took off their clothes on stage, and where men came to watch it all in living color.

A Visitor

It was afternoon, just before the 4 o'clock opening of the club. Electric saws still buzzed along with the banging of hammers, even as calypso music was blaring from the club's sole source of music, a box radio. A short, stocky Italian in his mid-40's walked up through the entrance, into the club full of activity, most of it illuminated by a single halogen lamp. The visitor had black hair, protruding cheeks and eyes, and a know-it-all expression. The knot in his tie was pulled halfway down and his dress shirt was opened so that anyone could see his few gold chains and the t-shirt. And since his oversized blazer matched his navy knit pants, the big picture here was that this guy meant business. He could've been a salesperson of some kind, since salesmen were approaching the club with increased regularity—sometimes 4 or 5 per day—peddling bathroom accessories, bar stools, chairs, liquor, soda, beer, chips and most every other imaginable need that a human could think up. Then finally the guy spoke.

"Hey . . . anybody know where the boss is?" The question was more or less shouted into the busy room, but with little more effect than a careless whisper. It was a busy day, with more than 20 workers huddled over their individual tasks. The guy raised his voice; more affirmative this time. More of his native accent.

"Yo! Anybody seen Gil around?"

With sawdust covering most of his body, a Jamaican carpenter stopped his circular saw and pulled back his protective goggles. The saw lost power, sounding like a falling, dying missile until it came to a halt.

"Whey yuh waaant!" The worker looked frustrated and ready

to curse the stranger for interrupting. In response, the visitor widened his eyes, slightly traumatized, and cautiously chose his response.

"Is Gil in?" he answered after adjusting.

"Him de ya maan . . ." The worker kissed his teeth and replaced his goggles.

"Mind if I wait around?"

Again the worker kissed his teeth, gave a casual wave as though he could care less and mumbled.

"Man, just watch where ya goin'." Without another second of interest, the worker returned to his saw. His mind was obviously on his money and getting that stage finished as soon as possible. Besides, the girls were fed up with dancing on blankets on the hard floor.

The visitor's name was Tony. He knew how to humble himself. Although, by far, he had been to more construction sites than he could count. Twenty years in and around *his* business brought him to many clubs, restaurants and numbers joints. Many, many construction sites. Fish markets. Gambling casinos. But today his mission was to speak to Gil, the owner of Fool's Paradise.

While Tony swaggered about the sawdust, pipes and tools on the floor, he took in an eyeful of the surroundings. Two of three bars were almost complete. One was a circular bar positioned almost immediately to the right of the entrance. The stage inside of the bar could use some carpeting, Tony thought. And he wondered if that was it; the giant roll of carpet to the rear of the club and bagged in plastic.

To the left of the entrance was a service bar which reached about twenty-five feet into the club. Behind the bar was a weak display of liquors. Maybe 5 or 6 brands. The bottles were set on a miniature staircase of stained wood alongside various makes of soda. On the wall behind the bar and the liquor were mirrors which reflected the setting far across to the other side of the club. It created a fascinating illusion of endlessness.

Wandering, Tony walked through an underpass towards the opposite side of the club. This area was darker; illuminated only by a halogen lamp angled towards the floor. There was a giant, 15-foot movie screen affixed high on a rear wall onto which sports scores and replay highlights were projected.

"Can I help you?" Gil emerged from a rear office. He was clothed in his usual navy khakis, with a white button-down shirt, tucked in with sleeves curled back.

"Hey there . . . Gil?" Tony wasn't so sure, but he had a clue.

"Who wants to know?" Gil was slightly evasive, sizing up the stranger. *Salesman or creditor?*

"Well, I came to offer you a nice deal for your club."

"Like what?" Gil wasn't a novice when it came to these sales tactics. He'd heard thousands of 'em through all of his years in the store and the club. However, he was still willing to hear the pitch. Tony readily opened a leather folder and presented Gil with a professional brochure. It was a colorful presentation of a coin operated basketball shoot.

"For 50 cents, a guy gets sixty seconds to sink as many basketballs into the hoop as possible. Something like foul shooting," said Tony. Already, Gil warmed to the pitch.

". . . There are six basketballs, see. And the balls are small enough for anyone to palm. Like they was on the court themselves . . ." Tony pointed out the various benefits on his brochure. ". . . if a person makes more than fifteen baskets, they receive a bonus of thirty seconds to score more points." Tony spoke fluently, as if he'd done this a hundred times.

"Hoop shoot, huh?" Since Gilmore was already a basketball fan and found himself captivated by the bold type, the imagery and the idea that he could have this clever amusement in his establishment.

"Yeah and it's a monster. Customers love dis here, and it would fit nice into a spot . . . er, a club like yours."

"How big is this machine?"

"'Bout fifteen feet. But it's narrow and doesn't take up much standing room. Like in a corna or sumpthin'."

"How much?" Gil inquired.

"Well, that's the beautiful thing here. You don't pay us, we pay you."

Gilmore let out a murmur.

"Dat's right, Gil." Tony was becoming more talkative by

now. "We could give you three thousand and have the game in here in three days. Brand new."

All Gil could think of was his enormous debt and the cost of living. Every day, every hour was one that required money being spent. Some way, somehow. Gil's dreams were even consumed with spending money whenever he managed to squeeze in a few hours of sleep.

"Could you do five?" asked Gil. "Cuz I could use it right about now." And Gil's audacity led to a handshake. There would be a $2,500 payment up front and 50% of the take from the machine would settle the deal until the full $5,000 was paid. After that, all but 25% of the proceeds went to Tony.

Although Gil agreed and shook hands with Tony, he had no idea who he was associating with. He did not know that Tony was with the Bianco crime family. It was through Tony's efforts that the Biancos planned to finagle a percentage of the club's profits. It was a hidden agenda that Gilmore didn't even detect as he signed the agreement with Tony "the HoopShoot salesman." As Tony pivoted to leave the dusty air he heard Gilmore ask his name.

"Angelo," Tony lied.

Finally

Four months after the struggles, the hard times and the tears, Fool's Paradise was bustling with business, as if all of those challenges were just an illusion. The Certificate of Occupancy was finally obtained thanks to Jeff Weiss, the attorney whom Douglass had contacted with the help of his friend. And Jeff sure knew his stuff. He pulled more strings than a puppeteer. A few payoffs and some promises. And finally, the club was now legit. All required paperwork was in order for Gilmore to showcase tits and ass as well as sell liquor. White collar workers and auto mechanics patronized the club from 12 noon till 4 pm. Blue collar workers, civil service workers and more auto mechanics piled in after 4 pm. By 8 pm, the night crowd was a mix of hustlers, lady-killers (just another title for playboy) and unfaithful husbands. And although these were the only hours a nightclub was permitted to open, it was a sure bet that, if the law allowed, Gil would have been open 24 hours a day, 7 days a week, just like the donut shop next door. He was already repeating his old Mt. Vernon ritual; how he opened the club every day of the year, including Christmas and New Year's day. And Gil's non-stop, relentless approach paid off in spades. The regulars became regulars once again, as well as they began to bring in new customers. Besides auto mechanics, the area was loaded with drivers. There was a Fed Express depot whose drivers serviced more than 100 cities and towns. There was the department of sanitation and the New York City Bus Company which accumulatively housed and dispatched over 2,000 vehicles. There were oil companies, bakeries, dairies and tow trucks. There were depots for both the telephone company and the electric company. Add to all of these critical services the six lane traffic, and the end result turned out to be the deepest money-well imaginable.

In the club on a busy Friday night, the colorful lights, as well as the infectious bass and drums of urban music, fueled this saucy, sexy atmosphere inside of Fool's Paradise. Dancers gyrated on 3 elevated stages, conversations and outbursts of laughter competed with the music, and all of this mixed with this hazy, crazy fusion of temptation. Also interesting was the reality of how this erotic experience forced a culture clash that had white men, Latino men and black men, both young and old, to sit along-side one another in perfect harmony while being consumed, constrained and put away by violent and aggressive hip hop beats and lyrics. The sound system and a house deejay were a standard now, creating an ultimate impact.

In the meantime, Sadie, China, Cinnamon, Moet, Champagne, Dynomite, Extacy and close to 80 other black and Latino dancers filled the club day and night. Sadie, China, Dynomite and Cinnamon were considered top-shelf dancers. Moet had been part of the old Gilmore's crew, along with Champagne, Extacy and Juicy. Dynomite, on the other hand, was considered the craziest, loosest, wildest entertainer on the stage. She was always good for the most unexpected exhibitions, often pointing at a particular customer, indicating that he could have her ass. If you blinked your eyes you might miss her pointing to another customer, winking at him, promising him that she'd take him in her mouth, between her legs, or wherever, however. To say the least, Dynomite left very little to be imagined, and was received well because of it.

Most other dancers were visitors to the club. They had no specific schedules or commitments with management, sometimes coming from other boroughs or states. There were also the local girls who added to the huge selection of flesh for customers to feast their eyes on. But, aside from the "top shelf" girls, it was clear that Gil allowed most any shapely woman onto his stages. If you could at least stretch a bikini, a teddy or a lacy bra—even cut-off jeans—you were good enough to work at Gilmore's Fool's Paradise.

Naturally, this was a very sexist trade. And when desperate or out-of-work women came to the club they would look forward to immediate tips from lap dancing, wall dancing or be paid for merely becoming a customer's so-called date for the night. The whole scheme of getting a man's money was a well-known science among prospective dancers—

"All you gotta do is grind and wiggle in a man's lap or up against his groin for ten minutes. But you gotta be good enough, real seductive-like, cuz you wanna sell 'em the fantasy. Do it right, and the tip could be ten, twenty or even fifty dollars. Sometimes more if the guy ejaculates in his pants . . ." Women had developed a talent for encouraging men who were too timid. And if the dancer was creative enough, she could make a week's salary in one night. She'd hustle her ass off, being aggressive with the conservative man, or even straight up demanding with the humble types.

China, in particular, always had that certain attitude and charisma.

"You need to come with me," said China, her eyes speaking louder than her whisper as she directed her prey to the wall-dance area. And naturally, the patron followed obediently while China sought out an empty place up against the wall.

There was lap dancing and table dancing, but not until Fool's Paradise tripped over that next level of innovation was there such a thing as the "wall dance." Sure, couples had most probably turned a "slow dance" into something of a wall dance, maybe in some quiet cove in some dark corner of some night-club somewhere in the country. However, Fool's Paradise made it a routine "service," actually setting rules and regulations for wall dancing so that the recreation didn't turn into a "slow screw up against the wall." So, while the lights and music flickered and pounded; while the stage shows and porn movies and closed-circuit sports events kept everyone's eyes and ears busy, the illusion of simulated sex went on against every available wall in the club.

Punish Claudine

"Go home," exclaimed Gil. And he was serious *this* time. There would be no more excuses. Claudine was *certainly* not a top-shelf dancer and had acted up many times in the past. Late for work; missing items from the dressing room; altercations with other girls over who owned what G-string, and various other incidents with dancers and staff. Claudine was a nuisance. Claudine was the type who tried to copy the styles of the top-shelf dancers, trying to be aggressive with the timid customers. In most cases, that customer found the courage to snatch his hand back and catch his very own attitude. *Her nerve!*

If the popular adult entertainment venue was known for the best-looking girls with the best moves, Claudine certainly didn't qualify; not even with her double-D breasts or the piles of makeup she wore to make herself look like something that she wasn't. At 6 feet tall, Claudine was taller than a lot of customers but very disproportionate. Her 19-year-old body still carried excessive body fat. Her ass was also excessive; similar to the side of beef that you'd see hanging up on sale at the butcher shop. And not that there's anything wrong with excessive fat, an excessive ass, or simulating a side of beef; it's just not that type of party at a topless nightclub. Moreover, Claudine, whose hair was always plastered in wild, swooping styles with a pound of sticky gel to keep things in place, often made customers laugh at her, always trying to be something that she wasn't. Up on stage doing the Cabbage Patch dance or the Harlem Shake, as if she knew what she was doing. Frankly, if not for Gil's "anything goes" attitude about who could and who couldn't dance at the club, Claudine would be shown the door. She'd end up working down at The Goat on Hunt's Point—a hole in the Bronx where girls were giving head for crowds of onlookers.

But Gil tolerated Claudine. Until now, that is. This was a busy Friday night.

"Not a night for your shenanigans," Gil had to tell her constantly. "This is not a nursery school, and I shouldn't have to watch over you like a little kid. You're a grown-ass woman." Gil ripped into her. He was very focused on making money. The club had quickly become New York's premier adult entertainment complex and his objective was to get through every night without a hitch. His take-home for Fridays had grown to a steady $10,000 a week. And that was after expenses.

So Claudine's antics sho' nuff wouldn't be tolerated. Gil repeated his order before shifting his eyes toward club security. Claudine finally took him seriously, standing with her hands on her hips. The black Spandex she wore was stretched to the stitches, covering all but the cellulite on her waist and reaching down to her calves where a furry pair of pink socks stood out. Her pink blouse was stained and discolored, pressing into her cellulite to create a pseudo-cleavage.

"Fuck this place. And *fuck* you, Gilmore!" Claudine was arched to one side and then the other. Doing her damned best to create a scene. She was stuttering now, knowing that she had reached a limit and that her future in Fool's Paradise was now questionable. But her 'tude flipped a switch within her that said FUCK IT! And she snapped. A few more profanities were spit and exhausted, and Claudine swung out of her hooker's pose, almost crashing into a customer on a stool. Onlookers peeled out of Claudine's way as if a drunk driver had come through. She strutted across the floor through dazed patrons, finally disappearing into the dressing room.

"No question, that broad's drunk. She's acting up, as usual, Jimmy. So she's barred for a week," said Gil to the head of his security staff.

And indeed Claudine was drunk. Earlier that evening, she swallowed a few shots of Hennessy straight up. Maybe it was in response to her poor financial status for the night. Or her poor financial status forever.

Nevertheless, that scene between Claudine and Gil went virtually unnoticed in the adventurous atmosphere. The giant screens to the front, side and rear of the club were projecting the usual sports of athletics and sodomy. Sadie was on the main stage with old-assed Juicy to the side. Juicy was laying on a blanket, spreading her wrinkled folds for her small fan-base. She was a mismatch in comparison to Sadie's youth and beauty, but Juicy could care less. She had her own thang goin' on, slithering and seducing her group of three aging onlookers.

The instrumental of the club classic to *Rapper's Delight* (or *Good Times*, depending on how you looked at it) kept the walls and floors vibrating all the while. It had been a few minutes since she argued with Gil, but Claudine was now dressed and half bouncing along the club floor with her knocking knees. She swished her Amazon frame and toted her travel bag towards the club's entrance. Gil shrugged off her obscene gestures with a gradual blink of his eyelids. And now he signaled Jimmy.

"Jimmy, I don't want her back in here. Put her in a cab or something." Gil was leaning over the circular bar, his elbow and forearm planted on the Formica surface. A lukewarm black coffee was within reach. At the same time, the ousted dancer finally lowered her middle finger and worked her way into the foyer, under the metal detector and towards Jimmy, who was holding open the front door. She looked Jimmy directly in the eyes and sneered.

"Jimmy, you can keep yo' dick in yo' pants. I can handle myself tonight." With her palm raised and flagged inches from his face, Claudine passed Jimmy and stepped through the doorway. Jimmy casually accepted Claudine's snide remarks as nothing unusual, and he stood outside the club's entrance, leaning back against an exterior wall. Two fresh customers were thrown for a moment, but didn't hesitate to scurry right through the entrance. Jimmy lit up a Newport and watched Claudine as she turned into the parking lot.

The parking lot was the least of the priorities in renovating the property. It was still unpaved, with loose dirt and gravel on its surface. Claudine rested against a Mercedes and fumbled in the dark for a joint from her artificial Gucci purse. From the short distance, Jimmy could see how sorry she looked with her fake fur half-on and half-off her body. Claudine's left breast was showing almost to the nipple, just barely ready to spring from her tight, pink halter top. This was one of *those* days when she raced out of her boyfriend's place. So the blond wig had to suffice. Even *that* wasn't on straight.

Finally having an opportunity to relax, she slipped the strap and travel bag from her shoulder and dropped it to the ground. She searched her pockets for a book of matches and eventually lit the stick of weed in the cup of her hands. Squinting her eyes from the fumes, she sucked in the smoke. After a long drag there was a mild burn in her throat as the marijuana found its way through her body. With her face tight, as if she was pressing out a rocky bowel, Claudine was now high as well as intoxicated. She was out here at a time when the last of the after-midnight crowd had paid their $10 admissions. It was now 2:30 AM. Jimmy had returned to his indoor post and Claudine had begun to talk to herself, alone, under the cool moonlit sky. The hum and drone of Cameo's *Candy* filtered through an exhaust fan in the wall and could be felt like a soft tremor in the parking lot. There were close to 50 spaces in the lot with every one of them filled. The stillness in the lot seemed stranger with all of that excitement only feet away, inside the wall. Like a wake for shiny vehicles.

"*Fuck Gilmore.*" Claudine was slurring her words now. Just above a mumble.

"He just mad cuz I didn't let him eat my pussy tonight . . . fuck 'em." She took a last pull from the blunt wedged between her thumb and forefinger until the orange flow touched her skin.

"Shit . . . Fuck. Fuckin' shit!" She shook her hand furiously like she was trying to force the ink down in a malfunctioning pen. "He ain't the only motherfucker payin' . . ." Claudine was disoriented, now blaming Gil for her burnt fingers. "Fuckin' stud . . . man, my hand is hurtin' . . . fuckin' killin' me!" She looked up to see two full moons and then cradled her head into her inner elbow, reaching her hand to the back of her neck.

"I need a break from this shit. Wack-ass, cheatin' men. *Dogs!* All full of shit." If Claudine wasn't high and twisted, then maybe things were in fact spinning fast around her. Maybe all was wrong with the world, while her little universe was fine and dandy.

"Motherfucker gonna give me a dollar tip and ask me for change. Got his fuckin' nerve." Claudine opened her eyes again, swearing that relief was somewhere. Somehow.

"I'mma wait for Sadie . . . she 'bout it. Take me home, girrrl . . ." Claudine moved her legs like they were weighted down with sandbags, and eventually she reached the rear of the lot. She could barely keep on her feet as the hallucinations fought with her want for sleep. With different sets of black tires and spirals of whitewalls to guide her, Claudine came to a halt and leaned against a black Cherokee jeep. She wasn't conscious of the tear sliding down her face, creating a path down through her layers of makeup.

"Hi, Moet. Wassup wit' chu? Tired or sumpthin'?" Claudine asked. There was very little light back here, not even enough to see that Moet's eyes were shut. Still, Claudine carried on like this was a usual conversation. "You need to fix yo'self, chile, wit yo' lame ass . . . guess Gilmore threw you out too, huh?" High as a kite, Claudine was having a one-way conversation with Moet—Moet, one of the top-shelf dancers at Fool's Paradise.

Moet began dancing for Gilmore at age 13, but nobody suspected her of being a minor. She was short and physically gifted. Cocoa-brown skin. C-cup breasts. She had the stage presence of a pro, demanding a man's unquestionable focus. Her alluring gaze and provocative dance swerves did it for a man. Her on again-off again "ghetto attitude" only helped to spice up her performance. She wasn't into the flashy outfits that Sadie or Dynomite wore. She was simple. Some denim short-shorts and a bleach-white brassiere might do it; as if she just threw something on. That was all she needed to make money. For sure, Moet had grown up in the business. She was 21 now and a seasoned veteran. One of Gil's top moneymakers.

Claudine assumed Moet was sleeping—sleeping?! *On the dirt of an outdoor parking lot???*—

She slumped down to sit beside her friend on the dusty ground, offering her companionship. Moet looked comfortable to Claudine; so peaceful with her eyes half closed like they were. And she was stretched out on the gravel like she was at the beach. Moet's right leg was cocked and leaning against the jeep, with part of her body exposed under the oversized

sheepskin coat she wore. Claudine thought Moet was lookin'
sexy for real. She relaxed against Moet's leg and the Cherokee,
pulling her knees to her breasts.

"Did you make yours tonight? That motherfucker didn't
even pay me . . . I wish he would get a life, huh? Yo, *you feelin'
me, Moet?*" With the club music making a dying transition,
from uptempo to slow jams, R. Kelly's "*You Remind Me*" now
drifted through the air, and the beats were strong enough to
have the ground thumping. Claudine reached over to Moet's
torso, her body now twisted and hovering over the dancer.
Then she stroked Moet's elevated knee with her free hand and
glided it down her stocking-smooth leg and thigh.

"Hmm . . . silky baby. I always liked your legs, chile . . . and
you got that chocolate-ass skin too." Claudine put her hand to
Moet's forehead, realizing a bit of moisture. She never *really* got
to touch Moet like this before, and didn't mind the frisky feeling she felt—like she was moving from first to second to third
base in record time.

"Damn, baby, I don't know if I got a feeva or if you just
makin' me hot all ova." Claudine moved her breast closer to
Moet and pressed her forehead into the area under Moet's chin,
looking again into the sky. She warmed Moet's cool body with
her own heat while her hands and palms freely caressed and
pried for easy access into Moet's crotch.

"Oh, Moet . . ." Claudine moaned. "Let's be together tonight." Claudine's mind was drifting, still disoriented as she
lifted her head to Moet's. Now completely covering Moet's
body with her own, she pulled her own coat over the both of
them and began to probe her bitter tongue into Moet's half-
opened mouth. The force of Claudine's weight caused both
bodies to move and rock on the ground in slow unison as she
wiggled on top of her. Sleepily, Claudine kissed all over Moet's
neck, cheeks, nose and forehead. Moet's forehead was extra
moist now. Gooey even. Claudine changed her focus to Moet's
breasts until she had a nipple in her mouth. She eventually fell
asleep there with the nipple feeding her . . . drifting finally
into unconsciousness. Claudine was asleep. Out cold. But she
wouldn't have any idea that Nadine Butler (aka Moet) was stiff
as a rock . . . and as dead as a doornail.

CHAPTER FIVE

A Letter to Mom

Dear Mom,

I finally got the chance to write you . . . after all these years. It's just that I've been so very busy building my empire, my life and my future. Since I came out to visit you in California a lot has happened. I hope to come out there again to spend more time with you. I didn't ever remember having one of those mother-son talks, like you see on TV and stuff.

Besides, I'm an adult now!

Meanwhile, I just wanted to take the time (at the beginning of my letter and on my 28th birthday) to say 'I love you' and that I'm doing everything I can with all that you have given to me. You always bounced back, Mom. With so many hard times that you faced. Financially, you struggled as an entrepreneur's wife; forced to be resourceful. You were the homemaker, making our clothes and taking on the most stressful jobs to help keep the bills paid when Dad didn't carry us. And you were strong, coping with Dad's infidelities. You are so strong, Mother, and you have survived regardless of the odds.

One thing that I have indeed inherited from you and Dad is the initiative to work hard. Working hard for me is a natural: doing and being the best I can. I'm pursuing my talents relentlessly and by far, I'm feeling like the most resourceful black man on earth. All because of you. I don't have one job, but so many responsibilities. Now, I haven't been making my own clothes, like you once did, but I have been good at penny-pinching (being conservative) and cooking. When Stacy says she's in the mood for pancakes, I know that means one thing or the other. She wants to be taken to IHOP (my lazy alternative) or I've got to get my black ass (oops!) out of bed and start making the batter. What a life! But just the same, thanks again, Mom.

I'm enclosing my latest videocassette of the TV show. It has an exclusive interview with Nancy Wilson that I know you'll appreciate. Yes, Mom! Your son is reaching for the big time! Enjoy the tape and I'll write to you again soon.

Oh! Stacy says hi!
Kiss, kiss,
Hug, hug.

Your son,
Douglass

Writing to his mother was a stretch for Douglass, since he'd been so far removed from the concept of family for years. His father was the nearest immediate member of the Gilmores that he related with on a day-to-day basis. And yet, despite how close they were with business affairs, the two were farther apart than they would have liked to admit. Convenience. That was the only "why" that kept them in close contact. But in the meantime, looking alike and (sort of) living together didn't substantiate a bond. Being father and son was more or less coincidental.

Home Sweet Home

The Gilmore family, in the past 2 generations (at least), had never grown into a position of great wealth. Douglass couldn't ever recall any relatives having more than a working man's luxuries. At best, the really consistent aunts and uncles maintained their own homes, cars and middle class lifestyles, if merely due to hard, diligent work. But for sure, nobody moved to that level of affluence to deserve a 10,000-square foot, 24-room home with a 4-car garage. Not until Douglass learned about real estate.

In Douglass's teen years, the family began to break out in different directions. Different destinies. His mother eventually sought a divorce. She left for sunny California to live with her parents who had retired there from New York decades before. Douglass's two sisters simultaneously followed their mother to eventually marry into their own separate family start-ups. But, all told, the divorce between Mr. and Mrs. Gilmore left the family in shambles. With everyone left to sow their own oats in their very own mismatched worlds with no backbone, and no sound leadership or role models to turn to or rely upon.

Against those odds, Douglass still managed to spend many hours learning sales techniques and the many strategies of buying real estate with "no money down." From seminars to the mail-order cassette courses, Douglass absorbed himself in the basics of finding distress properties, identifying the "don't wanters" of these parcels, and he drew up his own offers for them. Before and during the issues which led to the breakup of his parents, Douglass was searching for a home. Inspired by pain that was pervasive and self-perpetuating in their Mt. Vernon home, he thought that closing on a new deal, a new home, in a new area might encourage a new family attitude. So for Douglass, although the Gilmores always had a roof over their heads, finding a home was necessary. And it wasn't merely to keep the family together either because Mr. Gilmore was so busy with his own lifestyle that he had been neglecting the rent payments for 3 or 4 months.

Douglass searched for days, concentrating on the neighboring towns of Pelham and New Rochelle. He spent the most time in New Rochelle, where his parents had arranged for him to attend junior high school and part of high school. One day he stumbled upon a huge property that showed all of the signs he'd been looking for: Tall-as-hell grass. Dingy windows. Need for a paint job. This was the "don't wanter" that he was trained to look for!

At first the home seemed unattainable because of its size. A four-story Colonial with a breathtaking panoramic view of the town's main artery, North Avenue. This was a four-lane road that connected one end of New Rochelle with the other; the only road to do so. Just across the street was the town landmark, the Thomas Paine statue. It stood 25 feet tall and represented the history of the Huguenots, the army which battled under the leadership of then-General George Washington. To the immediate right of the house were two mile-long lakes, divided by a small bridge and walkway. Finally, just behind the lakes was New Rochelle High School, known best for its state championship-winning football team. It was also known as the #1 school in the country for its impeccable curriculum and grade-point average. Douglass also attended New Ro (the pet name for the high school) and kept no more than a A or no less than a C average in his classes. Yet he was an above average girl watcher. It was well after his school years, and his stint in the Marine Corps when he found this vacant corner property on North Avenue.

Part duty and part nuts and bolts know-how, Douglass sought out the homeowner. Digging into the town tax assessment records he discovered that the owner was a Japanese doctor who practiced acupuncture. He could not obtain a license to practice his profession in the United States as he hoped. He actually gambled on the process, but found himself caught between a rock and a hard place. Forced to continue his practice in London, the home which he'd purchased sat unoccupied for over 2 years. Thus, the New Rochelle home was useless to him and became the best-kept opportunity for an entrepreneur looking for a home.

Douglass contacted the doctor, and taking advantage of the circumstances, offered him $1,000 a month in a lease-option deal. The doctor appreciated Douglass's aggressive approach. He wasn't offended by the below-market offering. Instead, he was happy to have a committed buyer. Bottom line: this deal would be a family in the home, one that would hopefully take care of it, and the investment would continue to appreciate in value. This residential neighborhood was an attractive one, to say the least. Immaculately kept. It was quiet during the day *and* night, with the exception of garden workers, gas-powered mowers and leaf blowers in the early mornings. Every home had a large front yard. If the front yard was small, it was because of an oval driveway or a massive backyard. Most every home in the area had these amenities and all of the benefits of affluence.

950 North Avenue was no different from the rest. There was a great lawn in front, accentuated by a 230-foot oval driveway that curved around from one road to the other. The backyard was long and wide enough to fit another small home on. The house was an all-white Colonial with a crimson-red clay tile roof. There were even two addresses since the home sat on a corner property. 950 North Avenue faced the main road, while 11 Braemar Avenue enjoyed the scenery of the lakes.

The icing on the cake (a boost to Douglass's ego) was to live just across the way from his old school where high school acquaintances used to tease him about his homemade orange tie, his high-water jeans and the overall miscoordination of clothing. The youngster had no sense of detail and nobody to show him style. But if those hecklers could only see Douglass *now*! He was living in a damned mansion! And it only added to his ten-ton collection of "last laughs" for everyone who was curious enough to ask themselves, *"How the hell did he do that?"*

Unfortunately, the doctor's acceptance of Douglass's offer did not come in time to salvage the family unity or to support whatever could be salvaged. So while his mom and sisters traveled westward, Douglass was left to live side by side with his father in this big home, with the most lavish living conditions, and his only responsibility was the fun and excitement of managing the ever-popular family nightclub, Gilmore's Fool's Paradise.

The Beginning of an Empire

New Rochelle, New York, was and is considered suburbia. And yet this community, with its *Good Morning America* ways, has fast become a melting pot where residents from every other country have sprouted up faster than vines. Many Spanish, Haitian, Oriental and Caribbean immigrants found New Rochelle to be an even mix of city-like resources in the most suburban surroundings. Grass. Trees. Lakes and streams; all of these elements lending their energy to the clean air that contradicts the realities of the big city only 25 minutes south. That once-upon-a-time all-white town, with its all-white infrastructure, has been forced to rub elbows with and adjust to the realities of culture and all of the spices that come with it. These realities have even forced New Rochelle into an economic surrender, where over half of its commercial businesses, including banks and restaurants, have bailed out. Four big nightclubs closed permanently. So while the majority of the city's large businesses fled or shut down, the new opportunities opened up for niche businesses which could adapt to the shift in this town's new cultural realities.

All things considered, with his new home, his know-how and business savvy, Douglass embarked on a new plan. This would go further than his selling shoes door to door when he was 7, or his mining for Cabbage Patch Kids when toy store shelves went dry. This venture (he planned) would be a multi-media empire which focused on an experience that the world could not escape. Black entertainment. A fan and a student of black entertainment, Douglass enjoyed recording the events through the decades. The icons stood out like massive bill-boards: MOTOWN; BLACK ENTERTAINMENT TELEVISION; NO LIMIT; DEF JAM & ROC-A-FELLA RECORDS. Douglass observed the growth of these institutions, much like millions of others. But unlike many who simply observed, he vowed to be a part of it. The growth and popularity was becoming so obvious. Black artists were now being seen more on video. More and more, week after week, black artists would strike pay dirt until it was no longer unusual. Now, instead of rock and pop artists, urban music became a fixture on the world's top pop charts. Finally, America was realizing the creativity, richness and longevity of black music, regardless of the skin color behind the sounds. This was music and entertainment that was just plain addictive. The beats, the bass, and the grooves were enticing. The days of K.C. & the Sunshine Band and Hall & Oats (groups that relied on soul) were replaced by a sea of newcomers. Not just The Whispers, Temps, Tops or Miracles. But new editions like Luther Vandross, Whitney Houston and Stephanie Mills. In their shadows came Boys II Men, Babyface, Toni Braxton and the many productions of Jimmy Jam and Terry Lewis. These groups among others moved into the top ranks of popular music. They were the *new* A-list, to the point that rock music began to question its own mainstream appeal. And bigger than that, this all had a pro-found effect on impressionable young men like Douglass.

He soaked it all up, absorbed it all. He knew that the world (overall) was accepting the truth. Black talent and black cul-ture, as expressed through black entertainment. He watched how MTV even changed its format from a rock video channel, in order to keep up with black videos, black artists, rap artists and the many events which embraced the genre. Douglass recognized all of this and he vowed to play a strong part in it. In his manifesto—unsaid and undocumented—he pledged to create that vacuum which would inevitably seduce and attract the black community en masse, inviting one and all to his empire. SuperStar Communications. Brainstorming for a substantial company name wasn't a tough task. The name would have to have some "umph". It would also have to indicate technology, future and endurance. The name would have to flow. It would have to look good in bright lights. Yet it would have to be pleasant enough to be accepted as a household word. And finally, the name would have to stand on its own and overcome any shadow of a doubt by its mere mention. So Douglass chose "SuperStar." He picked the word for its many meanings and for its self-prescribing decree of *the very best*. The "communications" tag on the company name was a natural, indicating there was information to be shared.

To claim and register this title as his very own universal address was a great feeling for Douglass. He felt as if he'd created a new, unprecedented home for the black entertainment experience. A simple $35 filing fee and some forms were the only necessary criteria for operating such a business in Westchester County. No specific licenses or permits were necessary, just a visit to the county clerk's office and some deliberate ideas to create a cash flow.

Douglass tried to begin a singles organization, thinking that a weekly gathering of lonely, horny people would create that cash flow he wanted. But when that seemed more wayward than not, he did a little research and thought up a plan whereby amateur performers from the tri-state area would come together under one roof—one event. He formatted the event as a variety show so that any age and any talent might attend. Next, he set up an inexpensive registration fee of $10, affordable to most anyone. After an onslaught of street advertisement, there was a big reception and audition, after which over 500 performers were scheduled for an ongoing theme of shows with 25 or 30 acts per night. Furthermore, each entertainer was required to sell 10 tickets for each of their appearances. That would create revenue and bring a consistent audience of hundreds.

So it was settled. This would be a big event. And New Rochelle would be the home of his idea. Douglass went about addressing the event with a title; one with some credibility, because surely *anyone* could throw together a talent show. To lend some sort of traditional edge (without the need for any such approval or permission) and to additionally create the climate of a "community atmosphere" (as opposed to a business venture), Douglass named the event *The Westchester Talent Competition.*

Business and Pleasure

Talk of the big audition spread throughout the county and the state. The ads in the local newspapers, in pennysavers, on posters and by word of mouth, created the blitz of attention. The event was coordinated from his home office, and ultimately became the most talked-about talent showcase in the county's history of entertainment. All along, he'd tell himself: *"It's going just as planned. Now, make it better."* He also placed ads on the local cable television community bulletin board. And as the $10 fees began to pour in, Douglass put the money back into television commercials that were placed on MTV, CNN and various other highly visible cable channels. But to his surprise, the print ads, television and word of mouth attracted nothing close to the amount of responses that the hand-made tree signs provoked. These were his most successful tools; those 400 modestly sized slices of sheet metal with an 800 number and the words "TALENT WANTED."

So many signs were put up in so many high-traffic areas that the message became a nuisance. People began to call just out of curiosity, and even then, some signed up and got involved. Phone calls came day and night, and along with them came the flow of innocence and naiveté, ignorance and fever. A script was created, telling the average caller everything that an amateur performer with the fever to perform would want to hear. The script made no unfounded promises, but it was attractive and suggested that most anyone should ready their $10 application fee for a try at fame. Another technique which Douglass executed was to put the caller on hold momentarily. Douglass's girlfriend Stacy would conveniently handle calls from the male respondents, while he accepted female callers. The idea worked well. They were both passionate about the event, and they both developed savvy as they became comfortable with the routine. Stacy always kept the guys' hearts pounding. She excited them so much they called back frequently, asking for her by name. In the meantime both Douglass and Stacy were focused, asking all callers for their full name, address and phone number. The duo talked to callers for long enough to ensure that application fee would be in hand within a matter of days.

Although she was not experienced in any management capacity, Stacy handled the tasks of organizing and arranging like a pro. She maintained a certain wisdom, but was nonetheless subordinated by Douglass's high expectations. Somehow, their relationship was overcome by need. Stacy needed a dominant figure in her life. Douglass was boosted by Stacy's charisma, her submissiveness—how she put on that "little girl" act—and he was allured by her dancer's features; the results of her formal training as a youngster. She had the look of a fitness instructor, with well defined calves, good posture, and that hip-hop-video ass. Stacy's other assets were the tight B-cup breasts, the alluring, full lips and doe eyes.

Douglass sensed an air of adventure about Stacy when they first met. She was a tagalong of a mutual friend who was just stopping by the Gilmore home. Perhaps she was more like a delivery, since that mutual friend had been planning this all along. But once she made it to the house, Stacy mentioned something about knowing Douglass's family.

"I went to school with your sisters, plus I was in your mother's Girl Scouts group," she told Douglass. Such words quickly earned Douglass's confidence. And he easily soaked it up so that it didn't take two days for the two to get intimate. Yes, there were those obligatory gestures of courting, like the flowers and phone calls. The also did lunch at a classy Japanese restaurant. But eventually Stacy returned to Douglass's house without playing "hard to get."

"This place is crazy! It's all yours?"

Douglass shrugged, not trying too hard to be humble.

"It's so spacious," she went on to say. "So much . . . atmosphere. And it matches you and your free spirit."

"If that means it looks like a bachelor's pad, then, yeah . . . I agree with you."

"Nah. This isn't a bachelor pad. Far from it. And besides, I never met a guy as organized as you."

"Organized, but single," said Douglass with that smirk.

Stacy stayed over that night. It was a long night of personal, but not intimate, conversation. The two even fell asleep fully clothed on Douglass's humongous waterbed. In the early hours of the next morning, with the daylight barely showing through the bedroom window, Douglass woke up to find Stacy in heat. She was hovering close to him with an exploring gaze. From that moment, cruddy breath and all, the two connected with plug-and-play perfection. They began kissing and touching. The stimulation was both original and exciting, progressively taking them into a wild and frenzied session of feverish grabbing and groping. If there was skin exposed, it was covered or palmed or squeezed. They stretched their bodies and limbs to the limitless levels of their desires. They swelled with passion, and had no regard for birth control or prevention.

Stacy finally pulled Douglass's naked body into hers. The thrusts invoked her cries, followed by a heavy stream of tears and sighs. She didn't want to admit that she needed him, but he convinced her again and again that she did. In the heat of the moment, Stacy expressed that she *did* need him and backed it up with an emotional testimony.

"It seems like I knew you for so much longer. I know that sounds like a line or somethin', like out of a movie, but it's true," she said tearfully. The confession hit a peak, and Stacy abandoned every discipline, giving into a flow of affection. She pulled herself even closer to Douglass, until they could be no closer—as if she altogether wanted to be inside of him. The heat between them was part of that soft yet aggressive friction between her Camay skin and his, two shades darker. There was an instant when Douglass continuously entered her, as if in some race for a power-finish. She bounced with him until they were both breathlessly waiting for an answer . . . for a finale . . . or for some July 4th explosion. There was a definite end, and then neither of them wanted to move, if only to linger there in that ecstasy.

After a time, their bodies shifted and they rolled over so that she was on top. She circled her arms around Douglass's neck, then in a soft-spoken tone, Stacy explained, "I'm not sad, just . . . just in disbelief."

"Huh?" Her sincerity slowed him and a lone tear fell from her eye onto his cheek.

"Douglass, that was my first one."

"First what?" he asked, bewildered and frustrated. Stacy looked directly into his eyes, expecting him to understand. Then she exhaled.

"My first orgasm," she said with her eyelids contracting, finishing her sentence. *Silly.*

"Ooo-kay," said Douglass before his own eyes asked, *Now what?*

Expecting the moment to be more eventful, but settling for whatever, Stacy began to kiss Douglass's bare chest. She delicately lowered her head to his waist, observing his limp penis, still shimmering from all the sex. Then, with a certain determination about her, Stacey embracing him with one hand, she pushed her straight black hair to the side, but stopped to look up into Douglass's eyes.

"Have you ever had any diseases?" She was bashful, but still had that sense of hope in her voice. As though his answer was irrelevant, Stacy unconsciously massaged him with her palm fully gripping his erection. Douglass looked at her inquisitively thinking that *This must be some doctor shit.*

"I mean like sexual infections or whatever?" Stacy affirmed her position with a more determined tone.

"N-no. *Hell*, no." Douglass was simple and truthful and sincere. His face expressed that *yuck!* as if he'd envisioned the images of puss and infection.

"You sure?" She looked at him. Her eyes smiling and not really requiring an answer.

"Sure, I'm sure." he answered definitely. But Stacy had already begun to lower her head. She purposefully took him into her mouth, devouring him with her cheeks tight and tongue consumed with his erection. She bobbed her head up and down on him, doing her best to maneuver on the water-filled mattress.

Meanwhile, Douglass was trying hard to maintain his sanity, all but rupturing with gasps and quivers. Stacy took things a step further, overwhelming his greatest expectations. She licked and kissed her way around and below his testicles.

She adjusted his legs and knees until they were comfortably cocked. Then she kissed and slurped at what had (until now) been forbidden and taboo. Having never experienced the feeling before, Douglass was hit hard with feelings of exhilaration. He shuddered. He was speechless. Part of him was a little frightened. Yet Stacy became engrossed as if she was trying to impress or gain his approval. He couldn't open his eyes because he was squeezing them too tight. He was tense. Squeezing his face like a weightlifter.

Stacy eventually revisited his erection with her swollen lips and she massaged him with both hands until he was completely spent within her jaws. Douglass just laid there in a state of comatose, stunned at how this woman just swallowed all of him just as easy as if he was her favorite milkshake. There were no questions left in his mind. Stacy was convenient. She was a freak who could curl his toes, and now (so to speak), this nymphomaniac belonged to him!

For two years the talent showcase went from small idea to a big bang. It grew rapidly into a cornerstone of New York's entertainment world, introducing all things amateur. People traveled from as far as Florida and Canada to be a part of the weekly showcase. The videotapes from each weekly performance created footage and content which was neatly edited together into a 60-minute TV show. The show was named *"The SuperStar USA TV Show,"* starting out as a cheesy video production with poor lighting and sound. The continuity was horrible and choppy—as if a naive 2nd grade student put it together. Even the response to the cablecast was discouraging. However, the core audience—families, friends and those performers—had no other choice. Gradually, even if viewers had to cope with the growing pains of an aspiring TV producer, the show eventually developed into an entertaining, hour-long presentation.

To accommodate the needs of performers, as well as to carry out the operations of this ever growing enterprise, Douglass had gathered a small but reliable staff of supporters. Darryl was the public access studio manager who originally showed Douglass basic studio use. Greg and Lou served as publicist and public relations directors, respectively. Huey was the stage manager for the various stage shows, and Rick hosted each live event. With this support, Douglass was inspired to grow and better his labor of love. Otherwise, the project might not have progressed past a few months. But it *did* survive. The t.v. show aired at 9PM every Saturday night—prime time airtime—on a channel that was wedged between CBS on one side and NBC on the other. This made it inevitable for any channel surfer to "stumble" into the world of SuperStar.

In time, the production of the show began to improve, and its regional audience also increased since Douglass began to syndicate the show; making copies and then distributing them to other stations throughout the tri-state area. Many hundreds of thousands of people were now tuning into SuperStar USA, forcing Douglass to get his shit together. He was on the front line, where he had no choice but to improve—improve or perish.

The benefits from the pressure was that Douglass not only grew as a talented producer, he also sharpened his skills at editing, camera angles and hosting. As the host of *The Super-Star USA TV Show*, Douglass performed hundreds of interviews with aspiring artists and debut artists, until he was very good at questions and interacting with just about anyone. Soon, major names began to fill the entire one-hour show.

The toughest interview, his first major (quote, unquote) celebrity interview was Phyllis Hyman. She originally declined his request for an exclusive. But perhaps the exposure to over 2 million viewers changed her mind, and she agreed—at least, over the phone. However, when Douglass and his 2 man camera crew showed up at the Blue Note Jazz Club for the interview, Phyllis still hadn't completely agreed. Finally, Douglass confronted Ms. Hyman's road manager, and addressed him with that same relentless desire—the drive of a man who had confronted rejection time and time again—and in the end the interview went down as scheduled. The dressing room, an intimate setting with classy couches and mirrors and flowers, Douglass handled his questions nervously, but somehow maintained an on-air professionalism. Halfway into the interview, he became more confident. He realized that it was actually the diva herself who was having the difficulty. He slowly took account of her off-stage realities and the problems that she encountered. Yes, this was his toughest interview. But only up until Douglass found that she was human too.

That first celebrity interview virtually broke down every conceivable barrier that Douglass had, or that he *thought* he had. In agreeing to come on the show, Phyllis was actually endorsing the show's existence with a clever interview and stellar stage performance. Subsequently, Douglass's struggle to earn SuperStar's star-power, acceptance and notoriety virtually vanished. That particular episode of the show led to further interest. And suddenly, the show became appealing for big names. Nancy Wilson, Chaka Khan, Stanley Turrentine, Rachelle Ferrell, Pam (Foxy Brown) Grier, Ice Cube, Nia Long, KRS-One, Brandy, Shabba Ranks, Queen Latifah, Glenn Jones, and Keith Washington. The stars flowed into New York and SuperStar was the magnet, as there were no other New York–based shows that claimed such a diverse audience and track record of varying interviews. The popularity of the show expanded with bigger, live audiences, regional popularity and resources that promised a successful future in the music and entertainment industries. Douglass's dream was becoming reality fast, without end.

CHAPTER SIX

Dyre Avenue, Bronx, New York

Dyre Avenue is a busy commercial strip which connects the Bronx, one of New York City's five boroughs, to Mt. Vernon, a suburb of Westchester County. Because Dyre is also the last stop on the northern tip of New York's mammoth subway system, commuters who are headed to homes in the North Bronx or into Mt. Vernon are forced to transfer to or wait for a bus or taxi. With so many itineraries concentrated in one area, congestion cannot be avoided. High traffic, grocery stores, newsstands, tailors and most every other kind of impulse service imaginable was a part of the flurry on Dyre Avenue. From an aerial view, the activity on a bright, humid day might engross the most uninterested eyes. All the loud noise, bustle, the two-way stream of cabbies and thicket of pedestrians was suddenly interrupted by a different person. A different attitude, not aggravated or tense, but friendly. Different clothing, loose with an unrestricting flow. No straps or elastic hugging or trapping body parts for definition. Different skin color, glowing with the color of a healthy redwood tree, not blemished or sulking with stress like some ol' worn oak. Valerie was like this alien walking up Dyre Avenue who was fulfilling a simple task, a quart of milk for Mrs. White. Twice Valerie's age and a home-owner who was a friend of a friend of Valerie's mother. Mrs. White, who insisted that she be addressed with her maiden name in place. *Okay . . . Mrs. Brown-White then. So be it*, Valerie submitted. Since $60 was certainly below market rates for room rentals, Valerie would grin and bear the extra drama. *Going to the store for these sudden needs? Well, all right.* She could tolerate that. Valerie thought about these various extras as taxes, while she headed for the grocery store purposefully.

Nearly every person who caught a peek at Valerie strolling down the sidewalk, whether they were alone or with another, gazed at her for extended periods of time. Even inside the window of the local laundromat a few women nearly pressed their faces to the window. Then came a loud, obnoxious para-keet whistle that cried out into the air. Valerie looked over and thought this guy was just acting silly, how he was standing up with his upper body extended through the passenger's win-dow of a moving Chevy Caprice. It appeared to be a taxi mov-ing about 10 miles per hour—that is until those next few seconds. Nothing but confusion. The car in front, also a Chevy Caprice, either put on his brakes or merely decelerated. Either way, there was this loud **CRASH!** Headlights, backlights and directional signals from both vehicles were strewn about the Dyre Avenue blacktop. The back and front bumpers of the ve-hicles were lip-locked under and over one another. Instead of whistling, the rude boy was now moaning and still hanging from the window. And, although he looked like a damaged, human jackknife, wiggling from his circumstances as best he could, he still mustered the audacity to pursue Valerie with his eyes. Killing himself over a piece of ass.

While the drivers argued, Valerie hardly noticed. She turned her head away from the loud noise and returned down Dyre Avenue with the slim brown bag cuddled between her arm and breast. Before long Valerie whipped back around the corner to

Mrs. Brown-White's house, not having any idea of the commotion she'd just caused. But then, there's no telling how many men have stumbled, tripped or stuttered upon approaching or passing Valerie. Even her ex-boyfriend used to have those nightmares about her stifling the economy of Canada when she sneezed.

Mrs. Brown-White may have also come to envy Valerie, realizing how much attention her new visitor was attracting during her first months in the Bronx. She first thought that spring fever had something to do with it. But now in Valerie's third month as a live-in, men began surfacing with even more consistency. Mrs. Brown-White's home had never been a site for tourists, nor was it near a traffic light. Nevertheless, car horns, the doorbell, telephone and even the extra nice "hellos" that Mrs. White was herself receiving was becoming a bit much. The activities pushed the woman to be more of an overseer than a landlady. Valerie, on the other hand, was overwhelmed, and she welcomed the kindness, the flowers and the attention. And she wasn't cheesy about it, but she wasn't interested in anything serious at the moment. Basically, the flurry of interest merely helped her to forget Canada and the obsessed boyfriend she'd escaped from. Besides, she wouldn't be here for long. The house was too close to her job; she was making good money, and she was an independent woman, not the type to overstay her welcome. Not to mention she'd already begun searching for more appropriate living conditions.

The New Job

Valerie figured that finding a bedroom couldn't be any harder than it was to find a job. But of course, this *was* Valerie. And things just kind of happened *for* her—like a flower receiving its timely shower of sun and rain, no more, no less. She didn't think this way; that's just the way it was. She was in a perfect rhythm with the universe around her. It was the type of assurance that made anything possible, where she could cope in just about any circumstance. For instance, when Valerie had initially sought out a job, you'd think she won the World Series or something, with how employment applications show-

ered her ticker tape parade-style. Coincidentally, Valerie sort
of stumbled into her new occupation compliments of her landlady. She joined Mrs. Brown-White for a weekly food buy. And
on the way home they stopped by the local Dunkin' Donuts. It
was then that Valerie recognized a large building, painted all
black. On the exterior there were bigger-than-life artist rendi-
tions of bold, voluptuous women. A 10-foot sign hung from an
extended beam, where passing traffic couldn't miss its big
black, beveled letters.

GILMORE'S
FOOL'S PARADISE
The Leader in Adult Entertainment.

Valerie avoided the obvious and gave her chaperon no indications. But in time she'd learn more.

It was the next day, only a week after her arrival in New
York, that Valerie took a cab—it was a ploy, just to make Mrs.
Brown-White think she was traveling far. But she didn't go
more than 4 city blocks to Boston Post Road and the building
called FOOL'S PARADISE. She tipped the driver, left him dumbfounded, and carried herself casually through the front entrance of the establishment. It was about 4:30 PM. Once
inside . . . once her eyes adjusted from the extreme light to
instant darkness, she realized the blur of men throughout the
room. There was a moment when she measured the intensity
in the club, most of it caught up in the stage show where a
couple of shapely dancers performed in sensual, eye-catching
motion. One was cherubic with tobacco-brown skin and
pointed breasts. The other was more like mocha chocolate; a
girl with slightly chiseled facial features, glistening under the
concentration of colorful spotlights, and selfishly caressing
herself with excessive baby oil. Some men by the stage were
suspended in amazement, giving each other affirmative high-
fives and bouncing with merriment, all of them appreciative
enough to swing dollars at the entertainment until the money
either stuck to her beautiful curves or floated to her feet like
feathers.

Valerie peeped a customer tapping another on the shoulder.
Soon, many pairs of eyes eventually shifted to her location by

the club's entrance. The attention made her feel as if she was on stage herself, only without the spotlights. Maybe thirteen or fourteen men were looking her way, but with the ultra-violet lighting in the room causing all things bright to illuminate in the dark. In a nearby mirror Valerie saw how her teeth glowed and how the whites of her eyes seemed to light up like the girl from *X-Men*.

"Can I help you?" A bouncer stepped to Valerie.

"I was . . . just looking." Valerie's expression was still asking for time to take all this in. "But do you guys have jobs open here?" Valerie had spent quality time at Mrs. Brown-White's vanity to look impressive, and now she only hoped the extra time would pay off—how? She had no idea. In the meantime, she listened for a response knowing that, as was usually the case, her thick Caribbean accent would be respected or rejected. Predictably, Americans usually did one or the other.

"Well . . ." said the bouncer, not wanting to point out the obvious, "I'm sure there is." As though he might be a little ashamed, the bouncer's body was conveniently positioned to block Valerie's view of the stage. It made her smirk, wondering if there was something about her that made her appear to be a prude. Now another bouncer passed by, taking one long shameless look at Valerie's body. *No shame in his game,* Valerie assumed. She wondered also just how much the other guy could see past her long, black fur. Again she smirked.

"Do you dance?"

"I don't . . ." She stretched her eyes to find the stage again . . . "know if I'm as good as some of—"

The bouncer made a gesture, as though he were brushing away the competition. With a sweeping eye, Valerie gave a closer look, scanning the room while the bouncer—

"Name's Jimmy," the bouncer finally said. And he helped her away from the entrance. At the same time, various men were still peering on with nostrils flaring. Other dancers and lingerie, costumes, sexy gowns, thongs, stilettos, boots and all manner of hosiery, silk and lace were sprinkled throughout the crowd of men. Most of the girls were slender and voluptuous, like what you'd find on a beach. One girl was champagne and elegant, while the next was ghetto, and looked like she might be ready for a street fight. Aside from that strange mix of attitudes, there were many complexions of brown, like chocolate pudding, fudge and creamy caramel all working for the same green.

There were sensual expressions, as well as the erotic ones, and they addressed customers with the confidence of long-legged ostriches or the determination of stallions, or silky smooth Cheshire cats. Asses bounced throughout the club— an ass-*fest!*—and dancers cupped their breasts or stroked themselves with satisfied expressions in their eyes, as though this was normal to do this in front of absolute strangers. A couple of special effects devices projected colored rays of light in various directions, swinging wildly and rhythmically, while bartenders stayed busy pouring, popping bottle tops and serving the drinks atop of cocktail napkins across the bar. Handshakes took place here and there along with kisses and hugs. A look to the left, and you'd see dancers onstage, mostly naked, with thongs—nothing but lace to keep a patch of fabric to hide the pubic area. With her back to the audience, there was one dancer leaning up against a walled mirror. By the looks of things, she seemed to be mostly amusing herself, jiggling her tits and ass for tips.

"Is *that* what you mean?" Valerie gestured towards the stage. Jimmy agreed with less-then a nod of confirmation. Now, Valerie looked over at the main stage with more at stake. "How much does it pay?"

"Well, I'll let Gil tell you. He can get into that with you. But I'll tell you now, girls make hundreds a day. Some make as much as a thousand. It depends on you and how much you hustle." Valerie didn't really understand the meaning of "hustle," and it really wasn't Jimmy's place to discuss these preliminaries with her. But without explanation, Valerie was confident. She *always* worked hard for the things she wanted.

When Gil emerged from the back room, Jimmy waited before introducing Valerie. He could see that Gil needed a second or two to tuck his shirt in and adjust his zipper. Eventually, Jimmy flashed a gesture at Gil until the proprietor understood that his zipper was down.

"Go on and make some money, girl. This ain't got nothin' to do with you." While Gil pulled up his zipper he still managed to swat some knock-kneed dancer from the area; the same girl who came from the back office with him. This sudden activity threw Valerie for a spin, telling her at once exactly *who* Mr. Gilmore was and how she'd approach him. With *extra* caution.

"Later, Gil," the dancer signified and smiled towards Valerie. She moved in extra slow motion, her eyes on Gil's zipper, and then she addressed Valerie with that same contemptuous, sarcastic smile. Valerie could read between the lines, how the dancer was letting her know that there was more to the boss than meets the eye. But it was the kind of thing that Valerie was too focued to care about. The girl finally squeezed past Gilmore, but not before she reached between his legs.

Gil pushed her hand away, sucked his teeth and said, "*Alright,* now." Then, to Valerie, he asked, "So . . . what's your name?" The question didn't come without a quick examination.

Valerie answered while she looked directly into his eyes. Eventually, she graduated from a firm gaze to her usual, pleasing smile.

"Ever dance before?" asked Gil, maybe waiting for her answer. In the meantime, Prince was growling and screaming over his music,

> *I looked all over, and all I found*
> *was a phone number on the stairs.*
> *It said, "Thank you for a funky time,*
> *Call me up whenever you wanna grind."*

And while the "Purple One" was screaming over the club's sound system, a dancer was gyrating and thrusting and humping to the music, performing every lyric of the song as though she was the one who created it . . . as though she meant every word . . . (and ultimately) as though she was actually fucking some invisible person up there on stage.

"Well . . . not like . . . *that.* But . . . I'm willing to give it a try."

"Okay." Gil rushed into specifics, scaling a fish he'd just caught. "Do you have an outfit or anything?"

"No. But I could try to get some—"

Gil cut in.

"What size do you wear?"

"I'm a seven . . . or six," she replied with a coy smile.

"Hold on. Let me get one of the girls over here to help out. Maybe you can audition today."

"Now?" Valerie's eyes opened wide. "But I wasn't expecting—"

Gil had already motioned for Jimmy. He spoke to him in a low tone, out of Valerie's range. She could see that this was activity related to her, and she watched as Jimmy circled around to the rear of the club, into what could've been a dressing room. The deejay was now playing a record, scratching a lyricless rock beat over the end of Prince's song. Seconds later Phil Collins faded in.

"I can feel it comin' in the air tonight, hold on . . ."

"Oh, that's my *song*," mentioned Valerie. The deejay let the record go and the transition melted in like some musical design. It was in the next few moments that Valerie's life took a fast-paced spin into the world of topless dancing.

Cinnamon

Cinnamon was summoned from the dressing room and in no time at all she was in deep conversation with Valerie. Valerie asked, and Cinnamon answered. They talked about economic possibilities, setbacks, the sleaze, the most effective dance moves, the boss, the busiest nights and other topless clubs too. The two even got in to their own experiences of how each arrived at Gilmore's and what their future plans were. Cinnamon was paying her way through nursing school with just 3 and 4 days of dancing per week. That's all Valerie needed to hear!

While the girls continued to chit chat, customers and club staff alike waited anxiously for the new girl's audition. Many customers waited for this very special time; when that "fresh meat" got up on stage, all afraid and green. Hence, the word on Valerie spread quickly throughout the club like an airborne virus. Jimmy, suddenly famous for his introducing the new girl, looked towards the two, catching Cinnamon's eye, casting that all important question on behalf of everyone else in the club.

When is she gonna be ready???

Cinnamon got the message, but all good things must wait. And Cinnamon got every indication that Valerie was a *very* good thing.

"How does it feel to show your stuff up there in front of all those men?" Valerie went deeper, craving a sincere answer.

"I don't even notice it anymore. It comes natural. Ever since that first time on stage—and I was scared out of my skin, girl—but it was all good afterwards. Once you realize that all of these men are in here sweatin' your ass, your ego starts to take over. You start taking control. You even feel liberated. And it helps with your hustle."

"How did *you* deal with that first time, Cinnamon?"

"I wore a cat mask." They both giggled heartily. "But it didn't last for more than two days. More and more, men began to tell me how fine I was and that I was the most beautiful girl they'd ever seen." Cinnamon feigned a yawn. "Some wanted to give me things like jewelry or clothes. One guy even offered me a fuckin' BMW. *Girl*! Do you know I would have let him fuck my *asshole* to get the car? *Especially* then, 'cause times was hard, you know? But I caught myself. I said to myself—when Moet introduced me to the game—that I would never receive gifts. And somehow I was able to stick to it. I don't wanna ever *think* I owe anybody *anything*! And to think I almost fell for that shit." Cinnamon took a *deep*, deep relieving breath while her mind wandered back in time.

"What did you tell the guy?" Valerie was curious.

"I had to swallow first. *Reeeal* hard. And you know I was choked up, and *giiiirl* . . . I imagined doing him one time. Just *once—reeeal* good, and then disappearing into the sunset." They both laughed hysterically. "But a second later I had flashes of him stalking my ass. You must have heard the stories and seen the movies. I just didn't wanna be no movie of the week."

"I heard that." Valerie's raised eyebrows also agreed.

"Now the guy's my best customer. Probably paid my whole tuition by now. I lost count of the C notes."

Valerie raised her hand to give Cinnamon a high-five. They both got up from the cocktail table and proceeded back towards the dressing room.

"Listen, I'll give you something nice to wear. I'm gonna be up on stage for the next set . . . and if you . . . well, take a few

minutes and then come up and join me. Trust me, it'll be easy."
Cinnamon looked over her shoulder at Jimmy with an assuring wink. Jimmy went back to Gil, most likely to inform him
of the inevitable. From then on, the excitement in the club
turned electric.

Valerie followed Cinnamon through a door that was branded
with a modest silver star. Meanwhile, she couldn't resist throwing a playful jab.

"You wouldn't happen to have a cat mask for me, would
you?" Valerie bubbled, suppressing a laugh. Cinnamon wagged
a finger at Valerie. Smiling.

"Okay, girl. That's one for you."

In the dressing room there were two card tables with
makeup tubes and jars, Heineken bottles, ashtrays, and a
cheap vanity mirror scattered about them. Four dancers were
preparing for the evening, sitting in folding chairs at various
areas in the small room. The carpeting was a dark, dingy red,
very worn and stained as if matted by somebody's steamroller.
The walls were bare and still gray with sheetrock, except for
the off-white plaster at the seams and grooves. Big shoulder
bags were propped side by side along the base of the wall. A
bright fluorescent light above was also substituting as a clothes
dryer, so that it helped to dry out a recently and hastily washed
G-string. Apparently, one of the girls used ingenuity, wedging a
writing pen into the fixture, using it as a hook. Meanwhile, the
air in the room was thick and murky, confused with cheap
perfumes and a twist of funk from the busy garbage can next
to a pair of soiled panties in a corner. The fight for clean air
immediately challenged Valerie's senses, and she intentionally
held her breath as she took a seat beside Cinnamon. Eventually, once she realized it was no use, she abandoned the effort,
forcing herself to cope with it all.

Both girls settled down as Cinnamon got into her little prepa-
ratory rituals, while the room took on a dead air. Valerie could
guess that it was her, "the fresh meat," that was the cause of this
tight apprehension. After all, she was the new girl, and they'd all
have no choice but to get along with her. A couple dancers whispered judgments amongst themselves, but Cinnamon rushed
things along, ignoring the lack of charm. After securing her
bag of outfits, she dabbed her face with a cloth, checked her

face in a mirror, and touched and teased up her hair with a comb. She cupped the undersides of her breasts, pulling them higher, subsequently driving her thumbs up under the bra straps to tighten the slack. Cinnamon methodically slipped out of her loafers (shoes she wore in the club when she wasn't on stage) and into a pair of black stilettos. She lifted one heel, and then the other, to pull the strap over her ankle before heading out of the dressing room for her session on stage.

"Ya'll be good. That's Valerie, she's auditioning today." Cinnamon took a second to bend over for a whisper into Jasmine's ear. Jasmine shook her head and Cinnamon rushed through the door. The muffled voice of Luther Vandross instantly turned from hum and drumbeat, and it quickly filled the dressing room with the clear and melodic lyrics of *"Never Too Much."* Cinnamon shut the door behind her, returning the room back to the dead.

Valerie flashed an uncomfortable grin and ignored the tacky surroundings as she began undressing. The others looked on as Valerie roughed it. She recalled her days in the high school locker room back in Christ Church, an attractive community in her native Barbados.

"You new?" blurted China, with the stupid question of the day. Valerie didn't complicate things the way she wanted to; she didn't turn around to flash a raised eyebrow. That would have been too black and she didn't want to go there unless she absolutely, positively *had* to. Instead, Valerie politely answered, *"Yesss!* My name is Valerie. And you?"

"I'm China. This is Sadie." China didn't bother to introduce the other two dancers in the room. She didn't even know them herself, alienating them all the more. Sadie just gave a head nod and kept occupied, changing panties, wiping, spraying, observing. China dug into Valerie a little more.

"Girl, you need a stage name in here. You gotta protect yo'self. Give as little information to customers as possible. Even to other dancers." Valerie nodded her response while slipping into a two-piece costume that Cinnamon loaned her. Suddenly, remembering that she was supposed to watch Cinnamon on stage, Valerie stood up to adjust the pieces comfortably.

She threw a grateful glance at China and headed out of the door.

Leaving the dressing room was like being sucked into a vacuum. Chubb Rock's *"Treat 'Em Right"* was sending vibrations through the walls and floors, as if the entire club was the inside of a sound system. Every banging bass beat was pushing through Valerie's body—out of the floor, up into her spiked heels and into her nervous system. At the same time, the whites of so many pairs of eyes were glued to her as she shut the dressing room door. It felt as if every centimeter of her body was being touched by total strangers. A tremor shook her body. Her feet were getting cold. Freezing. Goose pimples began to show on her smooth, mocha skin. She wanted to quickly turn around to run back into the dressing room. But the eyes around her just beckoned. Her body was uncontrollably obedient as if some powerful, magnetic force was pulling her through this.

Wobbling slightly on her first step in Cinnamon's shoes, Valerie was able to steady her posture, trying her best to remember what elegant was; trying to maintain what Cinnamon called "control." Through a huge opening in the wall, where the oval bar was situated, Valerie could see Cinnamon in the distance. She was at center stage, twisting her body to this fast-paced bass beat—*"Rock Creek Park"* by the Blackbyrds. Cinnamon encouraged the excitement, her arms waving and swinging on time like an excited traffic cop. The sight of Cinnamon gave Valerie some more confidence. *If Cinnamon can do it, so can I.* Only Valerie didn't see herself as *quite* that physically entertaining. She'd give it a try though. The main stage became her focus, as she did her absolute best to avoid eye contact with bystanders. Valerie found a spot adjacent to the stage and stood with her bare ass pressed up against a wall, folded arms, consciously concealing what she could of her breasts. She also crossed her legs, feeling insecure about the next-to-nothing G-string she wore.

The hell with it, she thought. *I may as well be naked!* Although Valerie left Mrs. Brown-White's home fresh and sure, and despite how the air conditioning in the club was pushing up goose bumps on her skin, she swore that there was a pound of perspiration lingering there under her arms, between her legs and across her brow. With so many eyes on her, challenging her comfort . . . even questioning her existence and whether or not she was worthy of being here, there wasn't much she could do. Again, she said *the hell with it.*

For the second time Valerie got a good evaluation of Cinnamon. Cinnamon was brilliant on stage with so much confidence. She didn't speak a word, but her bedroom eyes spoke volumes of fantasies fulfilled to the audience of onlookers. Cinnamon kept such a flawless appearance. No scars, tattoos or blemishes. Her skin was brown like the soft leather of a suitcase. Her breasts curved up as if inclined, with eraser-shaped nipples as peaks. Her curves were accentuated by the stagelights and lasers swinging to and fro. The definitions, her navel, her cleavage, collar bone, waist and spine were all sculptured chocolate delights. Targets for soft, dark and sensual shadows.

Cinnamon toyed with her G-string, hinting that it was removable at will and that there was more to see. She was creative, never removing it totally, but revealing shades of her most erogenous zone. The fire-red outfit that she wore, including the top lying on the stage floor, was small enough to fit into a 6-oz. glass. *Wow,* Valerie thought to herself. She observed her new friend, and now appreciated her even more. There was a second where Valerie looked closer, concluding that Cinnamon had to be clean-shaven and hairless between her legs because the G-string was no bigger than a *Star Trek* insignia and there was not a hair to be seen. Again, she said *wow* to herself.

A customer raced up from his front row seat to tip Cinnamon. But she kept her pride and made him wait a few seconds. Soon after, she belly-danced her way over to him, leaning over and down to drape her arms as she shook her marvelous breasts inches from his nose. Cinnamon turned around with her legs spread apart and the customer's eyes strained with his arm and a $10 bill extended. She bent over to touch her toes, giving him an exclusive view, while looking at him through her legs. She jiggled her butt cheeks at him, requiring his appreciation. Then, backing up her ass to be inches from his nose, Cinnamon reached between her legs and grabbed the man's wrist so that it was snugly wedged in her crack. Slowly, Cinnamon guided the man's hand, sliding it southward until releasing him precisely as he cupped her mound. Leaving the tip with her, the customer returned to his seat half crouched as if he had to pee.

Unsympathetically, Cinnamon resumed her dancing, spreading herself to other areas of the stage as if that little intimate moment with the ten-dollar tipper never occurred. Valerie smiled to herself, feeling more encouraged and remembering Cinnamon's words.

". . . All these men are sweatin' yo' ass . . ." *I can do this,* Valerie thought, loosening the grip of her folded arms.

"You ready to give it a try?" Jimmy's voice caught Valerie off guard. She dropped her arms to her sides before shrugging in agreement.

"Could you ask the DJ to put on something slower, like an Isley's tune or something?" Jimmy chuckled a bit, knowing that that was a far-out request. The DJ was 40 minutes into a jam session that boosted the crowd into moments of spasms. It was a busy after-work crowd that craved release and excitement. And the DJ was feeding the frenzy with the sensational mixes. Now, he was fading from *"Rock Creek Park"* to *"I Get Lifted,"* the classic by K.C. & the Sunshine Band. As they say, the DJ had the house rockin'.

"Sure. I'll ask him. But he usually does his own thing. That's the boss's son, you know." Valerie turned her eyes up to the DJ booth, hoping to make eye contact with *whoever.* As she was helped up the steps to the main stage, other dancers, the bartenders, bouncers and Gil watched with intense anticipation.

"Please welcome Valerie to the stage . . . Valerie!"

The heavy, hollow announcement startled her. She looked over towards Gil, recalling his voice. He was laying down the mic and lifting a half cup of Guinness Stout to his lips as the club full of men applauded and Cinnamon stepped down.

The Audition

The crowd inside of Fool's Paradise was usual for a Friday evening. Maybe 70 or 80 blue collar, white collar and greasy collar workers were concentrated close to the bar and main stage. The club or the dancers could not want for a more appreciative audience. Hungry, full of desire and pockets full of money. The mirrors in the club, along the walls and behind the dancers on stage reflected the incredible illusion that everything was more than it was. The capacity, the activities, the impact of it all . . . everything was MORE.

Valerie felt every bit of the illusion, because to her there seemed to be thousands of faces in the audience. All men. Her imagination was exaggerating the worst. With the heels, Valerie stood almost 5 feet, 10 inches, and on the 4-foot stage she towered over the crowd of captivated and bemused patrons with every dimension, color and age of working men. Valerie took a deep breath, doing her best to wait for a change of music. No waiting was tolerated, however, as men continued applauding to build her confidence. She stepped and swaggered smoothly, in contradiction to the boom-boom-bap of the deejay's latest musical selection. He was on a roll now, blending in the instrumental version of *"California Love."* Valerie addressed Dr. Dre's hardcore drums with her own trademark elegance, swaying, swerving and swishing her hips. Projecting a sense of maturity with her smooth moves, high cheeks and sweet almond eyes. She captivated all without any of the usual hip-hop dance moves or clever neck and shoulder shifts. She simply followed and drifted into her own complete rhythm. Eventually, the DJ got soft and changed the music to fit Valerie's mood. He allowed the pitch of the record's speed to slow to a stop. Simultaneously, Marvin Gaye's *"Let's Get It On"* changed the vibe of the club into a desirable melancholy. Soothing the excitement to a slow groove. The changeover suited Valerie just fine and fit her sensual movements. For half of the song Valerie began to play the crowd. She toyed with men at the edge of the stage, picking a cap from the head of one balding patron in his 50's and then adjusting it on her own head. She pulled her hair through the adjustable strap in the rear, instantly creating a ponytail with her long hair. The elderly man was thrown for a spin of his emotions, suppressing his embarrassment with a gulp from his bottle of Budweiser.

By the time Valerie canvassed the front row of tables with her provocative approach, the DJ was mixing in Sade's "Sweetest Taboo." Determined that these would be her last moments of the audition, Valerie wrapped her arms to reach behind, hugging herself and pulling at the string that supported the top which she wore. It quickly came loose and she continued hugging her breasts along with the furry, white bikini top. She was playful, and slowly let her arms drop with the clothing. Her breasts stood out despite the lack of support. She eventually let her hands down casually, comfortable now with erotic, sexual expressions in her eyes.

With most of Valerie's body exposed, customers turned to each other, while staff and dancers shared comments. Most everyone was amazed by Valerie's perky breasts. She was thick and thin in all the right places as every man's fantasy, and it was all right there on stage at Fool's Paradise. If you weren't present then you missed out.

She was a heavenly sight, passing her hands slowly through her hair and winding and wiggling her curves as if the music was carrying her. The hat which she snatched from the customer was glowing and stood out against Valerie's jet black hair and dark coffee tone. There were subtle indications of Valerie's innocence, thrown off by her being half naked in otherwise raunchy circumstances. Even more innocence was cast by this being her very first topless audition. But that too was contrary to her sexual expressions and the innate confidence that eventually surfaced on stage.

The music made another transition. Valerie bent over to pick up and tie on her top. She already noticed Cinnamon waiting by the bar, and she approached her. At the same time, there was applause from a number of patrons as Valerie left the stage. She hardly noticed as Jimmy the bouncer came over to help her down. Cinnamon rolled her eyes at Jimmy's "extra shit," but reached out to embrace Valerie.

"You were great, girl! They love you. See how they're all

looking at you?" Valerie took the small stack of cocktail napkins from Cinnamon and began dabbing at her brow and neck and underarms.

"Really? I was so—*nervous!* I couldn't even dance at first. But I started getting into it after a few minutes." Valerie was a little gleeful, trying to contain herself.

"Girl, you did all the dancin' you needed to do. Just keep doin' what you were doin'. They love that shit."

Valerie's spontaneous audition quickly earned her a slot on the busiest nights at Gilmore's. She filled a significant void at the club, even more so than she knew, considering her genuine elegance and that Caribbean flavor that the club needed. Sure, Moet was the top girl. And Sadie was an easy second place pick. But perhaps, Valerie would be number three one day.

Within a week of Valerie's employment, she moved into a room; a room that was in the home of a club patron. With that, she broke rules number one and two.

"*Never mix your personal business with a customer, and never accept any gifts like cars, apartments, or huge diamond rings,*" Cinnamon told her. "*Not unless you plan on fucking the guy. And if you do that, they got a whole 'nother profession for that type a shit.*"

Even as a teenager, Valerie's uncle told her, "*Nobody gives you something for nothing.*" However, Valerie ignored those early warnings and went with her own gut feeling. The room she rented was about as close to the job as Mrs. Brown-White's home, which was convenient. But, of course, Valerie had already recognized this arrangement as too good to be true. And she had her guard up just in case the fat slob that she moved in with was not as altruistic as he appeared to be. All the while, Valerie had to wonder: *Do books live up to their covers?* Only time would tell.

The room that Valerie rented from the guy was lightly furnished with a mattress on the floor, a dresser and a chair. Simple enough to build upon and for Valerie to get a good night's sleep after the evening hustle at Gilmore's. She was making three and four hundred dollars from an evening's work. But already things had to change up. Her new (so-called) landlord became a nuisance, always picking her up from work instead of the usual, how he used to stop by every now and again. Furthermore, he was taking her out to eat more, as though they were a couple. Eventually, he propositioned her for sex. Before she busted out laughing in his face, she caught herself and simply uttered an uncompromising "NO." Even the way she said it to him was like a warning to *back off*, which was exactly when the shit started to hit the fan. She declined his favors and even lost a sense of security that she felt behind a locked door. After all, this was his house. But especially, breaking rule number three (*don't sleep with the customers*) wasn't even a distant idea. So while the man remained in heat, his soft hearted, wimpish nature nowhere to be found, Valerie again faced inevitable changes. Not only that, so consumed was she with her living situation and keeping her impact at work, that she had no idea that all the while (even at Mrs. Brown-White's home) she was being followed.

CHAPTER EIGHT

Wake Up!

At 11:20PM, Mechelle was situated on a rickety wooden bench, under a swinging sign that read "BUTNER, N.C." A halogen lamp above the sign attracted various insects that bounced on and off the lamp window. The 70 degree weather would have been bearable, except Mechelle had to constantly shoo the flying, buzzing annoyances from her face and legs. She wanted to move from the light, but the spot where she sat had become warm from her behind. She decided to remain there until the next bus pulled up. Maybe she'd take a quick stroll later.

Otherwise, the climate was calm. The environment was still. There was no more sleep left in her, but she tried awfully hard, pulling her legs up to her breasts and propping her forehead between her kneecaps. Mechelle squeezed her eyes tight, looking to create designs in the darkness of her eyelids. All she could envision was an empty lot to the side of the Greyhound station. An ice machine with a padlock securing the door. A sign, erect at the entrance to the terminal: JD'S REST AND GO. Mechelle wondered if the old fart who locked her out was J.D.

There was a red and blue Greyhound logo at the top portion of the sign, and all that did was make things worse—*does Greyhound know the type of people they partner with?* A Coke machine stood tall at one side of the bench she occupied. The entrance to the station was to her right with shades pulled down on the inside of the glass doors. The loud red sign wedged in the door was a harsh reminder of the bastard who locked her out earlier. CLOSED.

"Asshole." Mechelle cursed him for the 50th time.

The station was shack-like with a shingled roof stretching over Mechelle's head, just enough to shield her from any potential rain. But no hint of that tonight. Her view of the silent, moonlit sky was a pleasant one, even though she was just bored of looking at the stars. Now, she was no astrology student, but these stars seemed to be saying something to her. What, she couldn't say. And, if listening to stars wasn't driving her crazy, then the trees were next, since every other inch of her surrounding was occupied by trees, trees and more trees!

As the midnight hour came around, halfway through Mechelle's frustrating wait, she began to hear some humming in the distance. Moments later, the humming turned into muffled tones, and then voices. She wondered where they were coming from. People? *People!* Mechelle lifted her head and looked towards the left and right of the main road. A slight tremor in her chest warned her of possible danger, but she felt it too late to run and hide as three figures came into eyesight. It was dark, and they were merely shadows for a time, but Mechelle was quick enough to know they were white men. She wondered if it wasn't *she* who was being the suspicious one. But nonetheless, she returned to her seat and remained there as still as a cat with her eyes begging for compassion.

"Lookie there, Bo. Somebody's over on J.D.'s bench." Mike was the first to notice Mechelle. He was also the youngest of the three white men. A delinquent since his early teens, Mike was a pimple-faced eighteen-year-old now. With the crew cut, spectacles and thin build, he maintained a schoolboy appearance. But inside of his head he was conjuring plans like shooting his high school principal and some of the other wiseasses who graduated without him. He even figured to use Bo's rifle to do the job. However, the plan was on the backburner for now, still leaving him with the images of suicide and his own body falling on top of a small pile of 10 or 15 other dead bodies.

"Yep. That's a somebody, alright. Ifn' it ain't a greezy ole groundhawg, it might be a lil' ole nigger-girl." Bo was the heaviest of the bar-room buddies. The local paper mill had laid him off just two months earlier. Meanwhile, he'd be sittin' home with his mother or spending idle hours at the local tavern, making noise, creating conflicts or just bein' plain ole lame-ass Bo. His beer belly was extra luggage, and he rarely kept good health or hygiene. So, his older appearance was but a lie since his neglect made him appear much older than 34.

"N'yall just hold on a cottn' pickin' minit now. The lil' nigger girl might need some help sittin' there all 'lone." Jed was the eldest of the trio, at 42. He spoke real fast, like he was always on the run. He also earned himself an artificial limb as the contender of a tree-cutting contest, pulling and pushing a 6-foot saw against the county champ.

During the final seconds of the feat, with the stainless-steel blade glowing hot-orange from the friction, the champ lost his grip. Jed made the last pull out and down, he fell back to the ground, and in one quick, freakish motion, the scorching sharp blade melted halfway into his leg. The town of Butner and neighboring Daneville heard his hollers for almost 3 days after the accident. But that was 8 years back. It took a few years for him to get comfortable with the prosthetic leg, but he was never the same Jed that worked at the local hardware store; that happy dude who helped the elderly or who mowed the lawn. He just gave up and turned evil. He didn't care anymore. Or as he would say it, *"I don' give a flyin' fuck!"* And from the time he emerged from the hospital, everyone looked at him differently, like he was an abomination. The champ on the other end of the big saw was Big Blue; a monster of a black man who Jed never did forgive. Jed blamed him and every other black person for the mishap.

And now, here they were, strolling along the road at the most awkward hour; Jed and Mike with their dirty blonde hair; Bo with his grassy, jet black mop. The three of them wore clothes that could've been thrift store specials; holes, stains and faded colors. They also carried the same rubbery, intestinal odor that you'd smell in the corner alley where men urinate.

This mangy trio stepped off the main road and approached Mechelle as if they were lazy gunslinging desperados. But, really, all they were looking for was trouble.

"Hey, Bo, I gotta go piss sumpm' awful." Mike made a twisted face at the other two. Bo ignored him while Jed did the introductions.

"Hey, whatcha doin' there, lil' nigger-girl." Jed spoke at his normal rat-tat-tat speed.

Mechelle didn't catch most of what this hillbilly just said, although she did hear the "girl" part of his inquiry. She assumed that the older man was offering help.

"I . . . a . . . I missed the bus."

"Idn' that right," one of them said, pouting as if concerned. Meanwhile, the same guy bobbed his head, appraised Mechelle from head to toe, and even seemed more comfortable now. Now, all three of them felt more comfortable easing closer—about 5 feet from where she sat. The boyish looking one propped his foot up on the wooden walkway in front of Mechelle.

"Where's ya headed?"

"New York."

"Idn' *that* right. A little ole *city* nigger-girl."

Mechelle heard all of *that* comment, with her legs still pressed up against her chest in an upward fetal position. Her arms and her jaw tightened. No words to express what she was thinking.

"Oh really?" Truth be told, Mechelle couldn't believe what she'd heard and didn't really know how to respond. If some of her school friends, or even her sister, were with her, she'd *surely* be singing a different tune to these meatheads. Oh, Mechelle could *get* loud and vulgar if she wanted to. Don't get *that* twisted. But this wasn't school, and she wasn't at home. She was in Buttfuck, North Carolina, with no money, no friends, no help, nowhere.

"Yeah . . . sure." Mechelle's answer had an attitude. She slightly chuckled, but this was Mechelle's way of replying to *anyone* who challenged her. She was always so instantly sarcastic. Even if this was a different situation, she was the same ole Mechelle.

"Oh, so you's a funny city-nigger-girl, huh?" The heavy one turned things up a notch. Meanwhile, the slim one whispered to the older, balding, funny-walking man.

"Well, go the fuck on 'n piss, kid! What the fuck!" The older man spoke as if he was looking to reveal Mike's big secret. Embarrassed, Mike looked around and then settled for the dark area behind the ice machine. He moved in a backwards motion, then turned to scoot to the spot. Just then, the fat one cursed him out again.

"Fuck-no, Mike. Comeer." Mechelle was finally able to put a name to one of these faces.

Mike.

Mike hesitated at Fat Boy's order.

"I said comeer!" Fat boy pointed at the porch where Mechelle was huddled like a rock.

"Whachawant, Bo? I gotta *go.*" Mike stressed his eyes down towards his zipper.

Bo. So, the fat one's name is Bo.

"Alright, missy from New Yawk. Tell ya what. We's gonna play a little game since you wanna be all smart-assy . . ." Bo guessed that this girl was trembling now, regretting the attitude she displayed. But he didn't care a bit since the occasion was making his pecker harder and harder by the second. He wondered if her head was rushing like his was. Maybe that was just the beers fucking with him since they had just been to Joe Bob's bar a mile away . . . since they were boozed up enough to feel a little above the law . . . and boozed up enough to not give a shit.

"Oh, don'cha be puzzled, little city-slicker . . . don'cha be scrrd cuz a few crackers done run up on ya. We's a few good boys, we are . . . we just out to have a good ole time . . ."

At this point, Mechelle couldn't hear any more. She was frightened, afraid for her life, and about to panic. She had no idea that these men were intoxicated, but even so, it didn't make a difference. This appeared to be nothing less than their very own unprovoked, malicious actions.

Mike's eyes widened, wondering what Bo was up to now. The last crazy thing that he had Mike do was to hotwire Joe Bob's car and drive it into Kessler's Pond when Joe Bob denied them any more credit. Credit was reinstated the next day, along with Bo's ego. Ever since, he began exercising this notion that he was above the law.

"Alrighty then, missy . . . relax yo'self. Put your legs down like a nice little nigger-girl." Bo eyeballed Jed as if he was planning to make him proud. Jed blinked unconsciously, in slow motion, while turning his head back towards the girl. Bo took that as agreement from the elder of the crew, then he twisted his head contemptuously towards the girl—zeroing in on his prey. And while these looks were being shared, Mike was simply bloated with piss. The girl was apparently procrastinating, exercising her belligerence, and Mike didn't see what any of this had to do with *him* having to pee!

"Ah sayd, put yo' fuckin' legs down, bitch!" The man they called Bo emphasized his words, simultaneously pulling a palm-sized, 9 millimeter pistol from under his shirt. He stepped up on the wood platform and pressed the tiny barrel to Mechelle's forehead. There was a burning sensation in her stomach now as her every limb shivered. She slowly let go of her legs, easing them down below her, sitting perfectly still with hands dropped to her sides on the bench.

Mike seemed to shrivel, and he dropped his shoulders to put his hands in his pockets. Both the older and younger sidekicks simply stared at Bo. But why did Mechelle sense that there was no stoppin' this guy Bo from whatever he was gonna do?

"Mike . . . you said you had to go? So go." The skinny one, Mike, quickly turned around to head for the ice machine, the piss just about to explode from him. "Nah, boy . . . here! Go here! Here, on the nigger-girl's legs." Bo looked toward Mike, with the gun pressing harder into Mechelle's skull until it cocked back to its limit. No doubt, Bo wasn't fucking around. Whatever he was getting to . . . however he intended to get his rocks off, it was about to commence.

Mike fumbled for his zipper and pulled it down. He reached into his pants and boxers as if he had to search for it; he grabbed his penis, exposing the twig-of-a-thing to the two others, and pointing it in the direction of Mechelle's ankles, Mike stood there with his eyes squeezed closed.

Bo shoved Mike with his free hand. "Gowan' . . . thought ya had to piss?"

"It's comin'. It's *comin*'." Mike tried not to look at Mechelle and it was obvious that he never did this before. But all Mechelle could do was grovel before him.

"Please. Don't listen to—"

"Shut up, city-slick bee-atch. Git'er, boy!"

Mike simply had to go. And go he did, with his steamy stream of urine hitting the girl's bare legs and flowed down into her sneakers. She let a tear drop down her cheek, even if she remained still and somehow still proud. The urine was thick with fumes—a combination of rotten eggs and burnt rubber. It splashed about the porch under her while Mike looked over at Bo for acknowledgment. But Bo was steady smiling at Mechelle—getting his rocks off and still pressing the gun snug against Mechelle's head. Bo was also breathing fast and heartily, realizing his own personal neurotic pleasure in the moment. The look at Bo threw Mike off in a way that caused his urine to change directions, now spraying Mechelle's knees and thighs. He was taken aback by her expression, her tears flowing more rapidly now. Suddenly jolted by the expression on her face, the kid adjusted his direction, now almost a minute into his relief, and aiming back at her ankles as if that were the lesser crime. Once his rush slowed, he shook the remaining drops, then quickly tucked his assault weapon back into his pants.

Mechelle was distraught now, overcome with the lurid stench that was about her waist and limbs. She was breathing harder than a doomed hot air balloon and still trembling with fright. At the same time, the one they called Jed was wide-eyed and grinning with fascination. And now he added *his* two cents to the malice.

"Might as well leave it out, Mike. I got a feelin' your virgin days is over." Mike swung his head around to Jed, his zipper halfway up. He was outraged at Jed's big mouth. Bo lowered the gun and stepped back to watch with his hearty laughter.

"Jed!"

"Don' act like it ain't so, Mike. *Sheeet*, the whole friggin' town knows you's a v, Mike! And you knows *we* known it all along. You's a punk-pussy till you grown up to be a man. And you ain't no man if'n you ain't had no pussy."

Mechelle's body shook and shivered; she was no less than a shaved poodle deserted in a winter snowstorm.

"Please . . . stop this. Don't *dooo* this. What did I do to you all?" she cried.

"Shut d'fuck up, nigger-bitch!" Bo's piece of wood turned even harder at this point. He was in control here; likely the only thing he had control over other than his mouth. "Shoulda stayed your ass on the bus."

"But *please* . . ." she said, but then she quickly suppressed her cries when Bo reached his pistol back over his shoulder as if to whip her.

"Shuuut *uuup,* nigger!" His words came out like a loud echo. And the utter fear raced through her at the thought of her dilemma.

"Git up."

Mechelle pushed herself up from the bench and immediately felt the sticky wetness in her Reebok sneakers. Beads of urine continued to trickle down her calves. Bo flicked his pistol, indicating for her to move on, and the 3 men trailed Mechelle towards the Coke machine and then around to the lot at the rear of the station. Back here was a gas pump against the wall, a stack of used tires and some empty oil cans. Beyond the lot were trees and darkness. Mechelle considered running, but the thought of endless woods and her fear of bullets detained her.

Bo poked Mechelle to move faster, and in the moon's glow, their four shadows were cast onto the station's dirty white wall, all of them moving in unison so that the four bodies look like eight. When they got to the rear of the station they faced an old Bentley parked and rusting. The tires on the vehicle were flat, evidence of a decade's worth of neglect.

"Open the door," Bo ordered.

Mechelle obeyed, but the door was locked. Bo pushed Mechelle up against the car and her upper body bent over to the front hood. He pressed the pistol to her temple and smacked her wet ass with his full palm nearly covering her all.

"Keep your head on the car and don't fucking move." Bo turned the small handgun so that the barrel was extended from his fist. He pulled up the flap of his flannel shirt to cover the barrel—maybe to lessen the noise—and smashed the driver's side window. With the glass scattered like crystal chips onto the front seat, Bo reached in and felt for the lever. But what he was reaching for was on the front seat along with the broken glass. He went for the back door lever and eventually got a door opened.

"Alrighty then . . ." All these sounds—the clicks and tugs and broken glass—were noises that continuously startled Mechelle, as if a knife was poking at her. She could feel the sequence of it all; the progress towards inevitable pain and peril. When it would end, she couldn't imagine. But already, she felt as if there'd been hours of torture. Her tears had stopped and she became lost in the whole theme of events. Just going along as she was told.

Bo pulled Mechelle's hair back and her body jerked back too.

"Get them pants down, bitch. And don't give me any problems or you'll get a slug in yer ass." With the pistol again to her temple, Mechelle began whimpering. The piece of steel was starting to feel like an extension to her head, she was so conscious of it. She did as she was told. She pried her wet shorts and panties from her waist until they dropped along her legs to the dirt floor.

Mike stood by Jed, still with his zipper open and his inexperienced penis shriveled up and hiding inside. Jed pulled a half pint bottle of Jack Daniels from his back pocket and swigged at it. Refreshing himself.

"You fine'ly gonna get you some. Be a man, boy. Here, this'll tighten ya some." Jed pushed the bottle to Mike. Mike was as stiff and scared and speechless as his pimples. He took a swig and grimaced at the bitter strength of the liquor.

While Mike and Jed carried on, Bo was in his own world.

"This too," said Bo, and he reached out to Mechelle, grabbed her denim top and pulled—hard enough for two of the three buttons to pop—so that the clasp of her bra was ripped and her left breast was exposed. Hype as ever, Bo pushed Mechelle back against the Bentley to observe.

"Gimme some . . ." Bo reached out to Jed for the bottle of Jack Daniels, then he threw his head back for a quick swig. Between drinks, Bo eyed Mechelle, as if to reconsider this event, standing with his legs spread chauvinistically, and the bottle pushing his head back and eyes to the sky. Meanwhile, standing naked in her soggy Reeboks, Mechelle was still that flawless, chocolate prize, humbled and scared before these local hicks.

"Now this is *real* simple, missy. You're gonna take all of us and we're gonna let you go like a good girl. In the morning you'll forget all about us. Do the job right and you don't get a cap in yo' ass. Do it wrong, I'll kill yer ass juss the same. Try anything stupid, I kill yer ass. And bitch, if you scream once, I'mma shoot you and then kill yer ass again . . . Jed. Give 'er some Jack." Jed screwed his face a second until he met Bo's eyes. Then he pushed the bottle to Mechelle.

"Take it, gowon." Jed softened and handed the bottle over. Mechelle reached for the bottle and held it. She couldn't decide if this was her chance—to break the bottle and start cutting everything in sight, or was this even threatening enough to save her at all.

"Drink," Bo ordered. "All of it." No choice in the matter, Mechelle put the whiskey to her lips and slowly sipped. Bo moved closer, not wanting to dilly dally, and he pushed the bottle up until Mechelle gurgled the liquor down. Some spilled about her lips and cheeks, dribbling down her body. Mechelle could only shed tears that slid down her cheek and neck, blending with the beverage, soaking into the skin about her shoulders and breasts. She felt so helpless and alone, wondering if praying would help. Wondering if *anything* would help. Her swallow was followed by a heavy, ripping burn.

"Okay. You git in the car first, Mike. And you take care of 'im like a good nigger-girl. This is his first time."

As told, Mechelle crawled into the dusty cabin of the Bentley. The leather cracked under her knees. She didn't hesitate anymore, and intended on submitting enough to at least get out of this alive. She was in too much shock to think about protection of any kind—she just wanted this to be over.

Just as Mike started after the girl, Jed pulled his shirt to slow him up.

"God sakes, Mike, drop yer drawers, boy. Ain't no otha way."

"But she's . . . she's a *nigger*, Uncle Jed."

"A bitch is a bitch, boy. One day you'll learn. Plus a nigger-bitch is better, 'cause she's as good as a slave. She'll just do any ole thing ya say. Just watch."

Mike dropped his pants, leaving his boxer drawers on. With a doe's eyes, Mechelle sat up in the back seat, arched by her arms and elbows behind her.

"Get in there in front'a her, boy . . ." Jed was calling directions. ". . . Now take his whistle out, girl. Gwon." Mechelle did take Mike's penis out, thin and limp as it was. She couldn't ever remember feeling this inhibited about holding a man's dick, even after 5 or 6 other men in her life. It was the thought of this kid's innocence that eased her fears, but it also made her wanna puke. *What harm could he do with this?*

"Suck it . . . put 'em in your mouth and make 'em hard." Mechelle leaned over to take him as he kneeled between her legs, there on the back seat. His tall body, head and shoulders were leaning, collecting cobwebs over top of her for lack of headroom in the car. Mechelle barely enclosed her lips over Mike's grungy-smelling penis before he began to expand. All Mechelle could think of was keeping her tongue and gums away from his prick. But it didn't help. She was quickly growing nauseous from the cruddy odor of his pubic hairs right under her nose.

Meanwhile, Mike's eyes got bigger and more excited. If he stretched his eyelids any more, the sockets of his eyeballs could have held golf balls. Mechelle tried to steady him, attempting again to clasp his penis with her outer lips. Surely, he couldn't know what a *real* blow job was. Instinctively, Mike held Mechelle's head, pressing her closer to him. Now her tongue was flat against the underside of his prick. Eventually, Mike was moving about wildly, until Jed spoke up.

"Easy, Mike . . . easy. There's more, kid. Show 'im more, bitch." Now, Bo and Jed stood looking through the car windows like peeping Toms with their hands in their pants. Mechelle took the opportunity to remove Mike from her mouth. She let a mouthful of spit drool from her lips, oozing down her chin and chest. After a few deep breaths of mildewed air, she adjusted her body. Mike came down off of his knees and bridged his body over top of her. He was apprehensive about being face to face with a "nigger," but he had also seen plenty of movies to at least know what went where.

Arching his upper body, Mike mashed his groin against her pubic area. Body to body, he began to rub around and around, applying more friction. Meanwhile, the audience outside was too preoccupied to know that there was no penetration here; they even square-danced around the car, laughing and drinking wildly. Inside, Mike was rocking on top of Mechelle. He was too frantic and desperate to realize that this was not sex. And this began to break the spell, injecting a bit of humor into the escapade. If this wasn't so horrific and devastating, Mechelle might just have to laugh out loud at this young fool. Was this really happening? Was this guy actually coming closer and closer to orgasm?

Finally, there was a finishing point, with Mike ejaculating and letting out a cry of exhilaration. Mechelle found her tummy and waist dressed with a serving of the 18-year-old's semen, while he slumped down onto her body. His face molded into her neck as if they'd been longtime lovers.

Seconds later, Mechelle pushed Mike up off of her thinking that the worst was over. He scrambled out of the car while she lay there propped up on her elbows, wondering when these three would leave her be.

Bo slapped Jed on the shoulder.

"Gowon, Jed. I want the bitch last. Sloppy, sloppy thirds." Bo let out a big laugh as he buddied up with Mike, who was just recuperating from his part in the ordeal. Mechelle's eyes squinted, suddenly aware that this was not over. And then she realized just what abuse was, now that the older man climbed on top of her. He felt scruffy and smelled of nicotine and whisky. He'd opened his shirt and merely pulled his trousers to his thighs. Jed reached between Mechelle's legs, knowing what he wanted. He felt wetness, but didn't know that it was only spent semen from Mike. Still, Jed wiggled his fingers around in the opening and seemed to be preparing himself at the same time with his other hand. Mechelle just lay motionless, crying, barely able to breath.

"Now don't you worry, girly. This ain't gonna hurt a bit."

Mechelle's head began to pound, with the liquor and the raunchy stench taking her senses more and more. She was close to blacking out, but she was still aware that a total stranger was mounting her; inviting himself into her and violating her. The man's fingers felt so foreign and impersonal inside of her. Then, without a moment's notice, he was prying her open and entering her. And consequently, the semen that Mike left on her actually helped to ease the pain, with the gluey consistency actually making things slick and bearable. But the more Jed got into Mechelle, the bigger and wider he grew. She felt more than his potential as he expanded inside of her. Mechelle braced herself up against the opposite side of the car, holding onto the front and back headrests for support. Meanwhile, Jed forged himself again and again, getting harder and stronger with each of Mechelle's whimpers. Mechelle began to moan and wail louder, even as Bo and Mike square-danced outside, the two of them celebrating Mike's newfound manhood. It was at the same time that Mechelle "*oohed*" and "*aahed*" like an overdramatic porn star, only she wasn't faking. She wasn't enjoying the act, and yet the act was increasingly overcoming her as she endured every inch of his anguish, his abstinence and his hostility towards blacks.

"No . . . no . . . no," Mechelle bawled. But Jed did not let up.

"Shut up, nigger-bitch—" With all of his issues on the front line, he continued thrusting and pumping this woman's hole. It didn't matter who she was. "—shut-the-fuck . . . up." Jed pumped his anger deep, turning this stranger into his personal human dispenser for all those many shortcomings. And while her head thumped against the car door, Jed thought about Big Blue the log-cutting champ. Jed's chest hairs were coarse, sanding her bare breasts as he thought about all the women who'd rejected him over the years. He gripped her hair with one hand and silenced her cries with his other palm over her mouth, pounding her and driving her as he thought about his missing leg. At that moment, he ejaculated, like a leak had cracked his pipe. He yowled and subsequently pulled out, his sperm still dripping onto her chest and belly. He worked his way up to Mechelle's face until the two of them were crowded there, pressed up against the window of the back door, and he rubbed his penis in her face until she was painted with his semen.

"Yeeeehaww!" Jed shouted an eerie, howling celebration. He jumped off, adjusted his pants, and crawled out of the car, past Bo. Bo was rubbing his hands together in energetic, malicious anticipation. He poked the 9 millimeter into Jed's hand and climbed into the Bentley.

Mechelle lay helpless as ever now, moaning there on the back seat. Both sets of her lips were swollen, and her eyes were rolling lifelessly in their sockets. Her arms and legs were strewn over the edge of the seat. Her calves and feet were dangling out of the open car door. She looked like an overdose victim; and still, they weren't done with her.

"Please . . . no more. Please. I—I can't . . . take any . . . more. I'll do any . . . thing. But . . ."

WHACK! Bo smacked her with a swift, open palm.

He was already in the backseat, shirt off and pants to his ankles. His belly was pressed against her abdomen and he was volleying with her legs, lifting one up over the front seat and one over the back. Bo was going in like a tank and his victim was uttering her last chances for reprieve.

"Say '*no more*' again, nigger-bitch. *Say it!*"

"No . . . more. Plee . . ."

SMACK!

Bo hit her again, leaving her cheek and jaw even more inflamed and red.

"Say it again. I dare ya. Gowon!" Bo was ruthless. And now he had her on her back with her legs straddled and elevated as if she was ready to give birth. Her body was glistening at the mid-section, but mostly from the perspiration and semen of the previous visitors. Her body was also numb from so much pressure. So much abuse and pain. Bo could care less. He fondled himself to erection and pressed himself into Mechelle's gooey vagina. She was loose now. Sticky.

Bo was short and stout. He held her one leg in place with his left hand and smacked her ass with the other. With each thrust there was a sigh from her lips. Bo was trying to make it exciting by the ass slapping, but she was too out of it to be revived. Not only was Bo raping her but he was also smothering her. His weight was so unbearable that she no longer sighed. Now, there were merely those effortless gasps for air that came from her mouth and lungs. Mechelle's body was totally senseless now. No feeling at all. Her world was spinning and her eyes rolled back into her head until she was unconscious. She didn't feel Bo ejaculate, nor could she feel any more of his smacks to her ass and face. She didn't even realize the worst, that he had pissed on her face and body when he was done fucking her mouth.

Mechelle might as well have been dead.

The Morning After

At 6am, Mechelle woke up on a cot, with old man Riley holding a smelling salt capsule under her nose. His face came into focus, shaking Mechelle into paranoia. Because he was white, Mechelle associated him with her pain and torture of a few hours earlier. But Riley held Mechelle down, calming her as best he could. He told her that she'd be okay and that he was helping her, not hurting her. She looked around at what seemed to be a back room or office of some sort. There was a steaming cup of coffee on a nearby table. Some warm towels were in a bowl of water, plus she was covered by a clean white blanket. He reached again for a towel to dab on her mouth and cheek.

"You were a mess out there in the back this morning. I cleaned you up as best I could." Riley smiled, but not selfishly.

Mechelle felt cozy, but if she budged at all there was that sharp pain between her legs. Her vagina was throbbing, and so was her cheek and mouth.

"Looks like you're outta pocket here." The man who said he was sorry had introduced himself as Riley; and now he was trying his best to strike up a conversation with Mechelle, perhaps wanting to relieve himself of the guilt he felt. Maybe, Mechelle wondered, there might even be grounds to sue the pants off of him *and* Greyhound.

* * *

When Riley found Mechelle at 6a.m. laying on the porch moaning, he knew that she'd been hurt and that it was his fault. So he took her inside quickly before anyone saw her. He didn't call the sheriff, for fear that he'd be the talk of the town. Everybody would find out what a creep he was for what he did. Maybe *he* would even be implicated for assaulting her. So, Riley kept it all hush-hush. He cleaned her up with a hot bath, and she had 4 hours of rest. It was nearly 10 AM now.

When Mechelle realized who Riley was, she wanted to get away from him more than anything else. But she couldn't. She accepted Riley's complementary meals and TLC. When he was in the shop tending to a customer, Mechelle took it upon herself to dab the hot cloths on her pubic area and face. She'd already missed the 9AM bus. But, damned if she was gonna miss the next one at noon.

Her shorts were still damp from being hastily washed, but Mechelle wanted them back on her body. She began to stretch her limbs and eventually worked her feet into the shorts to pull them on. Riley walked in on her, not realizing that she was mostly nude and turned his head away.

"Sorry, missy . . . I thought you might like these." Riley handed Mechelle a set of brand-new sweats. Fresh from the shelf in the souvenir area of the bus depot. The sweatshirt had a bold, scriptive black print against its pink color: *"Welcome to North Carolina!"* Mechelle thanked him with a somewhat sarcastic overtone. It was obvious by now that he'd seen Mechelle's body through and through. But it was no time for quarrels or cursing. Mechelle just wanted to walk again, to be mobile and dressed and away from North Carolina altogether.

Riley left the room, leaving Mechelle to indulge in the newness of the sweatsuit, as though she'd just received a new cheerleading uniform and that it would brush away all the pain—not to mention, she felt like the entire high school football team ran a train on her. She did some stretching, some aerobics, and she drank a lot of the bottled water Riley had set beside the cot. Slowly, the headache disappeared. 11:30 came. Mechelle tossed her soiled clothes, pulled on some flip-flops, and she grabbed another blueberry muffin from the tray before heading for the door. Out in the station, Mechelle pretended that nobody was watching her. She noticed Riley at the register where a large variety of candies and cigarettes were displayed.

"Thank you for the food. I'm gonna wait outside—get some fresh air, ya know."

"Here . . ." He passed some change to a customer and reached under the counter for something. ". . . I put this together for you." It was a travel bag with various snacks, cakes and sodas. There was a towel and washcloth set and a number of other convenient feminine needs.

"Oh . . ." He passed her an envelope. ". . . and here's a ticket so there'll be no problem with the bus driver. Have a nice trip." Riley offered a hint of a smile and Mechelle was less than appreciative. She waited outside the depot until 12 noon, determined not to look anywhere close to the left; where it all started. She just wanted to erase that whole encounter from her mind. She never wanted to come through here again. If she did, she wouldn't be without a gang of girlfriends; girlfriends, weapons, and a wicked vengeance.

Mechelle snuggled and curled up in a rear seat of the Greyhound headed for New York. She sought sleep to maybe dream away the nightmare which she lived through. But she couldn't trick herself. She leaned up against the window, gazing indirectly at passing images and reviewing the events of the previous night. She felt humiliated and used, hurt and violated. No doubt, this had been the most tragic night . . . the most tragic moment of her life. Mechelle wiped away a single tear.

After what felt like the shortest trip ever into New York City, Mechelle weaved through the sea of faces at the Port Authority Bus Terminal, suddenly facing new realities. She still had to find her luggage and her sister, Nikki. Nikki was to be waiting for Mechelle at one in the morning at the appropriate gate. But 1AM seemed like a history book away. And if she *did* find Nikki, what would she tell her? Would she notice the bruises? Ask questions? Get all nosey?

Mechelle wanted to keep whatever humanity she had left. If that dissolved, she could always cut her wrists.

Between 4:30PM and 5PM, Mechelle did her best to juggle 3 or 4 tasks; she had to learn to walk again, she had to find her luggage, and she had to get home. If she could manage all of that and maintain her sanity, the day might be a success. Life might just continue for her. Eventually, she roughed it, dealing with the sore feeling between her legs. At one point, she grabbed for her tummy. And the queasy feeling eventually made her toss up her breakfast.

After a momentary cleanup in the public bathroom, Mechelle pulled on a Southpole hat that Riley had stuffed in her bag. She fixed it low on her brow and headed off to look for the lost and found office within Port Authority. The attendants there told her to first go through the baggage area, just down the counter. Her most pleasurable sight in the past 24 hours, Mechelle immediately identified her bags. She unconsciously checked her pockets for stubs, but quickly recalled that they were in her shorts, the ones she trashed. Nonetheless, the attendants were helpful, asking her to identify a few items that might be inside the bags. She did, and they let her retrieve her property without I.D.

Mechelle got to a payphone and called Nikki's apartment collect. No dice. Nikki's phone would not accept collect calls. No long distance provider. *Ghetto shit*, Mechelle reckoned. Stranded again, Mechelle decided to rely on hope as she window-shopped at many of the terminal stores. Perhaps Nikki was around or she would at least return.

The New York terminal was impersonal. Nobody gave her a second look and nobody else seemed to care. It was evening, but Mechelle kept her sunglasses on. (Another of Riley's souvenirs). Announcements were barked over a loudspeaker. Gate numbers and destinations droned and echoed throughout the corridors. Incoming and outgoing buses. People with shoulder bags, luggage carts, attaché cases and strollers, all of them rushing to and fro. The scent of sweet, roasted peanuts mixed with Cinnabuns and fresh popcorn in the air.

Mechelle parked herself next to a monstrous red contraption. Its iron foundations were glossy red like the skin on a cherry. Inside the four walls of glass there were simulated gumballs, the size of baseballs, sliding down rails, climbing up miniature conveyor belts to a high point and then twisting and turning down a colorful maze to a bridge. The bridge led the various balls over a mini pond until they repeated the entire process over again. With so much turmoil in her life,

Mechelle watched the attraction in awe, amazed at the simplicity of the design and how the balls kind of resembled people; people who go through all kinds of twists and turns, ups and downs, only to go through it all over and over again, through the very same colorful, gigantic maze called life. Mechelle wondered where she was in that equation. But as she did, she noticed a man on the opposite side of the great big toy. He had his black hair tied back into a ponytail, and he was looking through the glass at Mechelle. Apparently, he'd been watching her all along; maybe ever since she was at the lost and found? Now he was moving in for a closer look. But Mechelle was too wrapped up in her own issues to give any more attention to her admirer.

Stranger

David was not a traveler, a wanderer or an employee at the nation's biggest bus terminal. This was not his first time focused on a lost young woman either. David was on his usual stakeout at Port Authority. Looking for lost souls to benefit him in his own way. He knew what signs to look for in identifying lost souls. Moreover, his focus was not on just *anybody*. He was looking specifically for young, attractive women of color. There were some who he bought coffee for, took to lunch and helped with baggage. He forged relationships with those he considered to be aimless and vagabond since, in those cases, there'd be no challenge or demands for independence. Mostly, what he'd find was desperation, in whatever way, shape or form.

In a nutshell, what David was attracted to was weakness and convenience of lonely hearts who arrived in New York to make it big in entertainment. David befriended Mechelle in just that way, hoping to find out more about her. But he held back his sexual aggressions. That was always kept on the back burner—his ulterior motive. He sensed something different about Mechelle, and so he had to be cautious. Her eyes said a lot more than the average vagabond at the terminal. This chick had a sense of knowing and a sharp wit, however hidden under her current issues. There was a greater potential here;

more than just sex. For now, David figured, Mechelle was at her weakest. He didn't know why, but he suspected a shattered story of some sort. A tale that had some whup-ass at the end of it.

The two had coffee. Then more coffee. Then David offered Mechelle a ride to where she was going. Hell, she wanted to go to her sister's apartment in Queens, but she didn't even know where that was.

"I didn't think to take down Nikki's address because everything was set up for us to meet at Port Authority," Mechelle told David. "But I always had an alternative. I mean, I could stay with my mother. But I can't . . ." Mechelle didn't want to say it—there was no way she could let her mom catch her in this condition.

"The truth is, David, I don't have any place to stay right now." Mechelle was critically frank. David comforted her by deliberating, as though he had a number of options. But he spoke up, not wanting to lose the opportunity.

"I take care of this building in the Bronx. It's close to everything. Even the baseball games and the subway. There are a few apartments still vacant. The entire building was recently renovated. It's nice . . ." David had every bit of Mechelle's attention. "I work with the landlord. Good terms. I know you don't have a job or money just yet, but I can get you in now, and we can work it out down the road, when you get on your feet." David seemed sincere, without a hint of contempt or larceny, but any of this would work for Mechelle, considering where she came from and how much healing was required to get her life back in order. Finally, she could do nothing but melt in the presence of such good fortune. David was like some guardian angel with a ponytail, how he appeared in her life with such good news at this time of dire need. Maybe he was being nice. Maybe she'd have to be concerned down the road. Whatever. One sure thing was that this was her time of need, not a time to try and discover any possible underlying motives.

David felt he was impressive with his platinum Cherokee, perched up in the driver's seat as cocky as could be. Dropping signs about his access to money, power and respect. Mechelle could have uttered a dramatic yawn, but she wasn't herself at present, and she was certainly in no mood to be sarcastic. Not for a long, long time. She merely expected that David's description of the apartment was another dream he was trying to sell her, a mirage that he cooked up with the help of his jasmine-scented jeep with its soft reggae sounds consuming them.

"Okay, if you don't believe me, just watch and see," said David as the two zoomed up the West Side Highway, onto the Cross Bronx Expressway and a few exits up the Major Deegan throughway until they pulled up to the building on Locust Avenue. The complex was stupendous at first glance, even in the dark. Actually, there were two buildings joined together by a big courtyard. The entrance was secured by a tall, black wrought-iron gate and a lock that was combination controlled. David helped Mechelle with her bags, leaving his truck double-parked on the street. He directed her to the 5th floor.

"It's not much," David warned as he put the key in the cylinder. "Remember, no furniture, no phone, TV or stereo." David turned the key and opened the door to 5B.

"That's fine. I'll make due." Mechelle would have time to be resourceful later. But for now, she waited to hear what strings were attached.

"Here it is," said David, surprising her. The apartment was even better than he had her imagine. She inhaled the newness of the studio with its warm and inviting comfort.

"Make yourself at home. I have 2 blankets down in the jeep. I'll go get 'em." He did bring blankets back and promised to check with her periodically. "You have my numbers," were his last words. David must've expected to have access to Mechelle whenever and however he wanted to. So he played Mr. Laid-Back, handing her the key before shuffling down the hall to the elevator.

Meanwhile, Mechelle was left to indulge in her very 1st apartment. It was secure. Simple and spacious. Shiny, polished wood flooring. New fixtures in the kitchen area and bathroom. She felt ultimate independence, even if she was lonely and distant from family and friends. At least she could soak in a hot bath and brush the horrors from her teeth and gums. After a 2-hour bath, Mechelle felt bold enough to trek to the stadium diner at the corner where she phoned her mother collect. Her mother (always dependable) gave her another number for Nikki's cell phone and an access code for her to use so that she could make coinless calls for the time being.

Later, over a turkey club at the Stadium Diner, Mechelle and Nikki brought each other up to date. Nikki was a single mom with two kids. She had a 2-bedroom apartment in Queens and was relieved at the revelation that Mechelle had somewhere to stay. Even if temporarily. Nikki also revealed to Mechelle (the first in the family to know) that she was a stripper at a club in the Bronx called Gilmore's Fool's Paradise. Mechelle became even more interested when her sister told her about the money she was bringing home, how the profession was paying her way through college, rent and for child care.

"*Sometimes I make four hundred a night*," was the statement that stood out most in Mechelle's head, encouraging her with thoughts of a furnished apartment, a car and paying off her own college loan. Nikki gave her sister $150 to help her get on her feet. Mechelle looked at the money, and the stash that it came from, like it was a pile of sparkling diamonds. Nikki's lifestyle very quickly became infectious.

A New Friend

Mechelle joined Nikki on a visit to Fool's Paradise and she was quick to audition. She wore a cat mask loaned to her by another dancer, and was able to face those initial fears with ease. She did a cute dance routine, more like a deviation from some cheerleader sequences, and caught the attention of Gil's son, Douglass. Douglass was spinning records that day—just a hobby for him, using the busy lunch hours to improve his music mixing skills—and he immediately took a liking to Mechelle.

Long story short, Mechelle was hired. And after speaking briefly to Gil, she left with Nikki and returned the next day for a booking on the 12noon to 4PM shift.

Following his hormones, and contradicting his very own discipline of not fraternizing with the dancers, Douglass approached Mechelle on that second day. On the outside it was

Mechelle's tight body and pretty face that sparked Douglass's interest. However, once he got to know her and listen to her, Mechelle's wit won him over. On the other hand, Douglass also won Mechelle's heart. She saw him as a breed apart from those other men who had already approached her with familiar, played-out pick-up lines; men who were no deeper than a one-slice bologna sandwich. But Douglass was unique and different to her, which is why she agreed to his offer for a ride home.

"Wanna take the long way?" Douglass asked.

"What's that? The long way?" Mechelle asked with a cute, curious smile.

"Well, the long way means I cook dinner . . . at my house—"

Mechelle chuckled.

"No-no . . . don't judge me yet," he said. "I don't have any sneaky plans, I just wanna be a cook tonight."

After she came down from the laugh, Mechelle said, "Depends on what you're cooking." And that statement came with a raised eyebrow.

She thought about all this; dinner with Gilmore's son; his secure approach; and the invite to his home. His home . . . that was another thing, entirely. Mechelle got to wander through the house while Douglass cooked and she realized that she had never been inside of a residence of such magnificence. It was enormous, with more rooms than she had fingers to count. There came a point when she got a little dizzy and needed a seat. Not just because of the house, but for so much else that crashlanded into her life all of a sudden. The events seemed to escalate so abruptly; from being the victim of a rape only days before, to the easy money job she now had, to this new adventure, and how the boss's son was embracing her with treatment she long deserved, craved and desired.

"*Denworth never even cooked dinner for me*," she told herself. The apparent power and wealth that she was now absorbed in had her ask, *Denworth who??* Having another man kiss up to her like Douglass surely reminded her of Denworth. But, then again, it was so easy to erase Den from her mind and to bask in the treasures of the moment. Dinner with Douglass. Mechelle inhaled, then exhaled.

* * *

Once the spaghetti disappeared; Douglass took the initiative
to soak Mechelle's feet in warm salt water. Then he massaged
them with a menthol lotion. Little did she know, amidst the
dreamy sensuality of the moment, Douglass Jr.'s actions were
mostly a case of him missing his water when the well went
dry. Stacy had left him only days earlier. She discovered a list
of women that he'd been with, along with a 1 to 10 rating he
marked beside the names. The evidence was the work of an
ass; like Douglass was *asking* for a breakup. He may as well
have taped the incriminating list up on Stacey's make-up mirror, because there were two names on the list that were new;
two women whom he and Stacy met while they were together.
What's more, he had a 5 marked next to Stacy's name. Not a
"10" but a 5, in essence saying that she wasn't all that hot, not
compared to some of the others.

Needless to say, the breakup was hostile. They had made a
child together, but to these two young lovers that meant little
to nothing. He didn't know how to put his ego away for long
enough to calm her; and she didn't have a rational bone in her
body to get past his infidelity. To add to the confusion, Stacy
took the child, moved out of state, and was never heard from
again.

Along with Stacy went all of those conveniences of having a
good woman around the house. So Douglass, too, was a man in
need, which was why he strongly considered offering a room to
Mechelle when he heard of her hollow arrangement in the
Bronx. And even if Mechelle pretended to "think about it," her
answer wouldn't take long.

Following dinner, Douglass drove Mechelle back to her studio
in the Bronx. Out front, their conversation ended with an intimate and promising kiss. She informed Douglass that she
was "involved," and he backed off. Nothing ventured, nothing
gained. However, Mechelle subsequently invited him up to see
her place. He accepted, and while Mechelle went upstairs Douglass spent close to 10 minutes searching for a parking space.
On a block full of apartment complexes, finding a parking
space was like mining for gold on a public beach. Eventually,

he struck oil about a block away, on a busy street over which Yankee Stadium towered. It was a short walk back to the apartment building, yet long enough for Douglass to talk to himself.

"Don't play y'self, big dog. Don't expect or anticipate anything more than companionship. She's just a friend. Nothing more." With that, Douglass stepped through the front gate, pressing in the simple combination which Mechelle provided.

Inside the foyer of the building to the right, Douglass pressed 5B on the panel. Mechelle buzzed him in without verification and he instinctively moved towards the elevator. On the 5th floor, he found the door marked 5B opened and awaiting his entrance. Douglass simply pushed his way in.

"Oh, sorry," explained Douglass. He peeped Mechelle coming from the shower, casually reaching in a closet for a towel, then heading back into the bathroom. Seconds later the shower water was cut off. Douglass immediately appreciated the newness of her studio. A polished wood floor, fresh paint, new appliances, fixtures and plumbing seemed to be the only complementary elements of this Bronx nest. There was a pillow and comforter laid out on the floor in the center of the room. Mechelle answered Douglass from the bathroom.

"Not a problem, please. You practically watched me all day," she said. "Grab a drink. I have some things in the fridge."

He pulled open the refrigerator door and took a gulp from the quart of orange juice. He began to make himself at home, fiddling through her small stack of cassette tapes, then he turned the knob on her portable radio to WBLS for the familiar mix of rhythm and blues. Meanwhile, Douglass took note of the surroundings. Curious to know how this new woman in his life was living. The view from Mechelle's window was but a voyeur's exclusive perspective into the building and window of the couple next door. A fire escape was the only separation between the two addresses. However limited the view of the city, the depth of it all was filled with alleys and pockets between buildings, and all the while there were those monstrous subway cars rumbling nearby.

"I think they know we can see them," Mechelle said, catching Douglass off guard, approaching him from behind while still drying her own dipping body off with the oversized bath towel.

"Uh . . . who? See what?" Douglass was practically tripping over his words, while trying his best to be as blasé as she was about her nudity. Mechelle turned her back to Douglass and handed him the towel to wipe her back. As she explained, he traced her back contours with the towel.

"The couple . . . I'm talkin' about the couple down there . . ." Mechelle pointed to a window in the building next door. Douglass had not noticed earlier, but down below there were two lovers feeding on each other in a very involved sexual embrace. From Mechelle, to the couple, and back to Mechelle, Douglass's eyes couldn't make up its mind. Then, Mechelle eased her perfectly sculptured figure over to the light switch. She dimmed the lights and stepped over to the comforter to lay facedown.

"Could you massage me?" Mechelle placed a bottle of lotion beside her and laid her arms at either side of her head. Douglass shrugged humbly and approached her. He knelt down beside her and began to lotion her neck and shoulders. Meanwhile, Vaughn Harper's *Quiet Storm* theme music filtered through the room. That meant it was 10 PM and that the next 4 hours would be all slow jams and dusties.

Douglass was fighting discipline now, realizing that he had fed, chauffeured and touched most of Mechelle's body, all on one day. This was slowly affecting him as he kneaded and caressed her curves and contours. The electricity was very personal, very intimate. Douglass became excited and aware of his erection. Mechelle also noticed him, in spite of his jeans. Eventually, without words, the two molded and tossed on the floor, sharing each other's tongues. Lips volleyed for positions. Mechelle was soon caressing him as much as he was her. He softly fondled her breasts and she laid back on the pillow, loving this, breathlessly stretching herself out for his full access. Douglass began to kiss her, progressing from her cheeks and neck, to her breasts and nipples. Teasing, gentle and unselfish, until he realized an immediate need. *A condom!*

"You gotta excuse me for a minute," he told her, leaving Mechelle and himself titillated. His pants were unbuckled and pushing down off of his hips, but he ignored the indiscretion and rushed through the front door. He hobbled down the staircase, not wanting to wait for the elevator, and left the door to the foyer ajar. Mechelle was in no position to buzz him in. Besides, he wanted nothing to mess up that image that he left in 5B. Molten, sweet chocolate on the floor, ready for him to eat until he was sloppy with her affection.

Fortunately, Douglass's oversized hockey jersey covered his erection all the way to the glove compartment of his car and back. When he returned to the apartment, Mechelle was still dreamy-eyed and filled with anticipation.

Thank God!

Feeling the overwhelming heat in the room, Douglass lifted the window a few inches and reclined back to Mechelle's side. He reignited their fire with tender kisses from her forehead to her toenails. Just in time, that phat jam *"Long As I Live"* put their action on blast. Mechelle was beginning to erupt when Douglass reached her toes. There was some pain below her tummy, and she realized what was about to go down. She wanted him inside her, but she couldn't. Not yet. And she didn't want to let him down. Her intentions had nothing to do with his position, or who his father was. It was that she wanted to give herself to him . . . he was a good man, and she wanted him to have her vote.

Mechelle put her palm to Douglass's chest when he came up to hover over her. She switched positions with him until he was under her. Shamelessly, with tears falling, Mechelle took him into her mouth. She stroked him and massaged him and made her mouth as wanton as her walls were. It seemed as though he was holding back and that he didn't want to cum in her mouth, but she encouraged his orgasm. When he eventually came, Mechelle took every drop down her throat. With no words shared between them, this was her way of showing him her passion for him. And in the cool night air, the two embraced until the morning.

Over breakfast, Mechelle agreed to move in with Douglass. Late that morning, they packed her things and she was on the move again. This time, to the Gilmore home in New Rochelle.

CHAPTER NINE

Queens, New York

The overall talent of David Turner could be best described as networker. Not only did he scout out vagabonds at Port Authority, not only was he a frequent flier with a few of the hot properties from Fool's Paradise, but he also had his claws sunk into the web. The Internet was where he came to know Debbie. It wasn't too long before Moet's murder that David would finally get to meet his "long lost love."

It was during an autumn rush hour that David waited there at LaGuardia Airport for Debbie. All he had to go by was a digital photo, loads of e-mails, and almost as many phone calls. All of the technology helped him create a mental picture of Debbie. His perfect 10. And now, he praised his imagination for not failing him as he sifted through the many heads and eyes of the crowd milling up the airport corridor. Debbie was one of the last to emerge. But when she did, David turned on his charm. He called her name, smiled and went as far as the metal detectors to embrace her. Debbie felt relieved within his hug, as though she was soaking into his arms. A perfect fit, thought David. She was shorter than David. Almost a foot. Her Camay skin was just a shade lighter than his own complexion. And even with jeans and a jean jacket on, David recognized her shapely contours. He disregarded her body for the moment (almost certain that it would soon be his to explore), and allowed himself to become a victim to her wide, attractive smile.

"Let me help you with your bag," said David, as he took hold of her shoulder bag. Then he led the way through the airport lobby, to the baggage area. After picking out 2 pink and black suitcases and then loading them onto a baggage cart, the two glided out through 2 sets of sliding glass doors onto the walkway outside of the airport's "arrivals" terminal.

David's jeep, with its dull-platinum finish and worn tires, was parked across the pavement and close to the curb. While Debbie waited by the cart, David started the jeep and maneuvered it backwards and diagonally to meet her at the entrance.

Moments later, the couple were weaving through the maze of roads and byways that led out of LaGuardia Airport with Debbie melting into the leather seat and blushing with her big, glossy eyes and round cheeks.

"So . . . finally." David cut through the awkwardness of their first physical interaction.

"Yeah. Seems like forever, huh?"

"Well, it has been a while since we've first met . . . or communicated, anyway. But somehow it seems like we've known each other for much longer." David tried to be as cool and manly as he could, working hard on creating a good first impression. This is what mattered, even more than their year on the Internet and the lil' chat room rendezvous that frequently took place.

"This trip even seemed like forever," said Debbie. It had been an hour and a half flight from Chicago's O'Hare Airport. But instead of weightlessness and jet lag, other things occupied her thoughts. To some degree, Debbie felt that she was abandoning her mother. On the other hand, she knew she had only one life to live. And she was determined to live it to the max. For her mom, and even for her brother, Ray Ray. The thoughts in her mind spun once again, and she thought about Jackie.

"Do you know where Ninty-fifth Street is?"

"Actually, I've already been by your friend . . . Jackie's?— house. We've met and everything. Didn't I tell you?" David *knew* he hadn't told her. He was just being cute.

"No. You *didn't* tell me. What did you guys talk about?" Debbie uttered a hint of jealousy. Tempering her words.

"We talked about Southside Chicago and . . . your old boyfriends."

"Boyfriends?" Debbie was sure that the neighborhood knew about the high school jock turned college hunk, Robert Bass. But *what* they knew exactly, she wasn't sure. And what else did they know that she didn't know they knew? Debbie was suspicious and skeptical too.

"Well, not really *boyfriends*—as in many—but there was one guy."

"Oh really?" Debbie felt a bit betrayed, folding a mood with her arms.

"But Deb, it was all good, baby. She just gave me an idea of the kind of guys you like." David consoled her.

"Oh . . ." Debbie softened her anger into guilt. His saying "*baby*" helped a lot, reminding her of their Internet chats.

"Debbie, relax. Jackie can't wait to see you, okay?"

"Well . . . I just . . . you know us girls."

"No, not really. What about you girls?" David uttered his lie with a playful sarcasm and a raised brow.

Debbie took a dive into the subject, revealing some of the ghetto in her. David never picked that up on the Net or through the phone calls. It was all nostalgic to him, arousing even. He'd met a full string of attractive women and grew a talent for stereotyping them. Even if they'd hide their characteristics. Meanwhile, he allowed Debbie to be talkative and used the opportunity to take closer looks at her. Great skin. Well kept hair. The perfume was counterfeit, but David could sense that Debbie was trying hard to fit into the groove of big city essence. Even though she wasn't quite cutting it.

While she conversed with David, Debbie kept an eye on the landscape of Queens. A lot of small homes stood in close proximity to one another. Meager lawns, many trees, and that equal mix of both city and suburban. It almost seemed like back home, which made her all the more comfortable. As they arrived at Jackie's home, Debbie instantly sized the residence and surveyed the block. The house was a small, brick one-level, identical to those to its right and left. The surroundings were stapled with well manicured shrubbery and lawns. There were no children in the streets, like she was accustomed to on her block in Chicago, and there was a certain ease and seclusion that was infectious.

Before Debbie could pull the lever to get out of the jeep, Jackie came flying out of the screen door, down two steps and through a waist-high wrought iron gate. Debbie hopped down from her seat and they both embraced, each shedding their own silly tears. David unpacked the back of the jeep with that all-systems-go smile, and he followed the two as they chit-chatted their way into the house. Debbie fell silent, taken by the atmosphere inside. There were artifacts of every sort on the walls, on the floor and on the tables. The tables and chairs themselves were even cluttered. In a slow-motion ballerina twirl, Debbie became preoccupied with surroundings.

"Hi!" A man about Debbie's height popped out from the hallway. He could've been a young Sammy Davis Jr., with his head so square. Reaching to shake Debbie's hand, the guy then turned to help David with the suitcases.

"Can I get you something to drink?" The guy was trying to do everything for Debbie all at once. And he barely acknowledged David's presence.

"Some water," Debbie answered with the unimposing voice.

"You just have a seat . . . I'll get you something nice . . ."

The kind man shot a shiny glare and smile at Debbie, and David could smell that something was up his sleeve. Debbie nodded, and she moved towards the couch, folding her ankle under her behind. The two men disappeared into the back of the home.

"That's Danny," said Jackie. "He's Mom's boyfriend. It's actually his house. But we're all family."

"What's with all these African artifacts?" Debbie nodded towards a mask on the wall and tall drum with animal skin stretched at its surface.

"He's into that stuff . . . collecting and all. But you ain't seen the end, girl . . ." And they went on to discuss Danny's tofu meals, super-nutrition drinks, mandatory Tai-Chi routines, and the sound effects in his bedroom after hours. Jackie made a face when she explained this, but the truth was that she was just happy that her mom was compatible with *someone*. The idea that her mom was getting the guts boned out of her in the next room was not as outrageous as the fits that she'd go into during her lonely spells *without* a steady man. A win-win-win situation, if you asked Jackie.

Settled In

A week went by before David had opportunity to see Debbie again. The vibe was kept warm with a phone call here and there, but there wasn't that same "Internet feel" about things. David was busy anyhow; inconsistent. Never content with any one woman. In fact, he was manipulating much more than he could handle. Eventually, however, David came back around.

On a chilly Friday evening, David pursued his promise to show Debbie a good time. His idea of a real good time was thwarted somewhat, because he'd encountered some unexpected sexual satisfaction just an hour or so earlier. But the date was already arranged. And so, even though he was spent, he went through with it. David just had that insatiable appetite for more and more.

"It's a surprise," was all he mentioned to Debbie, as they traveled northbound on the Grand Central Parkway. David actually had two surprises up his sleeve for Debbie. But for now, he was feeling that total control as he commanded his Cherokee over the Whitestone Bridge and through the toll. Unbeknownst to Debbie, David was headed for a full course menu of crab legs at JP's, one of the dozens of fish restaurants on City Island. But once she got in the restaurant . . . once Debbie sat down in front of her plate, she ate like a whale.

"Damn, baby! Where you puttin' all that?" David asked while assisting with a nutcracker, breaking the meat free from the crab's shell, dipping it into the red, spicy cocktail sauce and then feeding it to her directly. For David, this was nothing new; he'd been here plenty of times before with one chick or another. It was actually a while since David had been to JP's, and he'd almost forgotten how incredible the food was. But for sure, he had been to almost every restaurant on the strip with his crab-feeding, his under-the-table foot games, and the oyster slurping. Deep into his game, Debbie sucked it up like a sponge.

"Well, just how adventurous are you?" David's question came after their dinner, while they were traveling away from City Island, northbound on the Hutchinson River Parkway.

"Pretty damned adventurous, David. I can handle most things, if you don't recall; I'm a Chi-Town girl." Indeed, Debbie seemed excited enough to get into anything, so David took a shot.

"I don't know . . ." said David.

Then Debbie said, "Try me."

"Okay. Close your eyes." She did, expecting David to maybe reach over and fondle or kiss her. She braced herself for anything. Almost.

David had no such thing in mind. He was close to the

Pelham exit of the Hutch. He glided up the off-ramp as if by gravitational pull, made a left, caught a few traffic lights and parked.

"We're here," David announced. And with the motor still running, he relaxed in his seat, watching Debbie open her eyes to have a look around. Disregarding the various auto body shops that lined either side of the block, Debbie eventually zoomed in on a crowd that lined up outside of the entrance. Swinging over their heads was the bold and bright sign that read:

GILMORE'S
FOOL'S PARADISE
The Leader in Adult Entertainment.

Having no idea of the usual Friday night frolic that took place inside of the club, Debbie smiled inquisitively at David while her hands stretched out in front of her to her knees. Bashful, but game.

After a quick U-turn, David took a vacant parking spot. He ran around to open the passenger door for Debbie and upon closing the door, armed the vehicle's security system.

"*Bleep-bleep.*" The alarm called the attentions of many men who waited in line to pay their $10 admission. And that was just fine with David as he took Debbie's hand, arrogantly stepping ahead directly to the entrance. Debbie tagged along, in a black, short skirt and a matching blouse. The material clung to her body like cellophane wrap, merely outlining her breasts and curves with somebody's fabric. The excitement, attention and evening chill further provoked the impressions of her nipples through the clothing.

As usual, David displayed his familiar savvy at the entrance, attracting Jimmy's attention and preferential treatment in front of the eager crowd. Upon entering the club, the atmosphere all but sucked the two in, how electric it all was, with wall-to-wall people. Most of the focus was on the main stage where Sadie was twisting her body to the club banger, "*Over Like A Fat Rat,*" and tossing smiles to as much of the crowd as possible. She was sweaty and glisting. Her attitude was convincing and her dance moves driven. While Sadie captivated the customers, the bartenders and bouncers were politicking to increase their own popularity or stake in the game. Bartenders leaned into individual customers with concern and interest, while bouncers put on their bold veneer of Superfly and Superman, impressing one and all (or trying to) in their muscle-stretched STAFF t-shirts. All the while, two adjacent stages promoted similar hustles, with 2 dancers on each, vying for their own audiences. In the front corner of the club, Gil was counting singles for a customer. And behind that customer was another who also wanted singles. Above everything else, the DJ and his music, the movie screens featuring X-rated films, and the colorful streams of light that flickered throughout the club, made Gilmore's a completely electrifying experience.

David was jaded, accustomed to and no longer impressed by the euphoria in the club. Instead, he proudly weaved through the crowd, showing off his new friend, until he reached the VIP area. As an elevated area in perfect view of the main stage, the VIP section was enclosed by decorative wooden railings and accommodated five tables with respective seating. One table still had two empty seats, which David and Debbie quickly occupied. With their backs to a mirrored wall, the two looked on at the heat in motion. David was comfortable; Debbie, on the other hand, was new to this, set in her own moment of silent shock, and yet mesmerized by all the various activity. No words were exchanged as David bopped his head to the beat of the music, hoping that it would rub off on Debbie and that she would grow just as comfortable. He could see that she was apprehensive about this "surprise" and he refrained from looking her directly in the eye. Instead of facing the honesty of the circumstances, he asked her if she wanted a drink.

"Could you suggest one for me?" Debbie replied.

"How about a . . . a rum and Coke?"

"Cool." Debbie suddenly twisted her smile into a tight grimace, realizing that David was leaving her alone. *Now*, she could feel more comfortable! With arms folded, she let her eyes wander. Various areas along the walls in the club were occupied by groups of women, mostly in bikinis or negligees, with just about every one of them shamelessly hunched over, with their hands clenching their knees to brace themselves as they grinded up against the groins of those customers behind them. Those same men kept a tight grip on the dancer's love handles, hips and even their breasts. On the movie screens above, various porno flicks were showing. In one, a man and women were humped over and under each other, bobbing and bumping into each other's pubic area.

At the table next to Debbie were three men and a dancer. They paid that girl their undivided attention, each working hard to strike up meaningful conversation. Debbie peeped the girl concealing a yawn, which when they locked eyes, almost made the two giggle.

Debbie Meets Moet

Moet sat with drink in hand, legs crossed, with her attention on the porn flick. Close enough to touch, Moet eventually focused on Debbie and they smiled at one another.

"First time?" Moet asked.

"First time *here*? Yeah. *You*?"

"Nah, honey. Like, 10 years in this game. Started when I was like thirteen. I had *blessings*." Moet wiggled slightly in her seat, squared off her shoulders and pushed out her chest to emphasize her "*blessings*".

". . . But you know, the suckers never seem to disappear." Debbie tried to suppress her laugh, knowing how the three men were within listening distance, but Moet made it easier with her own deep, jolly cackle. And Debbie joined in.

"I'm Debbie." Debbie reached out her hand.

"Okay. And I'm Moet," and the ladies both shook hands. "My real name is Nadine, but please call me Moet."

"Ten years, huh? Wow. Do you like it?"

"It's a living. I wanted to go to college, but the money got so good that I stayed with this. Sometimes I wish I went to school. Other times, I love this shit. Depends on the time of the month, I guess." The two laughed.

"What's the money like?" Debbie was curious.

"I do well . . . sometimes fifteen hundred, sometimes two Gs." Moet pulled a cigarette from a new pack and offered it to

Debbie. Debbie raised her hand to say no and Moet put the white stick to her lips. One of her customers played humble servant, flicking at his lighter again and again; on the fourth try, a short flame popped up.

"Baby, you need to step your lighter-game together, fo' real." Moet brushed her admirer away and turned back to Debbie.

"A month?"

"No. A week."

"Wow. The club pays you that much?"

"No. The club doesn't pay, boo. Most of my money is in tips or bachelor parties." Moet sucked on the cigarette and released a relieved stream of smoke into the air.

"You thinkin' about gettin' down?"

"I'm just visiting, really. But the money sure sounds good." Debbie looked back towards Sadie. She was now pressed up against the mirrors on the wall behind the stage, arms extended, jiggling her shiny ass in rhythm with the music. The DJ mixed in *"Encore"* while, one by one, men stepped to the stage and tossed singles into the growing pile.

"Your . . . good love . . . deserves . . . an encore!"

"That is the jam," Debbie testified while Moet sang.

"Don't get me wrong, girlfriend . . . I make that kind of money . . . *she* makes that kind of money . . ." Moet pointed to Sadie with her nod. ". . . But she *doesn't* make our kind of money." Moet had directed her remark towards Claudine, who was nearby at a table on the main floor, practically begging with excessive fawning and flashing. Just then, Debbie could see that David was making his way back to the table with two drinks in his hands.

Moet also saw David coming. That's when she said, "Listen. I don't know *how* you got with that loser, but if you want to make some *real* money, meet some *real* men . . ." Moet fumbled quickly for a business card. ". . . call me." Debbie squinted, disturbed by Moet's comment. But David was back at the table by now. He curiously acknowledged Moet, as she did him, and he passed the rum and Coke to Debbie. The couple spent the next hour watching the excitement of dancers wiggling, gyrating and touching themselves in front of a capacity crowd of about 200 anxious men. Debbie tried to count the shower of money that fell at the feet of the dancers. By 1AM she lost count.

Back in David's jeep, he attempted to feel her out. For the most part, despite the euphoria that consumed her mind with images and sounds from the club, Debbie was quiet about the experience. She couldn't shake the comment from Moet. She kept thinking "*loser*" and "*real men.*" But her comments were contradicted by David's actions and words. The Internet, on the phone, at the restaurant. He was so polite; a gentleman. He was humorous and seemed to know a lot. All those months that Debbie had invested, believing that he filled voids for her. And his poem . . . David's poem set a fire in her heart. Nobody ever wrote or said anything so beautiful to her. Somehow, she found herself looking for a crack in such a perfect picture. *Was he putting on an act?*

The trip back to Queens was a confusing one. Debbie didn't have those same romantic feelings that she had earlier. She easily dozed off, awaiting the view of Jackie's house. She needed to know more about David before they went any further. She had let him get close to her heart, but did she really know him? Moet would tell her more, of that she was sure.

A quaint kiss and hug ended the night. But the next morning brought questions and concerns that couldn't escape Debbie's every thought. She had grown so callous because of the various nightmares back in Chicago and feeling the weight and responsibility of achieving in the name of the Rose family. Part of that responsibility meant being in good hands and on the right path.

Moet.

The business card Debbie received didn't even have Moet's name printed. There was simply a phone number in glossy, raised black print, in the center of the card. Considering Moet's blessings, less was certainly more. When Debbie finally connected with her, the two agreed to spend the night out. Moet provided the transportation, driving her brand new Mercedes Benz. They made small talk on the way to Moet's favorite restaurant, Mobay in Harlem. The journey was a short one, past LaGuardia Airport, over the Triboro Bridge, through the toll and down 125th Street. Moet double parked outside of the popular Harlem hot spot, which had already developed an early crowd. Unusual for a Saturday night. Many other sporty vehicles were also double parked in the vicinity of the restaurant.

Moet and Debbie stepped proudly towards the Mobay entrance, like celebrities deserving of fanfare. They blended into the night, a part of this impeccable Harlem night. Before Moet had a chance to step through the doorway a homeless man with dark clothing and crusty hygiene ran up as if to accost her. Debbie gasped under her breath, but then she realized that the scruffy man was offering to keep an eye on the car while they were inside. Moet always kept her car clean anyhow. Cleaned and polished. She also had a silent alarm built into the vehicle that was designed to alert the cellphone on her waist. But the guy was polite and humble and convenient for Moet to impress her present company. Without haggling, Moet agreed to let the guy take care of her car while she and Debbie disappeared inside of Mobay. The homeless man scurried to retrieve his bucket and rag.

Quickly becoming a cornerstone of Harlem's dining and nightlife, Mobay was suitable for Moet and Debbie to have a heart to heart talk. Tevin Campbell's classic song, *"Can We Talk"* was playing just loud enough to encourage customers to lean in for a little more intimacy in their conversations. Bartenders and waiters bounced from one patron to another, wearing neat black and white uniforms, pleasant attitudes and blending evenly with the buzzing, humming crowd. Every one of the seats, it seemed, was occupied. Some drinkers were standing shoulder to shoulder with one another for even more personal discussion.

Moet and Debbie made their way through the musks and perfumes of the thick, well-dressed crowd, and into the dining room where reserved seats were awaiting them. A maitre d' greeted the ladies and escorted them. Table candles were lit throughout the room, flickering about the faces of diners and silverware in use. Fine art hung about the walls. A few ceiling fans and flowers on each table and excellent Caribbean food completed the authentic and genuine dining experience.

A waitress readily stepped up to hand menus to the ladies

and suggested the fish of the day. After ordering drinks and finding themselves in their own intimate sphere, Debbie thought it as good a time as any to ask some questions.

"What's it worth to ya?" Moet tried to break the seriousness in Debbie's face. "Just kiddin' . . . loosen up, girl. He's just a man. I deal with men everyday—I damn near have a Ph.D. in the field."

"So I'll ask you again . . . what's wrong with David?" Debbie sipped at the glass of water that the waitress poured for her.

"I think he's a user. That's another way . . . another word for a pimp." (Debbie visibly gulped her water.) "That's right . . . I said *pimp*."

"What makes you so sure?" Debbie asked, a bit defensive. Chaka Khan's voice was now romancing the establishment.

"You mean, besides seeing him with a different girl every now and then? Girlfriend, listen, the guy's a fuckin' pimp-wanna-be-mack, *whateva*. He even tried to fuck *me*. He tried to . . ."

"So that's what this is about? Cuz y'all didn't hit it off, I'm s'pose to turn his lights off?" Moet restrained herself, aware that nearby tables were too close for her peak emotions.

"It's not even about that, Deb. I'm bein' upfront with you. You don't need him. Not as a boyfriend, not as a pimp . . . girl, he's not even good enough to be a *man*." Moet eased her attack, faced with Debbie's frown. "I'm tellin' you some good shit, Deb."

Moet reached across the table and placed her palm over the back of Debbie's hand, offering compassion. Not a second later, they were disrupted. The waitress laid down their drinks. Debbie had a rum and Coke, while Moet lived up to her name and had champagne.

After their red snapper dinner and some flirting at the bar, the evening's excitement escalated with a trip downtown to The Shadow nightclub in midtown Manhattan. Moet's Mercedes was extra shiny (well worth the $5 tip she'd paid outside of the restaurant) and it attracted some appreciation from the long line outside of the club.

It was now 1AM, and Moet knew that she was playing with fire. The club usually sold out by this time on Saturday nights, and the crowd was body to body along the ramp ascending towards the entrance. She rushed into the adjacent parking lot, paid the attendant and encouraged Debbie to get a move on.

"Come on. I know the doorman," Moet said. And just so, the two avoided the crowd thanks to Moet luring the doorman with her half naked body.

Once inside, Debbie could feel the drone of house music thumping and bouncing off of the walls and floors and ceilings. She felt her heart beating like a jungle drum under her breast as she looked up and out into the dark, captivating rotunda. Colorful strings of laser lights shot out into the fog above a sea of ethnic men and women. Heads bobbed and eyeballs roamed, while people wandered to and fro in their endless search for companionship.

The heaviest concentration—where most of the body heat was focused—was the large dance floor in the center of the club, where men and women shook and wiggled and dazzled one another. Blending the rhythm with some attitude was DJ Sugar Daddy, currently spinning the classic Colonel Abrams hit, "*I'm Not Gonna Let You*," and thrilling the venue of mostly 30-somethings. One behind the other, Moet and Debbie worked their way through the crowd of bodies, to different areas and designated rooms. In one of those designated rooms reggae music encouraged women and men alike to wind and grind against one another. Some men were standing back against pillars, or up against walls, merely observing the activities instead of actually participating.

Leaving the reggae room was like walking through a sound barrier or time warp, with the reggae and club music clashing, the beats and tempos conflicting and the vibrations at war with one another. From that room, the two climbed a case of stairs to an intimate wing on the second floor. To the left was a jazz room where the mood was smooth and mellow. To the right was a glass-enclosed balcony, complete with couches, cocktail tables and a few intimate couples. From that position those couples had a glass-enclosed, unobstructed view of the crowded dance floor below. Moet and Debbie occupied a table and soaked into the obscurity of the dimmed atmosphere, and they too looked down over the sea of heads on the dance floor below. Although the music was muffled to a low hum, the vibrations still thumped and bumped and penetrated the walls and floors throughout.

The night was just an ongoing movement for Debbie, now with this latest head rush to help her to forget the concerns at the top of her list; like suddenly feeling alone in New York; or like not being financially stable; and most of all, there were David's deceptions that somehow persuaded Debbie to veer from her mother, and from her wants and desires for a successful future. All of these concerns were now so easily whisked away, or at least subdued by the ever-intriguing Moet. She seemed to have influence with all the right people in all the right places. Yes, her acquaintances were mostly men, but from all walks of life. She had what Debbie was beginning to crave. Control.

That late night on the way back to Jackie's house, Moet pulled over into a service area on the Grand Central Parkway.

"Everything is . . . yeah, everything is fine. I just wanted to stop for a minute." Debbie shrugged at Moet's answer and sank back, relaxed in the passenger's seat. She settled into a mood of calm, with her eyes closed and her mind on the pleasant, infectious sounds of Tony Toni Toné's "*Slow Wind*," playing on Moet's Alpine sound system. Moet leaned over into Debbie's own field of warmth. Her lips barely touched Debbie's, prompting her to jolt and draw her head back wide-eyed and dumbfounded.

"Moet!" Debbie seemed more amazed than shocked. Suddenly folding her arms over her breasts, she shrank into the soft leather, at a loss for words or actions. Her jaw simply fell open.

"Relax, Deb. I like you. Just wanted to get with you closer— you know?" Moet maintained dominance, with her arm extended, resting behind Debbie's neck next to the headrest. Yet Moet held a concern in her eyes. She didn't appreciate the rejection. Nor did she expect it—not from anyone.

"Don't you like me?"

"Yeah . . . but . . . Moet?" Debbie widened her lids inquisitively. Her way of confronting a taboo. "I've . . . never . . . I mean, you know . . ." She tried to explain with open palms. ". . . like . . . been with a woman." As if these were words she was expecting, Moet placed her fore and middle fingers to Debbie's lips.

"You don't have to explain. I understand." Moet maintained control over Debbie's senses, now reaching over to the volume dial on the car stereo. You could hear a pin drop, the car turned so quiet. There were also those faint "*zips*" and "*whooshes*" of speeding vehicles darting past on the parkway. The force of the wind budging the vehicle ever so slightly.

"Close your eyes for me and relax. Let nature take over."

Moet leveled her serious eyes, and the moment made Debbie shiver a bit. Debbie also felt her nerves pricking under her skin and her lungs pumped harder and deeper breaths as Moet touched her fingertips to Debbie's lids, guiding them closed. Now, with that full feeling of the unknown, a wave of heat flushed Debbie's body. Moet rolled her fingers down along her cheek, then her lips, and on down her neck until she grazed Debbie's stiffened nipples. Debbie's whole body was stiff. Her nostrils flared—the result of sensations shooting through her . . . of being touched so delicately. Moet now had all of the girl's breast in her hand. One hand on Debbie's; the other on her own. Then she moved in and pressed her lips to Debbie's. Debbie's eyes twitched as if they were anticipating eye drops, but she slowly gave in and relaxed under Moet's pressure. She found comfort in the moment; a security and warmth that she'd been missing for so long.

Moet became more aggressive, prying into Debbie's lap and then her panties. It came to a point where Debbie jumped defiantly. Moet had gone too far. For now, anyway. And still, Debbie attempted to save face, saying, "This is . . . this is moving too fast for me. I . . . I need time." With puckered lips and eyes full of desire, Moet backed down. But behind her eyes Debbie could see some promise, as though she didn't want to chase away the future of this potential relationship. *Relationship? What am I saying?* And, now that Moet's intentions were clear, *is this the reason she said those things about David?* Moet didn't even need to try hard to provoke Debbie to change her mind about David; she discouraged her just enough, and then extended her own invite.

In all of New York City, there couldn't be anyone more confused than Debbie was right now.

CHAPTER TEN

The new Gilmore's, now widely recognized as FOOL'S PARADISE, was open for a year without incident. Incidents such as fights and shootings were not uncommon in many New York nightclubs, but Fool's Paradise seemed to steer clear of this. The women came to work to make money. The men came to the club to get the attention of those same women. It was a perfect cycle.

After such an impeccable track record, Murphy stopped by and he brought his *"anything that can go wrong"* song with him. The incident involved an argument with a correctional officer, and resulted in him retrieving a pistol from his car. But what made the incident all the more significant was not only the intensity or the potential violence. Also, there were special visitors who came by the club on that night.

For a long time, Douglass had been coached and advised by his friend and neighbor, Steve—the same well-known and very successful club owner who represented a major source of support for Douglass. Not only did Steve give Douglass consultation and technical support, but on occasion (and off the record) he provided thousands in financial support. Meanwhile, the two shared industry secrets, always discussing who would and would not survive in New York radio, clubs or concert promotions. Whether it was Douglass who called Steve, or if Steve called Douglass, the two could rant and ramble on for hours. And coincidentally, the two became wise and experienced as a result of their conversations, forever affirming each other's points of view.

As Douglass became his own man, building his own name in entertainment and spearheading the construction of Fool's Paradise, he'd always update Steve on the club's progress and development, always inviting him to stop by. Steve, on the other hand, was forced to comply with his own responsibilities with operating two heavily attended New York City nightclubs, spending time with his own family, as well as he managed various other business concerns. Besides that workload, Steve was also a tremendous help to his own father, owner of the world-famous Copacabana. All of these factors made it too difficult to just stop in and say hi, or to give hands-on advice at the drop of a dime. All the more reason why Steve's first visit to Fool's Paradise was both ironic and eventful. Finally, he'd get to meet Douglass's father, as well as he would get to offer his own analysis of Douglass's accomplishments. After all, it was with Steve's help that Douglass summoned during the development of the new establishment; all those problems he was having obtaining a license to sell liquor and other necessary permits; not to mention all the hurdles and paranoia as a result of the Happy Land fire.

Douglass had, for a long time, testified, "The club is safe, Steve. The licenses are all legit—come on, man. Stop by just to take a peek. I would have never gotten this club open without your help."

However, when Steve stepped though the entrance, with his girlfriend in tow, he may have well hit the lottery of circumstances. Douglass and his dad were already overwhelmed by the visit; but then, they were all dumbfounded to see the rush of activity. This angry correctional officer raced through the entrance, past the doorman, and he pointed his gun at everyone and no one in the center of the room. In the flurry of activity, a wave of patrons and staff opened up in a semicircle (or, maybe, something like the parting of the Red Sea) to keep their distance. Meanwhile, Douglass and his guests took quick leave through the side door leading to Gilmore's messy office. Messy or not, the office had its own back door which led to the sidewalk outside. The incident, despite what it appeared to be, turned out to be a dud. The guy never fired a shot. But for sure, certain images were left to reckon with; and needless to say, security had to be reorganized.

And still, no security overhaul could have prevented the murder that took place in the parking lot.

Detective Walter Wade

The history of Fool's Paradise was one of the factors which most intrigued Detective Walter Wade. A man in his 50's, with some Ozzie Davis likeness, Wade was graying with wisdom enough to expect a topless establishment to carry burdens of trouble. Shootings, anarchy, robbery, fights, and rapes were usual occurrences with many of Gilmore's competitors. How then did Fool's Paradise beat the odds? What chemistry or method had the establishment mastered? Or were there payoffs, or better yet, was this just a big, perfect front for other things? It was too good to be true. Wade smelled a cover-up of sorts and was suspicious of the club and everyone responsible for its existence. Perhaps the wonder of it all simply overwhelmed Wade, with his modest job and his modest paycheck. But this was not the time to bring his personal life into the mix of thoughts that floated through his mind as he watched the blitz of activities before him.

This was officially a crime scene. The area outside the club, in the parking lot, at the side and rear, everything was brightly illuminated by two Hollywood-sized halogens. Sunrise was only hours away, but the details of a homicide were critical in police procedure. The moonlight, the daylight creeping in, and the dim spotlights that hung from high up on the wall wouldn't be sufficient. Coroners from the Bronx City Morgue were now finished bagging the corpse. The zipper was pulled, sealing the long, dark, vinyl heap. Moet's body was carried to a black station wagon at the driveway's edge. Wade was casual about it all. Been here, done this at least a thousand times. And that was just his attitude as he sipped cautiously at his hot chocolate.

Another fickle thought now:

"How convenient; working a case next door to Dunkin' Donuts. Mental note." He juggled his cup while pulling out his short pad and Bic pen, and he wrote, *"Interview Donut workers."*

Wade flipped the pad closed and stuffed it back into his Army jacket. He looked back up to see Claudine, draped in a sheepskin coat and holding its flaps tight as if she'd just been pulled from the icy, murky Hudson River. So far, Claudine was the first and most important eyewitness, and she leaned back inclined against one of the seven patrol cars on the scene. An officer was standing a foot or two away, pad and pen connected as he interviewed her. In several other areas of the lot similar interviews were being conducted with staff members, patrons and the owner. Everyone exhaled their own levels of vapor into the cool air. A bright-yellow plastic strip with POLICE LINE printed in bold, black letters was tied across the edge of the driveway, keeping a crowd of 20 or so standing at the sidewalk.

The owner of the black Cherokee, the one by which Moet

was lying stiff with a bullet in her forehead, was irate. He was Jamaican, with a rainbow-colored, Dr. Seuss-sized hat, arguing with another officer about his vehicle. He wanted to go, and the police were preventing him from doing so. The jeep was currently being dusted for fingerprints.

Forensic specialists were hovering over and about the truck with what looked like thick blush applicators, stroking that white dust all over the hood, doors, tires and windows. The Jamaican could be heard in the distance, something about *"painting me jeep all white."* A few dancers were freezing their asses off, standing in a threesome huddle, legs bare, answering questions and chain-smoking.

Wade sipped again at his sweet and frothy hot chocolate, preparing to make his own rounds. First he'd get an update from the captain, then the officers. He wanted to re-address Gil and Claudine, because they were part of an obvious scene that took place inside the club earlier that night. It may mean something, so Wade had to know. Afterwards, he wanted to get back over to Dunkin' Donuts. This time, if he applied himself in a more official capacity, maybe the second cup of cocoa would be free. Wade's eyes passed back to Claudine. A fellow officer had mentioned something about her lying on the ground with the victim. Wade suddenly wanted to hear *this* one himself—directly from the source, if at all possible.

About 30 minutes later he spoke with Claudine.

"I don't know . . . I . . . was, you know . . . drinkin'. Maaaan, do I have to go over this *again*? My head is *killin'* me."

Wade wasn't yet growing impatient, but he had an urge; still he kept his composure.

"Listen, Claudine. I understand that you've got a headache and you're probably dying for a nice, comfortable bed. But the fact is that if you don't answer my questions here, you'll have to go down to the precinct and answer them." Claudine's face expressed another level of dismay in resignation.

"Now, I need you to relax and to be honest with me. You were found laying half naked on top of the victim. I'm told that's she's been dead since one AM. But you left the club at something past two. Now think back, Claudine. What did you see and how did you come to be so . . . so *intimate* with Moet, not more than an hour after she was shot in the head?"

Claudine was visibly shaken as the realities of her predicament were explained to her. Detective Wade offered her a cigarette and Claudine eventually buckled down and gave in to his
confidence. Once all of the physical evidence was accumulated
and interviews were completed, Wade reached for his cell phone
and called his ace, a doctor at St. Barnabas Hospital. He arranged for Claudine to be escorted there for a *just-to-be-sure*
check-up. But of course, there was a hook.

"Hi, Wade. Thanks again for dinner the other night." Diane was
as perky and alive on the phone as her breasts and curves were
in person. And she had that bit of daytime attitude to break
through the overnight monotonies.

"No problem, baby. I hope we can do it again, soon."

"You wouldn't be tryin' to push up on me now, would you,
Detective Walter Wade?"

"Me? I don't know what you mean." The two chuckled
slightly before buckling down to the business at hand.

"So what can I do you for this morning? You got a back-
ache?" Diane asked facetiously.

"I'm sending over a young lady. Her name's Claudine. We've
got a homicide case over here at Fool's Paradise."

"Fool's Paradise . . . hmmm. I know that place—wait a
minute . . . you're not going topless on me now, are you?" Wade
smirked at the pun and continued to explain.

"I need you to do a check-up on her. I mean . . . a *real*
check-up."

"Okay. So . . . the usual; blood, hair samples, urine?"

"Yup. And check under her nails and even her panties . . ."

"Was she raped or something?"

"I don't think so, but I have a few hunches. The only way I
can follow up on them is to get this extra-personal data. Know-
whadda mean?"

"You got it, boss. Does this mean I can go for a lobster next
time?"

"Sure . . . and listen, Di. This isn't pretty. She's had a bit to
drink. But take this seriously. Okay?"

"Always."

Suspects and Developments

A few weeks after the homicide Detective Wade found himself swiveling, idle in his leather executive chair, bent back and staring at his cork bulletin board. This was where he strategized all of his cases. The monument of his glory. And not one of his cases ever went unsolved. Maybe that had to do with his choosing whether or not to take certain cases and to refuse others, maybe not. Wade was indeed a clever man, and it was well represented right there on that wall. Newspaper headlines, clippings and photos scattered about the wall. All of it organized in a disorganized way. Some were tacked to the board. Others were scotch-taped to the perimeter of the board. Either way, Wade was accomplished with or without fanfare. If not for his 18 years on the force and his consistent success, he probably would have resorted to opening his own firm as a private detective. But the resources and fringe benefits as a well-received New York City police officer were limitless. The donut breaks sustained his potbelly. He could talk as much as he wanted on the phone—on the city's tab. He could walk into various city-run agencies and buildings without invite. All of this access to information on just about everything and everybody was nothing less than a pot of gold for a single man. Forget the badge. What about the women! How many gorgeous city workers did Wade know on a first-name basis? Such a resource was as good as having more money than he could count. It would never run out.

And Wade wasn't a user. However, he *was* a romantic. The abundance of police resources filled a tremendous void in His life. It was almost 25 years since he lost his dear wife Renee in a high-speed car accident on the Audubon in Germany. The two met while serving in the Army. They were so compatible, thinking and speaking alike. They were soulmates, and Wade always told himself that he'd *never* replace her. She was the poetry in his life. When she was whisked away, life just turned colorless and grey. Things were never the same after that loss. She was so young. So beautiful. Wade kept himself from every movie or song which Vanessa Williams was a part of. No more radio in his life, because he could never know when another of her songs would come on the air. And besides, the singer reminded him so much of Renee. They looked so much alike it was painful to see a Vanessa video or a movie.

Four years after her death, with a heart of stone, Wade left active duty with an Honorable Discharge, and he joined the police academy. He served his probation period walking the sidewalks as a flatfoot in the Bronx. White Plains Road. Gun Hill Road. Boston Post Road. He'd seen it all, walked in on robberies and delivered babies. He'd seen the same child who he delivered slain during an attempted car jacking as a teen. Yes, indeed, Wade had seen it all. And now, with close to two years until his retirement, and more than 50 solved homicide cases to his credit, Wade was suddenly stumped by the circumstances surrounding Fool's Paradise and the murder of Nadine Butler, aka Moet. For sure, Wade had a lot of facts and suspects pinned to his strategy board. Too many. It was time to crunch. Time to whittle things down.

Wade had his own way of working a case. First, he would detail his own idea of what happened based on witness accounts and evidence. Then he'd draw up a list of class A suspects, class B and class C. In whittling things down, he'd ultimately eliminate C suspects and then B suspects. The *New York Daily Post* gave only brief accounts of what cases Wade was working. That's the way he wanted it. That's the way it was. News of Moet's murder didn't hit the papers until Monday morning. Saturday's paper had already gone to press and any news blotter rarely made the Sunday paper, more or less designed for exclusives, Arts & Liesure, and (of course) *The Week in Review*. So Wade had his various contacts that won him a story here and there; it was his "edge" in crime fighting. But for this latest case he wanted enough attention to shine on the details so that any potential witness, customers from that fatal Friday night, might come forth. Ordinarily, a story like this would be lucky to get page 17, if it even made the obituary. But with Wade's juice, he pulled off a banner announcement. Bold white print on a black bar across the top of the front page.

TOPLESS DANCER SLAIN
Details on page 2.

The story inside was column length and went into details about Moet, the club and the circumstances surrounding the tragedy. The papers always had a way of sensationalizing a murder. But Wade could always see right through the fat. Especially when the case was from his precinct. As Wade observed the board, he recalled the extended details of his investigation. He'd learned a lot from his class B list, so it provided a good starting point. At least Moet was no longer a mystery victim.

She began dancing at the old Gilmore's when the club was in Mt. Vernon, operating out of a virtual hole in the wall. At the time she was 13 years old, she had left a home where her uncles, her father and her brother took their turns at sexually abusing her. She didn't attend high school, but was very bright and witty, nonetheless. Her rough childhood led to her degree in hard knocks. But surviving and overcoming those horrors resulted in her ultimately using her God-givens to manipulate men and women alike.

True, Moet was viewed as a competitor for the dollars that came through the club's entrance, but dancers still considered her a friend. Sadie was a close friend, and she didn't mind letting Detective Wade in on some realities about Moet's escapades with men. Or, at least, those *she* knew of. There was Bobby the fisherman. With him (so said Moet), it was purely money and sex. If Moet needed a piece of furniture, say a couch or an armoire, or help with her mortgage, Bobby easily dished out a wad of cash to subsidize her whims. In return (and this was in defiance of that "unwritten rule"), Moet would satiate his freaky desires. There was bondage and kinky sex. Moet even made a home video of an episode, according to Sadie. No, Bobby didn't live with her. He was even married with children, Wade had later discovered. Bobby was married to a woman from Iowa, named Joy. They had two children and tucked themselves away, snug, in the village of Pelham Manor. Minutes away from Moet's home and job. Too convenient? Or just convenient enough to commit murder? Wade wouldn't so quickly scratch Bobby off of the list.

On the other hand, Moet was deep in love and steadily dating major league baseball pitcher Ken Stevens. He was living out a 68-million dollar contract with the New York Yankees. He was in and out of town, according to his busy schedule. A second generation player of major league ball, following in his father's footsteps, Ken definitely had dough. But along with the wealth, he drove a player's lifestyle. He wasn't a one-woman man, but then, Moet wasn't a one-man woman, either. According to a bat boy at the stadium, Ken was swinging a couple of relationships himself. Bi-coastal. While numerous men of various classes in life continuously kissed up to Moet at Fool's Paradise, she pretty much did the same, kissing up to Ken. Maybe it was his money or the idea that he could claim any one of the thousands of female fans who pursued him.

"The intrigue or the jock status?" Sadie couldn't call that one, because she didn't sell ass. She said, "I can't even imagine what that's like." But she was informed enough to be of help to Wade.

As a top money maker at Gilmore's, as well as at the all-new Fool's Paradise, as well as hundreds of private bachelor parties through the years, Moet had accumulated true wealth, experience *and* money. She not only had her own two-level home, the Mercedes and a gold Toyota Land Cruiser that was used seasonally, but she kept mucho cash on hand.

The night of her murder, she still had $2,300 in her purse along with her house and car keys. At her house, there was a stack of Maxwell House Coffee cans lined up in a kitchen cabinet, air-tight with one hundred-dollar bills. Over $120,000 in total. So Wade had no doubts about the motive *not* being robbery. Remaining were those usual motives of jealousy, spite or revenge. Under jealousy, Wade considered boyfriends and customers. Under spite, there were dancers to question. Then there was revenge. Was there someone that Moet ticked off or hurt? Could be an ex-boyfriend or even a dancer if Moet stole another woman's man. The idea of outright, cold blooded, reasonless murder was out of the question.

"Murder has a reason every time." That was a quote that Wade's father shared with him before he died. All of those years of writing mystery and suspense novels rubbed off, finally put to actual use a generation later. But ultimately, it was up to Wade to choose the most likely motive. Even if it was one with the broadest possibilities. He leaned towards revenge. The bullethole at the center of her head made it clear that the

suspect wanted her dead. D.E.A.D.—dead. And to want someone dead that bad (in Wade's 18 years of experience) added up
to nothing more than revenge.

There seemed to be a month's worth of investigation squeezed
into 3 weeks, with Wade following dancers, staff members and
a few regular customers to their homes. He verified employment of those girls who were only moonlighting at Fool's Paradise. He accessed records from the Department of Social
Services, and he surveyed bank accounts of the owner and
some of his employees. He traced license plates from three
consecutive Friday night crowds. He even had an opportunity
to see . . . or *investigate* Moet's private library of video tapes. He
removed them from her house before officers had an opportunity to collect evidence. And in the three weeks he'd been on
the case, he was able to devote an hour each night to her videos.
Still—and this surely had something to do with the content of
the tapes—so far, he had only completed 2 of them.

Sadie

The dancers that Detective Wade decided to tail were the top-
shelf girls from the club. Laurie Hill, aka Sadie, was very helpful with her insights on Moet's relationships. Wade realized
that they were close friends. Regardless of whether she was involved or not, Wade could only become familiar with a dancer's
habits and routines by observing Sadie and others for a period
of time. Sadie had a 20th-floor apartment on 134th Street in
Harlem. During his interview with her, Wade was blown away
by her living arrangements. Sadie lived in *the* lap of luxury.
Walls of mirrors increased the depth of so many lavish possessions filling her spacious rooms. A monster aquarium was built
into a wall which separated the living room and dining area. A
cabinet full of crystal, china and silver was sandwiched between 2 tall and plentiful wine racks. The carpet was a deep,
lime green. Thick enough to hide a dancer's overworked toes.
An arrangement of plush couches were positioned against the
walls. Wallpaper was fabric and textured with soft, contempo-

rary designs. A 6-foot television screen was positioned beside a rack of 10 various stereo components, including compact disc players, AM/FM receiver, amplifier, 2 VCRs and other electronic accommodations. A 2-foot high, 5-foot wide, oval coffee table sat in front of the couch, while the surface of the table was a massive, polished ivory slab of the marble with off-white swirls. On top, a weaved basket was stuffed with dried flowers, providing a pleasant fragrance for the room. Attracting the most attention was a life-sized statue of an exotic dancer. It was sculpted of iron and held a black, glossy luster.

Amazing how at 22 Sadie was childless, but not without companionship. She was the driving force behind a threesome; a relationship with a man and another woman. The three lovers lived together and slept together.

Wade also discovered that Sadie's bank account didn't reflect her lifestyle, but it was a comfortable safety net. $10,550 in savings, $6,100 in checking. There were no out of the ordinary expenditures, so far as Wade could see. Tailing her, he noted her daily routine, how she took her cherry red Puget on various errands. The cleaners. The supermarket. A stop at a local lingerie shop now and then. Twice a week Sadie visited the video store and disappeared into the back room labeled "ADULT." Wade guessed that Sadie's life was full of passion and security. She was living life to the top and didn't seem to be in a position to be jealous or vengeful. If anybody was jealous, it would be another dancer jealous of Sadie. Or any of the dozens of customers whom she had to reject weekly. Wade made his mental notes.

It must be nice.

Juicy

The next dancer on Wade's list was Erica Miller. Her stage name was Juicy, and she more or less served as a lure for the old timers who had been devoted customers for over 15 years. Juicy was 42. However, she was fit enough to appear as though she was 20-something. On stage, she wasn't daring or exciting like the younger dancers. She moved slow and unconcerned, a slithery vixen. At her own pace, she was attractive enough for men age 40 and over. Some customers came specifically to see Juicy. Part of her following.

Wade had techniques for catching the individuals on his "hit list;" his, so to speak, *covert operational approach*. He'd simply follow them home from work and knock (conveniently) a moment after they closed their front door—as if he was the cab driver returning something left in his car. Most dancers took cabs to work. Juicy was one of those who did, so Wade played taxi cab driver to gain entry. Then the badge.

"Juicy? Detective Walter Wade. Mind if I come in and ask you a few questions?"

"Listen, man . . . I'm tired. My feets is tired. I ain't eat donuts and count traffic tickets all night—I worked."

"Whoa, there, lil lady. I'm not here to make a scene. I just need a couple of minutes of your time. Nothin' but a few questions, if you'll just give me—"

"Come in, man. And keep your own business."

The detective was apprehensive about this invite into Juicy's basement apartment. Her place was part of a 4-story walkup on Hamilton Terrace in Harlem. The outside of the dwelling looked as authentic and classy as the rest of Hamilton Terrace. Wrought iron gate. Clean, limestone facade with 18th century style carvings and moldings. But once Wade stepped through the entrance, at first sight his mind was thrown for a spin. The place was an atrocity. Ransacked and corroded. Compared to the elite appearances of the brownstones that lined the immediate area, with cobblestone accuracy and impeccable stained-wood entryways, Juicy was living in a pigsty. The basement was unfinished with encrusted plaster and paint on the walls and ceilings. The floors were untiled, unclean cement. Wires and pipes ran a maze along the ceilings and floors. Three steps past the front door led Wade through a dark hallway. A room to his immediate left was where the interview was held. Wade could have smacked himself for his so-called "covert actions," and for assuming that every topless dancer lived lavishly and organized. He wondered why he didn't just interview Juicy at the club. He cursed himself and reconciled that he'd be as quick as possible with *this* conversation. Wade had no choice but to record the surroundings with his four senses. His fifth sense was being challenged with every passing second as he stifled his breathing as best he could. While asking questions, his tongue even became preoccupied with the odor from the piles of spoiled clothing—a thick aroma that provoked a tart taste in his mouth.

A makeshift stand supported an outdated TV set which flickered between viewable and fuzzy. It looked as if Juicy kept it on all day as a form of security. Two milk crates were stacked with a slice of plywood placed on top as a flat surface.

Her dining room table? There on the wood were jars of peanut butter and jelly. The jelly jar was opened, with the lid just next to it. Fruit flies buzzed over and around the jelly, unchallenged. A half loaf of bread was also opened, with a few slices exposed to the murky absence of ventilation in the room. A mattress in a corner on the floor lay adjacent to the TV, and that shameless variety of feminine articles threatening to break a fragile, plastic shelf. Observing all of this, Wade remained still in an antique armchair while Juicy went along with the session. She appeared to be aggravated by Wade's timing, and in protest she remained busy as they spoke. She undressed as if he wasn't even there, took a damp washcloth from a shelf and wiped her underarms and vaginal area. Then she threw an oversized t-shirt over her head—apparently ready for bed. Wade almost wanted to barf as he breathed in the mix of her body odor along with the spoiled jelly, airborne asbestos and dust, as well as the soiled laundry scents. As if by clockwork, Juicy casually proceeded to count her singles on top of that same soiled mattress.

"So, this is it, huh? This is what dancing at Gilmore's gets you? After what—" Wade looked at his pad and produced a disbelieving expression. "—I hear you've been dancing there for twelve years?"

"What's it to ya, Pops? You got all the questions—you got answers, too? You ain't ever walked in my shoes, you come in my house like some super cop—probably ain't got no warrant—and you wanna cast judgment on me? For your information, I'm happy. I been there, done that. Been around the world wit all you men, and y'all ain't nothin' but the same. If you put on a good act, ya might hide what's in your minds; but I can see through all that there."

"Oh, really. And what is it that you see?"

"See, I been with more men than you can count on an army's fingers and toes. I know your lies, your insecurities, your fears and your denials. I know what makes you weak, and what sends your egos through the roof. So, you can't come in here judgin' me, Kojak. Cuz, I already know y'all ain't nothin' but some swingin' dicks lookin' to bust off down some poor girl's throat. Some of you ain't neva had it *that* good, so you'll settle for creamin' our tits or ass. And the percent a y'all that *did* have some type a *real* love in your life, well . . . y'all might wanna fuck us the right way, the way the Lord meant it to be."

Wade froze for a time, even disgusted at himself for digging down the wrong path. *I asked for that*, he told himself as he tried to block out a lot of the dancer's comments from his mind. And as Wade completed his interview, having endured more discoveries than he would have liked to, Juicy didn't even bother to see him to the door. She actually dozed off right in front of him, soaking into the pattern and impression left in her mattress.

And to think that Wade tailed Juicy for two days subsequent to this eventful interview. All that just to get to this latest decision to remove her from his list of suspects. Not only didn't Moet have an impact on Juicy's cash flow, but they had worked alongside one another for years. The younger and older woman actually complemented one another—part of the "old school" of Gilmore's stable of dancers. Meanwhile, Wade qualified Juicy's alibi for the time of the murder. She left the club at 1AM in a cab. The driver confirmed the same.

Claudine

Claudine was a simple subject to measure. She was a young and very naive 19-year-old who had been dancing for just a year at Fool's Paradise. She was attending the College of New Rochelle in an attempt to major in communications. She maintained part-time hours as a receptionist from a local entrepreneur, but even her boss treated her like the wannabe that she was. At the time of the murder, Claudine was but an underpaid intern, whose rationale for working for free was:

"I just wanna be part of somethin' legitimate," because—Detective Wade guessed—nothing else in her life was. Upon further discovery, Wade saw that she wasn't even keeping good grades in school. One of two siblings who came from a broken family, Claudine's father had died and her mother became a schizophrenic and unbearable to live with. Homeless for a while, even sleeping on the floor of her campus dorm, Claudine eventually shacked up with a young boy and his mother in a Bronx apartment.

Wade had noted that (if Claudine was the murderer—and he already guessed she wasn't) she might've been jealous of Moet, thought Wade, but it would've been more envy than anything else. If anything, Claudine was in awe of all the top-shelf dancers.

"She thinks they're fascinating," one dancer told the detective. "She's always aspiring to be like one of them. But she never could quite cut it. She's just Claudine. Plain Jane Claudine. She don't even have a stage name. Too naive to think one up, I guess."

Wade also found that she drank excessively at times, escaping the realities of her failures. Two abortions in 6 months. Forced to sex her boyfriend for lack of a place to stay. And besides (quiet as she tried to keep it) she couldn't succeed at the various jobs she applied for. Even the average Joe could get a job at McDonald's at the local mall or as an on-campus librarian. But not Claudine. She was a miserable failure. She felt hopeless, trapped and lacked direction and self esteem. Very often her boyfriend was in attendance at Fool's Paradise to monitor her activity, and likely helping with that esteem issue. But was he the jealous type? Or was he merely practicing to be a pimp mandating that she bring her earnings home only to hand it all over to him? Questions to be answered as Detective Wade dug more and more behind the scenes of the topless industry's activities.

On the night of the murder, Claudine's boyfriend was nowhere to be found. That could've meant a lot of things that evening. Wade assumed that, in Claudine's dizzy state that night, she was the first to stumble on Moet's corpse. Yet, she may not have known that Moet was dead. At St. Barnabas

Hospital, the physical performed by Wade's friend Diane came up with some hard revelations. Claudine had blood in her mouth. Moet's blood. Moet's blood was also soaked into Claudine's clothing. In taking samples from under Claudine's fingernails, Diane found that the girl had had her fingers in and around Moet's vagina.

Was she finger fucking the dead body as well? Wade wondered.

"Walter, the blood shows a nine percent alcohol content in her system. Her blood also revealed traces of marijuana. In all, the girl was toasted and high as a kite," said Diane following that fatal Friday. Wade concluded that there was no way Claudine could have killed Moet. Not only was she inside the club most of the night, even getting into an altercation with the boss; but she was also seen leaving the club an hour past the estimated time of death. The Dodo bird didn't even have sense enough to distinguish interactive sex from sucking on a corpse.

Cinnamon

Sheryl Moore took on the name Cinnamon once she came to appreciate the constant compliments from her customers.

"You sure do have fine skin, baby."

"Woman, just let me touch your skin. How much do you want?" Even dancers commented about Sheryl's alluring skin that was proclaimed as *"butter soft"* and *"good enough to eat."* So, she adopted the name Cinnamon and it caught on like fire. Even her friends outside of the topless world called her by her stage name. Cinnamon was an adventurous dancer. Much of what Wade learned about her, he picked up from her stage performances and comments from co-workers. Besides being a hit on the main stage, Cinnamon was well known for her girl-on-girl shows at Fool's Paradise. Although body-to-body contact was not permissible by law, *certain* entertainment at the club went on (despite rules) and became standards. Cinnamon did a lot of girl-on-girl stuff on Friday and Saturday nights, at the busiest hours. And mostly on a whim, she would put on her show with exclusive partners Sadie or Moet.

"You know, basically, just sixty-nine stuff. We used bananas, whipped cream and even cherries. You've never seen one?" Cinnamon answered Wade's curiosity as if it was normal for a man to have witnessed such an event.

"No," he emphasized, "I *haven't*."

"Well then . . . you don't know what you're missing." Cinnamon widened her eyes as though she had a passion for the subject. Wade had been on the case long enough to expect certain things, but he didn't expect *this* conversation. Nor did he expect the arousal that went with it. He expected that he was stronger than anything this case could bring his way. But Cinnamon was a trip. Her abrupt, salacious expressions and impulsive responses cut through Wade's demeanor. Cinnamon went on to discuss her enterprises; the bachelor parties, the private parties, the newsletter that she founded, and the lesbian pilgrimages that she spearheaded every year.

"I never heard of that . . . what all does that involve?" Again Wade was going beyond his detective questions, back to that predictable, horny-man status.

"Well, there's about four or five hundred of us that go out to camp grounds upstate . . . Bear Mountain."

Wade interjected with his silent humor, "*You mean more like Beaver Mountain*," he thought.

"There's three days of picnics, games, seminars and other fun activities." As Cinnamon explained all, Wade wandered off thinking, envisioning what "*other fun activities*" might mean. Adventurous was an understatement with respect to Cinnamon. Just as was the case with Sadie, she also lived with two companions—two female companions. Foxy and Monifah were a part of her permanent entourage. Within some of the most lavish standards of living, the ladies were lovers in a Brooklyn brownstone. Each of them fine, young and sensual, they all danced for a living, sometimes for club bookings, but mostly for the very best bachelor parties. Cinnamon was the ringleader of the trio, maintaining a simple yet warm atmosphere at home. The walls were kept in their original state, genuine red brick, while the floors were finished wood with modest oriental throw rugs in a couple places. On the floor there were only necessary furnishings; a long and sumptuous soft-black-leather couch. An expensive sound system. A 50-inch television; and about seven fine art paintings of African images at various areas along the walls and in the hallways. The art seemed to defy conformity, how it stood out, unfazed and purposeful, under tall, arched stucco ceilings and ceiling fans. There was a generous picture window that offered an ultimate, elevated view of the Great Lawn, the playground and clusters of blacks and Latinos in Fort Green Park. Wade figured that with three or four thousand dollars, the combined income which the three women took home weekly, it was easy to see how the three dancing dolls lived so well. Secure. Complete. Comfortable. Wade left Cinnamon harboring the same feelings he took from his visit with Sadie. Her bank account was just shy of $8000. However, Cinnamon *kept* credit cards. Her credit report showed she had 10 altogether—the gold and platinum plaques of her success. Cinnamon and her housemates also shared twin Volkswagen Rabbits and were close to paying them both off in full. Their cellphones were legal and they each had their share of man problems. But, according to their three's-company living, they managed to keep them at a distance. If anything, Cinnamon was endeared to Moet. Maybe the two even took it to another level. But she definitely didn't . . . wouldn't kill her. Just another attractive, sexy vixen relationship. And another dead end.

Wade shook himself from the stupor he was caught up in for at least a half hour. He didn't feel the need to doze off or rest, he just kind of gazed into the cork of his bulletin board and focused on his case. Reviewing. Deciphering. Contemplating. He decided to play more of the field. His class-A suspects. The first character was Debbie, since most of those he interviewed brought up her name as one of Moet's closest friends. Others said the two were lovers. Based on the various accounts, it wasn't unusual to see Moet and Debbie side by side for up to a month before the murder. But now, she was nowhere to be found. Wade had a vague description of Debbie. She had only been around Fool's Paradise for a month or so, and Claudine remembered seeing her with a guy named David. Claudine knew even more about this guy David and was apparently holding something back. Wade figured immediately that the two (Claudine and David) took their roll in the sack and that there were those inevitable issues between them. But as for Debbie, nobody knew much about her, which posed a problem for Wade. Almost a month into the case and all of the class-A suspects were accounted for except Debbie. Why else would she just vanish like that, unless she had something more to do with this. That was more than suspicious. How could someone who was *that* intimate with Moet just disappear? Surely she'd have been at the funeral, or at least the wake. These were concerns of Wade's as he headed home to view more of Moet's videotapes.

The first two tapes were exciting to watch. Candid footage of Moet's stage show, Moet in the dressing room with other dancers and Moet in her car. But there were at least nine other tapes to go through. None of them had dates or times or labels. So it was anybody's guess as to *when* they were shot. However enticing the subject matter, Wade focused for clues of dates. Maybe someone was wearing a watch or perhaps there might be a newspaper laying around. Whatever. Wade just knew that some serious investigative work was ahead of him. For certain, he had to find Debbie.

Video Voyeur

Wade lived a cluttered single life. Cluttered because of his many interests. First, he had an insatiable appetite for videos and books galore. There were his three dogs with accessories to complement their every whimper. And then there was his shitload of tools. Wade loved serving the public and solving crimes; however, to fill the void, instead of the sports or cars or the club hopping that other officers engaged in, he became a mister-fix-it at heart. Fixing and inventing things were the activities that consumed Wade's so-called leisure time; especially after Renee's death. This is where he devoted hours of patience and concentration until a particular problem was solved. But there was no future in trying to be Inspector Gadget. After all, that was just a cartoon. So the next best thing was creating push-button devices for his car and convenient gadgets for his fifth-floor apartment.

Wade cursed the elevator again as he finally reached the fourth case of stairs, wishing down deep that he'd kept up with Kiara's physical fitness show on ESPN. Dogs from various apartments always blew Wade's cover when he used the stairs. It was the same for the various buildings that he had to enter through the day, trekking up case after case of stairs . . . alerting dogs. It made him wonder if he carried a scent that called out to them, making them bark no matter what the hour.

Before he put his key in the door, Wade pressed his door bell 7 times, abruptly. Another clever invention of his, the 7th consecutive impression of the buzzer turned the peephole on the door into a visitor-friendly device. Now, the peephole made a 180-degree turn, giving a telescopic view of a mirror that was strategically positioned at the rear of the short hallway inside his apartment. Simultaneously, as the device on the door rotated, the house lights glared on, giving Wade a full, well-lit panoramic view of his apartment before even entering. Obviously, his dogs exploded with that routine, ruckus reaction. So the apartment was clear of threat and he could enter carefree.

Wade frequently asked himself what *all* the security was for. A covert peephole. Lights on. Dogs. *And* 3 guns?

Well, he reasoned, *someday you dogs won't be around anymore.* But Wade also knew, deep down in his heart, that one day all of his voids wouldn't be voids anymore.

Bells and Whistle were the names of Wade's 2 prized Japanese poodles. They were harmless; one black and one white. The 3rd dog was an English bulldog named Bones. Bones had an unusually long, sluggish figure. He moved like everything was a burden. More bark than bite—all three of them. And this was his so-called security.

After a brief walk, feeding, checking his answering machine, and his own relief at the toilet, Wade poured himself a tall glass of orange juice and sunk himself comfortably into his oversized, futon ottoman. To his side was a table and lamp. He swigged at the OJ, placed the glass on the table and switched on the lamp, instantly flooding 2 stacks of Moet's videotapes with more light. The poodles were now flat on the floor, pressed up against the door to the bedroom. Eventually Bones swaggered in; he posted himself in the middle of the room and observed Wade picking out one of the video cassettes. As if to be familiar with the sights and sounds about to play on the TV screen. Bones then made a semicircle, more or less chasing his tail before he spiraled to the floor, conveniently facing the television.

"*All-knowing bastard*," Wade huffed at Bones sarcastically before he fed a video into the VCR. His video system was set to go, with a cable running from the unit, down to the floor and under a Persian rug until it connected with a 35" television set across the room. On a handy remote control, Wade pressed the power button and awaited the next episode to be shown on the television.

Before he could see an image on his screen, there was music playing, accompanied by a few feminine giggles. This went on for a minute or so until Bones nonchalantly turned towards Wade behind him. With half opened eyes, the dog yawned and repositioned his head on the floor, his big nostrils contracting slightly after an expansive exhale.

Just then light appeared on the screen, as if a door had just opened to a tunnel. Wade was quick to realize that a camera's lens cap had been removed, as the TV screen came to life with light and color, unveiling the unfolding events in Moet's bedroom. The camera angle was unstable at first as someone tried to hold it steady, pointing it at a king-sized bed covered with pillows, a few teddy bears and a visibly soft comforter. Tossing about in the thicket of blankets were two women, with their brown curves and limbs in motion and harmony. They were holding, embracing, caressing and tongue kissing each other in a frenzy. A third female joined them after placing the video camera on a flat surface of some sort. The video was now steady and pitched perfectly to record the action.

Wade silently inhaled the imagery on his TV screen. Somehow, this was equivalent to closing his eyes, holding his nose, taking a deep breath and then jumping head-first into Moet's superfluous sex files. Bones was still as a statue, his head still flat on the floor, and his eyes still holding a glossy gaze. Wade adjusted his thinking, recalling the gruesome vision of Moet's dead body. He remembered the happy expressions she brandished in the various photos in her photo album. He couldn't immediately make out who the other two women were on the bed. One was somewhat familiar. She looked like she could've been one of the dancers at Fool's Paradise. A dark almond-toned woman with Caribbean features. The other woman had a caramel complexion. In his mind he assumed that perhaps this was Debbie. Considering Debbie's stage name was Caramel. Of the three, she was the light (yet tanned) adventurous girl in the video. Wade's intent on keeping business and pleasure separate was challenged by moans, laughter and cries on the screen. Bones raised his head after one of those passionate expressions. And he kept his head up in an interested manner. The dog's face couldn't change, however; still with that permanent frown weighed down by the layers of skin pulling at his jaw. Meanwhile, the poodles cared less about the TV and instead let their eyes volley from Bones to Wade and back.

Despite the attitudes of his dogs, Wade was becoming obviously excited. The three women entertained each other with what Wade imagined to be soft licks, tender caresses and light spanking. They inevitably built upon their involvement by creating that never-ending circle, connected only by their tongues inside of each other. They alternated positions. They alternated partners.

Click.

It was just as easy to turn off the excitement as it was to be absorbed in it. Thoughts of Renee were what moved him through his days and nights. She was the spirit now—the only spirit that made him smile and then cry, all within the space of a few moments. Wade knew deep down that she was the reason why he couldn't keep a love interest or a steady girl. Being single wasn't just convenient, it kept the spooks out.

Wade lowered his head and stared at the remote. Sure, shutting down the amateur porn was part of his personal issues, but it wasn't something that he couldn't get over. Apparently, it was the same for Bones, as he hopped up on the couch to comfort his master.

CHAPTER ELEVEN

There's No Place Like Home

Wade learned a lot about Moet in a short period of time. As if he was piecing together her biography. Moet was a dancer, yes, but that was second only to her being a nympho. She either loved sex, loved being with different partners, or at least she was practicing amateur video producing. More of her video library allowed for some new discoveries. Sometimes Moet would cry out her partner's name, other times there was role playing that provoked idle talk. Meanwhile, she was never at a loss for partners. Debbie (aka Caramel) and Valerie (aka Sadie) turned out to be those in Moet's famous threesome. One tape even recorded a *foursome*. It was Cinnamon and her two friends, Foxy and Mo. Cinnamon and company took turns satiating Moet as if they were lining up for a religious confession of some kind. Wade saw the event as a celebration for Moet, because from what was on video—a birthday present?—Moet was the only one being satisfied. Plus, everyone wore party hats and edible party outfits. There was lively music and a spread of party favors about the floor.

Besides the occasions with other women, Moet also had sessions with Ken, the gazillion-dollar baseball star, and Bobby, the fisherman from the South Street Seaport. Those tapes and escapades were helpful in providing Wade with images of the various associates in Moet's life, and yet they were also uneventful in the way of hard evidence. However, there *was* a controversial engagement with Douglass Jr., Mr. Gilmore's son. The video was short lived due to some vile name calling and a physical struggle which followed. The last image left on that video was of Moet throwing a potted plant at Douglass; then came a backhand across Moet's face sending her in the direction of the camera. The straw that broke the camel's back was when Moet got even more physical, shoving Douglass with all her might and shouting, "*Fuck you, daddy's boy!*" Then she swung a lamp that hit his wrist and the action was *on* from there. The video camera toppled over and fell to the floor. And there it was, Wade's first motivated lead; a disagreement which began with "*who would do who*," escalating into a battle of the naked egos.

The video and TV screen went black after the camera hit the floor, leaving Wade to assume this was the latest video tape. Maybe the camera broke. Maybe not. He'd have to figure that out. If the camera broke, then that was obviously the last videotape. Suspect. If not, and other videos were shot subsequent to the argument, then Douglass Jr. was off the hook. Maybe. It was also that tape which compelled Wade to revisit Moet's home for an intimate investigation. No forensic specialist. No flatfoots or rookie investigators. Wade needed to see things for himself.

At the Barnes Avenue home, Wade was already familiar with the layout. The block was a development of identical 2-family homes. They were all done in white, aluminum siding and had short driveways with short, manicured lawns. A model home at the head of the block was set up and furnished for new prospects to see. A sign hung outside, close to the sidewalk: NEW HOMES—INQUIRE WITHIN.

Every home was no older than 6 months, with new ones being built on adjacent blocks. The latest model automobiles occupied various driveways. Mercedes. BMW. Utility vehicles. No fences. No apparent need for security other than the private agency on regular patrol. The development was a diamond in the rough. A very suburban essence, smack dab in this overcrowded section of the Bronx.

Wade's discussion with the realtor was productive. Moet had lived in the house for no more than 4 months. Before that, she was on the waiting list for a year. To get on the waiting list, you were interviewed and scrutinized and then required to lay out a $15,000 deposit. The 2nd payment of $15,000 was due upon occupancy and a 1st mortgage of $1,500 a month was payable thereafter.

A sore thumb for the development, the sunny-yellow police tape was still stretched from border to border around Moet's home. As Wade parked out front he decided that if he didn't do it, the police line might stay up until trees grew around it. There was no more need for a police watch on the home—that ended during the first week of the investigation. Furthermore, there was tremendous aggravation still lingering. Moet's first floor tenants were paying her $1,100 a month rent for their 3-bedroom dwelling. And now that Moet was gone, not only were the renters burdened with various sessions of police questioning, but there was also the question of who to pay the rent to, not to mention, of course, that damned yellow police line. So much drama.

Wade made his way up the steps that led to the entrance of Moet's half of the house. The late Moet, that is. After balling up the stretch of police tape, Wade fit in the key he obtained from the property manager. He pulled open the front screen door, unlocked the second, and easily slipped in the entry. He climbed a long stairway that was plush with golden shag carpet. The daylight beamed down on the passage through the skylight above, illuminating his ascension to the top. Somehow, this climb was different for Wade, since having seen a number of videos and knowing Moet as he did, this dead person's home seemed a lot more familiar than it might otherwise. The detective humored himself, thinking about the guests that Moet had entertained (the various men and a bunch of dancers), and wondering why there wasn't semen seeping from the walls. Moet could have had a party every night, and if she did, it could've easily competed with the action at Fool's Paradise, just miles away.

Back to business, Wade passed through the kitchen, not really expecting much there. It was organized and appeared to be infrequently used. New pots hanging over the counter. All the accessories and cabinets were new and, except for a shelf of various dried spices and seasonings, the cupboards were bare. There was a freezer still packed with frozen dinners, some Cornish hens and many varieties of seafood, salmon, shrimps and crab legs were piled and stacked in every possible space. Wade thought briefly about Bobby the fisherman and how his premier video might impress his wife. Did *she* know that he liked to wear flowered panties around his neck and a pink ribbon in his hair while being spanked and straddled like a horse? Did she know that his favorite expression was "*meow?*" *Wow*, Wade thought of how easily he could get his own freezer filled with free fish for life. And while he was on the free-resource trip, he spotted that same set of cookie jars positioned on Moet's kitchen counter. They reminded him of his earlier visit and the day he found what appeared to be her savings.

There was at least one sleepless night when Wade dreamed of coming alone to the house after she was killed . . . he dreamed of finding the $120,000 that she had compacted in her cookie cans . . . he dreamed of keeping it, and of how his life would change ever so immediately. *Who would know?* After all, wasn't she dead? For now, Wade thought about karma and that perhaps the circumstances were meant to be as they were. So he wouldn't have to ask or think or wonder what to do with the money. It was kept from him as an issue that he did not have to address.

So why am I thinking about it now? Wade asked himself. And then, after making a mental note to see Bobby, Wade perished the thought. But not before he felt his feet soaking into the wall-to-wall carpet in the hallways, the living room and the bedroom. He flicked on the light in the bedroom, adding to the thin rays that already penetrated the partially closed blinds. Now Wade was feeling as if he'd come on to a movie set long after the crew had gone. He turned towards the closet and fingered through a healthy collection of costumes, negligees, bras and thongs, all neatly hung and coordinated by color, sequins, fluorescent, jet black leather and chiffon. It was all there—enough to corrupt a couple of high school cheerleading squads. Wade couldn't deny the thoughts; there were so many sexual fantasies that this closet contributed to. So much from just one woman. She must have been a walking, talking fantasy fulfilled.

The queen-sized bed was made of solid, black Formica, with drawers underneath and nightstands as wings. Wade pushed his hands down on the mattress as if he were an educated consumer, and the mattress gave in, absorbing his touch. There was a rolling reaction that only a water-filled tube would give. Wade sifted through the various drawers and then plopped himself down on the bed, evaluating the room. When he realized that he was actually laying on the stage—*the* stage—he immediately jumped up to his feet. He moved to the vanity, adjacent to the bed, assuming that this was where the camera often sat. Wade lifted his hands so that they were inches from his face, and connected his thumbs and forefingers to simulate a viewfinder. As if he was a director, checking for a point of view, Wade squatted down into a deep knee bend until he felt that he'd achieved his goal. Realizing the ideal position, Wade stilled himself, recalling hours of video footage. Switching his imagination on and off. On and off. And then again, he had to close his eyes a few times to make this happen. To make out what he was seeing now, nervous about what he'd seen on video. Either way, Wade was focused on the bed, its nightstands and a window in the distance. He inhaled the flowery scent in the air which escaped from the open closet and with investigative eyes, cut through the room's stillness.

"The answering machine!" Wade heard himself speak out loud, knowing that something was missing. It was in the videos, so why wasn't it in the room now? Wade searched the drawers again. Now on his knees, he moved a pair of velour slippers from the floor underneath the nightstand. Feeling around with his hand, he located the thin, electronic box. Wade figured Moet had hidden the machine just before one of her trysts. Why else would it be stashed away? And who did she need to keep secrets from anyhow? Wade's mind flipped through images of the major league player. Then Bobby. Lord knows who else, Wade concluded.

The machine was still blinking intervals of eight. *Eight messages.* Wade adjusted himself to sit on the floor against the bed, and pressed "PLAY".

"Bleep . . . Hey, Mo. I'm coming in on a seven-thirty flight on Tuesday. Maybe you can meet me at the airport. Beep me. Love ya." The male voice was masculine, sporty and abrupt. He was casual and spoke with a comfortable, presumptive tone. Wade figured the call was from Ken. And so far, Ken was the last on Wade's list of A-subjects to see. Usually airborn, and a jetsetter, Ken's interview was still pending. Wade knew he'd eventually catch him before or after a home game. Two messages which followed were propositions for private parties. The voices were unsure and insecure, and it seemed as though Ken and the other callers didn't realize that Moet was long buried in the ground. Then again, there were no dates on these messages. However, Wade's thoughts continued to reach; the calls could be the perfect cover-up for someone's alibi. As usual, Wade didn't let much pass.

"Beep . . . tell you what, you bitch. I'll teach you . . . you think you're miss hot shit, huh? Well, I got somethin' for you!" The line went dead. Wade replayed that message a few more times,

making sure to write down every word. Angry. Vengeful. Young. Male. Wade noted all that he could, not knowing whose voice it was—but presuming that it was related to the video he watched. There were 3 consecutive hangups without messages. One last message.

"Beep . . . Girl, I don't know what that shit was about but I was scared to death! I had to get out. What is going on? Why don't you answer? Where are you? I'm going back home—this shit is too wild for me. I can't take it. Call me at seven one eight, four five eight, eight—" The tape went dead without transmitting the remaining digits. The voice was hysterical . . . a female. *Go back where?* Had to get out? What was Moet into and who was the girl calling? Wade spun so many ideas in his mind and his heart beat just as fast. These were two critical calls that should have never gotten past the police who took inventory on Moet's house.

After a more thorough look through the room, Wade returned to the living room for a more critical evaluation. He sat on the butter-soft, white leather couch that was long like a stretch limousine. He sat back and observed the various authentic paintings, the entertainment center and the rack of CDs that were organized in a carriage that was curved like a vertical cobra. Just as Wade began to feel comfortable, he noticed that his grip in the armrest was unstable, like it was broken. When he looked closer he saw that the armrest was a variety of items. A few remote controls for Moet's rack of electronic devices. A paperback book and the infamous palm-corder. It was the type which accepted small cartridges. There was one still lodged inside. Wade uttered a sigh of relief, thinking that he'd moved a step closer to some solutions. He set it in his lap and switched on the power. The tape was used almost to its end, so Wade pressed REWIND hoping to watch the tape right there, through the eyepiece. There was a clicking sound that indicated the tape was stuck, rotating slightly back and forth. Wade pressed STOP. Then PLAY. No dice. He pressed RECORD. The tape moved and a red light went on. The camcorder was not working correctly, except for the recording command. In a rushed paranoia, Wade pressed STOP a number of times to be certain not to destroy the tape in the chamber and whatever was previously recorded on it. It did stop. And Wade was relieved, thinking of how to view the tape without the palm-corder. He pressed the EJECT button. The sound of a click and pop was followed but the side panel extending and freezing the tape inside. Wade was now at ease, carefully removing the tape. He dropped the tape in his jacket pocket and placed the palm-corder back in the armrest caddie. Viewing the tape would be easy enough. He found a cassette adapter in Moet's collection of commercial videotapes. And also pocketed that. Then he called it a day.

On the way back to the 45th precinct, Wade recalled the quarrel with Moet and Douglass Jr. Gilmore. He decided at that point to take a detour to New Rochelle.

Progress and Regress

The Gilmore empire was growing, indeed. After 18 months of rough edges and fine tuning, Fool's Paradise had become a staple in New York's adult entertainment industry. Advertisements were playing constantly on the city's most listened to black radio stations. The printed adaptations of the radio spots were running weekly on the big metropolitan newspapers, *The Daily Post* and the *New York News*. The club and its varied showcases seemed to be on the tip of everyone's tongue. From celebrities in film and music, to jocks in radio and sports, the personalities lined up to adopt and endorse Fool's Paradise as their weekly dose of entertainment. Even Ed and Dre, who (at the time) were hip hop's dynamic duo of television and radio, made the club a shining star by discussing their "in the club" experiences on their daily radio broadcasts, reaching in excess of 2 million listeners daily.

"Give me a sweatshirt I can wear on MTV, dude. I'll wear that shit proudly, for all to see," Dre told Douglass. Indeed, the subject of different voluptuous dancers made for interesting content on radio and TV. But all of those mentions accumulated to lift the club to sky high popularity. National magazines showcased the club in 2 and 3-page editorial spreads, while booking agents for the most famous porn stars called constantly to have their clients showcased exclusively. Accordingly, revenues and profits flowed in streams and then rivers, with no end in sight. Gilmore reinvested more and more, soon building an additional bar, additional offices, and he improved the sound system and special effects lighting. Many became aware of the influx of cash which Gil controlled, and idea-men frequently walked through the entrance looking to get their piece of the pie. There were contractors, handymen, graffiti artists, emcees, comedians, snack vendors, bubble gum machine vendors, soap dispenser vendors, payphone salesmen, and self-acclaimed specialists of every kind. Peddlers. Consultants. You name it and they came runnin'. Remarkably, the majority of these treasure-chasers *were* accommodated. Gil seemed to like doing business with the tiny, unsubstantial types who had never previously proven themselves.

"Let's give the guy a shot," he'd tell his son. "He talks a good game, so let's see if he can back it up. Doesn't hurt to try." Douglass had heard that story over and over again, wondering when the balloon would bust—all of these hucksters feeding off of the house that he helped to build. But he didn't need to wonder much, since it was happening right before their very eyes.

In the flurry of activity, most of it controlled by Gilmore himself, there was no way to see just how much the entire empire was being attacked. From the inside out, and from the outside in, Douglass realized some of the more obvious and indiscreet activity which happened mostly behind his dad's back. He sometimes had to maintain a stricter-than-most demeanor whenever he was in the presence of club staff, although the attitude wasn't a happy one. Douglass had to fight the show of emotions and be that only true Teflon that kept the establishment strong. And although Gil expressed recognition and pride in his son's experience and business savvy, sometimes turning to him for advice or support on certain business decisions, the bottom line was clear. Douglass had no control of the final decisions and little if any influence over the staff. Staff members became comfortable in their positions, testing their limits in various ways without any serious policies in place. Bartenders continuously over-poured drinks, making them stronger than required. Bouncers saw to it that certain people (like their friends and friends of friends) were admitted at no charge, avoiding the ten-dollar admission. Some bouncers were even brazen enough to accept a percentage of that admission themselves from those they didn't know. If a bouncer wasn't getting over in that way, then he was stealing cases of beer through the rear exit. Those who weren't outright thieves stole time instead, drinking alcoholic beverages on duty or smoking weed in the men's room, blatantly defying the "no-drugs" rule in the establishment. Hence, the bouncers projected nothing but a false sense of security. The club was better protected by the electronic alarm at closing time. If the negligence, corruption and incompetency of the club security wasn't enough, the bartenders were also stealing. Often pocketing money instead of ringing and recording the transaction on the cash register. Some even operated their own business, their own hustles on the side. To top that off, the dancers were becoming more aware of the various opportunities in the club, capitalizing on the freedom to carry on with *their* own cons. If not that, dancers were at least showing up for work late. They were appearing on stage late, if at all. They frequently left the club with men who made get-rich-quick offers for bachelor parties or sex. Sex with the customers. Sex with the bouncers. Sex with the boss. At a minimum, hundreds of dancers bounced through the entrance of Fool's Paradise; and of those employees, the boss was sexually involved with dozens of them. They'd come and they'd go like clockwork. Most times, the encounter took place right there in his office, behind closed doors and his busy, money-making nightclub. This all may have been satisfying for his ego and his loins; but for the future of this establishment, these activities led to nothing more than the poor, decaying moral of this million-dollar business.

Douglass grew ever arrogant with each passing day. His observations of the activities in the club, when brought to his father's attentions, were met with a casual attitude.

"If it ain't broke don't fix it," he'd say. Gil simply neglected the hard work that Douglass put into locating, developing and marking Fool's Paradise. Yes, Gil certainly established the original Gilmore's, its following and a decade-plus of continuity. But when the heat was on, when the locals in Mt. Vernon put pressure on the business—not forgetting the police raids or

the neighbors complaining—it was Douglass who suggested the move; it was Douglass who found a new location and suggested the new club name Fool's Paradise. And it was Douglass who brought that new energy that could keep up with the competition. Douglass virtually reinvented the flames of the legendary Gilmore's, and those flames blazed. Because of Douglass, that watering hole in the wall from Mt. Vernon turned into an institution that was welcomed by the big city, with its big city rules and big city potentials.

The Gilmore's staff was somewhat aware of Douglass's presence. But that virtual immunity prevailed in spite of him; that *anything-goes* attitude lived on in the establishment, with almost each and every employee out for themselves, could not affect his own protective shield. Douglass often maintained an attitude which checked or inhibited others from walking over him. He rarely fraternized with staff or dancers, since doing so might seem to condone their ongoing conspiracies. Instead—and this was entirely not healthy for the business, or his relationships with others—Douglass kept a skeptical eye on anyone whom his father had even remote trust in. In fact, these various challenges fueled Douglass's own artistic arrogance—the sort that inspired creativity, productivity and mystique. The kind that said loudly, "*Leave me alone and let me fly.*"

Short of the uncontrollable capital gains and the unexplainable fever that Fool's Paradise provoked as "*the leader in adult entertainment*," nothing was going according to Douglass's vision and intentions for a successful nightclub. Moreover, Gil kept his son at a distance from any proprietary interests or decisions having to do with the club. The frustrations continued on.

Porn Queens

Fool's Paradise was poetically licensed when it came to healing its own wounds with good times, euphoria and thrills. The second year in the Bronx saw tremendous growth despite the club's inner ills, mainly because of exclusive stage shows by some of the porn industry's most notable black stars. Angel, Jeanni, Nina, Ebony and Heather were all featured at Gilmore's and therefore also served to endorse the existence of the club, making Fool's Paradise their second home.

When it came to promoting Gilmore's, Douglass was the brand ambassador. In other words, he helped spread the word about the business. This escalated the stakes, and it helped to draw in bigger shows and names. He tried white porn stars and even Vegas showgirl types (complete with sequined pasties over their nipples). But the overall audience response wasn't pretty, and in some cases audience members nearly tossed their drinks at performers. That was the last mistake Douglass would make when showcasing performers. Even if the audience was a mix of cultures, they expected women of color here at Gilmore's. And not that color had anything to do with skin tone—just that there was a hunger for that down 'n dirty street savvy; that homegirl who knew how to shake her ass and bare all without shame. Ethnic girls with ethnic features—big butts, shapely breasts, wide, alluring and succulent lips. Even Latino and white girls with ethnic features worked well in the club. Those were the types that made Gilmore's shine. Those were the types that the customers wanted to get to know, to watch, and, if they were lucky, get to grind up against the wall with. To bring anything less than what the customers wanted was a learning experience for Douglass.

At the time, the newest, hottest performer in adult videos was Dominique. And Douglass had to have her. With no readily available directory of phone numbers for porn stars, he did some light research of video production companies until he was directed to a Hollywood studio that shot most of Dominique's films. She didn't have a manager or agent to speak for her, so, bemused at the idea of having skills in hunting for and finding hot sex stars, Douglass managed to reach her directly by phone.

"I never been to New York," she told him on the call. So instead of going through the usual routine that he'd grown accustomed to—agents, hotels and limousines—Douglass handled Dominique with kid gloves. For example, she didn't know what to charge for a stage show. So, naturally, he suggested a price *for* her. Not to mention, Domonique was so green in the business that she didn't even *have* a stage show to speak of!

"Don't worry yourself, baby. Take my word for it, any lil' wiggle and smile will work in my club. All the customers want is to see you up close, live and in living color."

Naturally, the phone calls led to their meeting at the La-Guardia Airport arrival terminal. And even if he didn't know what she looked like in her raunchy films, or even if he wasn't the one spearheading the promotion of her appearance, Douglass couldn't have missed Dominique standing in the baggage claim area of the terminal. She was larger than her movies projected her to be. Full of life, the porn star was not only taller, but more colorful in person. It could have been the heels on her yellow cowgirl boots, or the suntan that was common of westerners. But her presence seemed to call out to him, until moments later, for the first time in his life, Douglass was escorting a porno star!

Lanky, but stunning at first sight, with some obvious signs of breast enhancement (her breasts curved much too high and expanded too much at the sides), Dominique had an intoxicating, brilliant cocoa brown shine. Douglass could see that her hair was purchased, but he had to admit it looked good— natural and deliberately black and long, with the mane swooping down against her white leather outfit. The pants hugged whatever curves and calves she did have, and the vest was opened to permit an all-access view of her studded black brassiere, and the loop of gold that pierced her navel. Her loud appearance was completed by a yellow sombrero and those tassels that dangled along the sleeves of the vest.

Besides her packaging, Dominique was spunky and vibrant with enthusiastic eyes and a smile that seemed so willing to surrender. Then there was that pep to her walk and the adventurous attitude that had Douglass thinking that he'd commissioned a whore, since everything appeared so . . . *for sale.* But he easily dismissed it all as naive and dizzy.

Maintaining that trademark no-nonsense demeanor, Douglass chauffered Dominique to his home and designated her to a guest room. As though he was revealing a new pair of cufflinks for all to see, he then took his new guest out to eat, to some nightclubs, and even shopping. She was his ultimate marketing tool for all that men (shallow men, at least) loved in a woman. Big tits. Big, luscious lips, and big, alluring bedroom eyes.

At the time of Domonique's visit to New York, Douglass was still steady with Mechelle, his live-in girlfriend. And she didn't seem to have any problems with this other woman in his home. Besides, the idea of a porn star being so accessible in Douglass's house was at least novel to the two lovers. Mechelle did no less than turned on the charm. She also turned up her own sexual motors, somehow wanting to prove to Douglass that she was just as good, if not better, than Dominique was; or maybe, quiet as she kept it, she was insecure about her place in Douglass's life. But as hard as Mechelle tried, there was no need for persuasion. Douglass was a committed man and just not interested in fucking a porn star.

On the second morning during her two-week stay, Douglass made up a breakfast tray and carried it waiter-style directly to Domonique's room. Still getting over a slight jet lag and adjustment to the east, Dominique was sprawled across the bed totally nude, and the door to the hallway was partially opened.

"Whoa!" Douglass barely breathed the exclamation as he took one *real* good voyeur's look at her. His eyes bugged out to see how her breasts didn't relax naturally, how they took on box-like shapes. For a moment he stood there at the doorway watching her. He could even see the healed incisions at the outer edges of her nipples, where her enhancement operations were executed. The gross gashes on this woman's most precious jewels were suddenly aberrations to Douglass, confusing his foremost references of this woman's humping, shrieking, sucking and slurping. And to think that Douglass swore he knew this woman so personally. But standing so close to her naked body, no makeup, or crafty camera angles, and . . .

Where's all the hair!? A wig! Douglass quickly knew for sure that he really didn't know this woman at all. And what he *thought* he knew was but smoke and mirrors.

Knocking at the door, Douglass kept a respectable distance with the plate of soft scrambled eggs. That sweet morning aroma no doubt helped him to wake Dominique. Lazily, the woman didn't flinch or cover up; instead, she casually lifted herself, took the breakfast tray and began to eat and talk naturally, as if her body was nude like this 24 hours a day. During Dominique's breakfast she managed to put Douglass on the spot.

"Okay . . . don't hold it in."

"*What?*"

"You look like you got a whole lot of porn-star questions. I can see it in your eyes. So, don't hold it in. Ask away."

"Well, to be honest with you, no . . . I've never really thought about it," Douglass answered her reasonably.

"Your eyes are lying, Gilmore. You mind if I call you that?"

"They usually call my pop that, but—I guess it's okay."

"Well, Mister Gilmore, about your views, I can already understand *your* point of view," she said. "I'm sure you have a bunch of *whys* and *whats* and *hows* in your chest; all those questions dying to get out. Come on . . . I get this kinda stuff all the time. Plus, I'm curious about how you see me."

"How about if *you* start, Dominique. You tell me about how *you* feel as a porn star." Douglass was careful. He could hear that she wanted to have a big discussion about this, and he leaned against the doorjamb to lend her that ear she wanted. He folded his arms like a shrink looking on.

"I didn't actually grow up *wanting* to be a porn star. I like, wanted to be an actress and all. But I never thought I'd be acting . . . like *this*."

"Do you like *what* you do?"

"Well, I *really* like sex," she explained like a true fiend. "So there's very little acting that I have to do. But before I do a shoot, I've like, gotta get loaded first."

"*Loaded?*"

"You know. Like, I have to have, like, a six pack of Heiny or something. My first gig was like that. I was seeing this video producer back then. I was drinking, and one thing led to another. Next thing I know, I'm doin' it all the time . . . with *everyone*," she said, giggling.

Douglass stood dumbfounded, sneaking an eyeful of her each time she went to scoop food into her mouth, examining every area of her body as he listened to her go on about her 3 breast augmentations and her aspirations of crossing over into the *real* film market as a legit actress. *Tough chance*, Douglass told himself.

That encounter with Dominique wasn't the first or the last time Douglass would be exposed to porn stars. In fact, these interactions came more frequently with each passing month. His favorite starlet was Heather. Except, where Dominique didn't excite Douglass in the least, Heather did just the opposite. It was Heather's movies that jaded Douglass as a teenager. Watching her films taught him what to expect from a woman and also how to reciprocate a woman's attentions. Even as recent as a year before the club moved to the Bronx, Douglass was talking about Heather's talent (especially her giving blow jobs) with college students who actively traded her tapes. Heather was that fine, fair-skinned cutie who indirectly lured him to want to see more and more porn flicks, until he eventually OD'd on the practice. And by the time the club opened, by the time those endless loops of X-rated films played constantly on the club's giant screens, Douglass had seen it all. And still, Heather was that fantasy vixen who left very little to the imagination in her performing oral sex on selected male and female partners. With her sound effects and extremely passionate facial expressions, there was no doubt that she was not acting, and that she was enjoying it. On screen, Heather had perfect round shapes and curves, with no evidence of breast implants. She had those naturally large and erect breasts, and didn't seem to need any excessive accessories such as wigs, or piled-on makeup. She also had those full, luscious lips, and captivating doe eyes. All of that packaged on such a flawless, petite frame was attractive to Douglass. Bigger than that, Heather was always so adventurous in her movies, with all of the form and flexibility that a gymnastics champ would envy. She was simply that wholesome, girl-next-door type that could never disappoint you, with an innocent, youthful appeal; and yet, underneath that good-girl mask, this was the raunchiest, nastiest sexual being on the planet—at least in this young man's eyes. And nobody did it better in the fuck flicks as far as Douglass's eyes could see.

Demetrious

After 2 years of weekly talent showcases, Douglass became less interested in the production of his Westchester Talent Competition. Often feeling burdened by the monotony of the same ole performers, singing the same ole songs and following the same ole routines of expression. *The Wind Beneath My Wings, The Greatest Love Of All*, and, of course, all of Mariah Carey's songs. Week in and week out Douglass would have to go home and cope with those tunes conflicting with his sound sleep. Besides that, the amateur-talent end of his enterprise was outdone by his growth and consistency in the more interesting field of television and the maintenance and marketing of the family business, Fool's Paradise. Inevitably, time constraints and the overall stress was taxing. So Douglass consolidated his interests. Most of his cash flow was now coming from the club, and that enabled him to comfortably finance his ongoing television show.

Even the TV show experienced its growing pains, shedding its skin and excluding amateur talent altogether. Abandoning that format, along with all of its mixed nuts of aspiring entertainers was a huge relief, and it simply left more airtime for a more focused effort; a platform for more popular entertainers and icons who were cumulatively and essentially creating a steady stream of substance and power in music, television and film. Now, the show could *really* live up to its claim:

"THE MOST ENTERTAINING 60 MINUTES ON TELE-VISION."

Anyone who assisted behind the scenes in the live productions now contributed and took on the responsibility of learning the necessary tasks of television production. Those who were once stage managers, ticket takers and organizers now trained to become cameramen, assistant directors and on-air personalities. The SuperStar team kept an "open door policy," all the while allowing individuals with their own energies and input to join in on the good time.

Demetrius was just one of those who fit well within those channels. D (Demetrius's nickname) more or less became involved and joined the team as a natural component of the operations. He was once a model in a fashion show at the Palace—the same venue at which Douglass staged his talent shows. However, a chemistry ensued between Douglass and Demetrius, even if they were virtual opposites. While Douglass had his foot firmly planted in the booty business, and this business was somewhat spearheading and subsidizing his direction in life, D was a born-again Christian. He frequently read the Bible and did all that he could to practice what he preached. Besides preaching (only amongst his friends), D studied nine forms of martial arts and a single form of abstinence. Douglass admired his friend for his discipline, faith and enthusiasm for his beliefs and practices. D had that absolute power of a man who, despite all, was determined to follow and believe. It was a ritual that Douglass could barely imagine, much less follow. He was too busy having fun; too much a product of his environment. Sex and cash.

Within no time, Douglass had incorporated D in his life and his home. D not only became a best friend, but in a way, Douglass saw him as his own personal ninja. The camaraderie also served to fill the void that Douglass was feeling—how he was missing that genuine security in his life. The police couldn't provide that; he wasn't into guard dogs; and he didn't own a firearm. D, in so many ways, *was* that firearm.

When D moved in, it also created a buffer for him to catch up to his own lingering after-college financial loan responsibilities.

"They just keep calling," he told Douglass when they discussed the possibility of D moving in. "They don't even give you breathing room after college! They expect me to immediately get the job of my dreams and to cash in and pay that loan off."

"So, your solution was to max-out a credit card?"

"It wasn't like that. I was paying off the loan with the card while I was still looking for a job. Plus, I was still pursuing my modeling career, and—"

"Damn, D. It looks like you got swallowed into a black hole."

"More than you know. See, while I was working that one card I was being sent approved cards from other—"

"Oh no . . ."

"Oh, YES! They sent me seven other cards. Soon, I started to just live off of the cards. Taking from Peter to pay Paul and whatnot . . ."

"Lord have mercy," said Douglass.

"He is having mercy, now that I ran into you. You're my safety net right now!" And so, D found refuge after a year of surviving on credit cards, and the creditors who had been chasing him. Douglass quickly situated D with a position at the club where he could make some unreported income. And, as it turned out, D was probably the best and most valuable member of the staff. D wasn't hired in time to witness that corrections officer who stormed into the club that night, waving that gun like a madman. If he had, he would have likely snatched the weapon and delivered a forearm to the guy's chest in the same move. Nonetheless, even D's mere presence was acknowledged and respected by all.

It was during one of Heather's engagements at Fool's Paradise that this most unexpected relationship began. *The Porn Star & The Preacher-Ninja* might be an awfully long movie title, but it would be an appropriate one to describe this most unique occasion—how in this busy Fool's Paradise (with a mob of porn fans begging for Heather's eyes to find them, all of them in one way or another testifying their appreciation of her presence on stage before them), Heather almost lost her balance when she caught an eyeful of Demetrius for the first time. D didn't notice her interest in him since he was on the job and so much a disciplined soldier of the Lord—uninterested in lusting after the flesh like the majority of patrons and staff in the club. He didn't bother like most others to pay Heather the attention that her performance demanded. Even Heather wouldn't know that D was simply performing his nightly ritual of focus that the job required. Heather also wouldn't know that D routinely shunned propositions from the club's top-shelf dancers. But for certain she was about to become another victim, already magnetized and set afire by D's looks. Demetrius had that perfectly chiseled body of a stone sculpture. Not too big nor too small, he was something of a darker shaded Tarzan or Fabio. If not for his unconventional looks—the ponytail; that rough and aggressively wide step; and, of course, his unbreakable defensive demeanor—women could easily mistake D for one of the world's most popular soap opera stars. And that's pretty close to the way women treated, reacted to, and approached Demetrius; as if he was a movie star. Countless phone calls and jealous pursuits of fatal attraction were just some of the baggage D had to cope with. And if he wasn't at home to receive a phone call, it wasn't uncommon for Douglass to get cursed out for not uttering the answer the caller wanted: *Yes, of course he's here. I'll get him!*

But when Douglass gave them the truth, when he'd tell them "*D's not in,*" that's when they'd let it rip: "*Yes, he is there!*" "*I know Demetrius is there. I know it!*" And just maybe they *did* know on a few occasions, since there was at least one occasion when one of his stalkers was caught peeping into one of the windows of the Gilmore home.

"How do you deal with this?" Douglass asked D after he caught the peeping Jane.

"What can I do? I'm humble about it. Never arrogant. And all I do is try and steer them towards the Lord. Watch and see; some of these women need Jesus. And they don't know it, but I'm gonna lead them to their salvation soon."

"*Wow,*" Douglass said breathlessly, almost hypnotized himself by D's faith and commitment. He'd already witnessed firsthand how, during shifts at the club, Demetrius had dancers in moments of prayer, sharing with them a dose of *The Good Word*, even with the contradictions; the porn images flashing on the giant screens and the dancers flashing their flesh up on the stages. Douglass figured the dancers to be phony about their interests, figuring they merely wanted to get up close and personal with the preacher himself. So, Heather the porn star had no idea of the load she was after. The conventional "*boy meets girl*" scenario wouldn't apply here, no matter how many thousands of men lusted after her. If she wanted Demetrius for anything more than a moment of prayer, she would most certainly have to be the aggressor. And, bigger than that, the woman was even shy about approaching D herself. Instead (executing the irony), she approached Douglass to be introduced. Of all people, she was asking a carnivore (Douglass) to deliver her (the big fat juicy T-bone steak) to Demetrius (the vegetarian). But despite all that, Douglass assisted. Ultimately,

Demetrius and Heather became close. She even became a regular at the Gilmore home. Douglass joined D on visits to Heather's NYC apartment as well. Entertained by this drama— *a porn star after his best friend!*—Douglass kept his fantasies hidden, deep down and out of sight like a smothered flame. Now that Douglass's main man was involved to whatever degree, according to his own ethics, Heather was off limits. He couldn't even think of her in the ways that he once did.

"**What?!** You're telling *me* that you had Heather . . . *the* Heather, in bed . . . *naked*? Right there next to you? *And you didn't hit it?* Say it ain't so!" Douglass's whole body was choked up with exclamations, encouraged but twisted by the thought of one of the world's most admired and desired video vixens, in his house . . . making herself available, but subjected to the frustrations of being embraced by a . . . *preacher?!*

Douglass could only silently sympathize with Heather.

I feel your pain, girl!

"Douglass . . . I'm not lying to you. I'm just not into sex without marriage. It's unholy."

"D . . . you've seen her videos. You *had* to! They play all damned day at the club!"

"I hardly pay attention to those freakin' videos . . ."

"But Deee! Do you know that an army of men would *love* to be in your shoes? Including me??? Man, D . . . Heather being here is like *history* being made. It would suit me just fine if I was the indirect reason that she was here, one of the biggest porn stars in the business, and at least *something* went down. That's like the President of the United States making a visit to a local McDonald's, and all he buys is a plain ole milkshake. Man . . . He betta be buyin' double this and double that, extra large this and extra large *that*! The Secret Service betta be doin' their thing, too! Otherwise, *what's the point?* D, you got the one and only Heather on your case! She's like one big Happy Meal—a Big Mac, a Super-Quarter Pounder, extra large fries, and the thickest strawberry milkshake you've ever tasted! If she's over my house, I wanna know at least that *someone* was up in that ass! I wanna know that clothing and sheets got wet! Because, man, the damn walls and furniture are watching! For *real*." Douglass had to settle himself before he caught a conniption.

"I'm tellin' you the truth, Douglass." Demetrius was sincere, almost to the point of Douglass's visible stomach cramps. But in Douglass's perception, Demetrius was truthful, maintaining an expression that only close friends might share. And so it was legend; the river of phone calls, the outings and even the invite to one of her film shoots never resulted in that so-called inevitable outcome. And if ever there was a doubt, being neglected of something you really desire does nothing but draw you closer, making you want for more.

Vanessa Fever

If Heather represented the freshest new talent in the porn industry, then Vanessa represented the most *experienced* talent in the porn industry. And considering her status, it was a must (if Douglass had anything to do with it) for Vanessa to grace the stage of Fool's Paradise. Vanessa was to the adult film industry what Mohammed Ali was to boxing. Considered the best who ever did it, this woman held the top belt, the reigning title and the standing ovations in the porn industry, and Douglass was determined to first, locate her, and second, to promote the *hell* out of the event until her name rolled off of more tongues than all the dentists in New York would care to smell.

Once Douglass found her—*was there any doubt?*—and once he persuaded her to come out of her semi-retirement, they reached a verbal agreement for a one-time-only engagement at Fool's Paradise. Upon agreeing, Douglass immediately went ballistic with the street promotion. Not knowing the actual depth or extent of Vanessa's appeal, or how she crossed traditional boundaries of race and nationality, may have helped Douglass. But it didn't matter, since he pushed this event as if it was his last shining moment on earth; as if the Pope was about to play craps with Mother Theresa; as if the Statue of Liberty was about to strip naked. This was by far Douglass's biggest event.

With Vanessa's assistance, Douglass met with one of her former photographers. He had a case of more than 10,000 of Vanessa's 8x10 photos. And they weren't your average photos;

edgy, but tasteful enough for general audiences. She was lying on the floor with her head up and eyes straight at you; she was wearing a black, see-through negligee. However, because of her position, her body's shapes and curves faded into a distant silhouette. The intimate photos then went through one night of "autographing;" only it wasn't Vanessa but Douglass who scribbled a personalized invitation with gold and silver metallic markers. Douglass marked down the critical details on each photo until his hand went numb:

"AN EVENING WITH VANESSA . . ."

The message was bold. It stated the place, time, date and there was a phone number for more information. Douglass handed these photos to every delivery driver he could catch. At red lights he would hop out of his car and pass two photos each to UPS drivers. (Of course, the additional photo was for a friend.) And that was the whole point, to get people talking about the big event. At the gas station, he'd pull beside FedEx drivers and reach out with photos in hand as they gassed their trucks; he did the same with garbage haulers, bus drivers, tractor-trailer operators, firemen, policemen, auto mechanics, factory workers and postal workers. Douglass visited army bases and reserve installations. There were visits to radio stations and free tickets given to various male radio personalities. Photos and complimentary tickets were also given to select professionals in the music and porn industries.

Beyond the person-to-person promotions, there was a shitload of mass marketing. Douglass printed Vanessa's image to larger posters and tacked them to telephone poles from city to city. Very soon after the posters went up, admirers took them down to keep for themselves. So posting on the very same telephone poles became a daily routine, with hot spots and high traffic areas the major focus. Never slowing, Douglass also placed ads in the big city newspapers and he produced a television commercial for cable TV. If Vanessa was even *thinking* retirement, you couldn't tell.

* * *

On the big night hundreds and hundreds of men converged on Boston Post Road. Anticipation hung in the air like thick smog from well before noon until the moment the club opened. Business flourished throughout the day, including the sales of last minute tickets, and there was an after work crowd that beat all previous capacity records. And Douglass was prepared for today, where even weeks ahead he had appropriated some of those long, blue police barricades on the morning after the St. Patrick's Day Parade. Thinking optimistically as always, he obviously had his own anticipations about the event. But the results superseded his wildest dreams. When evening fell, the line of men waiting to enter Fool's Paradise was four bodies wide and two city-blocks deep. To be on the second block, looking forward over the sea of heads, was discouraging at best. From the look of things, it became evident that one show wouldn't be enough. It wasn't clear if Vanessa had plans to follow the event, but Douglass and his dad just held their breath. It wouldn't hurt to ask.

As planned, Vanessa was chauffeured to the club in a candy apple red 1969 Rolls-Royce. The driver performed his duties, opening the passenger door for the legendary film star. She emerged in fur and sequins with breasts pushed up to the sky. A thunderous applause ignited the atmosphere, while wonderment, excitement, and heat all joined together like some magical tidal wave of joy and anxiety. Vanessa glowed bashfully and waved as if she was entering the theater for her biggest film premier. A red carpet zipped down the sidewalk, the roll conveniently ending at her feet. She stepped across the surface with an escort on either side of her, and she strolled up into the club's entrance, disappearing behind the closed doors of Gil's office. Quickly, a deal was struck for two more shows for a total of $1,800. It was only when the money changed hands that the problems began.

First, Vanessa bickered about the stage lighting being too bright, apparently inhibited about her aging and how the audience would respond. Next, she had her own cassette tape of music that was more nostalgia than relevant and current. Lastly, she had issues with who would be preceding her on stage. While the discussion worked itself out behind closed doors, the club was filled to capacity. The boom bap of the music, the various top-shelf dancers, and the intensity in the venue was all choked up in the same space. Dancers added to the euphoria with their best moves, colorful outfits, and the best money making attitudes they could wear. Meanwhile, this was the greatest high imaginable for Douglass, who was watching all of this shape up into the most successful promotion he'd ever managed.

The wait to see Vanessa up close was a thrill for all. Finally, any man in attendance who ever got his rocks off watching the Latin sex goddess with 5 stiff, naked men hunched and gasping over her open mouth . . . or with chains stretching her naked limbs in a dungeon setting, with a black leather masked man torturing her with whips and feathers . . . or with black, white and Latino men filling her every orifice. Finally, the mob inside of Fool's Paradise would realize the legend in person. Vanessa, *live*.

For the die-hard fans who managed to get in and out of the club for all three shows, Vanessa delivered. It didn't matter that she got up there and showed very little; it didn't matter that she was over 40 years of age and hadn't done a new film in years. She graced that stage with her own mysterious power. And they were more than satisfied. Even in her airborn kisses one could see that she didn't need to contend with the younger chicks that preceded or followed her shows; in no way were they competing against her track record of enticing and exciting generations of men. If Vanessa was not a legend in the true sense of the word, then she was at least the trailblazer who was responsible for millions of dollars in revenue, and for the many, many ethnic porn stars who followed in her footsteps. And if nothing else, she was at least a chapter in the history of the sexual revolution; and the history of Gilmore's.

While the crowds waited outside on the sidewalk for the 11PM and 2AM shows, fire engines roared and car audio systems pumped street beats, provoking a pre-party before the big one indoors. After each show Vanessa took numerous Polaroids with customers. She signed autographs, listened to fantasies and issued sweet kisses. It was history at Fool's Paradise. On one hand, she affirmed her superstar status; and on the other, Gilmore's received the ultimate endorsement from the ultimate legend. Now and forever, Gilmore's Fool's Paradise was sho' nuff the leader in adult entertainment.

Detective Wade was also present on that big night, somehow knowing that he was getting closer, and that his culprit might also be present. He recorded all that he saw, more mentally than on paper.

And still, the Gilmore empire was under attack from yet another angle. Envy, jealousy and even revenge waited in the wings; all of those cats preying . . . watching, and looking forward to cutting into the success.

Tony—aka "Angelo"—was the wise guy within the Bianco crime family; or at least he *wished* he was. He was a low-level "earner" looking to become a "made member" by his efforts with Fool's Paradise, hoping to bring home a big chunk of cake without too much strong-arming. His plan was first to get the vending machines in the establishment. And, so far, so good. There were already 5 machines in the club, all of them grossing more than a thousand or so dollars a week. The next step was to extend a small business loan. Chances were, according to his experience, that the business would eventually be late with a payment, at which time the interest would skyrocket. Tony was absolutely *counting* on that. It never failed, one business after another, there'd be that one late payment that would turn the seemingly fair business loan into one that the borrower could never pay off.

For Tony, however, all of those expectations went down the drain when Vanessa came to Gilmore's. The success was incredible, and it didn't start or stop with that one show. Men continued to pour into the club every night before and after the big show. New dancers were showing up, uninvited, and all of it was making Tony sick to his stomach. The money that the machines were making was mere pennies when compared to the bar and the door admission. The $100-a-day cash flow from the hoopshoot was but a fallen leaf from the virtual money tree that the Gilmores operated. There was no way that Gil needed a loan with all the money passing through his hands. On one particular Friday, Tony personally witnessed over $18,000 dollars in transactions at the bar. He sat there and nearly drank himself into oblivion, and the amount of pretzels he ate to soak it all up could've filled two family-sized bags. The sudden success and popularity behind a project that he was so close to would now only make his bosses mad at him for not capitalizing on such a windfall. He'd been sent to establish an "in" with the proprietor, and to keep tabs on the growth of the business for an inevitable shakedown. Instead, Tony was coming up with nothing. He was sitting on a goldmine, but with no real grip on a piece of the action. That had to change. And the thought of what he'd do to get it to change made him shiver. No matter what, Tony would make this work to his benefit and his capo would be proud.

Following the *"Night With Vanessa,"* Douglass celebrated, counting money for hours. There were over a thousand admissions paid on that evening. They paid $25.00 a ticket in advance and $30 at the door. The event made oodles of money. The bar made 3 times what the door receipts brought in. Douglass further celebrated his glory in day-long, uninhibited sex with Mechelle. He bought a decent car. And he made various investments in the TV show. Furthermore, it was vacation time. Off to California to visit Mom. Alone.

CHAPTER TWELVE

California Bound

There were two other times when Douglass visited the west coast. He was much younger—only 8—and on both occasions he and his younger sisters Laurie and Julie tagged along with Mrs. Gilmore. His grandparents had settled in San Diego County for a number of years, having retired from the fast life of New York and their successful careers as doctors. In the hills of California, the elders lived well, in a one level villa that had an in-ground pool, and a terrace with a view that overlooked a valley of beautifully landscaped gardens.

The children's stay was enjoyable and pleasant for the first trip. Douglass had experienced the San Diego Zoo, Disneyland, and a series of museums. Although he may not have been old enough to appreciate these spectacles, he did forever remember seeing bunny rabbits, lizards and grasshoppers all roaming freely along sidewalks, yards and parks. Cactuses, and the widest variety of plants and flowers that he'd ever seen, were a wonder to a boy whose heart grew to appreciate the inner city. Still, it was a cinch to adjust to peaceful, spacious San Diego, California. Douglass got to sit atop authentic cannons, he collected and identified rocks, and he even experimented with electricity during his short vacation. Suddenly, his young life was full of new possibilities such as science, botany and chemistry.

He whimsically saw himself as a young, mad scientist with a fever to learn and venture. Even if his wild journey was short-lived, at least he got to experience another side of life. His grandparents recognized his potential as well; their first grandchild showing them just how worthy he was to receive that college tuition that they'd earmarked for him.

The second visit to Grandma's house wasn't as pleasant. In fact, it was somewhat hostile. Douglass was about 13 at the time. And because of some infidelity (which led to an inevitable separation and divorce between his Mom and Dad), Mrs. Gilmore took Douglass and his sisters on a long, drawn out bus trip to the west coast.

His father had just gone through a long down-sizing during the early years of the Gilmore Empire, consolidating some of the stores he operated so that he could focus on just one. For one man to stretch himself so thin, attempting to maintain control over a chain of five delicatessens, a laundromat and a liquor store was the equivalent of juggling seven sizeable watermelons day after day. Added to that responsibility was a family, and the burdens only got heavier. Furthermore, the signs of the times called for creative, and even drastic measures. A bulletproof glass foyer had to be constructed for the liquor store and deli that Gil operated, just so that he could operate late into the night. This was a new expenditure (necessary to prevent robberies), which forced the entrepreneur to consolidate his chain of delicatessens into the one large property on the south side of Mt. Vernon. Moreover, the Gilmore family was forced to move as well. Gil sold his four bedroom, two story home in order to subsidize the new foyers. A corner property on a major artery in town, the Gilmore enterprise now consisted of a grocery store, liquor store and a bar. Above the stores there were three apartments, the smallest of which his family occupied. From a private house with a front and back yard, the Gilmores were imported into a two bedroom apartment where the entrance opened into the master bedroom. When the front door to the apartment opened, it barely brushed the king sized bed.

With the apartment also came the mice and the roaches, the odors and noise pollution; the next apartment, the next door neighbors, and even the street was close enough so that everybody knew everybody else's business. Sometimes the hot water worked, and sometimes it didn't. There were leaks in the ceilings, cracks in the walls, and always . . . *always* things scrambling behind those cheap, plaster walls. True, this wasn't necessarily the worst that the ghetto could get; but it still wasn't pretty.

In time, the grocery store, liquor store and eventually the bar were joined by various secret passageways and doors. If the bar needed beer or liquor, it could be obtained in minutes. If the store needed change, someone could hustle up from the bar. There was never a need that couldn't be satisfied thanks to Gil's keen business mind, and how he linked all three of his businesses under one roof so that they fed one another. Every possible resource was available in this world within a world. *Every* resource.

Now that Gil had his family under that same roof, feeding, seeing, and communicating with his family was a lot more convenient. To get to and from work enabled Gil to manage life's ultimate freedoms. But because most of his time was devoted to business, the grocery store by day and the bar at night, he neglected his son and daughters; attention that was required for a growing boy. The result was the cold, harsh realities of the streets. At any given hour, Douglass or his sisters could sneak away from home. Although Mrs. Gilmore did her best to keep her children tied into various community activities, Douglass still became quite mischievous, whether it was his climbing fire escapes, exploring rooftops of buildings, or gambling with the boys in the hood. He even treasure hunted, scavenging through *his* family's possessions stored in the basement below the businesses. Such access exposed Douglass and his sister Laurie to a raw awakening.

Everyone in the neighborhood must have known that there was something "special" about that hole in the wall known as Gilmore's. After all, what man, if any, could keep from bragging about his sexual episodes with his favorite topless dancer in the infamous back room of Gilmore's? Douglass was too young to be aware, and was mostly oblivious of the adult activities that his father facilitated. However, the boy was mischievous enough to make his own harsh discovery. The teenager couldn't believe his eyes the first time he climbed the steps in the basement—the ones *waaay* back past the water heaters and furnace. But it was his second tour that dragged his younger, impressionable sister with him. The steps that Douglass revisited led to another secret passageway to the bar. Only at this time of the night, that passage was so much more. Taking turns pressing their eyes up against a crack in the doorjamb, the two could see the events on the other side of the door. There was candlelight. There were dark silhouettes. There were shadows moving, grinding and rolling on a blanket spread about the wood floor.

Douglass already knew this passageway from daytime deliveries in one way or another, and it never occurred to him that the dirty floor was soiled with varying degrees of musk, perfumes, baby oil and semen. But now it all made more sense as the activities produced some seedy fragrances that seeped from the room, fighting with the basement's mildew, the fumes from the furnace and, of course, Butch's bowels piled here and there. Douglass would often be responsible for walking and cleaning up after Butch, which lent him greater access to the basement. And yet, that was all the access he needed for this new revelation.

Despite the discouraging stench around them, the youngsters continued to peek. There was moaning and giggling and slurping and sucking and gurgling from a couple who sensually attacked each other. Both individuals had their heads buried between each other's legs while the candles flickered, casting shadows on the walls nearby. The two were positioned in such a way that the children couldn't see faces. But at just the right moment the truth hit them hard.

Daddy is cheating on Mommy!

The rest of the lust and sleaze was not as shocking as seeing Dad *doin'* it with another woman. It was a *monster* shock that had both kids stumbling over one another as they shot out of the basement undetected—or so they thought.

The experience in the basement turned the Gilmore world upside down. Douglass and Laurie shared their story with Mom. Mom was satisfied enough with her children's testimonies to immediately book those 4 bus tickets to San Diego. The children joined their mom excitedly, as though this was one big adventure—never mind that the family was in shambles—and they zealously packed all of their belongings in the family station wagon one early morning. As for the heavy furniture, Mother and children secretly cleared out the apartment until there was an echo. The four looked as if they were on a shopping spree, except the items were their own. Labels, stickers and packaging slips were tied and applied to every item or possession. The TV set, their bicycles. Suitcases. Everything. Mrs. Gilmore even gave her car to a close friend before making the cross-country crusade. From then on it was one bus station after another. For Douglass, it was one Pac-Man arcade game after another. A cooler full of fruits and veggies that Mrs. Gilmore packaged in little Ziploc bags kept the travelers fed, while Douglass was sedated with a cassette player and Stevie Wonder's "Hotter Than July" album. That, and an Elton John album were the two tapes that kept his headphones on his head for the whole trip.

Ten days later, after a long, funky journey, Mrs. Gilmore and her three children were on the front steps of Grandma's house.

More than 15 years later, Douglass found himself reminiscing about that last trip and how, after all that journeying, they ended up back in the same apartment just a month later. But this trip was different. Douglass was an adult now, almost 28. With some accomplishments under his belt. He simply wanted to relax. To escape the rat race, and to see his mother after so many years of distance.

New Rules

Wade closed the door behind him, suddenly facing Chief Washington, his boss, and two other men in suits and ties.

"Yes, Chief—you wanted to see me?" Wade was casual and unknowing.

"Detective Wade, meet Special Agent Walsh and Special Agent Olgen—?" Washington huffed under his breath, attempting to pronounce his name.

"Olgenhiemer. But just call me Hammer, sir." The suit was proud enough to ordain himself.

"Sure . . ." Chief Washington lifted his brows and grinned sarcastically. ". . . Olgenhiemer. These guys are here to pick up the Fool's Paradise case. Special orders from the high-ups. The organized crime task force in Jersey." Washington expressed discouragement and concern in his tone, while Wade shifted his eyes to avoid those of his boss. Chief Washington reminded Wade of The Rock, the wrestler-turned-actor. He was always so serious and down-to-earth. Then, Wade turned to Walsh, a puny man, for sure. Dark hair. Chiseled features. Cheeks, chin, nose and lips. He looked as if he had had a shave and a haircut only an hour earlier.

"Chief, if you will allow me . . ."

Walsh interrupted. ". . . Yes, Detective Wade. We have reason to believe that there is organized activity behind the Fool's Paradise murder. We've been following a drug case and an extortion scheme. These investigations somehow led us to Fool's Paradise. Now there's a murder . . . you can understand our interest. There's likely a link here."

Wade heard the man, but he wasn't really listening. Anger was bubbling inside of him. All he could picture was his hard work and time; all of it about to be kicked to the side because of two secret agent men. Puny man and boy Hammer.

"We'll need to see your notes and files on the case," said Hammer, immediately reading Wade's expression. Wade tried not to show any reaction, except to turn his head slightly towards humble Chief Washington, his eyes slowly trailing behind the motion. The chief said *My hands are tied,* if only with his shoulder shrug, and *"I'm sorry,"* if only with his defeated eyes. The chief's expression couldn't lie even if he tried.

Without an argument, Detective Wade led the two suits through the bright squad room and into the rear foyer. They made a left and then a right, until they came to the dim, haunting strategy room just ahead. The room was defined by 4 desks, a series of bulletin boards, a well worn black tile floor and some hazy windows that allowed little visibility. There was a table in a corner with a coffeemaker. A glass pot on the heating plate was tarnished and empty. Wade's desk was to one side, in front of another.

"I hear you handle a lot of the homicides," said Walsh.

"I guess," said Wade. And then, to change the subject so that he wouldn't start swinging on these federal agents, Wade went on to say, "Detective Block handles gang activity at this desk. And over here, Detective Warren handles—"

One of the agents tried to cut in, but Wade kept on speaking; rambling, really.

"—special projects like serial killers, politically related issues and others that receive heavy press and publicity. And *this* desk . . . you know who *this* desk belongs to? This desk belongs to Detective Baxter. And the reason Baxter's desk isn't as busy as the others is because it's a sort of shrine . . . see, he was struck down during a recent drug deal gone bad. Used to be my partner. And you know what my partner would think of you coming in here and taking this murder case out of MY HANDS?"

—Wade was turning a little red as the volume of his voice raised a few notches—

"HE'D THINK THAT WHAT YOU'RE DOING SUCKS ASS! THAT'S RIGHT, I SAID IT! IT SUCKS—ASS!"

The men all stood still for a time, before one of Wade's colleagues stepped in the room.

"Every—is everything alright, Wade?"

More than relaxed now, Wade performed his duties as though he hadn't just cursed out two federal agents.

"Oh, everything is just dandy, Rivers. Just dan-dy."

Wade proceeded to explain the details of his investigation to Walsh and Hammer. He covered Moet and her lifestyle; the men and women she'd laid, as well as her financial status. He calmly talked about her house and the recording on the answering machine. He deliberately left out the videotapes, as if they were his personal discovery. There was the list of dancers, staff, and the ownership at Fool's Paradise. And then there was Debbie. He figured he could share info on her because he honestly needed their help to find her. The agents seemed unimpressed by Wade's personal opinions and emphasis on Debbie, but entirely interested in what he might know about the Gilmores and possible links to Jersey's Bianco crime family.

"*A local family of entrepreneurs,*" Wade called them. "There's various business ventures of the father and son. The women by their sides. The successes . . . the failures. The possessions and bank accounts . . ." Wade hadn't yet pinpointed the actual owners of the Gilmore home, or just how many people lived there. He could only say that it was *big* and that *anything could be going on inside.*

Hammer's mind buzzed along, knowing that the Bureau had handled plenty of these situations before. He could see 30, maybe 40 agents storming the house. Dogs, shotguns, vests, and battering rams. He almost broke into a smile, knowing how equipped his unit was for a job like this. Wade went on about Douglass also being a B-list suspect.

"Then, there's this panty hustler named David who's a customer at the club and into it with a lot of the club's dancers," said Wade.

After a quick glance at one another for approval, Walsh and Hammer collected reports, statements, lists of physical evidence and the autopsy results. Then they left for the FBI's satellite office in New Rochelle.

The Whispers song was the perfect edge that David needed to serenade Valerie . . .

> "*Chocolate girl . . .*
> *oh, chocolate girl . . .*
> *play in my ice cream . . .*"

They were already caught up in the atmosphere of New York's acclaimed Kwanza restaurant, with its rich traditional imports of abstract Kuba art and rich Kente fabrics. Table coverings were done with fine mudcloth-brown panels, and complementing the theme for the entire dining room was an array of tribal art, baskets and exotic sculptures. Meanwhile, spicy, soulful music and incense set the mood for the couple as they awaited their dishes. David didn't mind expressing how his stomach was fighting itself for some food. But more than likely, it was tied in knots for the want to flirt with the gorgeous waitress. On the other hand, he was hungering for a deeper relationship with Valerie. Or was that just lust?

He'd nearly accosted Valerie every night she worked at Fool's Paradise—*a brother just wants a quiet night together.*

"No strings attached" he promised. And finally, after so many rejections and the three sets of roses, Valerie gave in. She wasn't *supposed* to give in, according to the unwritten rules that Cinnamon and others had warned her about, but David was *so damned determined.* At the least, she thought, she'd get a microscopic view of the guy. His defects might stand out, soon as she gave him the once-over, two times. Valerie wasn't looking for a new man, happy with the ten or so thousand dollars that she'd accumulated and stashed between her mattresses.

"It's nice to have you all to myself . . . you know, er—instead of a whole club full a' niggas. You know?" David was leaning over the table, giving Valerie his undivided attention and handling her palms with the tender touch of his fingertips. The lighting in the room was mild, as if the sun was going down indoors. The candles were scented, enhancing the dining room's intimacy—as if the rest of the establishment wasn't already doing the job. Valerie couldn't help but feel the romance in the air. She dared herself at first to be drawn in by David's lure. At least 100 people (men and women) had run the same ole boring lines to her in the club: *"What are you doing in a place like this?" "What do I have to do to get you to go out with me?" "If I could take you home, you'd never have to raise a finger—you'd never have to work another day in your life . . ."* and the one that Valerie heard more often than the rest: *"Girl, you so fine, I'd drink your bath water."* Blah, blah, blah. Valerie just knew she'd heard them all. But then David came in the club with his suave three-liner.

"I was never so weak until I first saw you. My heart stopped beating and then you breathed in my direction. You gave me life again." When she suddenly realized what David had said, her eyes turned glassy. She had to excuse herself. In the bathroom, Valerie shook the gloom and dizziness with a cold face cloth, plus a baby wipe here and there. He was making her hot. Fortunately there were no other dancers in the bathroom. A spray of Binaca Blast woke her up from the dreamy illusions that overcame her, and she went back into the busy club as if nothing happened. That was the night Valerie committed to David.

"Yes . . ." she said, almost choking on the word. ". . . I said *yes*."

David had a moment of shock. Like his heart truly did stop. He was all too prepared for rejection and for a tough 3 hours of some Keith Sweat-type begging. And then he agreed with himself.

*Huh . . . even **this** bitch falls for the Don!*

The sweet and sour chicken and collard greens were appetizing, along with side dishes of candied yams and yellow rice. The delicious meal helped to satisfy the hunger in David's stomach, but not the craving for Valerie. To be kind, David was staring at Valerie while she ate her chocolate ice cream. But to be honest, he was looking right through her, already secure that he would get in between her legs at some point. If not today, tomorrow. If not this week, next. It was that next, new territory for him to conquer, and the beast in him wanted to fill her until there was little room for the ice cream sliding down her throat . . . until gobs of it trickled back out of her lips and down her chin and neck. The chocolate would blend with the beads of perspiration on her neck and cleavage. That was where David imagined he would lay his tongue until it lapped up every bit of sweetness from her dark skin.

". . . David. Did you hear me?" Valerie couldn't be indignant, it wasn't in her nature. But she did raise her voice a stitch.

"Huh . . . oh—yeah. Yeah, sure. Let's get out of here."

David watched his manners and opened the door for Valerie. If he didn't observe high maintenance at these most crucial times in the . . . relationship, he'd surely blow his potential . . .

he'd ruin his . . . Long story short—he wouldn't get to fuck her!

Valerie hopped up into the jeep and reached over to pull the lever, unlocking the driver's door. She crossed her legs and rested her hands in her lap. The split in her black dress was open to all but her upper thigh.

As David eased out of the parking space, Valerie reached up to the visor, pulled it down and checked her makeup in the mirror.

"So where to?" Valerie was direct as she toyed with her eyelashes, using the tip of her pinky's nail to correct things.

"Well . . . any ideas?" David was being cautious, but he was also throwing the ball back over the net to Valerie. However, she wasn't for games.

"You could take me home. I *do* have a long day tomorrow. Laundry. Errands and stuff." She waited for the typical beggar's reply. She got none.

"Okay, great." David was reserved and polite. Not expecting. This threw Valerie off. Almost like he was going with the plan; her playing hard to get.

It was close to midnight and the quiet storm was well into its ritual of all-night-long slow jams. A half moon reflected a bright, unharnessed glow on the hood of David's jeep. Except for a Tevin Campbell song soothing the air, it was tight in the jeep; a silence between the two. David was being casual, while Valerie was becoming more frustrated with each passing traffic light. She tried recrossing her legs. She tried to doze off. None of that was working.

David couldn't miss Valerie's legs. Her defined, naked calves and the perfume that lingered about her were doing a good enough job exciting him, causing him to grow partially stiff.

"David, you're not upset or anything, are you?"

"No—why would you say that?"

"It's just that I don't usually mix business and pleasure. I try and keep the club and my private life separate," said Valerie, expecting a response.

"Okay . . . and?" he asked, looking for her to elaborate.

"Well, I . . . *damn,* David! What happened?" asked Valerie, needing to release some suppressed anxiety. "I thought you wanted me? What are you, fuckin' *gay?*" Valerie found it hard to break her proper Caribbean demeanor, but he pushed her to the edge.

David's ego was on blast, but he kept from smiling, thinking, *Now she's mine.*

"Hey, easy, baby. Of *course* I want you. But I want this to be right. I want just what you want. Nothing more, nothing less. Don't take me for a customer. I'm not just another John."

"Well, I'm not just another . . . I mean, I'm not a ho. You know what I mean? I *know* you do." Valerie was stumbling. Stuttering. It was unlike her. She couldn't . . . wouldn't admit it, but she was horny.

"I know. I know," David said as he zipped up the Major Deegan Expressway to the 233rd Street exit in the Bronx. Along 233rd Street and up to White Plains Road, closer to her address, Valerie seemed to be getting desperate. Maybe she *would* fuck David. Maybe, one day. At least he could show her that he was still interested. That she didn't turn him off. At least he'd shown her something besides dick. Valerie wanted so much to affirm her ability to have a relationship with a black man. But, it had to be right. It had been almost 2 years since she left Canada and Richard.

Oh, why did I have to think of him?

David pulled up to a double parked position outside of Valerie's place. She was now renting a room in a private home on Paulding Avenue. Finally on her own, she graduated and learned. First, Mrs. Brown-White. Then Josh, the obsessed, Radio Shack cashier who thought he owned her. And now she was in a semi-private situation. A basement apartment where she didn't mind sharing the bathroom and kitchen. *The price of freedom*, she reconciled.

It came time to say goodbye and to thank David. But she didn't want to go there just yet.

"Come in. See how I'm livin'."

"Well, I don't know, Valerie. Are you sure?"

"Are *you* sure?" she asked. But David didn't dare read between the lines on that comment. He dismissed it as "cute" and turned on his jeep's hazard lights to follow her inside. The two stepped along the walkway, around the side of the house, up to a doorway under a halogen lamp. Meanwhile, out of the couple's view, a rented Caprice rolled up to double park a few houses away. The headlights blinked off and the motor went dead, but nobody got out of the vehicle. Not yet, anyway

". . . And this is my sister, Beverly, and my brother, Jason." Valerie was pointing to her set of photos that stood in miniature plastic frames, all positioned in a small semi-circle.

David took account of Valerie's humble living quarters. A simple twin-sized bed. A small, movable wardrobe. A new 19" television, a VCR and a clock radio. There was a dresser with four drawers. On top was where she kept her photos, jewelry and makeup. A foot-high mirror was propped up on the dresser, against the wall. The entire room wasn't more than 40 square feet painted in an off-green color. A high window close to the ceiling offered a rectangular view of the fence where the walkway crossed. With the plants and shrubs just outside the window, a clean view didn't seem possible.

But indeed, with the lights on in the basement, someone *could* see inside. And indeed someone *was* on hands and knees, looking on with angry eyes. The two were on center stage and didn't know it. The Peeping Tom could see every slick maneuver and expression that Valerie's visitor made; how he worked his way up behind her, draping his arms around her waist. Valerie didn't flinch, but instead molded instinctively and comfortable in his embrace. He was gliding his nose against the crook at Valerie's bare neck and shoulders . . . he was raising his embrace to just below her breasts. The onlooker disappeared from the window once the light switch was flipped off.

A moment later, there was a loud sound of broken glass, then a police-like car alarm. The double-parked Caprice immediately raced away without being detected.

With his shirt half unbuttoned, David emerged from the side entrance of the house, expecting a confrontation. He ran up to his jeep, with its headlights flashing on and off. The alarm still blaring along with the foghorn on the truck. Someone had smashed the rear window with a stone.

"*Shit!*" David stood outside for a few minutes evaluating the damage. *Steaming*. Valerie came out and stood beside him helplessly. David thought of any immediate enemies, because vandals would have taken his $1,500 sound system and amps. But that was all still there. He wondered what woman he may have ticked off. *Was it Debbie? Was it Moet? Maybe it was Sadie or Cinnamon?* He walked Valerie back to the entrance, deliberating. Wondering. He gave her a brief kiss goodbye. She felt offended by the brisk show of emotion. But she'd have to understand.

Valerie was left with that strange, relieved feeling; somehow glad that there was no real collateral interest in David. By now, she was at least positive that a black man (even if he *was* high yellow) would still pursue her. And off he went, probably to some 24-hour auto glass repair shop. Nothing lost, nothing gained.

Caged

Douglass thought about Mechelle for most of his flight back to New York. He also imagined how he would approach his father with his proposal to buy the club. Investors, meetings, and a firm handshake consumed his thoughts when Mechelle wasn't on his mind. The images volleyed inside of his head like a tennis match. Sex. Money. If it wasn't the club on his mind, it was Mechelle's famous onion dip blow job. If he wasn't thinking about the club and new dancers with perfect bodies and brilliant attitudes, then it was Mechelle and her want for commitment. The club, with palm trees, waterfalls and a new snack bar. Mechelle, and making babies; lots of them. The club, and celebrity memorabilia in glass frames, Kente paneling and a brand new staff. Douglass's mind raced back and forth while his head was jerking, synchronized with his rapid eye movement. He jolted when the stewardess tapped his wrist, warning him about the plane landing and that he needed to fasten his seat belt.

Once the plane parked at LaGuardia, the fluttering and turbulence in the cabin brought Douglass back to reality, his nerves ambitious to reach solid ground.

Home, he thought. And his eyes eventually focused on the here and now. Douglass defied the STAY SEATED lights, despite all the warnings the stewardess mentioned earlier, and he reached up to retrieve his shoulder bag, knowing that most of the passengers would be competing to get off the plane ahead of others.

So impatient, he thought selfishly. Douglass, no less, the pot calling the kettle black.

As the airplane made its hissing sounds, Douglass weaved through other passengers as if he was a ballerina spinning, dodging and rushing with a football into the end zone. All the while, he vowed to himself that *the next flight has to be first class!* Down the aisle, past startled airline attendants and through the exit, Douglass stepped quick and steadfast towards the opening to the terminal where Mechelle would be waiting. It was a great trip. A chance to see his mother and sisters. A chance to get a grip on himself and to take in the west coast climate. The music on Douglass's earphones was appropriate for his pace, flooding his ears and senses with the mood setting transitions of jazz. He had mixed a special tape just for the trip and side B was playing now, with Herb Albert's *Rise* just finishing and fading into Grover's *Mr. Magic*. This was just the right rhythm for his attitude, because in a moment or two he was about to perform the actions that he reviewed in his dreams so many times while he was away. He'd run up to Mechelle, and she'd run to him. He'd clench her hips and waist with a firm grip, lift her up, spin around once and then lower her to his magnetic kiss.

There she was! The fantasy was beginning to play itself out as Mechelle was one of the first to be waiting for passengers to enter the terminal. She had those tight green shorts on that he liked so much. And by that look in her eyes, he'd bet his last dollar that she was going along with his wishes—

"Don't wear any panties, either. Cuz, when I get back, I'mma tear that pussy up!" That was what Douglass growled into the telephone when last the two spoke. "I want you to be ready for *anything*," he told her.

Douglass took that deep breath and exhaled the tensions from the flight—all of those ideas tossing around in his head. It was the way Mechelle looked right now; to be so willing and waiting for him, standing there in her white blouse and match-

ing baseball cap that was turned to the rear and on an angle.
Mechelle stood all of 5 feet tall, and although she was considered short for a woman, she was just right for Douglass; all
buxom delicious in her white Nike sneakers. One of her legs
was slightly bent so that she was posing, and her hands were
stuffed in her back pockets to allow that full frontal view—his
prize catch, all stretched out and perky; fine like creamy,
molten chocolate that he suddenly wanted to devour right
there in public. So fine, in fact, that Douglass was proud of
himself for finding her. And as he got close enough to grab her
he was beyond *considering* a commitment; instead, he was
ready to pop the big question at this very instant.

With his shoulder bag strapped securely across his torso,
the wire from his headset swinging aimlessly, Douglass
reached out to Mechelle for that welcome-home hug he so anticipated. Just then, two bystanders—one with shades, one
without—stepped in between the two before they could touch.
One pulled a shiny billfold out and flipped it open, stretched
out close to Douglass's nose. Mechelle's giant smile suddenly
turned to a distraught gasp. The other bystander pulled his
blazer to the side, brandishing his badge and holstered pistol.

"Mr. Gilmore, this is Agent Walsh and I'm Agent Hammer
with the FBI. You're under arrest. Please step aside . . ." The
two agents moved towards a side wall, deliberately cradling
Douglass's elbows so that he had no choice. Another female
agent with blond hair stood by Mechelle to be sure that she
didn't interfere. Mechelle was frantic with her expressions, but
temperate in her actions. Loudly, she addressed the ambush.

"What's goin' on here? *Hey!* Where are you takin' him?"
Mechelle tried to move past the blond agent, but she blocked
the move and opened her blazer to brandish a holstered
weapon. Other passengers were passing through now, side-
stepping the arrest and keeping that shameful hush amongst
themselves, somehow embarrassed for Douglass.

Hammer and Walsh didn't need to use force under the circumstances. There was plenty of airport security around. And besides, Douglass did not resist, even if he was arguing.

"What's this about? *Hey!* Why the handcuffs? What did
I do?"

"You're under arrest for the murder of Nadine Butler . . ."

"Nadine *who*? I don't even *know* anybody named Nadine! Y'all are outta your fuckin' minds!"

"You have the right to remain silent . . . if you . . ." Agent Walsh went over his Miranda Rights while Hammer secured the cuffs on both wrists, his elbow slightly pressed into Douglass's spine. Douglass stood still, his cheek against the wall, watching fellow passengers and their expressions. Some of them were shocked and paranoid, veering to a wider distance. Others shook their heads as if they expected this of him— more or less wishing this on him; as if he was that speeding car who passed them, only to be flagged and chased down by the state troopers.

The blond agent tried to calm Mechelle, but Mechelle was having a fit. Eventually, she directed questions to Douglass. The passengers were all but emptied from the corridor now, leaving a group of uniformed stewardesses and pilots who stepped in unison from the ramp.

"Douglass, what should I do?"

"Just relax, baby. This is all bullshit. Don't get upset. Just go home and relax. I can handle everything. Tell my father what happened. Otherwise, I'll be fine. Wait for my call." Douglass threw Mechelle a kiss with his lips only, and he was escorted down a service corridor of the terminal. Mechelle was left outside of the swinging doors, looking through a plate of glass window that she'd rather kick in.

Meanwhile, the agents brought their prisoner through a series of doors and passageways until they reached a blue Chevy Caprice sedan that had a clean, but dull, appearance. Hammer helped Douglass into the back and the blond sat behind the wheel. Walsh was in the passenger seat, with his upper body twisted so that he sat facing the back seat. He began to ask Douglass some questions, but he got a sarcastic grimace in response. Douglass remained silent in light of this nightmare, and he didn't want to help these agents in the least. Even under the circumstances, he was able to find patience enough to wait and see a lawyer, judge or some other authority.

As the Chevy zipped along, an agent explored Douglass's belongings. Pen and pad handy, he recorded cell phone numbers, license and bank card numbers. Watching every activity, no matter how simple, Douglass kept a blank look on his face. A few moments later, the agent named Walsh motioned to the lady agent to pull over. She did so, and the vehicle sat on the service lane of the expressway. The agents each got out and met at the rear of the vehicle. Someone raised the trunk, shielding view of their conversation. Douglass could see through the narrow space at the bottom of the rear windshield. Walsh was doing most of the talking, while the other two agents looked on obediently. When they returned to their seats, all eyes were on their prisoner. Walsh leaned over into the back seat as if he had revealing news.

"Okay, Mr. Gilmore. Here's the situation. We're bringing you to New Jersey for holding. That's where our office is, and that's where this case will be tried. Now, you can make this difficult, or you can make this easy on yourself. If we bring you to New Jersey, we must extradite you from New York. That means we would have to process you here in New York. Manhattan. That could take a number of days, a magistrate and an extradition proceeding. That's the difficult way. The easy way is, you can sign this waiver . . ."

—Walsh produced a printed form and whipped it in front of Douglass's face—

". . . which will put it in front of a judge today, and you may be able to get bail by five PM." Walsh looked at his watch as if he was timing Douglass, or rushing him. To Douglass, the watch looked overdone, one of those with about 50 features more than necessary.

"It's twelve noon now. We have just enough time to process you and get you before a magistrate." Douglass considered the situation.

"Whatever . . ." He looked over the form and twisted his face, misunderstanding much of it. ". . . what does this mean?" Douglass pointed to a clause with his nose, something about waiving his rights. Agent Walsh snatched the sheet from Douglass.

"Okay . . . problem. Take him to Manhattan," Walsh ordered the lady agent like a general.

"No . . . no—*alright*. I'll sign it. . . . I *said* I'll sign it." Douglass felt pressured, but he made the plea so he could get through whatever procedure and get back home to Mechelle. It was a sleepless flight from Cali, and now, it was likely to be a long afternoon in custody. Douglass closed his eyes, knowing that this was some joke. Somebody had to correct this mess. He was sure things—

A murder? Nadine Butler? Who's that?

Tucked Away

The trip to New Jersey was a relatively quick one. The feds acted as if they were on a chase, speeding like a gush of wind on the throughway, jetting through toll booths without obligation and plowing forward like some God-Almighty force that intimidated other drivers into moving out of the way or pulling aside.

The agents raced back to their home base in Newark, and once they made the transition from the throughway to the busy streets, the same high speed was exercised, only now in spurts between major intersections. Douglass began to feel like a diplomat in a motorcade, or even a controversial rap star escaping gunfire. He tried to close his eyes and imagine *why, what* and *how*. Perhaps this was just a nightmare and these were really expensive bracelets (and not handcuffs) on his wrists? Was this a bad dream?

Nadine who? Douglass still couldn't put two and two together. Next to a massive postal building (obvious by the fleet of white trucks on the street and lot) there was an even bigger building labeled as the Martin Luther King Hall of Justice. Douglass huffed under his breath, thinking, *sure . . . what a laugh. Martin's masterminding this?* But at the same time he was thinking that Martin's name in the hands of the enemy was the worst contradiction.

The Caprice rolled down a driveway at the side of the building. Agent 99 lowered her window and slipped a plastic ID card into a machine. There was a beep before a garage door lifted electronically. The vehicle eased down and into the basement of the courthouse, into an underground passage, and it stopped just short of another steel door. Douglass realized that he was entering a fortress, with all of the procedures and sequences of doors and gates and such. The garage door lowered behind the car. Seconds later the steel door rolled up in front of the car. The vehicle moved again, now settling in what felt like a small cave. As the door lowered, sealing the vehicle inside, Douglass could feel the presence and power of that blue and yellow insignia on the wall. It was the size and shape of an oversized basketball. It read "U.S. MARSHALS SERVICE."

Once inside, Douglass could have been entering a control center for a NASA rocket launch for all he knew. Just ahead was a glass enclosed command booth, containing 10-foot panels full of video monitors, recorders and electronic buttons, lights and switches. Surveillance, squared. There were some telephones and a uniformed attendant overseeing it all. On the monitors, Douglass could surmise briefly that cameras were everywhere inside and outside of the building, capturing miles of activities in one room. The whole facility seemed equipped enough to offset any possible terrorist activity. Cameras were focused on the perimeter of the building, jail cells, driveways, corridors and doorways.

Immediately breaking Douglass's fixation with the electronics in his midst, a burly, bearded, Big Foot–like type, with unshaven, prickled skin, stepped forward, ready to process Douglass. Fingerprints. Photos. Property forms. A prisoner number. He had 3 or 4 sets of handcuffs and a big ring of keys hanging off of his waist—had to be 30 keys on that ring. The cuffs and keys were attached to the dark leather belt that disappeared under Big Foot's gas-tank belly. Douglass was told to sit in a chair next to a desk. Reception. The marshal poked at some keys on his computer and pulled a series of forms from trays on his desk. Among the questions Douglass was asked included vitals like date of birth, home address and phone number, parents, children and occupation. Douglass wanted to ask if this was for the U.S. Marshal's special mailing list and if he should expect 4-color brochures. But the enormity of the surroundings, all served to prevent his freedom and liberty, was intimidating, daunting, and a step beyond any "smoke and mirror" campaign that he'd ever seen.

Once the processing was done, the FBI agents left Douglass alone with the marshal, who escorted him down an elbow of hallways to where a row of closed-door holding cells were located. The handcuffs were removed and Douglass was made to wait until he was called to court for an arraignment before a U.S. Magistrate. During an hour long wait, alone in the cell, he couldn't explain to himself how his life had so suddenly been whisked up into such a twister of adversity. He did his best to rationalize. What would Les Brown tell him *now*, in **this** predicament? Certainly not LIVE YOUR DREAMS! Douglass couldn't see it, but he could feel that he was caught in a chain of events that had nothing to do with him.

"Gilmore." A marshal twirled a set of handcuffs as he entered the cell. "Court." he concluded. He was casual about it, an everyday occurrence for him. This time, handcuffs *and* shackles were used. A chain was wrapped around Douglass's waist to keep the cuffs restricted to his waist. A second marshal joined the escort, and the trio went into an elevator, down a few halls, and through a rear entrance into a courtroom with polished wood, carpet and bright lights. Douglass was directed to a long table where he was seated adjacent to an identical setup a few feet away. The three familiar FBI agents were seated at the adjacent table in a strategic huddle along with another man in a black suit and tie. Meanwhile, Douglass sat wondering, counting the faces. The stenographer. The court clerk. Two court officers at the rear of the room. The marshals.

Why are these people involved with my life? Douglass took a well needed deep breath, waiting for someone of authority to dismantle this whole mess. Someone would inevitably put all of this into proper perspective, and for sure, Douglass would be sent back to his busy life in New York.

"Good afternoon, Mr. Gilmore. I'm Mr. Locca, here to represent you. Are you familiar with the charges that are pending in this case?" Out of the clear blue, another white man in a suit approached Douglass from behind.

"Pending?" As Douglass asked this, the two wooden doors, demarcations between freedom and imprisonment, were still swinging.

"Well, there's actually a complaint at this point . . ."

Locca was a short Italian man with dark hair and a round nose. He handed Douglass a yellow copy of the complaint.

"Next will be the indictment. I've read the charges and I've spoken to the government about your case. Their case is kinda shaky, but . . ."

"*Wait* a minute. Who called you to represent me? That's first of all, and second of all, slow down. Things are going pretty fast for me right now."

"Mr. Gilmore, the *court* has appointed me to represent you in this matter. I was once a district attorney in this court, so if you just work with me we'll do the best we can for you." Locca was leaning into the conversation as if he didn't care for the marshals or the opposition to overhear. But the court room was quiet enough to hear a mouse squeak. Douglass was reviewing the complaint as he listened to the lawyer.

"RECO? *Organized crime?!*" Douglass was loud. The clerk of the court and the others all gazed in his direction. A marshal in the back of the courtroom seemed to ready himself for expected trouble.

"Mr. Gilmore, these are just allegations. In a court of law these things must be proven beyond reasonable doubt. Relax." Locca leaned in once again, placing a concerned hand on Douglass's shoulder. They discussed the circumstances and procedures a bit more before a voice spoke out loud.

"**All rise**. The Honorable Magistrate Bernice Keefe presiding in the matter of the United States of America versus Douglass Gilmore." A frail woman in her 50's, with silver hair and horn rimmed, wire frame glasses posted on the bridge of her nose, stepped affirmatively towards the platform as called upon by the clerk of the court. At the forefront of the courtroom, she sat behind a large, enclosed, redwood bench. Douglass could only see her from the shoulders and up, even when he stood. The handcuffs were removed, but the U.S. marshals stood even closer now, as if Douglass (who, despite all, was calm and humbled) would escape in shackles. Observing everyone's actions and words during the proceedings., Douglass smirked when he finally focused on the bronzed, raised letters on the wall behind the magistrate. The words in GOD WE TRUST forced Douglass to wonder: *You all trusting in God, but you're all acting corrupt, like kidnappers right now.*

After the introduction, a blizzard of legal mumbo jumbo was exchanged back and forth between the judge, the lawyer and the assistant U.S. attorney. And eventually, without a word from Douglass, a decision was reached relating to bail.

"Bail will be set at five million dollars, cash." The magistrate uttered the words in a single, insensitive breath before she slammed her gavel down, putting an end to the session. Just like that, the court appearance was over. Decisions and discussions about Douglass Gilmore and his freedom had simply brushed by him, a snowstorm that he was neither prepared or dressed for. And now, he was left to suffer the consequences, naked and alone.

"FIVE MILLION DOLLARS CASH?!" Douglass attracted everyone's attention within the space of seconds. He was so loud that he made the court stenographer cover her ears. He wanted to bust out of the chains on his ankles. He wanted to bust out in laughter and in tears. He wanted to destroy every breathing person in sight. And that's when the marshals closed in with their hands gripping his forearms and shoulders.

"Relax, Mr. Gilmore. Don't make a scene here in the courtroom. Be respectful of the court and they will be respectful towards you. Remember that. This isn't as bad as it sounds—" The marshals had already jumped at Douglass, replacing the handcuffs and proceeding as though the conversation with the attorney was the least important issue in existence. "—listen, I'll talk to you downstairs in the holding cell." Douglass quickly realized that he was being rushed and that the forces were too mighty for him to compete with, all of it moving, manipulating and shifting him the way they pleased. To him, this was all wrong; kidnapping disguised as justice. From Douglass's viewpoint, it seemed as though the FBI had fabricated a suitcase of possibilities to impress anyone that was listening, and therefore Douglass was pigeonholed as just another flagrant, belligerent ne'er-do-well of society.

The lawyer and client went their separate ways. One in the direction of liberty, the other, into a virtual straightjacket. Lifting her robe from her feet like it was a wedding gown, the magistrate quickly made her exit, as if she was fleeing, disappearing through a door to her chambers. The courtroom soon turned lifeless again—the scene of a hit-and-run.

Douglass did his best to harbor his tensions along the walk

back to the holding cell. But when the chains and cuffs were removed and the door slammed, he found a corner of the room and sat on the stainless steel bench. Feeling helpless and abused, he lifted his knees and assumed a fetal position. He squeezed until his arms felt lifeless; until teardrops of loss and confusion rolled down his cheeks.

The boom-bap and grungy bass of D'Angelo's *"Brown Sugar"* was entertaining the customers inside of Fool's Paradise as they watched the dancers swing and swerve along with the music. But for Gil, things were miserable right now. He'd just received word about his son, and it was having an impact on him.

"What *murder*? My son wouldn't commit any *murder*. He don't have no enemies like *that*." A dancer was standing just next to Gil, rubbing his back, while at the same time a customer was trying to get Gil's attention, waving a ten-dollar bill at him for singles. His thoughts hardly interrupted, Gil went ahead and gave the customer change, except he carried on with his conversation, his train of thought never slowing. He was still playing Mechelle's phone call in his mind.

He said to tell you he'll be alright and not to worry about him. He would handle things.

Then, Gil had responded, saying, *how the hell does **he** expect to handle things? This is the federal government, not some fluzzie, local sheriff. He's gonna need a good lawyer to get him out of—**murder?** Mechelle, do you know anything about what's going on?* Mechelle said she didn't know a thing, but suspected that this might have something to do with Moet's murder since that was the only murder to speak of in the past month.

Gil thought of calling one or two patrons who also happened to work at the 45th Precinct. But by Mechelle's call he realized something; Douglass was a grown man who, apparently, could take care of himself. After all these years of ups and downs; all the business ventures they had together, inevitably building Gilmore's to become a staple brand in the adult entertainment industry—after the family break-up and the two eventually re-uniting—Gil saw that his son was independent.

* * *

For the days to follow, Mechelle did her best to maintain Douglass's priorities; the bills, the phone calls and the brief errands. Demetrius was helpful as well, maintaining security at the house and keeping a watchful eye (more than ever before) on Fool's Paradise. One thing Demetrius did not realize was that Mechelle was becoming sick. She was growing hungrier, eating snacks all the time. But she was also throwing up on occasion. Mechelle was almost sure that she was pregnant. But that wasn't her problem. Her problem was that she wasn't sure if the baby belonged to Douglass, or if it belonged to one of the men who raped her down in North Carolina. Not to mention how she was afraid to find out the truth.

Detective Wade reclined in his swivel chair, feet up on the desk. He gazed at his strategy board, and the calendar beside it. Zeroing in today's date reminded him that he had less than 18 months before he was to retire. That calendar also reminded him that he had to make use of his vacations and sick days that he never took advantage of.

Damn, he thought. *I could take a whole year off if I want to.* There was one more thing about the calendar; something he'd forgotten. *The World Series! Jesus!*

Wade jumped up to make a few calls, before it was too late.

CHAPTER THIRTEEN

Go Yankees!

A Sunny October afternoon served up brilliant daylight over Yankee Stadium and its flurry of activity. Earlier than usual, ticket holders swarmed from the subways, buses and parking lots, converging on the first game of the World Series. Police presence was extra thick with trucks, cycles, squad cars and horses. Usually, their first priority might be the teams of ticket scalpers who preyed on unknowing visitors. Counterfeit tickets were always circulating, and every officer was supplied with over a hundred plastic tie-cuffs to apprehend suspects. However, the higher priority these days was terrorists. Anytime a large crowd convened in New York, there had to be that additional police presence; some extra cops in paramilitary gear; all of them strapped up with the M-16 rifle, the helmet and the added armor. Things were off the hook these days.

Wade was off duty for the game opener. But he used his police clout, regardless, enabling him to stand nearby, to listen in on the briefing held out on the sidewalk, directly across from the stadium. Sixty officers and 150 auxiliary officers were either on post or on line at the roll call. This was *the* event that called all of New York to its knees.

Generally, baseball fans would leave the game with memorabilia such as programs, flags, souvenir balls, bats and caps. But today, just about everyone that headed into the stadium was dressed from head to toe in their finest Yankees attire, carrying their trusty baseball gloves just in case.

Vans, buses and taxis that arrived (each vehicle loaded with fans) were also dressed and printed with team logos, and other game-related convictions. Many devoted ticket holders spent the morning at the local team diner, trading stories about each player and each home run they'd witnessed throughout the year. And once the gates opened, fans had no choice but to stand in endless lines which wrapped around the stadium in two directions on the Bronx streets. Many were waiting in separate lines to buy programs, commemoratives, or anything else tangible to remember the event by.

New York vs. Texas

The series began with explosive tempers and activity from the first inning. Mike Lewis, manager of the New York team, was ejected by the home plate umpire, just three pitches into the game against Texas. Lewis was too vulgar in response to the ball and strike calls. Five minutes later, his starting pitcher, Shane Hargrove, joined him for shouting at the same ump after a suspect home plate call. From Wade's seat, 10 rows behind the dugout, he heard *"You stupid motherfucker! Are you blind?"* And then the general manager for New York stalked down onto the field to vent *his* frustrations. It was an early mess of poor sportsmanship, which reminded Wade why he didn't follow sports in the first place. All of this early activity made him feel like he got more than he'd bargained for—even though he didn't pay squat for the tickets. He was supposed to be there on business. (*His* business, since he'd been officially removed from the case.) And at the last minute, he was able to get a ticket before anybody (anybody, like Ken Stevens) knew that this was not an FBI case. And he was so sure coming here would give him a head start on the feebies—no way they were onto Ken this early. Such thoughts helped Wade to relax. A good seat for the game; no pressure against time; and now, all he had to wait for was the right time.

New York was behind, 2–0. They were now counting on their star pitcher to salvage the game. Ken Stevens replaced Hargrove earlier than expected. It was originally planned that he would come in after the fifth inning to bring the fireworks, whether they were necessary or not. But, now that he thought about the article he read earlier, Wade agreed that Ken's placement in this game was just right.

Critics had suggested that some injury may have been the reason that Stevens wasn't starting in the series opener. Others claimed that he wasn't worth the millions that his contract promised. Talk was his only challenge, however. Because when it came to action, Ken Stevens was the prophet. And now that the game was moving along nicely, Ken was stomping the critics, holding Texas to five hits while striking out six without a walk in $7\frac{1}{2}$ innings. His only blemish was a homer in the eighth, cracked by Rico Diaz. But that was after NY flexed their muscle to take a 7–3 lead. Steven's grand slam off Texas pitcher David Kranker in the third inning, and José Clark's two-run homer off a Texas relief pitcher in the fifth, keyed the New York comeback. New York added a run in the sixth inning with Baker's sacrifice fly, with one out, driving in Bobbie Blue who had singled, stolen second base and advanced on a Griffey single.

New York broke the game in the eighth inning. A relief pitcher came in for Texas. Their second. He walked three batters in a row. The crowds were ecstatic with energy on the fourth batter. The stadium seemed to levitate with applause as Stevens came up to the plate. Everyone knew that he was facing a lot. Even though the team was up by 4. Point was, this game was his second time facing a grand slam. It was still crunch time, regardless of the score. This was their million-dollar man. The highest-paid player on the team. So, they expected him to deliver; to make it all official.

Crack! The bat connected dead center, driving the ball directly over the pitcher's head. He tried to jump for it, but the ball was on an incline and still climbing, climbing, climbing some more. Now, it was in the air over center field and beginning to descend on the glide. Diaz, the centerfielder, jetted towards the wall, sure that the ball would either bounce off the wall; or maybe just barely clip the top. Still running, Diaz had to make a decision to jump or stand. He eyed the ball. It seemed to fade in and out of the sky. With cautious measure, he decided to hit the wall. He paced himself, picked up speed, and catapulted with the left foot while raising the right to climb the wall. His right cleat dug into the sponge wall and the speed, motion and drive took his body into flight. With his arm extended a few inches over the top of the wall and still airborne, Diaz timed the ball. It was falling fast and close to the glove. Feet away. Then inches.

Pop! The ball smacked the leather of his glove. Diaz came down in a tumble. He got up strong and amped. Excited. All of those emotions until . . . until he looked in his glove. No ball! In the fever, he didn't realize the ball only hit the top of his glove—he didn't catch it! The ball was on the other side of the wall with stadium workers already scrambling for it. Stevens had hit another grand slam smash and the stadium turned into an ocean of jubilation. A spontaneous combustion of erratic applause and uncontrollable jumping. The result was a roar that cut through the air like a rocket blast.

After the game, Wade followed a series of corridors and wings, until he felt as though he'd circled the stadium twice. Pushing his badge when necessary, he headed for the team locker room. On the way, he grabbed a small sack of peanuts from a vendor, still descending ramps. Finally, at the door marked "CLUBHOUSE," he muscled through teams of waiting reporters, spilling some peanuts along the cement walkway, until he was able to reach and knock at the door. A uniformed guard pulled open a small slice of Plexiglas, peeking through the portal. Wade mentioned his appointment. When the guard winced, Wade took the easier method. A sign even the guard could understand. The guard immediately became a best friend and even escorted Wade through the tunnels leading to the New York Yankees locker room.

Showers were steaming in the rear. Laughter could be heard from various directions. Some players were half in and half out of uniform. Others were wrapped in towels, headed for their personal shower stalls. Soiled team jerseys were draped here and there. Rows of pinewood benches lined the areas a few feet away from similarly designed lockers. Some lockers were opened and looked lived in, while others were very neat and organized. There were centerfold posters, family portraits, neatly folded towels, shirts and hanging team uniforms. On the floor outside of most lockers were pairs of dirty cleats. Meanwhile, team attendants and players' personal assistants were either collecting used clothes, or else setting fresh street gear out for the players in the showers. This was certainly a locker room, but it was a glamorous one. Carpet. Generous lighting. Very organized. Cell phones at the ready. Walls of sink and mirror arrangements. Towel boys. Televisions in the walls. And there was pleasing ventilation that accommodated these million-dollar men—pampering for million-dollar feet and hands.

Ken was just about to head for his shower when Wade recognized him without his team cap, wrapped in a team towel. Wade caught his attention and they agreed to meet after and leave together for a discussion over dinner. In a room which branched off of the locker room, there was a lavish lounge. Instantly darker than the fluorescent lighting in the locker room, the lounge could have been mistaken for a nightclub from what Wade could measure. Luxuries galore. Video games. Snack machines. A mini bar with stools. Waitresses, couch-side telephones and top of the line flatscreen monitors made Wade almost feel guilty as he soaked into the fine leather couch, kicking his feet up onto a coffee table. As he watched the screen in front of him, the 6 o'clock news was beginning. Ernie Anastos and Brenda Blackmon were the familiar co-anchors for the local news on channel 5.

"For our top story, today federal agents from the New Jersey Or-

ganized Crime Task Force arrested New Rochelle television producer and entertainment entrepreneur, Douglass Gilmore. They're charging Gilmore with the murder of topless dancer Nadine Butler, known as Moet . . ." Brenda turned to a different camera. A photo of Moet showed up beside the anchor. "*The murder of Miss Butler had been a mystery to New York City authorities for the past eight months. However, recently the Federal Bureau of Investigation took over the case—a case that is allegedly related to the organized criminal activities of the New Jersey-based Bianco family . . .*" Video footage accompanied the anchor's voice, showing the scene of the murder and various dancers huddled outside in the chill to be questioned by officers. The broadcast went on to detailed allegations of the link between Gilmore and his businesses being one of the many fronts for organized crime. There were mug shots on the monitor of the Bianco chain of command and known underlings. An on-location reporter fused the pieces of the story together from a position outside of Fool's Paradise with the camera panning over to the club entrance and its sign overhead. A few seconds of video showed Douglass being led out of the courtroom, and then there was an interview with the district attorney, appearing to bring some authenticity to the story. Wade smirked at the inferences and the impressions that the newscast left viewers with. He wasn't surprised. Typical propaganda, all pushed by the FBI. Nothing new, except that this was the first time in nearly 20 years that a case had been taken from Wade. But the TV hype did aggravate him.

Total fabrication, he thought.

Ken's Version

Ken maneuvered his way out of the stadium garage as if the world was after his ass, moving far and away from the throng of press and waiting fans in his armored, gleaming black Lincoln Navigator. The truck was bigger than life, appropriate for the way the million-dollar player lived. The inside was clean and expertly loaded for any occasion, whether a party for eight or a cruise for two. Wade felt his body float on air as he nestled in the soft, glove-leather passenger seat, his feet planted firmly on the foot mat. The floor was as close as he could come to any hint of solid ground while Ken moved along the streets with commanding energy. When he took that first hard turn Wade held the door strap, expecting to feel gravity pull him in the opposite way. Nope. The luxury vehicle seemed to defy gravity because Wade barely budged with the seatbelt holding him so snug. He did, however, need to take a deep breath, and for the want of occupying the drive time he stared at the bronze carpet that covered the floor and matched the interior throughout the vehicle.

Must be nice.

A low volume feed of classical jazz played over the hi-fi sound system as they headed for Ken's favorite grub spot. In the meantime, Ken was comfortable enough with Wade to freely share his background. Perhaps this satisfied the void he felt, escaping all those reporters stranded and strung-out back at the stadium. The jeep eventually rolled up to a stop in front of Jimmy's Café. A valet stepped up to take possession of the vehicle, but quickly backed off when he recognized who it was. Apparently, Wade guessed, Ken always parked on his own. And the valet stepped aside and indicated for Ken to go and park as usual. In the rear of the lot, next to the convenient exit, Wade and Ken hopped down and out of the vehicle, then they strolled into the eatery. At the same time, a maître d' was already waiting to seat them. The two settled, ordered food, and Ken continued to talk Wade's ears off.

"What attracted you to Moet?" asked Wade, feeling confident enough to jump to another subject. He also needed to give Ken some direction, to stop him from wandering back into his sports-celebrity world; the shit Wade had heard enough of.

"I think it was her obsession with me. I know that might seem strange to you, knowing that *I'm* the one who's always approached by fanatics. But Moet was the *right* kind of woman that a man, *any man*, would *want* to be obsessed . . ." Wade sipped at his coffee to save himself an expression. Since he'd seen a few videos, he already knew what Ken was saying. He even wondered himself if Moet could have affected him that way. ". . . even if we had a little spat or something," said Ken, "she'd call me right back the next hour or the next day. Even if

I was wrong." Ken explained how he met Moet, things they did and how long or how much. She had been to his loft a few times, but it was Ken who visited *her* home most of the time. After a game. After dinner. After a movie. And whenever he did bring her home, she usually stayed for a few hours of gratuitous sex. No more, no less.

Ken seemed to be thrown off a bit when Wade described (more in depth) how Moet was left for dead. The only knowledge that Ken had of Moet's death was by Wade's initial phone call. That was what initially brought Ken closer to Wade. Close enough to confide in him. Close enough to share *other* things.

"I've never shared this with anyone . . ." Ken leaned into Wade like a weeping willow; tall as a 6'5" tower, Ken had Wade beat by almost 10 inches of height. "Once when I was out with Moet I had to put up a fight for her."

"A fight?" Wade reached in his pocket for a pad. For a while, he didn't think he'd be needing it anymore. Not for this case anyhow.

"Well, I dropped Moet off at her house one morning . . . it was almost noon. The whole block where she lives was like, deserted. Except for a few cars. We kissed . . . we'd spent the night together at my loft in the Village, and I turned my jeep around, heading for the airport. You know, her block is a dead end. They're building more . . ."

Wade shook his head and acknowledged that he knew all about her block, the construction, and the house. *Just get on with it, dude.*

"Well, anyway, I had a game in Seattle that night. So, I had to go. But before I got to the end of her block, I peeked into the rearview mirror. I don't know why, but I saw a guy, a white man, running up behind Moet. I thought it was curious and stopped quick. I almost hit my head on the *windshield!* Anyway, I backed *up* on her block and jumped out to see what was up. The guy was pushing her, like, right in front of her door. I ran up and snatched this dude by the collar. He flung around and popped me in the shoulder with his fist. I mean, I'm not a wimp or anything, but I never expected *that*. I'm no boxer or nothin', but I moved closer to grab him or hit him or *something*. I'm always concerned about being put in the press for some assault stuff." Wade yawned, visibly tired of Ken's ranting and beating around the bush. "Got to watch my image, you know. There's big money riding on me . . ." Wade wanted to shake Ken to get him to finish the damned story.

". . . anyway, he was like, *fuck off, jock* . . . then he pushed me again . . . dude is like big, not big and tall, but wide like a freakin' truck! He was real light in the skin. Almost all—

Ken twisted his face, trying to recall. And Wade helped.

"Yeah, that's right. Like an albino. Anyway, the dude pushed past me, cursing at Moet like she was a prostitute or somethin'." Wade now turned *his* face, knowing that *Ken* obviously didn't know everything about Moet.

"He yelled something like, '*You bitch! You wanna fuck with my girl? I'll show you—you fuckin' dyke!*' That's when I was like, *dude!* I went to grab him again, but he ran back to his car. A Chevy or somethin'. I looked at Moet. She was okay, just out of breath and hysterical. That made me run after the guy. He already closed himself in the car and locked it. I was bangin' on the window, but there was this sharp pain in my right shoulder. And I was like, **shit, shit, shit!!! My shoulder!** All I could think about was the Seattle game. Now I was *really* mad. I ran after the car for practically half the block. Exhaust fumes were in my face and everything. But he got away." Wade was listening to the story in between the flubber, envisioning the scene. White guy tries to attack Moet. He's saying Moet is messing with "his girl," and he's mad, he's in a Caprice. That was the *real* story. Question is, who was Moet ticking off, and what *girl* was this guy referring to? The dyke stuff? He already knew Moet was bisexual. Nothing new there. Wade felt a little breathless himself, as if he was there. Hanging onto every word coming from Ken's lips. Maybe Ken was Wade's best lead, after all.

Wade and Ken both had Ken's favorite dish. Grilled turkey salad with cheddar cheese and croutons. After the meal, Ken joined Wade for the short trip to Moet's house. Sean Clancy, the police artist, met them there, part of Wade's idea to prevent publicity and to help Ken with recollection of the faces and events. There was no doubt in Wade's mind that Ken's run-in had something to do with Moet's murder. So once Ken was sure that the sketch fit the description of the attacker, he acknowledged Wade's office and pager numbers, then zoomed off in a blur of black. Now, on the way back to the precinct, Wade and the police artist discussed more about the drawing; but Wade had stared at the likeness long enough to know that he hadn't run across any suspects with this description. He also marked Ken off of his hit list, recalling that his alibi was as good as an alibi could be. On the night of the murder, Ken was stuck in a hotel room in Kansas City waiting for part 2 of a double header. Besides, his story about the skirmish fit perfectly with the shoulder injury that prevented him from playing a few games. Must have been a bad hit, thought Wade, since Ken had been through a month of rehabilitation therapy for his entire right arm.

As Wade absorbed the impact of the speed bumps at the entrance to the headquarter's parking lot, he shared some male trivia with Sean.

"Do you know that Stevens hardly remembers the names of the women he lays?" Wade expected Sean to be more surprised.

"Really?" Sean was neither here nor there about the subject, finally swinging into the nearest parking space.

"Yeah. Since he visits quite a few different states, he's devised a system that can prevent him from screwing up the names. He gives them 'pet names.' Like nicknames. It starts immediately when he meets them, so if he's in Atlanta, and meets a girl there, her name is Atlanta. If he's in Montreal, then that's *her* nickname—Montreal, or Montey. The women adopt the name like it was their own. Coming from a sports star and all."

"What if there's two girls in the same state?"

"I don't know. I never got to ask."

"Maybe you weren't cut out to be a detective after all," said the artist, and the two laughed as they entered the rear of the station.

Passaic County Jail

Going to jail for the first time isn't pretty. It's a culture shock, to be more exact. But for Douglass, the passage into Passaic County's Public Safety Facility was a death defying experience. To say the least, the jail was overcrowded. Something like a dog kennel, only for men. And as soon as he arrived there,

Douglass was packed in with everybody else, regardless of their crime. Even if you were a petty thief, you might be grouped with an axe murderer.

Notwithstanding his current legal woes, Douglass still felt he could handle the circumstances. After all, he had already been introduced to "communal living" at age 17—even worse than jail, as far as he was concerned.

It was just after high school that he signed up and enlisted in the U.S. Marine Corps where he endured 90 days of boot camp on the infamous Parris Island training grounds in South Carolina. So, he figured if he could take 24 hours of physical torture for 90 days straight—physical training, psychological pressure and shouting—then he could certainly withstand a few days in the slammer . . . at least. He had no choice but to do that; to face the challenge.

U.S. marshals drove Douglass from the courthouse in Newark to Passaic. Detained as a federal prisoner until bail was paid or the case was decided. One way or the other, this was home for now. Escorting their prisoner through an electronically raised garage door, both marshals unstrapped their Glock MP 30s from their waists and, like a well rehearsed ritual, they stashed them; one in the glove compartment, the other in the armrest, between the seats. They raised from their seats and out of the car and moved towards the rear doors, approaching Douglass from both sides. Closest to Douglass was a female marshal. She had long, Barbie-blond hair, and the good looks to match. She reached down to help Douglass from his seat, and he instantly inhaled a dry flowery fragrance like his elementary school teachers used to wear. She was cordial, too; so far from the abrasive, bounty-hunter types that Douglass had been so far introduced to.

If this marshal thing ever falls through, you can always dance for me. It was like Douglass to think the craziest thoughts at a time like this, if only to lessen the torment. And he made the same assessment with his eyes, taking a slow, slithery evaluation of blondie's features. In the meantime, the other marshal, stiff, with a medium build, led the way through a door into the jail until all three of them stood before an elevated, glass-enclosed operations center. Something like box office seats for a basketball game. There was an intercom system through which the marshals made their representations, sliding some papers and identifications through a slot in the wall. After the paperwork was signed, the marshals took a receipt in return, and just like that the transaction was complete; Douglass was passed and delivered to the hands of the Passaic County Sheriff's Department.

From one facility to another, the difference was as clear as black and white. From the moment that the door closed behind the marshals, Douglass was ordered around and manhandled like a runaway slave. Actually, slave masters would have been kinder; even if wielding a stinging leather whip. Within minutes, a 9-foot tall giant began barking orders. He had the uniform and a sheriff's badge . . . he had dark hair, was clean shaven, and there were those bigger-than-life hands. Douglass would never forget this guy, because of how he grabbed him. Douglass didn't dare voice his disapproval, but he was surely thinking of how his father always grabbed him up when he was younger.

"TAKE OFF YOUR SNEAKERS AND BELT, AND PUT YOUR HANDS UP AGAINST THE WALL." There was a small, plastic bin on the table nearby. A sign inside said "PUT PROPERTY HERE." Everything was unquestionable and clear. No misunderstandings, as though this had been exercised a million times in the past.

On the wall, there were a few sets of handprints. They were large, as if the titan-sheriff was the one who buried his hands into a bucket of red paint and slapped his palms on the offyellow wall three times in a row. There were also directions and orders (blown up and printed) and meant for anyone to understand, apparently prepared for all languages and I.Q. levels.

So tall was the giant sheriff that he had to bend down low in order to execute his procedures. He first frisked Douglass, placing his hands on his shoulders, then gliding them along the outline of his arms, torso, outer and inner thighs, and ankles. The sheriff attached a plastic wristband with the prisoner's name and date of birth in permanent marker. It was similar to a hospital patient's ID bracelet. From one of many cubby holes, with varying sizes of blue, laceless skips, the sheriff pulled out a 9¹/₂ pair and tossed them to the floor to be worn. Another grab from another cubby, and he flung a Ziploc bag of items on the table. Douglass still had his palms on the wall, doing whatever he was instructed to do. Still he could peek or at least sense the sheriff's activities. Meanwhile, behind the glass there were uniformed men and women flipping switches, ruffling through papers and answering phones. Some black, some white, and some Hispanic, everybody back there was a busybody.

Douglass was asked to sign a property sheet. Then, with a copy of the same, he was handed the Ziploc bag of hygiene needs (toothpaste, toothbrush and comb) and directed down a hallway to a door. The sheriff stepped ahead of him and with one of many keys on a brass ring, unlocked the door. Douglass intuitively stepped through and the door was slammed impersonally behind him. In the room alone, Douglass was left to vegetate in an atmosphere of grimy, pissy cement walls and floors. There was no natural light, just fluorescent tubes that glared from high above. Scores of graffiti signatures and messages were either inscribed with a pencil, scratched in with a sharp object or burned in with matches all across the wall. Similar inscriptions were marked into a trail of wood benches which ran the perimeter of the room. A stainless steel toilet-sink combination, a coinless payphone and an adjacent door with a thick glass portal were the only other luxuries in the room.

A payphone!!!

"Hi, baby. Are you alright? Where are you?" Mechelle's was the compassionate voice that Douglass longed to hear. Although she was far away, the phone made it seem that she was standing before him—a taste of the world he'd been taken from.

"I'm okay. I'm in Passaic, New Jersey. Got a pen? I'll give you the address." Douglass reviewed the receipt he'd been given as Mechelle scrambled for a pen and paper. Douglass relayed the information, asked for a $25 money order to be mailed out, and he left it at that. No mention of bail or the circumstances of the case. Nothing about his current enslavement.

But Mechelle had words for *him*.

"Douglass, everyone's sayin' you killed Moet."

"Moet? And whaddaya mean, *everybody*?"

"I mean . . . well, it was on the TV, in the newspapers and on radio 'n stuff. People are just sayin' stuff." Mechelle sounded distraught and unsure.

"Mechelle, that's not *everybody*. That's the press. But at least, now I know who this Nadine Butler is."

"Yeah. That's Moet's real name. I . . . uh . . . Douglass? What's happening here? How long you think you'll be in there? Will they let you go? Can I see you?" Mechelle was obviously upset, looking for something tangible. Douglass's voice was her only form of hope.

"Easy, baby. Just relax. That's the best way to handle this. With a clear mind. Let me work this out and you'll see. Everything'll be alright. We just have to be patient and . . . and . . . Mechelle, just look out for things for me, okay? I'll be fine. Love ya." Mechelle hung on to every word. Wanting more. Trying to draw a full picture. But when he hung up, all she could do was cry.

Demetrius walked into 950 North, startling Mechelle. She felt so alone and nervous that even his entrance caught her off guard. She was in tears on the living room couch at the time, thinking about Douglass, about her baby issues and about her future. She knew that she'd have to stop dancing soon, and now she couldn't stop thinking about the *worst*-case scenario regarding Douglass's arrest—she didn't want to be a statistic; another single parent raising a child. She was sure that such a circumstance was harder than it was supposed to be, and these ideas hurt her the most. More tears.

Demetrius sat by and embraced her, consoling her as a friend. It helped, but it wouldn't erase Mechelle's frustrations and tensions. Mechelle; the distressed pregnant woman.

"Boss, you got my word. I ain't had nuttin' to do wit dat murder at da club." Tony was wide-eyed and filled with fear. His arms were flailing as he begged for understanding from the Capo of the Bianco family. Tony's memories of the Capo's deeds—executions that left dismembered bodies—were the only images that he could think about. He knew just how easily and how quickly that he too could meet Doctor Death.

The Capo was a Ralph Cramden look-a-like. And, like the *Honeymooner*, he also had a hot temper. For now, he took a breath, as if to inhale some surplus faith for dealing with his underling.

"Well . . . I'll tell you what. You's been workin' dat dare Paradise club for almost a year now. All we's got is trouble from the joint. And all for *what?* A fuckin' *hoop shoot game?* And now the Bianco name is all over TV again. But now we're tied in with these . . . these . . . *moolies!* Who da fuck are dees Gilmore people? How we get caught up in their shit if a you's didn't have nuttin' ta do wit it?" Now, the Capo was visibly red.

"Boss, I'm tellin' ya dat this thing is all a fluke. It's got nuttin' ta do wit us. Plus, I put almost two years in this project. I's close enough to get my . . . *our* teeth in the piggy bank. I'm startin' to learn how dis thing ticks. I don't think we should blow this here for . . ."

"You don't think? You don't think? No! You **don't** fuckin' think!" The Capo got up from the crate he was sitting on. The warehouse was dark and a hanging light bulb still cast light on him as he approached Tony. There were other shadows, many of them standing at certain points inside the cavernous facility.

"Gimme your gun." Tony froze like stone while the Capo came closer still.

"I said gimme your fuckin' gun!" Now Tony's stomach quivered and his heart palpitated, almost jumping inside of his chest cavity.

"Alright, fuck it. I got my own." And before Tony could move, the Capo reached in his belt for a pearl-handled 9-millimeter and pointed it at Tony's head.

"Boss, please, **boss!**" Tony's accent was thick as he pleaded, with pearls of sweat beginning to form on his brow.

"Lemme tell you sumptin', Antonio . . . *I* made your fuckin ass. **Me!** You either produce, or I'll do da job myself. Then I'll do **you!**"

—the Capo was still pointing the gun at Tony's forehead—

"Now, git the fuck outta here." The Capo busted a shot off into the air. "*Git!*"

There must have been a dozen earners standing ready to

carry out a Capo order. His gumbada were on balconies, ranges, and on top of freight and cargo shipments, prepared to put their firearms to use. Everyone looked forward to the chance of becoming the next made man. Tony knew this, and partially pissed himself while leaving the Jersey warehouse, back first, his eyes rolling around scared and erratic like pinballs. Once he was outside in the night air and safe from the spray of bullets, Tony leaned up against the warehouse in total relief, wiping sweat from his brow. All he could think about was how he was gonna infiltrate the Gilmore empire.

Absent Minded

Wade's phone was buzzing and he rushed through the squad room to pick it up.

"Hey, Wade? Ken." Wade already recognized Ken's voice and that he was on his cell phone. What he *didn't* know was how much talking Ken was going to do before he got to the point.

"How are you, Stevens? How is the series going?" Wade even knew that New York was up 2 to 1, and that they were away for the next 2 games in Texas.

"We're almost there. I think I'm starting in Texas. My arm is working *magic*!"

"Okay . . . I'll go find a bookie. To what do I owe this pleasure?" Wade had magic of his own, more than ready to move the conversation right along.

"Well, there was something else I remembered." Wade thought to himself, remembering how the *last* thing Ken *suddenly* recalled was a damned bombshell. Maybe now Ken saw who really shot Kennedy?

"You once asked me if I knew anyone of Moet's friends . . . Debbie? Remember?" Wade controlled his temper, sure not to shit himself.

"Uh-huh . . . and?"

"Well, I didn't remember her name when you brought it up before because . . . well, you know how I'm not good with names . . . how I have to give them nick . . ."

"Ken . . . Ken! Yes! I *know*. Now, cut to the chase—" Wade had to catch himself; keeping his voice at a minimum so that nobody would be in his business; his *case*. "—Debbie. Please. Tell me about *Debbie!*"

"Well, I took her home one night when Moet brought her along to a game."

"Took her home. You took her *home*? Where? *Where!*" Wade was answering faster than he was thinking, clumsy and desperately searching for his pen and note pad.

"Well . . . I don't exactly know the address. But I'll never forget the location. See, they took me in the house with them. There were all of these African things . . ."

"*What?* What do you mean you *don't know the address?* But you *do* know the location? Listen, Ken. I want you to listen to me very carefully—Debbie may have been the last person to see Moet alive. Nobody knows where she lives. If you have that information we might be able to find Debbie and she may help us find Moet's murderer. Now please. Take your time and think about this."

"See, I never forget directions. Never. I *could* actually take you there." Ken seemed a little unsure with his own words.

"How soon could we do that?"

"The game comes back to New York in three days . . ."

"That's not soon enough. Give me your cell number again. I'll call you back." Wade reminded Ken not to ignore his calls like he had surely done to so many others who'd fed into his celebrity. "And, please . . . leave your cell phone on at all times."

Wade made a call down to Audrey. She was the communications specialist at the 45th. He had her initiate a process of elimination to hopefully find the location of the phone number left by Debbie on Moet's answering machine.

"Audrey Starr," answered a vibrant voice.

"Hey, Starr. It's Wade. Any luck on the digits for the Paradise case?"

"I thought you were off of that case, Walter?"

"Yeah . . . but I, I got a hunch. *Anything?*"

"I tried every one of ninety-nine combinations. There were

two people named Debbie. One was sixty years old, telling me her health problems and complaints about her electric bill. Another was a thirteen-year-old in Catholic school. Everyone else wasn't home; the phone was disconnected, or they just didn't know anyone named Debbie. I *do* know that the origin of the number is in Forrest Hills."

"Yeah? Great, Starr. You're a gem." Wade hung up and no sooner did he pick up the receiver to dial Ken back.

"Stevens?"

"Yep."

"It's Wade. Does Forrest Hills ring a bell?"

"Yeah. That's near the LaGuardia Airport, right?"

"Yes. Ken, don't tell me you already knew she lived out near—*Never mind.* If I call you back on a cell from the airport, can you direct me from memory?"

"*Can I?* Like a homing device on a missile!"

"Okay. Look for my call at six this evening."

"I'll be at the game. But I'll have my cell. Holla at me." Wade heard the beep indicating that Ken had hung up. He imagined Ken on the pitcher's mound, winding up for a pitch and then stalling in effort to retrieve a ringing cell phone in his back pocket. He would have laughed at his own imagery, except just as Wade was hanging up the receiver, the phone rang again.

"Detective Wade."

"Hello, Walter. This is Brenda from Channel Five News."

"Oh . . . hi, Bren." Suddenly swallowing, waiting for a verbal bashing. Still picturing her pretty black hair and aerobic curves.

"Wade, don't give me that '*oh hi*' stuff. I have a couple of bones to pick with you." A hint of fire in her voice, Wade puckered his lips and folded his arms, wondering what a "couple" meant. He already knew that he'd stood her up for dinner a few weeks back. Brenda Feather. The 90's version of Jayne Kennedy's looks and critical, investigative tact.

"You know . . . if I thought you were a scoundrel like some other men, I'd never have given you the time of day, you . . . you . . ." Wade stretched his eyelids in anticipation, but cut her off before she cut too deep.

"Wait a minute, love. This case has been kicking my ass."

"Not since the FBI took over it hasn't." Brenda delivered a paper cut to get shit started, wounding his ego.

"Alright, lady. That'll be enough of that." Wade wrinkled his forehead in a scolding manner.

"Sorry," she recanted. "I was hurt, Walter. All dressed up and nowhere to go. Plus, I haven't been stood up since high school."

"Probably because you've been seeing those know-nothing, do-nothing, ain't-never-gonna-be-nothings that don't have a life. But yet, they have enough time to run yours."

"Okay, touché." Brenda smirked to loosen the atmosphere between them. "Listen. You walked right past me last week at the New York game. You couldn't have missed me. It was a bright day and before any of the major confusion started. Don't you remember? I was across the street from the police lineup. What's up with that?"

Wade thought about all of the fever outside of the stadium and didn't remember her.

"Sorry, Bren. I didn't see you."

"Wade, what's going on? What's happening with Ken? There's news footage here showing you entering the clubhouse and also jetting with Ken in his truck." Wade smiled at himself remembering how descriptive and precise Brenda was—the reason he was attracted to her in the first place; besides her youth and beauty, that is. She continued pushing buttons.

"How come you're his personal escort? Is he in trouble? Threats? *What?*" The investigator in Brenda was backing Wade up to the wall.

"Bre, don't jump the gun. Easy, woman. There's nothing going on with Stevens . . ."

"Then why are you with him?" Wade kept *personal escort* in his mind—and rode with it.

"Yeah. Personal escort. That's it. I'm hauling players around these days, ever since I've been removed from certain murder cases. You know, gotta think about job security nowadays. Listen, love. I'm working on something hot . . ."

"Hot? Hot like what?" Wade could imagine Brenda's eyes flexing to their limits. He took a deep breath, knowing he put some fire on her gasoline. Time for a damp cloth.

"I'll let you know. You'll be second to know. Sorry about

dinner. Soon, okay. Gotta go. Bye." Wade's heartbeat slowed quickly. He felt like he'd escaped a croc's bite.

While Wade was feeling relief, Brenda cringed. *Wade an escort? Stevens is bigger and stronger than Wade.* —Brenda's mind was churning a million ideas. — *Why the protection? Something's up. Something-is-up.* Brenda could not rest.

It was early Sunday morning and 911 emergency Control Offices were cooling from a busy Saturday night. Shots fired. Auto accidents. Family disputes. Fights and burglaries. Nuisance calls. Not to mention that in a city of 7 million residents, every real emergency brings an average of 10 calls to 911 Central. To aggregate that, close to 3,000 (so-called) emergencies take place in New York City each night. It was just about 6am, and Dawn, operator 376, was ready to head home. At 5:56 a call came in. Dawn replaced her headset over her baseball cap to answer the call and simultaneously pressed a red button to record the particulars.

"Hi, this is Holly and I'm headed up a hill, like on east Ninety-sixth Street, heading west, and, like this red Blazer is going like the opposite way. Like, towards the East River. But just like *totally* kept going. I mean, like, I'm pulled over now in my dad's Lex, ya know, he let me borrow it for the weekend. But I'm, like, looking back down the hill and like this is *so* cool—there's, like, this opening down near the FDR. I think that truck, like, totally went through the wall and into the water."

Dawn had rushed to her supervisor's office with her notes from the call and her boss reviewed the tape. Meanwhile, three other calls came in that gave similar accounts. Dawn had already taken action. EMS and NYPD were contacted with a 96th Street location and a possible auto accident as the incident.

Down under the FDR, just a half hour after the 911 call, police units, fire trucks, EMS and news trucks were on the scene. Two tow trucks were positioned near the edge of the road with cables hooked onto the front and rear of a nearly demolished Blazer. As the wreckage emerged from the river, with water spilling from all parts of the vehicle, officers on location could see that the entire front end was destroyed. A body of a male in his 40's was floating inside the cabin amidst his own blood and water from the East River. The front windshield was partially shattered from where the driver's head had smashed into it. There was still hair stuck in the glass over the steering wheel. With his face full of lacerations and his body mangled and torn, even the emergency teams on duty, with their Jaws of Life tool cutting through the metal and steel, would not be able to identify him. But one bystander in particular knew exactly who it was, as he lifted a lighter to the cigarette stuck to his lip, cupped his hands and inhaled. He was celebrating a successful slaughter. Just to think, all he had to do was cut a hose here and there. And now, Bobby was gone too.

Detective Wade was revved up. He was so sure he was onto something, and he acted accordingly. After updating Chief Washington, he jumped in a newer unmarked sedan and headed for Queens.

CHAPTER FOURTEEN

Reality

"In everyone's life comes a time when some ultimate challenge arrives. It comes fast and furious and without warning. It comes at a time when all of our resources are tested. A time when life seems unfair. A time when our faith, our values, our patience, our compassion, and our ability to persist are all pushed to the limit and beyond. Some have used such tests as opportunities for growth; others have turned away and allowed these experiences to destroy their hopes."

—Dr. Dennis Kimbro

In Jail Without the Bail

The hours progressed, slipping away like globs of hot, thick molten gold, until Douglass became more and more a part of that so-called "*ultimate challenge*." The storm had already swept him up and out of his own world. Unfair though it may have been, he was now in jail, far away from home, with nothing to lean on but his own purely fabricated faith. In the course of events, if there was such a thing as a great challenge, then Passaic County Jail was it. Douglass was originally in that holding cell alone. But the morning moved into afternoon, and with it came more and more prisoners, until the room filled to capacity. *Beyond* capacity. At most, the room was comfortable for 20 or 25 people. Thirty-five, if they were standing shoulder to shoulder. However, buses continued to drop off men, as if there was free fried chicken being given away. Eventually, more than 70 prisoners were sandwiched in the cell. No cigarettes were permitted in the holding cell, and someone even had the nerve to put a non smoking sign on the wall above the door. But there was smoking anyway. With one vent high above the door, the ventilation was the equivalent of all seventy-five men breathing through a straw at one time. Meanwhile, the various body odors from the day's local arrests created a stew of sordid, wretched vapors. Everyone, whether nefarious and boastful or quiet and considerate, contributed to the busy atmosphere. Five hours passed while the heat and the hunger in the cell continued cooking. Tempers began to surface, as food became more and more of a priority. Men began banging on one door or the other, wanting to irritate the overseer. The banging, the angry, conflicting conversations and the yelps for a staff member represented the worst conditions imaginable. Even a kennel of animals would be considered calm as compared to this mess. The fights over the phone; the want for elbow room; all of it creating that deafening noise.

After one man fainted, and after two fistfights (one that left an older man unconscious), prisoners were released from the room five by five. They were paraded to another small room and strip-searched. That is, every piece of clothing or thread was to be removed as the corrections officer conducted with routine directives.

"Raise your arms above your head. Open your mouth wide. Lift your tongue. Back of your hands. Lift your nuts. Turn around. Lift your foot. Now the other foot. Bend over and spread 'em." Douglass silently wondered how a man could deal with looking at so many hairy, crusty assholes, and still manage a peaceful sleep with so many of those images in their mental registers.

During and following the strip search, officers prodded and probed prisoners, then escorted them to the next room where interviews were held for each. Questions. *Good health? Ever have diseases? Contemplating suicide? Tattoo? Psychological problems?* Next, on to the fingerprint room. Forms were filled out. Next of kin in case of death. Home address and phone number. After fingerprints, Douglass dipped his inked-up fingers into a vat of grease—it looked and felt like lard, except it wasn't. It was the type that auto mechanics used. He rinsed off in a nearby sink and grabbed a few paper towels before being directed, still naked, into another large room. This time, there were only three walls. A wall of iron bars confined the men until everybody was completed with their processing. At least the room allowed for free-flowing air, thought Douglass. And once the cage filled to capacity, there was even another, and then another to offer relief as men continued waiting for food. At least the men weren't squeezed together like they were earlier; not a pretty thought with no clothes on.

By 10pm, there was still no food. The cages were emptied one at a time as three men at a time were led to a cove with three showers. The water was continuous, running on cold only. A corrections officer stood by to assure that each person got under the water. Once assured, a towel was handed over along with an unreasonable amount of clothing. Then a nurse reviewed each prisoner, taking blood and administering tuberculosis tests. On to another cage. More barking dogs in the distance. The food finally came. A Styrofoam tray of two fish patties, a hamburger roll, a bag of potato chips and two cups of Kool Aid for each man. Restless and anticipating a next move, the group now listened to a roll call and shot out into the hallway when called. Once you were called, you were to grab a mattress from a big pile, a blanket, and a sheet—no pillows. A single line filed through the hallway, making their pilgrimage into a day room. Douglass was reminded of scenes from *The Planet of the Apes*, where humans were held in massive cages, left to scramble and cope amongst themselves. In a similar fashion, the caged gates at Passaic ran almost 20 feet to the ceiling and they were wide like a zoo exhibit of a lion's den. A section of the cage was unlocked and slid aside, while the newest additions instinctively straggled through the opening to claim one of the available bed spaces. There were already close to 50 men in the room, having staked out the best bunks. About 30 tri-level bunk beds were situated through the room. Bolted to the floor. The top bunks were only feet from the ceiling. Meanwhile, air and noise flowed freely from the hallway and through the bars.

A row of toilets, sinks and showers remained a busy part of the room; a corner that was visible to everyone, regardless of whether a man was taking a shit or shamelessly jerking off—no privacy.

With no other choice, Douglass quickly adjusted, maneuvering his mattress to an available top bunk. He climbed half-way up and dressed his bed with the sheet and blanket. Then he climbed up some more to rest himself. Finally with a soft surface to sit, Douglass crossed his legs and observed the large room. The different values of men were evident. Some were loud and unruly. Others were quiet and calculating. Most were black. A handful of whites. Prison workers (also known as orderlies) walked through the hallway outside the cage at various times, while individuals who recognized them ran up to the bars to beg and plead for cigarettes. When C.O.'s, nurses or counselors came through the hallway and stopped by the cage, prisoners ran up still with other requests. Forced to survive with bare essentials, inconvenience and desperation encouraged many to crave any resource they could get their hands on; it was a pattern of behavior that seemed like a frequent practice, and Douglass was quick to stay out of the rat race. An institution nurse announced her presence and a line of men quickly grouped to receive medication of this kind or that. Skinny, fat, tall, short, young, and old. Men were detained for almost any infraction; jumping bail, spousal abuse, traffic violations, probation issues or even failure to pay child support. There was no shortage of drug possession cases; more or less the majority of the population.

"What, you think you special, nigga?"

The braided fool, Douglass told himself. *And, pleeease: I know he's not talkin to—*

"Yo, lil' nigga. I'm talkin' to *you.*"

Douglass had been reading a used *Newark Star Ledger* when the braided dude approached the bunk. He tried to ignore him, but the guy shook the bunk.

I thought these were bolted to the floor?

Not to cause any conflict in the room, and considering he was a stranger to the region, Douglass ignored the nigga part of the inquiry.

"You want somethin'?" asked Douglass. He said it in a way to show he was being irritated.

"Yeah, nigga. I'm talkin' to you. How come you ain't get up from your bunk for the issue?"

Douglass twisted his face, not even interested in making sense of this guy's question. He at least knew what issue the fool meant.

"I ain't interested, man."

"Naw, fuck that, yo! If you ain't gonna get yo shit, then get up and get mine." Braids crunched his body in such a way that showed he was ready to fight. His jumpsuit sleeves were already rolled back, and the leg cuff on the right was rolled up LL Cool J-style. "Exactly! Nigga, next time they come to the gate for *whatever,* you betta get mine. *Word!*"

Douglass realized that he was quite out of place. He noticed that while most were locals with state and municipal cases, he was from New York; a federal prisoner. He was out of his jurisdiction, mismatched amongst a crew of riff-raffs, with no ties to any "buddies" or "homies." So, this was his defining moment; the instant that everyone who was watching would judge him by. He was being "tested."

Thinking quickly, Douglass remembered his days in the Marine Corps, how in boot camp he was forced to battle guys twice his size with a pugle-stick. When it was his turn to step up, he was already preceded by "Tiny," one of the biggest in the platoon. Tiny was seething and full of electricity from the past five fights he'd won—all of his contenders knocked down and dismissed from the pit.

That's how Douglass was looking at this guy in Passaic, as if he was Tiny. Sure, Douglass was a foot and a half shorter than Tiny, but he also saw the guys that Tiny knocked down. Douglass decided rather contemptuously that he was NOT gonna end up like them. And just the same, he was also NOT gonna be dragged out of Passaic jail like they did another guy.

First, to disarm Tiny—and this braided one—Douglass fixed his face. He put on a face of defeat; as though there were no way out of this.

"You're right. I'm bein' selfish," said Douglass as he climbed down from the bunk. He didn't want to seem like any threat, and that's just what his expression showed: submission. "Anything you need, just let me know. In fact, I got some commissary money comin', if you want some of that."

The guy turned around and looked at the certain audience that he attracted. He couldn't believe how easy this was!

"Yeah-yeah-yeah, that's right, lil' nigga. Mark ass, nigga. Matter fact, I want *all* your commissary."

"Aw, damn, man. Could ya leave me a little money? I mean, I do wanna get some real toothpaste, instead of the crap they give us."

Boldly, the guy turned to his homies and said, "You hear this mark-ass nigga? I should make him my fuckin' girl."

He had to go and say that? Douglass couldn't wait another second. The fool didn't notice that Douglass had no socks on—he had slipped them off before he got down from the bunk so that his traction on the cement floor would be better; better than the socks he wore; socks that he might slip in once he—

That was it. Braided fool folded his arms. And Douglass couldn't think of a weaker position. In the meantime, Douglass had already measured his distance from his victim. He wanted just enough room so that when he swung his left arm, the tip of his fingers would barely touch his opponent's nose. And the left swing was only a diversion so that—

Douglass spun around; his left hand clipped the tip of the dude's nose, and his entire body wound up, spinning still, with momentum enough for that rock-hard backside of his right hand to connect with the side of his victim's face. Douglass was hyped now, with the adrenaline of a lion. He didn't let up either. His backhand sent the dude crashing onto the metal picnic tables—the ones that were too few to seat the amount of prisoners in the room—but his right roundhouse kick was the blow that had to *really* hurt since that went right to the guy's groin. Another kick was delivered to the waist, and before that foot touched the floor again, the other foot was already attacking, catching the opposite side of the waist. Both kicks leveled the guy out so that he slithered to the cement floor, defeated. Douglass was in a semi-horse stance now, waiting for another challenger to step up and substitute for the braided one.

"I don't want no trouble, but I swear to God, you'll be right on the floor with 'im!" Douglass didn't believe his own hype and how it was taking over his lips, making him challenge the whole room? Nobody budged, but Douglass could see one or two smiles in the room. Perhaps he did the right thing? There was no time to assess things. It was midnight now, and the barking neared. Within minutes, two German shepherds were accompanied by a band of uniformed correctional officers. The gate was unlocked and slid aside.

"COUNT TIME!" shouted the head officer. He was labeled and tagged with various emblems and stripes, decorating his black baseball jacket. Maybe he was a confused war veteran. Douglass couldn't tell how the head officer had accumulated such merits and awards. He wondered what the test was in the prison environment that might substantiate such honors; and hadn't he just earned them?

Meanwhile, as the head man stood to the side and parked his foot up on a stainless steel bench, the other officers posted themselves at various areas of the room. Like clockwork, prisoners were busy climbing down from bunk beds and moving towards an F-Troop formation in the center of the room. Just then, the head man noticed Douglass's victim aching on the floor. The dogs were still barking and breathing through open muzzles, with tongues wagging and salivating, and their eyes zeroed in on all sudden movements by prisoners and guards alike. Leashes were tugged to quiet the barking, but it seemed as if it was all staged to support the illusion of immense danger.

"What the fuck are you doin'? Git your ass in the lineup!" ordered the head slavemaster. "Are you bums ever gonna learn?" A few seconds passed as braids cringed in pain, lifting himself up to his feet to stand in line. "Well, then . . . when I call your name you are to answer 'HERE!' You are to show your wristband to the officer, and move between the racks!" The names were rattled off and prisoners followed the instructions, squeezing between the bunk beds in lines of ten. The racks were already close to one another, leaving a space about a foot and a half wide. Nonetheless, prisoners followed orders and stood still and quiet until every name was called. Afterwards, the group of drill instructor initiators swaggered out of the room, closed the gate behind them and moved out of sight. That's when prisoners scrambled back to their bunks. Douglass included. He wouldn't be anybody's *girl* tonight, or *any other night* for that matter.

That first night at Passaic County Jail was hard for Douglass to sleep through, since he had to watch his back. He wasn't sure if any of the guy's friends would try and stab him in his sleep. Before he knew it morning broke. His head was dizzied by the morning hustle at 5am.

"CHOW!"

The signal for food quickly triggered a habitual response. Each groping prisoner who chose to eat struggled to join the line, wiping sleep from their eyes, showing their wristbands to authenticate the transaction. Once the name was checked on the officer's printout, that prisoner was issued a tray. Douglass's first breakfast was filling. A bowl of Froot Loops, an apple, a slice of chocolate cake and coffee. Then back to a sleep that wouldn't last long.

"COUNT!" In came the dogs and the whole F-Troop routine. Same as the night before. Back to sleep.

"CHOW!"

"DOCTOR!"

"COUNT!"

"NURSE!"

One announcement after the next, barked loud enough so that everyone could wake up and step to the gate. At midnight, the last count was conducted, marking another day of the madness past and another one forthcoming. The experience took a little adjusting to, but the fight (or, at least, the altercation) made things so much easier for Douglass.

"Yo, that cat was a fool, anyway. I'm glad you put 'em down," said one prisoner. Douglass pretended to care about the whole situation, but for real, all he wanted to do was deal with this shit and stay alive. He tried to treat the situation as one big test in his mind—just like in boot camp—assuming how every situation, process and emotion was fabricated in an effort to "break" him. Every breathing being at Passaic was an extra in the experiment, paid to play a roll. Douglass imagined that if he could just exist, breathe and dream harmlessly, he would pass the test. At certain instances he was so anticipating the outcome of the challenge and how he'd end up the victor, that he found himself elated and overjoyed by the experience. Day by day, meal by meal and count by count, the regimen became redundant. To break the monotony, Douglass wrote songs, poems and did his best to dream. He dreamed of the future, and of better circumstances and improvements in his life. He thought about past relationships. He even thought about Moet.

"I realize that, Hammer, there's not much evidence. Tell me something I *don't* know. You've been with the Bureau long enough to know that we've squeezed convictions out of people with less evidence than *this*." Walsh and Hammer were slouching a bit in their vehicle, parked across the street from Fool's Paradise. It was mid-evening. Just about the time their man Tony showed up.

"We've got this Gilmore guy on tape, angry as hell at the murder victim. We've got a known mob figure walking into the family establishment numerous times. We can push some of these dancers to turn against Gilmore . . ."

—Walsh was flipping through black and white photos of various women, fully dressed, walking into the club entrance—

"You're not new to this. Keep the guy stressed up in Passaic, away from family, friends and his power base, and I say we get a confession. Maybe even before we can convene a grand jury or get an indictment. I see a plea bargain happening before Christmas. This guy's gonna bring in the New Year with a rack of time on his hands. My kid may have grandchildren when he gets out of the pen!" Hammer was floored by his partner's determination to pin Gilmore. He wanted to get his teeth in on the case, to really secure a conviction; but there was nothing to go on.

"Well, Walsh . . . you just tell me what's next on the agenda. I'm with you."

"We keep tailing the Biancos, Tony, the capos and the other wise guys. We get the links together and form the chain, capisci?" Walsh was being facetious with the pseudo-Italian accent, but dead serious at the same time.

"Hey, there's Tony now." Hammer took the cue and began snapping away with his camera. Moments later Hammer straightened his blazer and baseball cap, to take his turn patronizing Fool's Paradise.

Debbie's Trail

Wade turned down the car radio and dialed Ken on one of the Motorola cell phones he borrowed from the precinct.

"Ken." Ken Stevens picked up on the third ring, answering in his usual arrogant way.

"It's Wade . . . I'm near the airport on Ninty-fourth Street."

"Near the Enterprise car rental?"

"Not yet . . . but I can get there fast enough." Wade swung a U-turn, ran a traffic light, and was soon approaching the block where the rental franchise was located. Still juggling the cell phone between his shoulder and ear.

"Okay, Wade. Let's do this fast. There's one out, man on first with two strikes on the batter."

"Yep."

"Go straight, as if you were headed for the Marriot Hotel. There's a long strip. It should be dark with no street lights, right?"

"Right. What, do you have a photographic memory? *Wait* . . . don't answer that. You're doing good . . . okay. I'm near a circle near the . . . I can see the Marriot." Wade was excited.

"Okay. Make a quick right turn."

"Halfway into the circle?"

"Yeah. Before the hotel. There's only one turn to make."

"A short hill?"

"Yep . . . go up about three blocks." Wade could hear a crack sound behind Ken's voice. "Yeah!" Ken yelled away from the phone's mouthpiece.

"What happened?"

"A double. Man on first and third. Still one out."

"Okay, I made a left."

"Alright. Go one block . . ." Behind Ken's voice, Wade could hear Ken being summoned. Ken was soon to be on deck to bat. "And make another left. Hey—I gotta hurry"

"Okay . . ." Wade pushed the accelerator, speeding down the residential street to challenge a stop sign. After the brief pause, he hooked a quick left turn at the intersection. "I made the left. How far down?"

"Not far. There are a few houses, maybe three of 'em on your right. It's the brick house. One level, in the center of the block. There's a beat-up van in the driveway."

"I see it. A gate out front? Black?" Wade's heart was beating . . . thumping inside his chest as though *he* was the one to step up to bat.

"Yeah. And the grass—"

CRACK! (The crowd put up a load roar.)

"—is unkempt. Hey, I gotta go. Good luck." The line went dead. Wade pulled the car to the right and then hooked a U-turn so that he was across from 99-01 95th Street. He rolled up further and parked. The street was infrequent with passing cars going in either direction every few minutes. A pedestrian was just passing the house, nobody else in sight.

It was 7pm when Wade popped out of his sedan, an unmarked car he grabbed from the station. He approached the gate, a waist-high division between the sidewalk and the property line. No lock or bolt. He pushed it open and made his way up the path, to the stoop and up to the front door of the house. There was a large bay window to the right of the front door. Some distinguished, African sculptures could be seen set on the window sill inside. Wade pressed the buzzer. The light inside of its small, plastic housing blinked off and then back on when it was released. He could hear a chime inside the door, and he leaned over to look over towards the window, expecting to see a head emerge. When there was no sign of life, he looked over to the van in the driveway. It had flat tires at the front and rear. There was visible rust about the edges, and dirt had accumulated next to the wheels. Wade guessed that it hadn't been driven in 18 months. Again he pressed the buzzer. And again the chimes sounded. Another moment passed. No answer. He looked up to the dark blue sky for some answer, and when it didn't respond, the detective followed Mr. and Mrs. Two Feet around towards the van and the rear of the house. He felt for his nickel-plated .45, pulling it out under the darkening sky. He checked the chamber and the magazine, then he replaced it carefully in its nylon holster. Further into the rear of the residence, Wade could see beyond the property line. Just over the fence there was a schoolyard. To his left, a screen door was propped open by a chair on the back porch. Surprisingly, the back door was also open, leaving a clear view of the kitchen. Wade announced himself.

"Hello . . . *hello*?" He stepped into the doorway, half curious and half expecting trouble. Door opened and nobody home? That would spell trouble in most areas of New York's inner-city. Wade gave the situation the benefit of the doubt and let his sixth sense guide him. He patted his weapon for security and stepped partway into the kitchen, blending into the eerie silence. A few more steps brought him into a hallway. And at the end of the hallway, Wade could see the front door. The home was a small one. A door was left open, partially blocking Wade's view of the rest of the hallway. His next step caught a cat's tail.

Screech! The cat clung to Wade's ankle until its claws dug into the nylon holster that secured a 9-millimeter under his trousers, just below his calf. Wade instantly lifted his foot to shake the cat off. The cat pulled away, running down the hallway like a doped-up rabbit. Just as Wade placed his foot back to the carpet, happy just to have escaped imminent pain, two arms reached from around the door; one of them reached behind Wade's neck, the other extended like a steel barricade across his waist. Before Wade could see the body that mastered the movements, he was tumbling through the air, flipping headfirst, until he completed a 270-degree turn, landing flat on his back. A man was suddenly standing over him with a firm grip on his Adam's apple and his foot on his right arm. Another arm was cocked, ready to deliver a lullaby blow.

"P-police." Wade managed to breathe the word with the little air left in his system and a dizzied state of mind.

"Lemme see a badge. And you'd better not make any sudden moves, either!" The man in control was grinding the words through tightened lips and chin, drenched in a sweaty tank top and shorts. Ready for action. Wade cautiously . . . slowly . . . pulled his wallet out with his free hand. The man was satisfied to see a badge and gave Wade a hand to help him up.

"Is this Giuliani's new program for quality of life or something? You guys just come in without being invited?" The homeowner asked this while wiping away beads of perspiration.

"Well . . . ungh . . ." Wade was still trying to catch his composure, stretching the knots out of his neck and back. "Actually, not too far from it," he said with his humor still very much intact. "I'm Detective Wade from the four-five—a little out of my jurisdiction, but NYPD, nonetheless . . . and you? I already know your last name is·*Lee!*"

"Name's Danni. And I . . . ah, live here? Own the house. Pay the taxes. Head of security . . . you see?" Danni escorted Wade as if the detective was a nursing home out-patient. They entered the living room, where the bay window was built in. A bevy of African artifacts and furniture also set a strong theme in the room. Wade could see the cat he recently assaulted hiding under the couch. Her eyes were cutting through Wade like he was soft lunch meat.

"Can I get you a drink, Detective?"

"Sure. Do you have, uh . . . *rubbing* alcohol?" Both men laughed while Danni went to the kitchen for some orange juice. Danni accommodated Wade while acknowledging that *yes*, Debbie had lived there at one time. He talked about the relationship between Debbie and Jackie, Jackie's mom and himself. But the relations between Jackie and Debbie somehow hit a dead end when Debbie disappeared with her belongings one day. No note. No calls. No nothing. Danni explained that Jackie and her mom were off on a mother-daughter retreat in the Poconos. Danni became as helpful as possible, feeling that there was some serious business at hand. He eventually went into Jackie's room to fetch a personal address book.

"Jackie didn't appreciate Debbie's desertion at all," Danni explained. "So she's been on a silent trip for the past eight months or so. She hasn't tried to contact her—in a hussy about her just up and leaving after Jackie extended every hospitality to her. Oh . . . here's the number, and even the address in Chicago." Danni was somewhat apprehensive about just handing the book over.

"May I ask you what Debbie's into?"

"Can't really say yet. But she's wrapped tight into the center of a murder investigation. *My* murder investigation. I just want to ask her some questions."

"Is there something I can do to help?" Danni was pulling his tank top up to wipe his face dry from hours of training in his basement.

"Well, for one thing, you can teach me that move you did on me a moment ago. But as for the case, I sure would appreciate you calling Debbie for me. You know, to break the ice a bit. Warm her up so I can talk to her."

"Sure. *Now?*" Danni looked over at the phone on the couch. The cat braced herself and kept an eye on the detective.

"That'd be nice. There's no time like the present." Danni went to sit beside the phone, picked up the receiver and poked at the black buttons on the inner panel while Wade sipped at the juice, still standing and stretching. He listened intently while Danni was diplomatic on the phone.

"*Her mother.*" Danni whispered with his palm over the mouthpiece. A moment later, Danni was re-acquainting with Debbie, getting deeper into a conversation.

". . . I just had to go, Danni. There were some problems that I didn't want to bring back to your home . . ."

"Nonsense, Debbie. You could have talked to us about *anything.* You're one of the family—*you know that.*" Danni gave a thumbs-up sign to Wade; even if he could hear most of the conversation. Wade returned the gesture. That motion alone pushed a button for Kissy the cat, and she raced away from the couch and frantically around the corner onto the linoleum tile in the kitchen. Wade could see how the cat almost slid into a wall on the way.

"Listen, Debbie, can we—can I come out to see you? Talk to you?" Wade with another thumbs-up signal.

"I don't know, Danni. Everything is so complicated. I really don't want you to get caught up in this stuff."

"I don't have a choice in the matter, Deb. You're caught up in it, so I'm caught up in it, too. Remember . . . family. *Okay?* Family?"

"Family." Debbie conceded and the two made plans to meet. Wade looked on, realizing that he'd just deputized Danni, now part of his one-man crew. Danni set down the cordless and re-layed the details of the call to Wade. They spoke about sched-ules, flights and the sudden, sensitive need to travel to Chicago.

David

As far as David was concerned, the night was a success. He didn't need to stretch his chances with Valerie any more than necessary. In the sequence of the *boy-gets-girl-back* phase of their relationship, Valerie was taking more time (this time) to find out more about David before she committed her body to him. She'd already been there once, and because of her whims, she got tied up with Richard, the obsessed Canadian. This time, she needed to know where David was coming from. Where was he going with this. And did he plan on taking her, or dropping her off along the way.

The two had three other dates after his jeep was vandalized outside of her crib. There was the Denzel Washington movie which got them talking about future and family over dinner at Dallas BBQ. Then there was the 4th of July rendezvous at Play-land Amusement Park in upstate New York. That was when the *boy-loses-girl* phase set in—some silly argument over how many unused ride tickets Valerie wasted. On one other occasion, David took Valerie out to Manhattan Proper Café in Cambria Heights, Queens. The comedy show was hosted by comedian and radio personality, Talent, who smacked his tongue and gums to make his trademark **CLUCK!** sound.

"Ohhh, he gets me all hot when he does that!" said Valerie. And now (weeks later) after an intimate jazz experience at Londell's Restaurant in Harlem, along with their filling south-ern fried chicken dinner, the two were satisfied and sleepy.

David kissed Valerie proper against the lips; he walked her to her door and cruised off into the midnight hour towards his loft in Brooklyn. Along the Grand Central Parkway and onto the Interborough, David picked up speed, wanting desperately to beat his sleepy eyes in a race to his soft bed. The exits passed by him in blurs. Cypress Hills; the cemetery alerted him that he was close and also reminded him to keep his eyes open for the last stretch home, or else. Then Bushwick; he had reached the end of the highway. Bright lights from another vehicle stayed in his rearview mirror for the entire trip. But David never noticed. At best, he overlooked it, not in the mood for road rage. Down Atlantic Avenue, over to Eastern Parkway, David finally pulled up to his building. David parked with the lip of his jeep reaching partially into the driveway and the rear of his vehicle still on the sidewalk.

Speaking out loud about his landlady, David said, "She could've parked her damned Fiat in the street. She *had* to know I wasn't home yet. *Bitch.*" David was too bushed to do what he wanted to—to wake her black ass up so he could get in the driveway. But he was too frustrated and drowsy to do that, much less find a space on the street. Too damned tired to even move his body, to hear him tell it. So he killed the motor and let his seat recline a little. Smooth jazz from 101.9 serenaded David into a much-deserved nap. The last thing David heard was George Duke's *"No Rhyme, No Reason."* The last thing he *felt* was his own limbs growing cold and hard. But somewhere, between the music and the cold limbs, a bullet entered the center of his face at point-blank range.

"There's a delay. See if you can get a change on the tickets. I'm gonna need another day. If you have problems, call me on my cell and I can try and use my clout with the airline."

"Ten-four, good buddy. Hope all is well." Danni heard the line go dead and wondered if Wade heard him.

Wade grabbed his windbreaker and fought the drizzle on his way to Brooklyn. Meanwhile, he and Chief Washington shared information about Wade's progress on the case. The first issue was Chicago, which he was on the way to addressing himself. The other was the death of Bobby the fisherman. It seemed probable that some sabotage was done to provoke an accident that sent him slamming into a wall before he and his vehicle took the dive into the East River. Wade was not so surprised to find that Bobby had an apartment on the side, up on 96th and York. Certain things he was already aware of—part of the ole wheels of classic detective thinking. Still, Wade fixed his focus on other elements of the puzzle.

When he arrived at the 136th Street murder scene, there was the typical yellow police line to welcome him along with a crowd of bystanders; all of them lobbying for a view, irrespective of the officers on post. Naturally, Wade trooped around the crowd and under the yellow line. The officer nearest Wade stepped aside when he noticed the badge appearing from under his shirt. Wade let it hang so that it could be respected by these Brooklyn officers, none of which he knew. Wade approached the platinum jeep with white-walled tires. A photographer was slowly circling the truck, snapping and flashing at different intervals. Chief Washington was at the front of the jeep, speaking with another detective.

Finally, someone Wade knew. He could see the detectives were having a deep-rooted discussion about the scene. Wade made his introduction, and the chief introduced Brooklyn's Detective Minor. Most other officers were scattered along the driveway, at the front and back of the residential complex. Wade diverted his interest from the victim, not wanting to seem ghoulish, but eventually navigating his eyes towards the windshield. There was a hole in the windshield at eye level, a web of shattered glass, and a sheet draped over the body of the victim. A spot of dark red made it obvious that the victim had a devastating head wound. Wade got the idea.

"Let me show you something." Detective Minor led the way as Washington and Wade followed. The three climbed a short stairway at the rear of the building and then traveled a series of hallways. The ceilings in the hall were towering with skylights situated here and there. The floor was all polished wood with a finish so brilliant it reflected the daylight that blasted from above. There was a series of doors to other lofts leading the way to studio 4. With ceilings as high as those in the hallway and a captivating scent of flowers, walking into the room felt like walking into a vacuum of freshness. On the walls were dozens of photos. All women; many nude, sensual poses and girl-on-girl scenes. Lots of outdoor takes. Many studio shots. A corner of the studio was sectioned off, designated for photo shoots. A lawn of red fabric was draped from high on the wall and sloping down in soft folds, wrinkles and heaps to the wood floor. There were pillows of gold, silver and black piled on the floor around a stool. A camera was positioned just right, with umbrella lights to the sides and rear of the central area.

More accommodations in the loft included a two-door refrigerator, a couple of 19" televisions, a sofa bed, roundtable with chairs and an executive desk. A giant picture window offered an abundant view, but only of the sky and driveway.

"Everything's so modern. The guy must have some dough," assumed Detective Minor as he led the men to a table where a photo album was displayed. Page by page, photo by photo was filled with candid photos of women. They weren't women who were expecting to pose for photos, but pictures that were obviously taken from inside a car, close to a tree and from inconspicuous positions. The targets were unsuspecting. For the three public servants, David Turner quickly earned the title of Peeping Tom.

"This is why I called Chief Washington. I know about the FBI and how they took your case . . . it was the talk of the seventy-first precinct for weeks. We all felt for you. Hopefully, this will help you. We're on your side. You're one of us."

"Does the FBI know about this yet?" Wade wondered.

"The book? No. The homicide? Some rookie-tryin'-to-play detective called. He totally jumped protocol. They're on their way here."

"Can I take this?" Wade asked respectfully.

"Take what? Did you see anything, Chief?" Minor's eyebrows shifted conspiratorially.

"Actually . . ." Washington addressed the officer at the doorway.

". . . Can you tell me where the bathroom is, Officer?" And Washington escorted the officer from the area.

"Let me know about the bullet." Wade made some notes to conclude his visit. Then he surveyed their surroundings before stashing the photo album in his jacket. Back in his sedan, he pulled the book from his windbreaker, he drove for a few blocks and then pulled over onto the service road of Eastern Parkway. Content that the cavalry of suits would not stumble upon him, identifying him in the neighborhood of the homicide, Wade reviewed the photos. Part curiosity, part duty, Wade looked for faces that he might recognize.

Specifically, Wade was looking for dancers or anything relative to Fool's Paradise. His suspicions were further substantiated as he flipped through the album. There was Moet getting out of her car and going through the front yard of her house.

There were close ups, full body shots and zooms. All of it was without her knowing, or so it seemed. By the looks of the album, David was an all-around-the-town type of Peeping Tom. More page flipping. There was Valerie. Wade remembered her face in Moet's videos. Different snapshots showed her going into the club and leaving her house. When Wade saw a Camay-toned woman, he knew it was Debbie. He pulled it out of the book. A closer look brought him back to his days on the beat. He *knew* where that picture had been taken. He knew . . . he recognized the red exhibit with the balls racing throughout the giant contraption.

Port Authority.

Many more ideas tossed in his mind. Although David was moving even closer to becoming a prime suspect, Wade still needed to speak to Debbie. He had to hurry and reach Danni for the trip to Chicago. There was no way of knowing for certain, but David may have had a partner who had a dispute with *him*. Killed him off, and was now in the progress of completing the job. Far-fetched maybe, but there was indeed something brewing. Something beyond just brewing. There were three people dead; Moet, Bobby and now David. And Fool's Paradise was the epicenter of it all.

How did Douglass play a roll? Wade wondered if a big mistake had been made on behalf of the FBI. He thought out the possible ingredients of tragedy. Sex, murder, money. *Where was the money element? The motive? What the hell was going on?* It was time to talk to Debbie. He pulled some additional photos of David, Moet, Valerie and another of Debbie. Then he stashed them in his shirt pocket and accelerated into traffic.

Chi-Town

Detective Wade and his new deputy, Danni, touched down in Chicago's O'Hare Airport at 6pm. Just a couple of days after David Turner's body was discovered. Wade brought along nothing but his pen, his previously-retired writing pad, and a pack of Doublemint gum. He wasn't expecting to be in the Windy City for long, 12 hours at best. Danni, on the other hand, brought his usual traveling bag. Anytime he left New York, in the states, or out, his leather shoulder bag followed. *Felix-The-Cat* had his bag of tricks. *Danni-The-Ninja* had his bag of certain death.

For instance, there was a chess set that he rarely used. But inside the thin, compact box there was an arsenal. A nickle-plated set of nunchucks, a self extending steel rod, and a variety of blades; 14 blades in all, including daggers, knives and stars. All sharp enough to cut through skin and bone on contact. The exterior of the class set was plated with a special grade of uranium, an alloy from the mines of South Africa. The metal was immune to x-rays or laser scans, so the various compartments and sliding panels on the chess set could not be detected. The invention easily passed through airport security many times. If a jealous attendant wanted to see more, Danni would simply open the casing for them, revealing the many scrambled pieces of the game. Meanwhile, the next dangerous piece of artillery had already passed the checkpoint. Danni's beeper also had blades concealed within its casing. No matter the weather, he was ready for prime time.

Through the corridors, an eatery, and hundreds of rush hour passengers mulling about, Wade and Danni moved at a steady, brisk pace towards the Hertz counter to obtain their pre-arranged rental car. Before long they were headed down Michigan Avenue, along the perimeter of monstrous Lake Michigan, towards the southside of Chicago. Conversation kept them occupied as Danni drove down streets he remembered from his youth.

"So what's up with all of the artifacts and what-not?"

"Just collecting. Here and there. Nothing too serious."

"Are you kidding? I know some people that haven't traveled outside of their backyards. It looks like you've been *everywhere*. I'm not trying to play investigator or anything, but your home is one big-ole museum of precious artifacts," Wade added curiously.

". . . Well, you'd probably find out sooner or later. I used to . . . I used to be a pilot. Worked for a big outfit. I was all over the world."

"Really. What did you fly?"

"Private planes and jets mostly."

"Oh. Executives?" Wade easily slipped into the investigative habit.

"Not exactly. I moved drugs," Danni answered, proud of his experiences, but ashamed still. Wade dropped his head an inch into his shoulders.

"You mean, *prescription* drugs, right?"

"No. Far from it. I was a trafficker in another life."

"*Another* life?" Wade was hoping for better news. Like, the guy worked with the CIA in a government arms deal or something.

"Yeah. I crashed. Bad weather. When I woke up I was in a hospital bed with those special bracelets you're so familiar with."

"Whoa . . . hurt bad?"

"Hospitalized for a year. In a prison for nine more." Danni held a slight grimace. Nothing shady or pretty about the truth.

Wade responded with another drawl. Still, the weight seemed to lift from the shoulders of both men. Wade realized that Danni had paid his debt to society. As far as he was concerned, Danni was still of value on this mission. Danni, on the other hand, was glad to be open and truthful.

"Well, obviously you're a hundred percent better. All that kung-fu stuff you did on me back in Queens."

"My body's a hundred percent. My pockets aren't quiet there yet."

"Join the crowd. I try to stay patient. Many temptations, you know? But the discipline is key. If you're standing on a cliff and down in the canyon there's a bed of diamonds, you can't jump. That's the quick way to nowhere. But you can take the time to climb and navigate towards the goal. And learn some things about yourself along the way."

"Well . . . thanks for the motivational speech, counselor."

"Don't mention it. I *have* to stay on point. My community depends on me. You've heard the song '*Better Days*' by Diane Reeves?

"I might have." Danni was now at the edge of South Chicago, working his way into the hood.

"There's a line in the song that says '*you can't get through those better days until you make it through the night . . . you've got to be patient.*'"

"Uh-huh. That sounds familiar."

"To complete my point, you've got to focus on your objective in life. If everything you think about and act upon throughout your every living day is based in your objective, you can adapt to hard times. Accepting them as a kind of 'Right of Passage' if you will. Or, par for the course. I just know that in the balance of life there's got to be night to have a day. A time when things rest and when they come to life. A time to live—a time to die. That's the mastery of the universe." Wade didn't mind sharing wisdom. Besides, he found a bit of affirming energy in sharing.

The men were silent for a few moments until Danni pulled out a note from his pocket. It was an address that Debbie had confirmed with him. He made a left and a right, accordingly. When they arrived at Willowbrook Avenue there was a police road block erected and a traffic cop at the middle of the intersection who directed and re-routed vehicles to proceed in opposite directions or straight through the light. Crowds had formed at different areas along the sidewalks, observing the police activity. In passing the cop, Wade could see down Willowbrook, straight to the other end. A road block and more police capped that end as well. There were no visible indications of *what* exactly was happening on Willowbrook, but trouble was evident. A stone's throw from the road block, Danni pulled into an available parking space.

"See down the alley?"

"Yeah." Wade nodded, wondering what Danni was up to. If it was crazy, Wade wasn't down. Not long till retirement.

"Well, that's the backside of all the homes on Debbie's side of Willowbrook."

"Yeah, *and*?"

"Her house is only a few houses in. I say we execute business as usual. Make sure she's okay. Protect our interests."

"I don't know. Police usually means serious business."

"It could be a gas leak or something. Maybe they're waiting for the gas company to show up. Besides, the *alley* isn't blocked off. Nobody said we couldn't take a little walk. You're not chicken, are you? Feeling out of pocket? Playing it cool until '*Better Days*' come along?" Danni threw Wade a curious glance.

"Okay. Alright already. Let's go." Wade grabbed Danni's arm before he could exit the car. "Just be careful."

Danni nodded and stretched over to the back seat for his shoulder bag. The two marched down the alleyway as the descent of the sun left an auburn sky. To the left was a block-long row of one-car garages. To the right were the fenced-in backyards to the homes on Willowbrook. There were telephone poles lining the alley and garbage cans at the base of each pole. The atmosphere was dim and gloomy. Lights were struggling to flicker on, as their time controls commanded. While approaching the back gate of 422 Willowbrook a sound of cracking and popping ripped through the sky. It was distant, but Wade knew the sound well enough. Heard them at the firing range all the time.

"Those are gunshots, Danni," Wade issued matter-of-factly.

"If they are, they're pretty far away." Danni put his hand on Wade's shoulder for support. "We're here. That's her back door. Four twenty-two Willowbrook. Let's do this and get out." Even Danni was concerned.

"How can you tell? There's no number on the door."

"The cans, Detective. The *garbage* cans." Wade looked down to see 422 on the heavy-duty plastic container. "Lemme find out you bought your badge at an auction and didn't earn it at the Police Academy," said Danni.

Wade lifted his eyelids at the joke, but remained alert. Inside the gate and up the short path, Danni and his shadow stepped up to knock at the pane glass in the door. Less than 10 seconds passed before a flowered curtain shifted to the side in the kitchen window. The two men could barely see the woman's face.

"*Who?*" She was abrupt and ginger.

"It's Danni. Here to see Debbie . . ."

'She's not in. I'll tell her you came by." The woman abruptly shot out an answer before Danni finished his introduction. The two men swallowed as though they'd just been sent on their way. Suddenly, from a window on the second floor, Debbie waved to Danni. She lifted the window.

"Hey! What's up, Danni?"

"What's up with *you*? Are you on punishment or something?"

"No. Why?"

"Aaah . . ." Danni held a question mark on his face. Tossed between Debbie upstairs approving, and her mother downstairs, disapproving. "Your mother says you're not home. So

maybe we'll come back later." Danni pivoted as if to leave.
Wade played along. They knew that eyes were watching.

"***Mom!***" Debbie yowled through the house so that her
mother and everyone else could hear her. Danni and Wade
waited anxiously for the back door to be opened. Some loud,
aggressive words were thrown between the younger and older
Roses. Wade felt awkward as he listened to the series of locks
and latches flip, click and unfasten. The back door sucked in
the outside air and Debbie pushed the screen door outward
to invite the two inside. "Sorry. Mom even tells the *mailman*
I'm not home."

"Well, you can never be *too* safe," Wade added as he followed
Danni into the kitchen where Mrs. Rose could overhear.

"Good evening, ma'am . . ."

"Hello, ma'am."

"Yes. Hi, gentlemen. I'm Mrs. Rose. Debbie's mother." Mrs.
Rose spoke authoritatively, as if to put the two men on notice
that security was in place for *her* daughter, in *her* house.

"*Mom.*" Debbie appealed with her tone. "Mom, this is Danni.
He's Jackie's mother's boyfriend, from Queens. Remember I
told you how *nice* and *hospitable* he was to me?" Debbie was
trying to indicate that some reciprocity was in order. But Mrs.
Rose was holding back a growl, not knowing whether to bite
or kiss Danni. *Was he the reason her Debbie . . . her only remaining child, left the house in the first place? Was he doin' the nasty with
her daughter*? Or *was he genuinely kind*? Not too many men were,
according to Mrs. Rose. She'd been through too much to jump
to conclusions.

"Yes. Yes. I remember. Hello, Danni. I'm sorry to be so
rude. You never can be too safe ya know . . ." She was growing
more comfortable now. ". . . and besides, that troubled family
is at it again across the street. I swear I'm gonna leave this
blessed neighborhood if it's the *last* thing I do."

"This is a friend of mine. Wade." Everyone completed their
greetings and took seats at the dining table cramped in a corner of the kitchen. Mrs. Rose went into the refrigerator and
grabbed a pitcher. Then she went into a cabinet for some glasses.
Wade looked over to Danni with uneasiness, knowing that
what they had to discuss probably shouldn't include the
mother. Danni winked at Wade in understanding.

"So what brings you gentlemen out our way?" Mrs. Rose wasn't letting down with her investigation. Danni looked at Wade without turning his way. But Wade slammed the serve back into Danni's side of the net.

"A photographer in New York had taken some photos of Debbie and . . ." Wade jumped in.

". . . and there seems to be some interest in Debbie doing some paid work, like runway shows of some sort . . ." Danni cut Wade off now, thinking that they shouldn't imply Debbie leaving Chicago again.

". . . and we wanted to . . . interview Debbie for possible opportunities . . . uhh . . . the guy would come out here and . . ." Danni was at a loss for words. Debbie read through the code and jumped in before they dug a hole any deeper.

"Mom . . . do you *mind* if I speak with them alone?"

"Honey, I'd like to know what's happening . . . is this some modeling thing? I know how this industry abuses—"

"*Mom!* Please give me some time alone. I'll fill you in. I'm a big girl."

"Alright. Alright. I'm going to do some tidying." Mrs. Rose was apprehensive, but got up from the table and headed for the living room. More shots could be heard in the distance.

"What's this block caught up in, some kind of stand-off or something?" Wade put the question to Debbie *and* Danni, as if he was still a resident of the area.

"I guess the dealers are at it again. It's like every other day we hear gunshots around here. You know that's how my brother Ray Ray died. A bullet came right through the front window."

"Wow. Chicago sure hasn't changed a bit."

"It's *worse* than when you were young, Danni. Sometimes I can't go outside."

"Road blocks are set up outside, for God sakes."

"That's small time, Mr. Wade. You should be here when the helicopters are buzzin' over the house. I need to get my mom the hell outta here."

"Listen, Debbie. Not to cut you off, but Wade is a detective with . . ."

"Let me, Danni. Debbie, please tell us what you know about Moet. We're not suspecting you of anything. We're actually here to *protect* you. We think you could be a target." Debbie suddenly realized the purpose of this meeting and all of its intensity. She was feeling all bottled up with information anyhow and needed to tell someone.

"You know, I've been wanting so much to tell *someone* about what happened that night. But I didn't know where to go or who to tell."

"Slow down, Debbie. What night are you talking about? Tell us what happened." Wade attempted to comfort her. Debbie seemed to recapture the grief or horror from the experience. It showed in her eyes and on her face. With her elbows on the table and her face in her palms, she continued.

"Moet and I went out with this guy. He booked us for a private party. Said his name was Rick. He was nice at first. Never took off his glasses. Clean-shaven. Black hair and real-real white skin."

Wade was scribbling furiously into his pad. "He picked us up from Fool's Paradise—we worked there and . . ."

—Wade interrupted, explaining that she could move beyond the job; he already knew where she worked, etc.—

"Okay, well, we went downtown to the Marriot, in Times Square." Debbie recounted the event in her mind. Nervously combing ten fingers through her soft, bronze hair. "When we got to the hotel room Moe and I went into the bathroom to get ready. We had these leather outfits, whips. You know . . . fantasy stuff." Danni tried to act surprised, even though Wade had schooled him about Debbie, her dancing and the erotic escapades with Moet.

"When we came out to start our routine, he like—had a whole 'nother plan. He wanted to play games with handcuffs and stuff. Moet was like, *alright*. But I was like, *naw*. So I did the first half of the gig. He *still* put the cuffs on himself, and we're like—*whatever*. We teased him. Danced around a bit. Moet and I started a lil' girl-on-girl thing. Then he insisted on the handcuffs. I said *no* again. Moet and I agreed to meet up downstairs in the lobby after the gig. So I left and she stayed with him. Before I went out the door, he grabbed me, askin' if I was sure I didn't want to play. His grip was so hard I tried to wiggle away, told him to *let me go*. Then I slammed the door. I waited and waited in the lobby. Nobody showed up. After an hour I went back up. They were gone. The place was a mess. Not like when I left, but like—*wrecked*." Debbie put her face back in her palms. Ashamed and embarrassed, Danni put a comforting arm around Debbie's shoulder. Brotherly love. But Wade didn't want her to stop.

"What happened next, Debbie?" Swirling his ballpoint across a notepad.

"I took a cab home. I waited for Moet to call. The whole situation confused me, so I just packed my things and took a flight back home . . . here in Chicago, I mean. I think I called Moet a couple times before I left." Debbie's sigh turned to tears that left moist impressions along her cheeks. Danni pulled Debbie into his collarbone and signaled for Wade to ease up. More popping sounds cracked outside. Then an answer-back crackle. Closer still. At that moment, glass shattered in the front of the house.

"*Mom!*" Debbie shook her remorse and sorrow instantly. She jumped up, darting to the front of the house. "**Mom!!**" Mrs. Rose was spread out on the floor of the living room. The giant picture window was broken at the lower left corner, a hole in it the size and shape of a foot-long asterisk. Debbie looked down to see her mom coughing up blood, holding her hand to her bosom where a splatter of dark red resulted from the bullet wound. Danni and Wade were just behind Debbie. Debbie was already on the floor, cuddling her mother's head and torso in her lap. She wiped her mother's brow, smoothing a strand of hair aside to her temple. Helplessly and hopelessly, Debbie rained tears over her mother's trauma-stricken expression, how she stared up to the ceiling for some divine guidance.

The men in the house had already sprung into action. Wade was guarding the extremes with a revolver in one hand; his cell phone in the other as he barked information to a 911 emergency operator. Danni seemed to have gone through a total makeover, putting the final touches in place. Armbands, ankle straps and a Velcro vest were already tight on his limbs and torso. The next five seconds were dramatic, where Danni kneeled to the floor, placing his chess set in front of him. He popped the latches and flipped up the lid as if it was a laptop computer. On the side of the case an additional latch was actually a switch that when twisted and pulled, released the interior locks that held the panels in place. Suddenly the hidden arsenal was exposed. Danni picked up just about every blade on display and slipped them in their proper pockets around his body. Even Wade's attention was lured by a reflection from a piece of steel. He turned his head towards Danni and jolted, thinking that he'd seen a ghost.

"Now just what are you gonna do with all *that*?" Wade asked. "You don't even know where the bullet came from . . . take a look out there . . ." Wade neared the broken window, cautiously standing to the side. "Police are shooting at dealers. Dealers are shooting at the police. It's like *New Jack City* meets the Hatfields and the McCoys out there!" Wade was bold and erratic, though logical. Danni was left no choice but to think about his intentions.

"If you wanna do something, you'll help me get Mrs. Rose out of the back door to the car. She needs a doctor, quick." Danni deflated some, although still not 100% convinced.

"Come on—use your head, *deputy!* That's the cliff and the canyon out there! You go out the door, you might as well be jumping over the edge. I don't care if you know Billy Jack, Bruce Lee *and* Jackie Chan! Unless you're Superman and bullet-proof, you can *not* go out there! What are you gonna *do*, collect all the guns, tell everyone to pipe down and ask them all *'Who shot Mrs. Rose?'* It's not logical. Use your head, buddy."

While the New Yorkers bickered, Debbie was moaning and sniffing. Rocking back and forth with her mother in her arms, soaking in a growing puddle of blood. Mrs. Rose was motionless, with eyes open in shock and tears. Danni and Wade finally reached to help move Debbie's mom. Not a minute had passed since they raced into the living room.

"Don't! Don't you touch her!!" Debbie held her mother tighter, demanding that they stay away. They tried to persuade her. Wade called 911 again, wondering how far away they were. Debbie brought her attention back to her mother—dying in her arms. "Mama? Can you hear me?" Debbie held her mother's hand, ignoring the bullethole and blood. Tears pouring still. Mrs. Rose lay still, more or less lifeless. But Debbie could feel some pressure on her palm. Moms was holding on with whatever strength she had left. Debbie anticipated her own words. "Mom. I don't . . . I don't want you to try to speak or answer my words. Just please listen. I know you can hear me. Mom, you've had a wonderful life. You've given us the best you could . . . your service was to anyone in need and you've successfully raised two loving children. Ray Ray has gone. But he lived while he was here. Life has been good to us." Debbie continuously choked on her words.

"Mom . . . if . . . if it hurts too much . . . if you can't take it, *please* . . . let go. Ray Ray needs you, Mom. I'll be fine. Let go, Mom . . ."

Wade and Danni looked at one another with disbelief. What was she saying???

"Don't hurt anymore, Momma." Debbie sobbed audibly, hurt by her own words. It seemed like hours had passed, but they were just minutes. Precious minutes. Debbie continued rocking with her mom, her lips pressed against her mom's temple in a long goodbye kiss. Eventually an hour *had* passed. Danni and Wade sat helpless on the floor for support. The ambulance didn't matter anymore. Maybe Debbie was onto something, since Mrs. Rose had long passed away.

CHAPTER FIFTEEN

Deal or Die

The days passed by slowly in the beginning. But in time, they glided by as nothing more than irritating pimples. Douglass had grown callous to all of the monotony. The shouting, jingling keys, electronic sliding gates, three square meals and the stand-up counts were now presumed as a way of life. However temporary. Communal living, warehousing, slavery . . . call it what you will, Douglass had successfully landed in this new world. He had so far survived the worst of it all with no suicide attempts, no extreme depression or nervous breakdowns. It was hard, but he *handled* it hard.

There was a T.V. in the big day room where he was left. He ignored the conventional soap operas and *Seinfeld* sitcoms, but highly appreciated *Soul Train* on Saturdays. T.V. was the only medium of entertainment next to loud, boastful banter that inmates slung around on a day to day basis. And Douglass wasn't claustrophobic by any means, but it *was* a survival course just to breathe. His first day was merely a challenge, how he was vying for air in the tiny holding cell with all those men smoking. And later, when that goon tried to "punk" him in front of other prisoners. But those wouldn't be his biggest tests.

Douglass's personal items consisted of a towel, a small slice of motel soap, and a 2-inch toothbrush. (The toothbrush wasn't the usual length because if it were any longer it could be whittled into a knife or dagger.) The slim pickin's he was issued to wear were not interchangeable, and there were no laundry services. So getting into a crusty shower only to change back into the same dirty clothing was fruitless. The best Douglass could manage was to lounge in underwear while his hand-washed shirt and trousers dried. And nobody would dare steal his drying laundry since word got around that he knew kung fu real good. "Knocked that Newark cat right on his ass," they were saying.

The hand-washing continued almost every other day, just so he could feel clean. As time went by, a prisoner here or a prisoner there would get bailed out or set free by a judge, leaving scraps of excess clothing or linen (resources!) behind for the daily scavenger hunt. So accordingly, Douglass learned to make ends meet with time. Fortunately, he was tall and lanky enough to handle the frequent climbs up and down, to and from the top of his three-man bunk bed. It was either that, or sleep on the floor with ten or fifteen others. It had been a long first weekend at the jail. And looking at things with some novelty made all the difference in the world. To write down as much as a note to the doctor, a pen or pencil had to be smuggled from a prisoner with better privileges. Douglass got hold of one, but he couldn't write a letter since he had no stamps with which to mail one. So he got creative and produced a chess set. With the back of some other paper scraps that he ripped into shapes, Douglass fabricated the game of strategy and even taught one or two others how to play.

The meals were always generous. That much he appreciated.

A thin, black man was quarantined by the rest of the room—visibly gruesome, with pock marks and lumps scattered about his face and body. He had discolored skin, and he was constantly coughing and vomiting. Word had already spread about him: AIDS. Another thin, white man constantly needed insulin and extra food. He even had a doctor's note that ordered him to have a second portion of food at each serving. Prisoners stayed away from him, too. A few days passed and Douglass was moved along with a group of others to a fourth-floor pen. He was surprised that there was an elevator to lift them there. Such luxuries included elevators, electronically controlled doors, and steel doors and gates to protect everyone. Any time prisoners were near to passing one another, a corrections officer made one stand with palms on the wall so that there was no free-flowing communication. Besides that, all movement was announced by accompanying officers into their all-empowering tools of confidence—their walkie-talkies; anchors which were held onto like life-preservers.

On the fourth floor, Douglass was assigned to 4B—one of three cages. The various cages were sectioned off by steel doors and electronic gates, creating one huge octagon of confined areas. There wasn't much difference between the conditions at the jail and a zoo, so far as Douglass could tell. And at the center of the octagon, with a hallway that looped all the way around, was an officer's station, positioned up a platform and enclosed with unbreakable glass. Behind that thick glass, an officer controlled prisoner movement with switches, buttons, clipboards and phones.

Cell 4B didn't differ much in comparison to the first-floor day room, but for an extra TV, more three-man bunks, and a warmer climate. There was a lived-in element, evidenced by the makeshift clotheslines and scattered personal effects such as legal work and articles purchased from commissary. Cigarettes, candy, cosmetics, etc. Unlike downstairs, where nearly everyone was a newcomer, and nobody was permitted to smoke, the occupants in 4B were long adjusted to the jail. They stared at newcomers with great curiosity and evaluation. Part defensive, part intimidation, one was either made to feel at home or snubbed as if they didn't exist. Since Douglass was both a newcomer and from a different state, the label of outcast might have fit him well, except that the word had gotten around. Yeah, *that* same old tale about the kung fu and the beatdown on the first floor. The notoriety was apparently good enough to make him an attraction, and in no time other prisoners were bringing things to him. Stamps, excess underwear, commissary items; he was even given another inmate's lower bunk. So much came to him so fast that you'd think he was the Pope here on a yearly visit.

It took a couple of weeks to settle in and to discover his own way of doing this time. He could see that 95 percent of the prisoners were locals, caught up in local trends, and he sat and watched them, inconspicuously, of course, just to figure out how to penetrate the psychological mechanisms. In one of his routine phone calls home, Douglass asked Demetrius to mail in some photos. Demetrius didn't understand why, but carried out the request nonetheless. There were 50 photos that came; and they featured an array of celebrities and shapely females to serve as incantations of success. Once all of 4B got a whiff of Douglass's associations with international icons of music and entertainment, and with the most popular porn stars in the world, he became a phenomenon at Passaic County Jail. And once the word spread throughout the jail, other prisoners were sending Douglass notes for one reason or another: *"Yo, I heard you a big willie up in New York. You know that nigga, Binkie? I need to reach that nigga bad, and I know he into the skin market deeep, like you."*

"Yo, I heard about you in the newspaper, man. I got connects out here, so lemme know if you need somethin'. Anything. Word." Douglass was getting these types of letters every other day, and that made him more or less a big fish in a small pond. He quickly earned greater bargaining rights than before, however whimsical. The drug dealers, bank robbers and violent offenders couldn't match the fame that Douglass lived on the streets. And he can kick ass, too? His was the type of notoriety that couldn't be bought. Moreover, it couldn't be denied. Now, he was beyond welcomed. He was more than gifted with fresh, clean clothing, underwear, slippers, stamps or extra food.

More introductions were conjured. Some common ground was established, which enabled him to cross lines of race, age and nationality. But, although Douglass settled in, the minor

comforts weren't getting him out of jail. And they weren't helping him to breathe better either. Out of the hundred-plus men
in 4B, ninety or more of them were chronic smokers. In Douglass's bed assignment, the bottom of a three-level bunk bed,
he could cover up, blanket over his head, and he was still
planted in the midst of a thick fog of cigarette smoke that followed breakfast, lunch, dinner and persisted throughout late-
night conversations. He wanted to complain. He wanted to
move to some no-smoking area of the jail. But he kept his beef
to himself. No sense knocking a good thing in the ass since he
knew for sure, no matter how popular he had become, these
men were stressed. And there was no way they were gonna
give up smoking for a short-term visitor. Instead of bitching,
day after day, for weeks, Douglass would erect his own makeshift tent with a sheet, attempting to shield himself from the
deadly cloud. But it was pointless. There was no escape. On
occasion, Douglass was near suffocation, tearing and coughing
with ferocity before the buildup of smog eventually dissipated.
A visit to the jail's physician went nowhere. The doctor even
hid his name tag when Douglass threatened to call on his attorney about the problem. And speaking of which . . .

Douglass's appointed lawyer was unreachable on most occasions, and had no answers on others. A bail hearing eventually brought the bond down to $350,000. Douglass felt that
the judge was unmerciful for a reason, and that she had ultimately pigeonholed him because of his dark skin. The experience for the most part, the smoking and the legal turmoil,
were similar to sleeping on a nail. With each passing week, for
over six months now, the nail had become less and less of a
discomfort, and more and more of a mere formality. The bottom line was that Douglass had to deal or die.

Mechelle coped with her position as just another dancer. Half
naked, in the same ol' murky setting, with men fawning all
over her by night and going to bed manless by day. She was
growing tired and unexcited by her circumstances. After three
months, she began to show. Her tummy could not be concealed
any longer. She quickly threw together a resume and persuaded
her way into a position with Bosuer Products, a creamy-white
makeup company down in midtown Manhattan. They respected

her, valued her and made her feel at home as their receptionist and gofer. She began to appreciate the standard of receiving legitimate paychecks. She grew more and more able to cope with her newfound independence without Douglass. Now, she had something more important to rely on other than a man. She had herself! Go, Mechelle! This was her very solid excuse to avoid visiting Douglass in jail. And his phone calls were even becoming inconvenient as she was out more; at the doctor's, at pregnancy classes or with friends that were lending her a hand during this very lonely time.

"Let me ask you something, Mechelle. What's more important, that damned job . . . or *me*?" Douglass asked her point-blank on one particular phone call.

"You." She hesitated and still answered cautiously.

"Well, then why can't you get your ass *down* here?" Douglass heard himself shouting, but muffled the volume as best he could, with so many ears close to him. Mechelle hung up on him when he paused for her reply. That infuriated him more. She left the receiver off the hook. It wasn't replaced until the next day when Demetrius found it on the floor. Mechelle quickly moved out, according to D. Douglass assumed that she'd be back, after all, she *was* pregnant, and she'd pulled this "*leaving*" thing before.

Still Ticking

In contradiction to the turmoil that Douglass faced, and the various tragedies that were connected directly or indirectly to Fool's Paradise, the energy of the club persisted. Income was still strong and consistent. Gil was in his usual routine; in the office with his choice for a quickie, or else falling asleep cuddling a bottle of Guinness Stout as he stood overlooking the various club activities. Sometimes he'd be the cashier in the box office window, accepting ten-dollar bills that were pressed down into the stainless steel tray. Then seconds later, he'd swing out of the box office window to see that the doorman was doing his job properly, taking the admission ticket from the patron. The same ticket was then handed back to Gil. This confused routine was a comfortable one. One that offered Gil the security of that total control. The same security that he in turn surrendered when he explored his sexual adventures behind closed doors.

A bizarre freedom persisted inside of Fool's Paradise when Gil was back there tucked away in his office, between some young dancer's legs. The absence of *true* organization and control made stealing easy. Douglass couldn't even do anything about that before all the drama with his arrest. Now that he was away, shit was *really* buckwild. In essence, the young Gilmore's original vision was never further from its mark. Even with the bouncers, dancers, bartenders and eventually the customers doing as they pleased, the popularity of the establishment continued to grow, with the biggest porn stars in the world endorsing the joint, and the lap dancers still drawing those crowds. Drink prices increased to $6. Even lap dances grew more expensive. Pushovers like Claudine were lucky enough to make $2 or even $3 when they took a customer to the wall, pressing their big balloon behinds into the guy's groin in a senseless quest for friction and an imitation of sex. But the top-shelf dancers like Sadie and Valerie were getting $15, $20 and more for the same dance. The top-shelf girls were so captivating that a little wind in a man's ear might make him explode in his trousers without so much as a brush against him—well worth that top dollar. This was why men came to Fool's Paradise in the first place; not simply to *see* the spectacles, the thrills on stage . . . but to touch some of it; to *interact*. To be touched and to feel the sensation all the way up until (and almost as if) they'd reached an orgasm.

Tony really didn't have any new statistics or methods to report to his Capo. There was little to explain; a club, some music, drinks, and a lot of black girls. Tony couldn't figure out how all those women were drawn to Fool's Paradise. He knew about the booking agencies. But what they sent in emergency situations was nothing close to the quality of women that showed up on their own. Tony wondered how the club became such a magnet for them. He could only stand around, buddy up with Gil, observe and remain consistent. Eventually, he expected to impregnate the sudden success with some loan sharking and some other vending contracts. It was clear to him that the Biancos would have to make more money off of the establishment, but Tony was challenging time. The time he was investing at the club versus the time it took for his investment to grow. On top of that, he was handling other deals and scams to meet his quota of $5,000 a week—money he was obligated to bring back to the family.

For now, Gil wasn't accepting loans. He was in a cash-rich position. So, Tony came up with an alternative plan: he planned to open a similar club, one that would be bigger, better and more exciting than Fool's Paradise. And shamelessly, he'd open the club across the street. Surely, such an attraction would lure the best dancers; and pay them more. It was a brilliant idea! That is, from Tony's mouth to God's ears. The question was, *would the boss go for it?* This was quite a proposal he was thinking up. His biggest ever for the family.

"This is Brenda Feather, signing off. Hoping that your news is always good news . . . " The channel 5 theme music for the nightly news jingled along to a close as Brenda shuffled and shifted her notes, waiting to walk off the set. She was focused for most of the broadcast, until the sports segment came on. "Ken Stevens this, Ken Steven that . . . " Home runs. RBI's. The bid for MVP of the playoffs. The many accolades just enhanced Ken's image; the physical one that swept her off of her feet. Brenda reviewed a number of magazine articles. She watched a stream of video footage and couldn't help but to imagine and fantasize how one day she might be *Mrs*. Stevens. And that one day might come real soon.

The playoffs were in the final game (in the best out of five series) when she first had the opportunity to meet and interview the hot baseball superstar. Brenda even led herself to believe that it was *her* inspiration that caused Ken to hit the game-winning home run. Ken was known to shorten his interviews to 15 minutes, allowing for the preservation of his integrity. Hopefully then, the press wouldn't have the opportunity to build him up just to break him down. And everybody in the industry knew the press could slam dunk a man due to any trivial foul. Ken was already hip to the "slam dunk strategy" that was put on his sports colleagues like Mike, Michael, Dwight, and

Magic. And it wasn't that sports icons *didn't* ever error in their ways. It was how the media had exploited those errors, even the tiny ones, as if they were international catastrophes. As if jocks weren't human. But things were different with the Ken Stevens interview. Ken gave Brenda a whole hour! She should have expected that, though, considering what she went through to prepare. She wore her favorite Kente pullover top. It was mixed with mudcloth and merged with tribal colors and patterns. She wore a pair of tight, black cotton leggings that hugged her ass and calves just right. And to accent that, she wore Cowrie shells, strung on a choker necklace of black leather strands and fixed with elaborate, brass medallions. Brenda did her best and succeeded at maintaining her on-camera composure. But whenever Ken moved his lips it was as though she could feel them on her—*whenever.* Every second of the interview was a tease for Brenda, as her loins curled and her folds turned moist between her clasped thighs. Right there in the studio, bright lights and all, she was getting hot flashes. She was going through more than facts and figures during the interview. More than dates and accomplishments, or the euphoria of the playoffs. It was there on the set that Brenda was wide open, with nostrils flaring. And it was also there that she decided *she* would become that extra *umph* in Ken's life. Beyond the fame, the money and the notoriety, she'd become *everything* else that he needed in the world.

The Cat Gets Out of the Bag

So now, a few months into the off-season, Brenda thought it might be a good time to approach Ken from another perspective. *Hers.* Maybe he'd appreciate that she was interested in him, outside of the media hype. After all, he *did* give her his home number—of course, it was supposed to be business related. But maybe it was an invite. *What the heck! You only live once,* she ventured. And that attitude had Brenda scurrying through the production area of the newsroom, headed for her office. She organized her desk, poked at her Blackberry for Ken's number. It was at that point, seeing his phone number, that Brenda got warm once again. Determined now, whatever

it took, she'd get closer to Ken. She grabbed her Gap windbreaker from the back of her door, flicked the light switch and
returned the endearing waves from the production crew, suddenly appreciative of the admiration which she'd earned as
one of New York's top anchorwomen.

If they only knew how horny I am!

In the parking garage, secluded from the hype and tah-tah
of her own celebrity status, Brenda made the shameless call to
Ken. There was a half a minute of jazz on his voicemail, nothing more. Brenda guessed it was Charles Mingus. Orange-
something, she recollected. Waiting for the beep, she keyed the
ignition and turned it enough to activate the car stereo. There
was a Mint Condition CD in the player.

> *"Put your head on my pillow . . .*
> *And just relax . . . relax . . . relax . . ."*

Her favorite old-school song was a fresh reminder of the
luxuries that she'd worked for. She lowered the volume, surprised that Ken immediately returned her call. A pleasant
shock. Her *fuck it* attitude remained strong, and she laid it on
the line. A *late nightcap*, she called it. *How 'bout Birdland, on
Forty-fourth Street?* Brenda suggested. Ken seemed a little shook,
but he went for her spur-of-the-moment get-together. It was a
Monday night. A brisk winter evening, no wind. The streets
were ashy from the city's salt throwers of the past weeks. The
moon was full, set against a clear, black and blue sky. Stars appeared to be as close as they were far. Meanwhile, Brenda commanded the smooth streets with her trademark platinum late
model Lexus GS, soaring up 57th Street and down 9th Avenue
as the traffic lights disappeared behind her. The night seemed
to flow for her, with street lights brilliantly reflecting down
onto the hood of her vehicle. So slick and presumptuous, she
caught a slight chill, wondering what the hell she was doing,
cornering a horny jock in midtown Manhattan for a booty call.
Perhaps it was the lingering church-girl that was asking the
questions. But as Brenda pulled up to the curb at Birdland, the
devil had the upper hand, reminding her of her physical needs.
She shifted into park and pulled the rearview mirror to check
her makeup. Her evening wear was nothing but the routine

broadcast fashion. Nothing near to what she wore on the day she first interviewed Ken, but *would it matter?* She pondered. Her black, meshed blouse was low enough to hint at her head-turning cleavage, and it played well against her black brassiere. The combination that was "flat" enough for the hot lights in the studio, but it was also provocative enough if close-up with a companion. Brenda also had on a matching skirt that barely concealed her thighs. Whatever the weather, whether Ken wanted to test the waters, or if Brenda needed to merely entice him some more, she was ready for business.

By the look of things outside, considering the open parking spaces and half empty parking lot across the street, it was an intimate Monday night at Birdland. Brenda adjusted her bra and pushed her healthy breasts up a little before she hopped out of her ride. Then, as if she had an important appointment, she bleeped her car alarm, glided through the entrance, and easily melted into the opulence, soft music and warmth of her favorite jazzy spot. The maitre d' escorted her to a rear enclave of the establishment where Brenda found comfort amongst an arrangement of couches and tables that were visible by candle-light only. She ordered a light salad and a Perrier water while she waited for Ken. Waiting and anticipating. A 3-piece band was working on stage, apparently overwhelmed by the oppor-tunity to play at *"the world famous"* Birdland. In the meantime, the warm-up tunes they played amused Brenda to the degree that her nerves were soothed with her body sucked into the ambiance. She smiled at the intimacy here; the audience wasn't thick and cumbersome, but average and sentimental to every element. Couples in the sunken dining area by the stage, and singles at the bar were all caught up in the mood that carried throughout the room. They were even too caught up to notice the tall, determined figured that suddenly slid through the front entrance. However, Brenda didn't miss him. She already had her radar up for the ever-so-casual Ken Stevens. Although she had to admit that his attire tonight complemented her own. He had the white turtleneck, the black blazer, and the black denim jeans. When he got closer she also peeped the wing-tipped, snakeskin boots. Ken had a palm-sized cell phone clenched in one hand and he wore a white baseball cap with the NY insignia low, just above his brow. Now the movie that she played over and over in her mind was coming to life—Ken nodding and whispering to the maitre d'; Ken being told where his guest was seated . . . Ken gliding across the carpet, directly towards Brenda.

Brenda inhaled as if to pull the tall, deliberate and masculine Ken Stevens ever closer to her. And for an instant, she could read his walk and expression; how he moved as though he knew himself, his capabilities and his wants. She hoped it wasn't an act and she exhaled once he neared the table. He was now in her zone. She welcomed him with a kiss on the check; close enough to the lips to offer promise.

"Thank you for coming out on such short notice," she said. And they chatted briefly about the atmosphere and the music of Birdland. Eventually, the conversation eased into the evening's broadcast. A post-season story, and that hint of contract renewal. Ken addressed the subject like it was a secret forthcoming soap opera episode. Yet, in so many words, Ken made it clear that he couldn't discuss the issue at all. Meanwhile, Brenda watched his lips, smiling at him with her eyes and winking at him with her mind.

Don't worry, big boy. I'll get it out of you.

After some hot apple pie and cocoa, with the jazz winding down into the 1am hour, Brenda turned her head from the stage to catch Ken staring. It caught her off-guard and she feigned modesty and crunched her shoulders in with a slight giggle. The reaction, she felt, was overdone. But it was too late now. She was feeling like she was in college again; that dizzy, weather girl wannabe. But, at least she had his interest. And damned if she was gonna let that go.

"Wanna get out of here?" By Brenda's suggestion, the two left for Ken's place. She told him that she'd never been to a village loft and was looking forward to the experience. Maybe more than that.

And in their black and silver toys, the two complemented each other as Brenda followed Ken's Navigator down 42nd Street to the West Side Highway. They raced each other playfully, aware that the road was virtually empty, until they reached Green Street, next to New York University. *Is Ken tasting from the fountain of youth?* Brenda wondered as she rolled down and into the garage behind him, the sub-level of Ken's building. He explained that he owned the entire property, but that he only occupied the top floor—a penthouse overlooking the Hudson River. The first through third floors were leased to artists, performers and fashion designers.

As the garage door automatically lowered behind the vehicles, Brenda's eyes adjusted to the smear of lights that bounced off of a dozen or so vehicles that reached into the farthest corners of the basement and gave a fair indication of the massive length and width of the building.

"Yours?" Brenda asked after parking aside of Ken.

"A boy's gotta have his toys," was his reply as he led her into a freight elevator.

"This is the only way to get from floor to floor," Ken explained, very much into his property. "Unless you wanna use the long staircase to the side. And, trust me, you don't *ever* wanna walk from the basement to the penthouse." Ken pulled a gate across and reached up to tug at a strap until it pulled down half of a heavy, steel barrier. An identical barrier simultaneously lifted from below until the two parts met like closed lips. Brenda watched the ease with which Ken executed the process, wondering to herself (suddenly feeling captive) if she could do it like Ken did.

As the car moved slowly and silently up, and to break the uncomfortable silence in the car, Brenda expressed her awe of Ken's living arrangement. It was so rough and rugged. No personal driver or bodyguard, she noticed. No doorman or red carpet treatment at home. And that turned her on even more so, besides being the only other thing they hadn't discussed besides sex. She talked enough to fill the void until they reached his penthouse loft. Ken went through the motions again, this time in reverse. The steel lips separating, revealing a dark cavernous room, with only blacklights in the far reaches, glowing against various framed artwork. The paintings were illuminated at different intervals throughout the loft. And the only navigation in the room was the reflection and hue from the art, along with the moon that glowed down through a huge picture window at the outdoor balcony. Tiny red indicator lights could be seen about the facing, some electronic devices here and there—all of this building an anticipation for Brenda. She couldn't wait for the lights to reveal all.

As Ken stepped from the elevator and onto a section of red-pile carpet fit for a king, the sensors reacted from the pressure of his foot, activating a series of mood lamps throughout the loft. Prerecorded music also began to play over the Bose speakers that were posted in various areas of high ceilings and expansive walls of the loft. *Gothic*, was Brenda's first impression of Ken's habitat. Her second impression was *hulking*. She could see that he liked to live large. She had a career full of Donald Trump sensations, Presidential invites, and at least one Kennedy interview—the extended family that is, but until now, she just didn't know what large *really* was! Ken never exposed the true size of his world, and she never realized his absolute financial influence—how eccentric, excessive, and monolithic—until she came to his house. From the white Italian marble floors, to the towering ceiling and tanned granite. Part of the cavernous loft was sunken, with broad Aztec rugs, an enormous couch of suede and plenty of throw pillows. All of this was the setting facing a six-foot fireplace. Only Paul Bunyan could soak up so many abundant luxuries!

A graceful, spiral staircase, with birch-wood treads and rust-colored iron, led up to a study that overlooked most of the loft. From the study, a walkway ran against the wall (opposite the entrance) and afforded access to tall, sliding glass doors. Outside was a balcony that contained an in-ground pool below, as well as the best-ever view of New York City's twinkling lights in the distance. To the left of the entrance, Brenda could see a hallway. She was free to explore the stretch, and in doing so, discovered the kitchen and dining area. She could've fainted! Above those rooms, at the top of a hidden staircase, there were a couple of bedrooms; guest rooms, Brenda reckoned. Further sniffing lured her to Ken's fairytale master bedroom. Cast-iron pillars spiraled up like four thick branches, leading to those high arches from which white chiffon was draped on either side. Adjacent to the bed was a huge, velvet curtain with golden tassels and ropes. Brenda was almost afraid to open them. But when she did, she was smacked with a higher-than-high, breathtaking view of the large living room down below. Just over the balcony, she could see where she had entered. Above where she stood, a 25-foot movie screen was tucked up to an angle, apparently commanded by some electronic remote that called it to swing down into vertical use. There was also a walloping, black wood stove to the side of the bed on a pad of ceramic tile.

Brenda had all the intentions of concealing the impression Ken had on her. However, that idea went out the window along with every other possible prevention of falling, sinking, or submitting to the awesome realities and freedoms of the Ken Stevens universe. She wanted to dive onto the bed! She wanted to swing on the railing, and dance up and down his spiral staircase! And if Ken wouldn't take possession of her in every possible way, then she hoped that his home would!

Standing on the balcony, still soaking this all in, Brenda was rattled when Ken snuck up from behind and clasped his hands around her hips. He eased up even closer, brushing the small of her back with his bulge. Brenda began to relax, in his arms, and they just stood there, king and queen, discussing things. The conversation graduated into talk of groupies, the many what-ifs and myths about sex, celebrities and . . . well, just things that a top anchorwoman wouldn't expect to discuss with a celebrity bachelor. At the two o'clock hour the two toasted, clasped wrists to sip at their drinks and dissolved into one another's lips. Brenda almost spilled her martini. Ken took hold of the drinks and then, he took hold of her. Eventually, he spread her out on the floor, amongst the pile of pillows in front of a blazing fire. All of Brenda's defenses and pretenses were abandoned. She didn't just feel submissive, she *wanted* to be submissive. Either that, or else she had no other choice but to be caught up in the spell, serving him unconsciously. But then, Ken must have wanted her that much more, because the way he took Brenda . . . he took her as if he had something to prove. He grabbed her and worked her body as if she was new, foreign, undiscovered land to conquer and claim. Again, again and still again, Ken robbed Brenda of all her sensibilities. He turned her out! Even as he spent all of himself inside of her, he desired more. And she was just as delirious and mindless with her own responses. Out of control, still writhing from Ken's incredible abuse of her, Brenda extended the post play, nibbling at his torso, nipples, genitals and even his toes. The teen-iest bites built to a crescendo of salacious slurping and sucking. Every plateau excited Ken more, not expecting Brenda to turn out this freaky; freakier than he'd ever imagined! Even as freaky as a groupie! And just to think, he saw a church-girl in her.

Brenda fell half asleep somewhere between his thighs and his ass, not even aware when Ken got up to shower and complete his nightly rituals. Through watery eyes, Brenda later imag-ined that Ken was way across the loft, in the study, with a lamp over him. Writing? A question mark twisted in her face. The last expression of the night.

She was the first to wake the next morning. 10am. And like a thunderbolt just struck, she jolted, thinking she'd over-slept her errands and duties for the day ahead. Yet, that sud-den impulse that woke her was merely a pinch of reality. She *wasn't* dreaming. She'd lain with Ken. No. She *fucked* Ken like she'd never fucked anyone else. Like she'd never fucked anyone in her *dreams!* Not convinced, she told herself, "*Hell no.*" The truth was, Ken really fucked *her.* And he did it like a triathlon athlete. But then, *he had to get out of the bed and write?* Brenda was a maze of desperate emotions with the morning's daylight disturbing her peace. She rose from under Ken's draping arm and eased over to the window to fold the blinds upwards—pushing the "pause button" on Mother Nature's sunny wake-up call.

Brenda jumped into the shower, slipped on a pair of Ken's boxers and a clean, official baseball jersey over her bare breasts. She investigated more of Ken's living quarters. The kitchen, the bathrooms, medicine cabinets and eventually the study. Ken left a book. . . . a journal open. Maybe he fell asleep writ-ing and carelessly left it exposed. Or perhaps it was there for her to discover? To find out certain things?

Naw . . . Ken wouldn't be that extreme.

With the very little daylight that bounced down through the balcony doors onto the marble and up to the study, Brenda peeked through Ken's written entries. His latest entry was both anemic (for its lack of depth or meaning), and robust (in its passion and sexuality), describing how excited he was about a relationship with a real *live* news anchorwoman. He was actually more into *her* than she even realized. There was talk of her perfect shape, her sparkling eyes and dark, bronzed mane. Brenda was a toss-up between satisfied (with his interest in her) and abandoned (by his open-mindedness.) And—

How **dare** *he document my blowjob!* **Fuck!** She felt violated. But on second thought, this *was* his *personal* journal. Wasn't he able to write what he wanted? Brenda gazed over towards the balcony and bedroom in the distance. Ken had turned over, but was still asleep. She began to flip back through the days, weeks and months, very interested in Ken's other trysts, or even his feelings during the playoffs.

There were two or three others. She was afraid of that, still curious as to who she was sharing him with. There were relationships in Atlanta, L.A. and New York. In New York, surely of specific interest to Brenda (because of location), a dancer named Moet was noted in the journal. Realizing that he was detailing accounts with a topless dancer, Brenda found herself flipping too fast, skipping pages and hoping to stumble on some juicy revelations. Her heart pounded as she flipped back to the latest entry and worked her way backwards.

Ken was surprised about the dancer's murder. Okay. Brenda's mind continued to spin. *Was he really surprised or was he just keeping notes to cover his ass?* He knew so much about Moet. *Did he kill her? Moet is Nadine Butler.* Brenda recalled news coverage with one side of her brain and calculated Ken's involvement with the other. *Damn! Ken Stevens . . .* **the** *Ken Stevens was involved with a murder victim! Coincidence?*

Aloof with reckless excitement, Brenda flipped back through the journal. There was a skirmish with a white man after a long night with Moet—a date with Moet and a friend.

Camay from Queens, Ken wrote.

Wow. Brenda felt she'd stepped deep into a treasure chest of answers to life's most pressing mysteries, and that the map to some hidden secret was opened there in front of her. She'd forgotten all about the playoffs. And now, she even felt uneasy about the sex from a few hours earlier. That was all pushed aside by her ambitions for a hot story, and the improprieties of how she was getting it.

"Did you find what you were looking for?" The journal fell

to the floor, swept there with the rush of paranoia that drove through Brenda's body. Ken was towering over her, just a few feet away, at the top of the spiral staircase. In most other circumstances, a half naked man—tall, available, and wearing a frilly pair of boxer shorts, would be enticing; inviting. But Brenda was dead wrong here . . . and she was the one in violation, not Ken.

Fear (with a capital F) filled the space between the two. Distress pumped Brenda's heart faster still, until Ken spoke again.

"I'm shocked at you, prying into my personal life like that. I feel so . . . so violated." Ken approached Brenda, her expressionless face, and he casually picked up the journal to replace it on the desk. Capitalizing on the engrossing shadow that he represented, hovering over Brenda like a vulture, Ken leaned down with his nose inches from hers. His approach was peaceful, harmless even, but it made Brenda even more uncomfortable. What her shower washed away returned with a quickness to her armpits and the folds between her thighs.

"I . . . I just . . . it was opened and . . ."

"You know what this means *now,* don't you?" Brenda was as still as stone, shaking her head slowly and unknowing. "Lemme show you." Ken lifted Brenda like a casualty and her arms circled around his neck submissively. He carried her carefully down the steps, maintaining a playful expression of utter disgust. Brenda was calmed by the warm embrace of Ken's strong arms, still holding her wrongdoing in her eyes. Across the main floor and back up to the bedroom, Ken placed Brenda down (as though she were his prey), on top of their soiled sheets, and he assaulted her with the wicked smile of a nemesis. Intrigued, but not afraid, Brenda put her palm to Ken's chest.

"You're not going to hurt me, *are* you?"

"You've been a bad, bad girl, Bree. Where I come from, bad girls get *punished.*" Ken pressed himself past her ounce of prevention and growled, then barked loudly.

Brenda's body jerked with fright just before Ken dug his teeth dramatically into her neck while restraining her hands with his—overpowering her to the point of surrender. Just enough to make an impression on her skin, Ken continued growling and snorting and gnawing as if he were Brenda's personal bloodhound.

"No! No, *please* . . ." Brenda wriggled underneath Ken, her eyes widening, her face smiling with pleasing anguish.

"Ken! *Pleeeease* don't leave any marks. Oh, Ken, pleeeease—ahh!" Half screaming, half shrieking, Brenda was helpless and pinned against the silk sheets. Ken adjusted himself on top of her. Lowering himself as if to enter her. He pulled Brenda's wrists to her sides, and began nibbling, biting and teasing her nipples through the jersey. Now straddling her, with his knees forcing her arms against her waist, Ken sat lightly on her pelvis and began beating his chest Tarzan-style. He let out a roaring, echoing yelp, as if *he* had just transformed into the American werewolf. Brenda gasped, not knowing whether Ken would eat her whole or just ravage and rape her. Either way, she didn't mind.

"Now. You dare invade my privacy?"

"Ken. Stop. I don't know what you're about to do, but you've got me pinned. I can't do a thing. I shouldn't have looked through your journal. I'm *sorry*," Brenda pleaded, seriously wondering if Ken was a killer. "What do you want from me? You're scaring the *daylights* out of me!"

"What do I *want*? You've just violated the most personal, intimate details of my life. Who the *fuck* do you think you are?" Ken changed from jest to no-nonsense.

"Ken . . . I'm sorry . . ." A convincing tear spilled from Brenda's eye. "Just tell me what you want—I'll do it." Brenda didn't see the excitement forming in Ken's boxers.

"Slave hours. You owe me three slave hours."

"Slave hours?" Brenda wiped her cheek against the sheets.

"Yes. You do . . . as I say." Ken's fists went to his hips. Brenda's tongue poked around under her left cheek while she deliberated just how extensive her penance would be. Then she silently agreed by giving in. She let herself go, not really wanting to hear Ken's commands, but obediently complying to every beck and call. Brenda was Ken's sex slave for more than an hour, and she loved it. Exhausting not only every possibility, position and taboo, but her energy as well. In so many ways, Ken was Brenda's breakfast.

* * *

Ken allowed Brenda to nap into the 1 o'clock hour, while he made waffles and turkey sausages. It was late, but it just seemed politically correct to have breakfast. The sweet aroma woke her, as Ken stood over her overworked body with a tray of edibles. She hid her guilt of the prying and the slave labor by busying herself, smoothing the sheets and tossing the base- ball jersey back onto her naked body. Ken went to retrieve another tray for himself and they both sat comfortably on the bed facing each other, hungrily feeding their appetites.

"Listen . . . I really *am* sorry I went through your per- sonal stuff, but I just couldn't help noticing . . . umm..Moet. The dancer."

Ken continued chewing, thinking about all he wrote in the journal and what possibilities could've come to Brenda's mind. He spoke through the food. Casually

"What *about* her?"

"Ken, she was murdered. You obviously know *that*."

"I do."

"And you've been speaking with Detective Wade on the subject."

"Mmm . . ." He let off a sigh, neither agreeing or denying.

"Alright . . . let me be perfectly honest with you . . ." Brenda wiped the sausage juice from her lips. "If there's a story here, and I suspect there is, I'd like to get first dibs." All sincerity surfaced in Brenda's face as she maintained eye contact with Ken.

"And that's why you're fucking me? For a *story*?"

"Ken! I did not know about your relationship with Moet until a few hours ago. You're not being fair; I'm with you be- cause I *wanna* be . . . I loved every minute I've spent with you. Every minute." Brenda let some ghetto slip through her all- American TV facade. "I'm not with you for a story, or for any *other* reason but to *be* with you. Can't you respect me that much? Do you think I'd *honestly* go through with your slave hours if I didn't feel something for you?"

"*Sounds* good anyway." Ken was still for her convictions, but then went back to his waffles; unaffected. Brenda pushed her tray aside and reached to take the fork from Ken's hand. She set it down and moved the tray in one swift motion, before she ad- justed herself so that she'd be sitting in his lap with her legs around his waist. She also draped her arms around Ken's neck, close and intimate enough to feel him exhale a maple syrup scent into her nostrils.

"Listen to me, Mr. Stevens. Mister star pitcher and marathon fuck of my life. Can't a career woman have the same insatiable desires that the groupies do? Can't I want you, have *and* **do** you because you fine . . . not for some ulterior motive? Can't you see me for me, and not a woman with a title and a mission? Maybe I was wrong to talk shop with you so early, but my instincts want the story. *My insides* want you. So if you want, we can forget about the story. That's my day job. But *you?* I want you for my night job." Brenda followed up with an all-out tongue-in-his-mouth assault on Ken. It wasn't meant to be convincing, but it did convince him. Brenda was a flying free spirit now, just letting herself go. Breakfast got cold as they became preoccupied with other things; like part two of the slave hours.

Back at Channel 5, Brenda sat with the director for the evening news. She was staring into space while they reviewed the forthcoming broadcast.

"Brenda, snap out of it—"

Brenda shook her head.

"—You okay? Want me to get a fill-in tonight?"

"No, no . . . I'm fine. I was just thinking about something."

"You sure?"

"I'm double sure," she responded. Only, her head was indeed elsewhere. Right about now she was wondering what her producer would think if he knew about her activities during the past eight or so hours. And she had to smile to herself about the idea of it . . . *the churchgirl. Hahaha*!

Segments had been airing for a few days now, relating to the delay of court proceedings of Douglass Gilmore. The case was going nowhere. And the follow-up stories and the investigative strategies for the broadcasts were at a loss for significance. It was called "*running*" in TV terms; just filling airtime. But Brenda Feather was curling with information, all of it forming knots in her tummy. Ken shared a few things with her, but he also demanded that she keep him anonymous, as if he never existed. Brenda also knew that Darryl, her news director, would insist on sources; legitimate verifiable sources. Brenda had the biggest, most verifiable source in all the land; problem was that she swore to confidentiality. Question was, how was she gonna get her information to broadcast? Because . . . she *was* gonna get the story out. Brenda knew that her details would be important for a few reasons. Number one: Douglass Gilmore, who was the FBI's only target, was sitting in a New Jersey jail. And two: there was a crime to be solved. Pity, that the overall investigation seemed to be a battle between local and federal law enforcement agencies, playing tug-of-war with Gilmore's son. A mix of egos and miscommunication. Most importantly, the public trust and interest was being violated and misdirected because someone concocted a twisted story.

CHAPTER SIXTEEN

Southern Discomfort

Mechelle was desperate for associations when she returned to Atlanta. It had been easy to come back to Denworth since, after all, he was so head over heels for her. So, nothing really changed when Mechelle went down to see Denworth just a month after Douglass was carted off to jail—

They didn't lie when they said "*the flesh is weak.*"

—And naturally, Denworth served her as if she'd never left. The day she arrived, he tore that pussy up as if it were his last. No condom; no apprehension.

"I miss you . . . so . . . much," Denworth tried to say while he was thrusting himself inside of her. "And I want . . . you to . . . have . . . ***ooh, God!*** I want you to . . . have my . . . ***baby***!"

But, even though Denworth sprayed every drop of himself on the downstroke, Mechelle wasn't concerned about getting pregnant; that *already* happened. If anything, she wondered if her college love would realize that she was starting to show. There'd *sure* be a lot to explain then. However, to have him there, virtually waiting for her while he still pursued his degree, was extremely convenient for this fix she was in.

And two weeks after they rock and rolled, Mechelle dropped the bomb.

"Den, I don't know how to tell you this . . . but, I'm pregnant." And now that she told him that it was *his* baby, there was no end to his kindness and testaments of love. He was ecstatic about the news, and he showed it with plenty of tears and promises.

To throw a wet rag on her flames of guilt, Mechelle found refuge in a local church, only two blocks from Denworth's place. Church provided her with more to do than sit around a kiss-ass all day and night in a two-family house. Volunteering with the locals made her feel legitimate and worthwhile, because there were so many things about her that weren't.

And now that Mechelle was in the thick of things, there was no stopping her. Two days after she told Denworth the news, they found the nearest Justice of the Peace and tied the knot. Just like that; as if Douglass Gilmore and her new beginnings up in New York never mattered. Denworth had no way of knowing Mechelle's reasons for the hasty elopement, and she didn't reveal how desperate a move this was for her to have a man in her life—a father for her child, with all of the resources that came with it. Here she was, entering her second trimester, with no promise for the future. She *had* to leave New York if she was gonna keep this baby. And *damned* if she was gonna give up *this* one.

It was her pleasure to see Denworth suddenly so proud to be an expecting dad, regardless of the lies she harbored. He got more and more into Mechelle as her physical changes became more obvious. Her cheeks were glowing. Her color was a rich brown, and her breasts were growing into grapefruits, one step up from the healthy Sunkist orange shapes that she was used to. Denworth was so head over heels that he became the infant, sucking (and even drinking!) from her nipples. He was naïve to the ways of a woman; gullible even. These thoughts were dangerous thoughts for Mechelle, unhealthy for the most part. She began to feel stress and anxiety about not being truthful, as if her lying might reflect on the newborn. She had nightmares of the infant being retarded, with one arm. All of it was too much for her, and soon she felt compelled to tell Denworth the truth. This was particularly heavy on her mind during one stroll back home from her volunteer schedule. Her soul was having a discussion with her conscience, wondering if she'd be kicked out the house, or worse, forced to move back to New York. Now, there was a throbbing headache, and she changed her mind again.

"Tomorrow's another day," she said aloud. And it was practical to think this way since today, at least, she knew what she'd be coming home to. First Denworth would have her sit back on the sofa with an herbal tea to soothe her. Meanwhile, he'd have her shoes and socks stripped and her feet soaking in some luke-warm water with menthol crystals giving off penetrating, soothing vapors. As her feet soaked, Den always melted her heavy thoughts with soft kisses about her calves and thighs, always paying special attention to her lower body. One or two times he got zealous, but only after she approved. Of course dinner was already warming, and by the time Mechelle was totally relaxed, Den would play waiter, bringing the food by the tray, so that she didn't have to budge. After dinner, there was a stress-busting bath and a follow-up massage. Naturally the se-quence relaxed Mechelle into a deep sleep. When she woke in the morning, there he was, with breakfast and fruit juice. Serving her hand and foot, hour in, hour out. He didn't even *ask* for sex, probably not wanting to interfere with or induce labor. *Labor?* She was in her second trimester! Mechelle thought Den was so *dense* sometimes, but he was grounded with that good city job; good benefits and insurance. *Insurance!* That was a big word for Mechelle. It rang bells of security. And what black man from the hood had those kinds of benefits? She was tired and exhausted of dead ends. Den was her only ray of light in a tunnel of uncertainty. So much was going through Mechelle's mind as she stepped along the sidewalk and up the walkway to see her Denny-pooh after a long day.

As she ascended to the second floor of the house, she could hear the phone ringing continuously. She thought that to be strange, because it was after 6pm. Denworth should have been home waiting to pamper her, dinner cooked, soothing waters and herbal tea ready to absorb her. So far, Denworth's pampering hadn't faded or slacked in the weeks after the vows were exchanged. This was strange.

Mechelle hurried with the keys and then to the wall phone in the kitchen. She caught her breath, observing the surroundings at the same time. She tried to be patient with the cordial greetings to and from Den's parents; her in-laws. *Man!* She hated adopting that title; *in-laws.* Denworth's luggage and family fixtures. Like she didn't have enough problems of her own. His mom was obsessive, as if Den was born yesterday; and his father acted as though he had a speech problem and couldn't say hi to her. Mechelle couldn't ever recall if his father had said more than two words to her in the three years she'd known Denworth. Maybe he was an in-the-closet homo like his son was. That is, before *Mechelle* turned him out.

Scratching her head and wondering why there was no food waiting on the stove or kitchen table, Mechelle continued to make small talk and assurances with Denworth's mother as she stretched the coiled phone cord to the limits in either direction, looking for her husband. Who'd have guessed. Was *this* what the "*having your cake*" part of the saying was like? She could have yawned, finally disconnecting with her mother-in-law, Mechelle searched the house for Denworth, suddenly feeling alone and unusually deprived. Seconds later, Mechelle's scream could be heard well into the next residential block as she found Denworth, keeled over on the bed. He was 8 minutes into a severe asthma attack, his frozen blue image clutching an empty inhalor pressed between his lips.

Mechelle raced to various cabinets, the extra weight in her tummy bouncing like a Nerf football. She went through draws and the medicine cabinet, but that was useless. Denworth's lungs had already contracted for the last time. His last breath had already come and gone, however short.

The police and ambulance arrived to find Mechelle in a state of shock, sitting for a series of officials with their dutiful inquiries.

Jailhouse Romance

Valerie suddenly regretted the circumstances to which she'd committed herself, standing in line amongst a crowd of other women. There were mostly mothers, girlfriends and a few wives with their noisy children. She waited apprehensively for her turn to be permitted through the metal detectors, but some women were holding up all the processing, insisting that they be able to visit with their children.

"No children permitted." The guards kept affirming the rules on the wall of Passaic County Jail.

"Damn you, Demetrius," was all Valerie could say to herself while she stood amidst the noxious perfumes and body odors in the air. After all, she'd only met Gil's son once at the club. And frankly she didn't get that much of a vibe from him—arrogant and cold as he was. But if it weren't for Demetrius, with his kind request and rewarding looks, along with the fact that she *did* work for the Gilmore family, Valerie wouldn't have hired a town car to take her all the way to New Jersey. Nor would she have gotten up so early—6 AM!—to beat the rush of locals who converged at the jail every day. The deep breaths and long, relenting sighs helped her through it. Might as well follow through with it since, after all, it did take her nearly an hour to do her make-up.

And now there were other women staring at her. It was really nothing new for Valerie, always the pretty one in any group, attracting widened eyes and hungry expressions. The stares also came from corrections officers at the jail. They looked like (or at least dressed like) policemen, with navy blue uniforms and bright yellow, embroidered patches. But how could she tell these were law enforcement officers with their nostrils flaring like the customers who salivated before her at the club? She may as well have come naked. But then, that's really how she learned to look at men *and* women, as if she could see right through them. It was the only way to look at a person honestly; the only way to get past people's smoke and mirror campaigns. And besides, Valerie was forever comfortable when she looked at people in this way. It was a disarming skill, and at the same time it enabled her to recognize a certain control over men and women who were so predictable; so transparent.

As she followed procedures to enter the jail, men bent over backwards with all that extra *nicey-nicey stuff* to accommodate her, which told Valerie what she already knew: that the jailers were no different than regular civilians. *They're hungry, nasty and horny like the rest of us,* she told herself, getting rid of the uneasiness that occupied her belly. After an identification check, and the completion of a series of forms required of all first-time non-family members, Valerie was allowed to pass through where she joined a group of others and an escort, to file into an elevator. On the fourth floor, she was directed to a room with 10 diner-style counter stools. A long Formica counter ran the length of the room, and a Plexiglas window separated each prisoner and their visitor on the other side. Thinner and more humbled than she remembered him to be, Douglass emerged from a door and assumed his seat in the closed room. Both Douglass and Valerie picked up a telephone that enabled direct communication. They greeted one another, and made cautious conversation until they established a rapport. It eventually became more than rapport, as Valerie found herself visiting again and again. The same formalities, executions and precautions. The dialogue usually started out as small talk.

". . . to tell you the truth, I couldn't fully remember what you looked like when we spoke on the phone." Valerie's brute honesty came out that first day.

"Well, you'll have to excuse my presence. This is not exactly your ideal blind date," Douglass said, and they both smiled. "I'm not exactly in the best body I could be in, either. There's little room for opportunity to exercise. The food is so-so, and the company is yuck." Douglass attempted to appeal to Valerie's sympathy with his sense of humor. She shot back a compassionate response before he said, "But I'm doing my best to get by."

As weeks went past, they became closer. Valerie became an advocate, not just a dancer pretending to be good company. There was more concern now. She cared.

"When will they let you out of here?" Valerie eventually asked that most obvious question.

"You've got to look me straight in the eyes when I say this to you, Valerie . . ." Douglass could simultaneously picture himself in the reflection as he looked through the Plexiglas, focusing sincerely on Valerie's eyes. ". . . I am not a murderer. I have never killed anybody. The worst thing I've done is close the lid on the garbage can at home; I trapped a couple of raccoons in there, because they were a nuisance. They would scatter garbage all over the driveway. In the morning they were picked up by the garbage truck; and that still bothers me to this *day*. They are entitled to live, to make mistakes and to create noise while they're here on earth . . . just like you and me. I had no right to kill them, but honestly, I've never done anything worse than that. I don't belong here with real murderers, bank robbers and rapists . . ."

"I'm sad for you, Douglass. I feel so helpless with you caught up here. This place . . . these guards, the dogs and the guns . . . it's all like one big monster. Like I'm in this giant cage, coming in to visit you. But I've got to leave you here." Douglass put his palm to the window. Valerie matched the gesture. They were connected, but not connected.

"I know, I know. Valerie, you've gotta know something. You're the first person to come and see me here. My girlfriend . . . my *ex*-girlfriend, Mechelle, didn't even budge. You've been the first to show me compassion. To show me that I'm cared for . . ."

"Please, Douglass. People *do* care about you. It's just that they have their own priorities . . ."

"But if you know what I know, then you'd see that the majority of people's priorities are out of whack in the first place. See—Valerie, let me tell you what being here did for me. I didn't need any *reforming*. What I *did* need was to weed out all of the bullshit in my life. Like the tag-a-longs that were unproductive to my agenda. The toxic people . . . the energy drainers who were around me as quote-unquote *friends*, and the weak hearted who couldn't stand by me when times got tough. Now, all of those clouds are gone and I can focus on *me* . . . that means finding my purpose in life, setting short term and long term goals, keeping an agenda and lastly, maintaining discipline so that I can continuously follow through with my plans. *That* is priority for me. If you ask most people on the street today, they couldn't tell you what their purpose in life is. I guarantee you their face will twist up in a knot like, '*whaddaya mean?*'" Valerie leaned into the receiver and moved her palm from the window to support her chin. Douglass was emphasizing with convincing pokes at the glass, pounding on the counter to drive certain points home.

On another visit, Douglass threw his heart out to Valerie with a sudden, passionate statement.

"Val, I don't mean to say that I might've *shriveled up and died* if you hadn't come along, but you have made me feel whole again. If there is such a thing. Knowing that *someone* cares has made me feel more comfortable in a place where I'm not even supposed to be alive. I have to constantly fill my mind with reasons why I *must* go on, reasons why I *must* survive, and reasons why I must reach my goals, fulfill my dreams and accomplish my purpose in life. Not only to get by on a day to day basis, but to maintain a perspective; how this time here is only a minute in my century here on earth. The time I'm spending here—learning about me, learning how to love—is the challenge to achieve my own greatness in life. This is it. Here and now. Time to plan, to organize and to aspire. *Fuck* that judge and the FBI and all their claims! The circumstances that put me here are the same that will set me free. And the **ultimate judge** runs **all** that shit! *Are you with me?* This puny man, with his puny laws, and his puny ways, have *nothing* on the methods of the universe." Valerie's eyes received some of the passion and energy in Douglass's words. Her eyes were watering and her body trembling. She felt electricity passing through the phone and down into her spine.

"By the way . . ." Douglass added after a pause, ". . . how's the weather outside? I haven't seen daylight for a while now." Valerie was aghast, but amused by Douglass's sudden change in direction. As if she had to shake sleep from her eyes, she shook the riveting sensation with a self-imposed jitter and recalled his question. Shortly after Douglass's heartfelt testimony, Valerie walked away from her 20-minute visit floating on clouds of inspiration. She was looking forward to reclining in the back of the waiting Lincoln town car, a reminder of the drastic difference between freedom and captivity. She wondered if even she was taking freedom for granted. She also thought about Douglass and how worthy he was to have her; as she was to have him.

When he gets home, she declared.

Manifesto

Douglass was invigorated by Val's visit. He began to see her more frequently; even as much as every other week. He didn't want to overkill the novelty of it all, but he knew he had to compete with the hordes of men who already had two advantages over him. They were free *and* they got to see Valerie half naked; maybe even touching her on a lap dance. Douglass's battle wasn't as much with the customers as it was with temptation itself. Temptation and loneliness, just the same, were the forces he was fighting.

To make up for where he was lacking, Douglass purchased some writing materials from the jail's commissary and began to write to Valerie. That's how he made the most of his time, writing songs and poems (regardless of being forced into becoming a second-hand smoker).

So focused and filled with emotion was Douglass, that he completed four letters a day. He also began putting together his business plan and drawing up diagrams of a new, bigger Gilmore's. A new empire. Douglass often dreamed of his future and recollected his past, a big picture of where he'd been, where he was now, and where he was going. He thought about his contributions to the world and how, because of his existence and input, many had benefitted. He was certain that many had forgotten. But in his heart, and the war chest that was his memory, he felt blessed and accomplished. By age 30 Douglass had a heavy hand in most every element of black entertainment. Now in jail, recollections and visions poured through his brain as he slept and dreamed by night, contemplating the future. By day he continued with songs and poems, based on his own experiences of love and life.

One day he was deeply involved in pencil sketches for an all-new 10,000-square foot adult entertainment complex. Just over his shoulder, a prisoner named Fumi inquired about Douglass's project. Thin in mass and thick in culture, the Nigerian was quite interested in the imaginative perspectives, insightful knowledge of the business, and Douglass's strong desire to see it though to completion. Even if only in jail, Douglass created and devised a full-scale, step by step plan for his new club.

With a manifesto, drawings of various angles, costs and financial forecasts, it was clear that Douglass fully intended to see his dream through to reality. Fumi was even more inspired that Douglass's dream had the foundation of experience. As the two came to know each other better, Douglass learned of Fumi's homeland and practices. The African maintained certain traditions. He had been jailed for an alleged financial fraud and was awaiting trial. The judge denied him bail on the basis of him being a flight risk. In the meantime, the two shared each other's knowledge on a daily basis. Douglass talked adult entertainment, black entertainment and the Internet, while Fumi spoke of polygamy, double standards in America, and the spiritual wisdom of Afrocentricity. He felt strongly that the United States and the rest of humanity owed a huge debt to Africa, or else they just had no idea and didn't recognize those debts and obligations to Africa.

"There's a myth and misconception of Africa as a dark and barbaric continent; less civilized and profiled as separate from the rest of humanity," said Fumi with his rich African dialect. But as amazed as Douglass was about Fumi's knowledge of history and the state of humanity, so too was Fumi flattered by Douglass's recollections of his Grammy award interviews, celebrity functions and his family's near-domination of the adult entertainment industry. Fumi was spirited in sharing his rights of passage, the teachings of his elders African mentors and how the African—the black man—was actually the ultimate man. *The first man*, Fumi explained. *Every man's origin is African.* And although Douglass's experience paled when compared to the African's, in the end, the two learned much from one another. There was a promise of friendship that went without saying.

New Jersey, U.S. Attorney's Office

"Mr. Cipriani speaking."

"Yessir. This is Mr. Locca, returning your call."

"Oh yes. The Gilmore case. Has your client decided to cooperate? I won't hold this deal open too much longer."

"My client is not budging, Mr. Cipriani. He maintains his

innocence and says there's nothing to cooperate about. I'm ready to take this to trial if you are."

"I'll let the judge know so that he can set a date."

"Thank you, Mr. Cipriani. Have a nice day." As soon as Cipriani hung up, he picked up and poked at four buttons on the phone—lightning fast.

"Hammer, I need to see you and Walsh in my office, ASAP." Mr. Cipriani, the assistant U.S. attorney handling the case involving Gilmore, was sitting adjacent to his boss, looking desperately for answers. In need of a scapegoat. He had just hung up the phone at the conference table.

"I sure hope your boys have something. If they don't, they'd better *find* something. I've got pressure coming from the public and I've got political pressure from the higher-ups. These Biancos have been raping our communities for years and all we have is a New York arrest for a New York murder, with no trial date. You *do* realize that if I call the judge on this case he's gonna set the date for tomorrow, don't you?" Cipriani sat stiff in his seat, suddenly more agitated by their boss-slash-employee relationship.

"Sir, I understand. I trust my guys on this case. I'm riding with them all the way, until there's a conviction."

"Tell me something, Mr. Cipriani . . . if you will . . ." The U.S. attorney leaned over with a lower volume of concern in his voice. "If this is gonna be the big RICO-slash-organized crime bust that you've promised me . . . one that the *governor* can even be proud of, then where is the union involvement? Where are the wire tapes, the highjackings and the political payoffs? Where are the snitches, the territorial battles and the savage killings?" The U.S. attorney leaned in even more, and now he was down to a whisper. "If I wasn't in the business of law enforcement, I'd swear that the mob . . ." He raised his volume. "The mafia . . ." Now he shouted. ". . . the fuckin' La Cosa Nostra was INVISIBLE!"

Cipriani took the verbal stabbing personally and speechlessly strutted to his own office down the hallway to await the agents.

Celebrate Life

"Hee-Hee-Hee-Hee-Haw, Hee-Hee-Hee-Hee-Haw! That was some old school for ya, with Miss Supa-dupa Fly, Missy Elliot, rapping over Gina Thompson's slammin' joint, '*The Things You Do*'."

That familiar rock-the-bells ring, along with the bass-beat and groove of music moved the party crowd of 50-something into a somewhat delirious joy and dance celebration of the life and times of Ms. Brandi Rose. Debbie was even showing signs of a sweet and sour delight. A good thing, and a relief to everyone who gathered today at the Rose home. Only hours earlier, even before the final trumpets of traditional black spirits ended the funeral, Debbie was uncontrollably shaken. All of her mom's best friends, her co-workers and colleagues gathered in her honor, in their Sunday best, smelling good, looking good, with hair in place and shoes sparkling; the send-off was the ultimate killjoy. Everyone was there at the end, but in the end, that wouldn't bring Mama back!

"Ms. Rose, the homemaker . . . Ms. Rose, the mother . . . Ms. Rose, the model of progress for a community of single black women and children . . ." Her boss, Mr. Felton, showed gratitude through his words and appreciation from his pockets. Ms. Rose was his ace employee, and accordingly, he footed the bill to the end and beyond, paying for all expenses, as well as the celebration after the funeral and more.

Mr. Felton went on to say, "Ms. Rose was an example that a single mother *can* achieve greatness . . . she *can* accomplish . . . she *can* make great contributions in life!" The scatter of compassionate eyes were glued on the gentleman's every word. Everyone was attentive and still. Danni embraced Debbie with a warm, huddled closeness. ". . . I could stand here all day and blurt out overwhelming objectives and descriptions . . . but, in *all* of my years of living, I've learned that life is one big book. The big book is filled with many other books and stories. There are those that are written, others documented by accomplishments, and some are *never revealed*, but every book or story, whether it was complete or not, is however founded on love. Love is always at the root of the plot, so too is the story of

Brandi Rose. In her existence, in her freedoms and in her captivities, each moment was a reality because of, or for the purpose of love.

". . . When we seem to lose love, or if a loved one leaves us, we will indeed miss the moments, experiences and human interaction. But for sure, we have not lost the intangible, ever-lasting, ever-growing love that we have felt, are feeling, or will feel in the future. We are filled with love from head to toe, whether we admit it or not. Whether we *like* it or not! This is the mighty force that motivates our movements and our existence . . .

". . . Give and receive love in its fullest, most imaginable form and you will never be at a loss for love, no matter what. Life's book is called *love* . . . and every story in that book . . . just like the Brandi Rose story, is complete to whatever degree, because her story too was LOVE!"

The eulogy served its purpose, evoking a flutter of glory and praise for the deceased. The heaps of flowers, green ribbons, and the blue sky created a calmness about the ceremony. Most in attendance held a dazed expression, neither sad nor happy, just there, experiencing. A musical interlude, with three violins and an organist, caressed the audience as a young male vocalist emerged in an all-black tuxedo. He was hairless, except for sharp eyebrows and a slick, entertaining mustache. There was sincerity in his brown eyes and a brief glimmer of sun reflecting off of his coffee-brown scalp as he stepped up to a platform at the center of the floral arrangement. The music swelled to a familiar melody and carried the singer into a tailor-made version of the Ojay's song: *Brandy.* "Tony G" was introduced, and accordingly, above the open grave, the singer delivered his riveting tenor, and heart-wrenching soprano vocals. He pierced all senses with the tasteful vicissitudes of his range, eventually reaching a crescendo that caused Debbie to scream.

> *"Our best friend's gone,*
> *and we're so all alone!*
> *Oh, how could it be,*
> *they took you away from me,*
> *We real-ly miss you,*
> *Brandi,*

*We're so all alone . . .
when are you comin' back home?"*

Tony ripped and rolled his emphasis into the air, blending in with the birds that fluttered nearby. It was all poetic. Eventually, Danni could no longer suppress Debbie's erratic wails and outbursts. He tried to pull her even closer, but she just continued to let herself feed into hellified moments.

Some time later, the worst had passed for Debbie, who was now teaching Detective Wade the Electric Slide to the old school mix of *Rock, Skate, Roll Bounce, Must Be The Music* and *I Want To Thank You.* When everyone seemed exhausted, the deejay caused the record to lose speed until it stopped. Then she changed the mood with the mellow rhythm of Luther's *Don't You Know That?* By any means possible, Mrs. Rose's passing was accepted as a celebration.

By the end of the occasion, Debbie huddled with Wade and Danni to prepare and psych herself for the forthcoming announcement. When the music was cued to stop, Debbie took a deep breath to announce that she'd be leaving Chicago. Probably for good.

"There's an opportunity for me in New York, and my two friends here will be helping me to get along and build my new life." Wade snuck a conspirator's glance at Danni. Debbie was simultaneously sharing the attention with the two. At the same time, Wade was feeling a little guilty, knowing that there was little that he'd do for her new life. He also needed her assistance for some unfinished business, so it was more than convenient to have her back in New York.

Debbie went on to say, "I'll be donating this house and the equity that my mom had built here to the new *Block Watch Organization* that Mr. Felton has started in my mother's name. He's gonna convert the house into their headquarters. They plan to name the house the Rose Center after they reclaim the community . . . There will be a day-care center for children and resources for the elderly . . ." A tremendous applause erupted after Debbie's announcement. It fulfilled her beyond words. Her mom's boss, Mr. Felton, and the block watch director shook hands. Danni and Wade gave each other a buddy hug.

* * *

Halfway back to New York, Wade recalled the week and a half of events. It wasn't difficult for him to focus on his objectives since, for one reason or another, he'd been to many funerals in New York. He realized that everyone would eventually experience that one particular funeral which would tip the boat. For Debbie . . . for sure, this *was* that funeral. For Wade, that one particular funeral had been many years ago with Renee. He didn't even get to see the body because it was a closed casket ceremony. Renee was too damaged by the car accident. Sometimes Wade felt a little guilty that his emotions were absent from events like funerals and death. He was callous. The Rose funeral also reminded him of his friend, Detective Baxtor. A casualty of New York violence. And there were so many more.

That thought sent a quick surge through Wade, telling him that there was business at hand. And while the three waited at O'Hare for their midnight flight to New York, Debbie shared the rest of her experiences at the time of Moet's murder. As it turned out, the assailant that hired the girls to dance privately was the same burly man who attacked Moet when Ken dropped her home; and that was even the same man whom Ken Stevens described to Wade and Sean the police artist. Moet apparently didn't realize who he was. When she did, it was too late. She was handcuffed to the bedposts, practically naked and definitely helpless. In police terms, Wade could see past the dramatics. The two had been kidnapped. Wade had learned to weave through Debbie's emotional tangents, just as he had for Ken's talkative tangents, redirecting him from wavering. According to Debbie, she tried to contact Moet after the engagement. No answer. She eventually felt like she was abandoned, so she returned to Chicago.

If Wade could verify all of Debbie's story (and he expected to), then the FBI would need to be contacted. They most likely arrested the wrong person, because as Wade had come to find out, there was too much evidence popping up, indicating this white man as the culprit. A culprit that Wade wanted to find bad. Bad enough to solve this case.

As the airplane from Chicago descended into the New York City skyline, Wade looked across the aisle at Debbie. She was sleeping, purring against Danni's shoulder. Danni caught Wade's concern and returned an expression which shrugged back about the circumstances. Wade knew that he should inform Debbie about the dangers of returning to New York. Danni also knew that same naked truth. But both agreed that the time and place would have to be right. She'd already been through so much. After a few days of relaxation, Debbie would have to begin work. She'd be looking through mug shots, working with the police sketch artist, and perhaps she'd have to dance again at her former hot spot. In order to fish out the suspect, Debbie was the most appropriate candidate as a decoy at Fool's Paradise.

CHAPTER SEVENTEEN

Southern Discomfort

Daylight savings time. Fall back. Wade made the best of the extra hour. Lying in bed with eyes open, recounting the events of the short trip. The front door of his apartment was unlocked, and he could feel the slight change in the climate as the door swung open. The echo from the hallway told him that his sister was bringing back his mutts. How inconvenient could she be, just when he was beginning to wiggle his toes against the soft white sheets. The first conscious moments of his deep sleep. Wade could hear his mutts racing through the apartment to greet their master. Bones was no doubt straggling behind, sluggish and lazy. Bells and Whistle pushed through the bedroom door and buried Wade with their slick, slimy homecoming. Nancy peeked in the bedroom after them, satisfied that things were back to normal. She didn't mind dog-sitting, but not longer than absolutely necessary. And a week and a half was *too fucking long*. She felt like she deserved a vacation, offering her big brother a shameless smile and then escaping back out of the front door, back across the hall to her own apartment.

After a brief *hello*, Wade brushed them off of his bed and headed to the bathroom for the usual hygiene. While he attended to other odds and ends, he reached for the cordless phone to affirm his return to duty with Chief Washington. Chief informed

Wade that the FBI had returned to the precinct looking for additional details. Washington admitted that he assumed them to be pulling at straws. And then Wade commenced to share a few new revelations with his boss. Nothing like teamwork.

"I don't know what you mean. You'd better check your directory for the right extension, Mrs. Cantalk." Wade's receiver went dead midway into his discussion. The Chief heard as much as he could, until the two agents coincidentally stepped into his office. *Whew.* Quick thinking.

"Chief, how are you today? Listen, we're awfully sorry to bother you again. But we *really* would like to see Detective Wade."

"Well . . . uh . . . last I knew he was away in Chicago. On leave. I don't have any contact numbers."

"Do you know when he'll be back?"

"Should be soon . . . I'll make sure to let you know." There was a pause. "Is there anything else I can do for you?"

The chief was a little more condescending, looking out for his detective and also protecting the new information. Agents Walsh and Hammer left the office in quite a huff. Disgruntled by the little they had to work with and perhaps a lack of all the facts. They resorted to making their rounds. A couple hours at Fool's Paradise. Some hangouts of Tony the Crow. A spin through the FBI's New Rochelle branch, and then lunch at Subway for a couple of meatball subs.

"Alright, Hammer . . . let's go over our stuff."

"We've got a message on the answering machine. That's motive. We've got Junior at the scene of the crime. He *was* inside the club that evening. I know nobody has placed him next to the victim, but many have seen him nonetheless . . ."

"Why the lack of confidence on your face?" Walsh asked.

"What if the defense brings in support to say he never left the club?" Hammer played devil's advocate.

"They won't hold up in court. If they do, we'll drag their wives in . . . subpoena them as character witnesses." Hammer seemed to accept Walsh's plan. "Besides that, we can get some dancers into court . . . a few with past criminal records. Then we'll have them confirm Douglass Gilmore's dislike for Moet. At least one has seen them argue. Then of course, we have his own criminal history."

"You mean the copyright infringement?"

"Yeah. He got a year probation for that. But it still shows past criminal history. Now . . . what about fingerprints?"

"Yes! Of course. I forgot about that. Fingerprints at the Butler home. There *were* a lot of different fingerprints picked up there, but who's counting?" Hammer smiled again before he buried his teeth into the wedge. "And we can tie in Tony the Crow and the Bianco family—"

Hammer tried to swallow and speak too.

"—by his various visits to the club. We've got photos . . . there's organized crime here for sure."

"As soon as we get to the courtroom, Junior will flip his plea. I'm sure of it. See . . . if all of the defendants that we've arrested throughout the years only *knew* what little evidence we had on them, the prisons would be almost empty today. Throw words around like '*life in prison*' and they're scared shitless. We've got 'em by the balls. Remember Johnson, Brown and Robinson, uh . . . and Billings? All those guys copped out. Even Gilmore copped out on the copyright misdemeanor when he was younger. I hear he could have walked away from that scott-free. This is a fearsome machine we're a part of, partner. One that makes these heartless fools croak time after time." The two finished their meals and headed out of the entrance. North Avenue was busy with traffic in both directions. Hammer's head jerked right.

"Hey, Walsh . . . look there." Hammer pointed to an unmarked squad car, just passing them, and headed east on North Avenue. There were three people in the vehicle, and Hammer was sure that Detective Wade was driving. The vehicle was moving too fast to recognize the others, but still, the agents moved on the hunch, bolting to their Caprice across the street. With the siren and emergency light on, they backed out a few feet and recklessly swung into a wide U-turn. Walsh had no regard for oncoming traffic that was instantly thrown into a jam. Weaving through other cars, at an above-the-law speed, they charged down the median and eastbound on North until they could keep Wade within a 100-foot distance. They trailed by three car lengths and continued on for about four miles.

Team Gilmore

Debbie and Danni were with Wade, in his unmarked squad car, headed straight for the Gilmore home. A meeting had been arranged between various Gilmore supporters, friends, girl-friends and his television production crew. The car moved eas-ily onto the oval driveway and found a place to park amongst 5 other cars already situated. The three stepped into the en-trance, through the foyer, and were greeted by all in atten-dance. Demetrius was the closest, with his pectorals slightly bulging, pressing though a black, silk kimono and its oriental embroidery that marked the breast pocket in red and white. He shook hands with Wade, returned Danni's shotokan greet-ing, and then welcomed Debbie back to New York with a quaint peck on the cheek.

The SuperStar home office was busy with familiarity and purpose. Valerie was there, elegant as could be in a mudcloth V-neck sweater and a headwrap of olive, black and orange tribal colors. Mechelle had returned from Georgia after the cremation of her husband. Her multi-colored pullover was oversized, lying gently against her growing belly. Her hair was twisted into large cornrows, pulling back into a wild bush of curls. Everyone could sense that she'd been through a lot. Valerie knew about Mechelle, the baby, and the problems she had with Douglass. But despite the issues, she remained cordial, sincere and loving. With not a care in the world, Valerie played co-host as well, mingling in the semi-circle with Demetrius and Dino. Dino was a good friend of Douglass's. He was originally a customer, but eventually, he became an employee and a trustworthy bouncer who didn't feed into antisocial behavior amongst some of the staff. Douglass recognized his genuine efforts and the two soon became best of friends. Dino would escort Douglass to various celebrity functions with that *just-in-case* attitude.

Naturally, Dino and Demetrius also became close friends. They also knew and associated with just about everyone else at the gathering. There was SuperStar staff, like Darryl, who handled much of the camera-work for the TV show. And Greg, who was that college-educated publicist and writer for the SuperStar magazine. He also served as a commentator for the

TV show. And Lou was also present with his stellar personality and shining attitude. He generally hosted celebrity events and he also emceed many of the live events which the SuperStar firm sponsored. Beyond those tasks, Lou also contributed columns, and performed public relations for the magazine.

All 8 supporters (including Detective Wade) occupied themselves in various discussions about Moet's murder. They paired off in conversations about Douglass's jail-house situation and the slow court proceedings. Nobody spoke about the bail, as it was beyond the imaginations of all in attendance.

Eavesdropping

"Can I have your attention, everyone?" Demetrius was casual and sincere. Some took seats on the couch. Dino sat in an executive chair behind the only desk in the room, while others stood or perched themselves against a bookcase or the door jam. Everyone was attentive and concerned.

"First I'd like to thank you all for taking time out from your schedules to come here today. You should all know one another by now and why we're here today . . . our friend, my friend and colleague, Douglass, has been in jail for the past seven months for something he didn't do. There are a few people here that know more about the case than I do, and they'll be speaking out momentarily. But, before Detective Wade speaks to you, I wanna say this. Douglass is not only my friend and yours, but he's also given himself . . . more than what ten people might give. I'll put myself out there right now by saying that *everyone*, except for our two guests, has been at the receiving end of Douglass's generous actions. He's the most productive person I've ever met. In the past ten years he's been the promoter, the TV producer, night club developer, and an all-around entrepreneur that each of us has looked up to. Let us all reciprocate that love and consideration which he's shown us selflessly . . . Detective Wade? You'd like to say something?"

"Well, I've met most of you already, during my investigation of this case. And I have to admit that as of recently, I was misled. However, you should know that it wasn't *ever* my intention to arrest Douglass. I didn't have all the facts; and more than that, the case was taken out of my hands. The FBI's organized crime task force—from Jersey, mind you—is behind the steering wheel, and they're driving *backwards*. I don't have any say-so in the matter, but I *would* like to solve this case myself and bring Moet's killer to justice . . ." Wade grinded his teeth and with sleeves folded up, went on to describe his plan on how the group could compel the New Jersey authorities and certain political powers to release Douglass from jail. They would use the press, television and even picketing to spread the word: "FREE GILMORE!" The theme was a bold and worthy plea. And once the story leaked, the interest and concern from the general public would surely generate a positive reaction.

A parabolic mic is a device that law enforcement agents use to listen in on conversations which occur inside dwellings of up to 100 feet or more away. Walsh and Hammer kept one in the trunk of their vehicle for a rainy day. It even collected a little dust.

Today, after following Wade's vehicle down North Avenue, Hammer pulled the black metal case from the trunk and carried it into the woods, behind an embankment that was directly across from the Gilmore home. He began to erect it as quickly as possible while Walsh stood over him with a pair of binoculars. The two looked like a pair of toy soldiers. One spread-eagled on the grass; the other looking over him like a scout. Hammer was fumbling with the mini satellite dish, trying to adjust it to a precise degree of focus on the big house. He plugged in two sets of earphones and began to listen attentively while adjusting the volume and frequency of the device. The battery pack was low, but at the moment, the agents could hear a guy named Greg speaking to the group. He was both angry and passionate about the events, voicing his aggressions to all. Hammer began to hear parts of the transmission as it popped in and out.

"We're gonna make this happen. Before this is over everything is gonna flip our way. The only captives will be the judge, the D.A. and the FBI. They will be forced to play our game. We're gonna squeeze and squeeze until we get blood from them . . ." Greg was convincing. He was passionate. And the words brought a fresh sweat to Hammer's brow. Again, the reception fizzled out, provoking a sizzling noise in the agent's ears. Detective Wade readdressed the group effort, confirming assignments and the overall plan of action.

"We're back up!" Hammer was loud and excited about getting the mic working again. Relieved, Walsh was glad he didn't have to try and read lips through the windows of the house anymore.

". . . Ladies, you know what you have to do. Dino, Demetrius and Danni, you will be the eyes at the back of my head. I'll have to be ready to take him out. We've already got two down. If there has to be a third, so be it. But nobody else has to die here. Do we have an understanding?"

"Wade is the shooter?" Hammer's eyes grew by 10 percent. Walsh was jolted by his partner's high pitch and heavy volume. "*Wade's the shooter*! No **wonder** we can't get anywhere with this case. He's probably been holding out because he's involved!" Hammer was so excited by his revelation, he almost bit his tongue.

"Calm down, Hammer, I'm trying to hear what they're saying. *Shhh!*" Walsh emphasized with the sound effect.

Greg was speaking again. But the device also popped out again.

"Let's reach out to our friends in the press and television. I know . . . over at . . . and I could . . ." Wade was shook by Brenda's name coming from another man's lips. Walsh couldn't explain the expression on Wade's face and he didn't hear much of Greg's statement.

"Let me handle Brenda. Please," Wade interrupted. The device popped back on, following a sizzle and a fuzzy sound. Greg nodded. Walsh was becoming restless, not clear about all of the dialogue. He wasn't *that* good at reading lips.

"Keep the dish focused on the window. The *windows!* That's why we're not *hearing* everything. You keep moving that thing . . . keep it *still*." Walsh blew his commands like he fired a gun.

"When all of our people are in place we'll drop the bomb on these fools! They won't know who hit 'em." Greg was strong and vocal with his convictions. Walsh swallowed *real* hard. Hammer shifted his head and eyes into Walsh's direction and they both exchanged expressions of concern. The two agents knew for certain that they'd walked into a room full of dynamite. When it would explode, they didn't know. But they were confident that they'd be there to witness it. Hammer, ready with his long-lensed camera, snapped photos of those leaving the meeting. License plates of the various vehicles were recorded. The entire investigation seemed to take a leap to another level.

On the way back to the New Rochelle branch the two discussed their request for a bigger budget for the case, how they would substantiate the funding, and the new information to be figured into the equation. More agents, better equipment, wiretaps, transmitters, and especially (the one thing they needed most) more time was all a part of the request which they contemplated.

It's On!

Wade and Danni agreed that they would stick to Debbie like a respirator. If one had to leave her then the other would pick up the slack. On the day of the strategy meeting, both men escorted Debbie to the 45th precinct. Sean was waiting in the detectives' division for the trio.

"Hey, Walter," he said, raising up from where he sat on the edge of Wade's desk.

"Hi, Sean. This is Danni. Debbie, meet Sean." Debbie was humble, while Danni was a little edgy about being behind the closed doors at a police station.

"Sean, we're gonna chat with Debbie for a few moments. If you'll excuse us, we'll come down to your studio as soon as we're done." Sean made his way through the door. Both men seemed to clear their throats in preparation for the inevitable.

"Debbie, do you remember David? A customer at Fool's Paradise?"

"Sure. He helped me get a job at the club when I just came to New York. We met on the Internet."

"Debbie, David is dead. Shot once in the face . . ." Wade paused for a reaction. Debbie exhaled what little air she had in her lungs. Not as disturbed as Wade anticipated. ". . . but there's more that you should know. We think it might be *more* than a coincidence that Moet and David are dead. Did you know a guy named Bobby?"

"I can't remember," Debbie answered after a few seconds of thought. "That might be someone Moet was dealing with."

"That's right, Debbie . . . and he's dead, too. Someone rigged his vehicle and he crashed. It seems that these bodies are turning up as people that either you or Moet knew. There could be some psycho-secret admirer out there who's been killing people associated with the club in some way."

"But I don't know this guy Bobby, and I never . . . I mean David and I never . . . well, you know, *fucked*. We spent some time together, but never in bed."

"That's not so much the issue, Debbie. The killer could *think* you've been with David. He could even want you for himself. We don't really know what makes these fools tick. We just know that they do exist. They're excessive and extreme. There's no tellin' how or who they'll strike next." Wade made enough of an impact on Debbie to keep her undivided attention.

"Sean is downstairs with an artist's rendition of the suspect. We need you to come down and add your opinion. We'll also need you to look through some books . . . mug shots, we call them . . . to try and identify the man who kidnapped you and Moet. This could be a long day." Wade was direct. No nonsense.

"That's . . . that's okay. I *wanna* help catch this guy. Moet wouldn't hurt *anybody*. And I'm sick and tired of seeing people die, only so that killers can get away with murder."

Debbie followed Wade and Danni shadowed her. They stepped intentionally through the squad room, down a wing of the building. In the rear, Sean's office was filled with technology. Computers. Monitors. Scanners and an overhead projector. There was a large drafting board with lamps stretched up and across the work area. Sean was seated at his desk where a 21-inch flatscreen was anchored and supported by an iron swivel arm. Wade and Danni stood behind him and Debbie took a seat next to Sean. On one half of the screen was the virtual image changing with different hairstyles, eyeglasses, mustaches, and hats. The artist's rendition on the left had all the features of the suspect, except she remembered lighter hair. She remembered shades . . . *the Terminator look,* she told them.

Sean took Debbie's directives and made the adjustments. Debbie described the man's eyes as *squinted, with a lot of white in them, and a grey spiral around the pupils. And thinner lips*, she said. Sean maneuvered his mouse while a tiny pointer skated across the monitor, back and forth, to and from various electronic tools as the virtual image on the right went through an instant metamorphosis.

"That's him!" Debbie blurted abruptly. Then a chill slipped through her when she thought of her friend Moet. Sean pressed his thumb into the ALT button on his keyboard and simultaneously, he smacked the "p" key with the pinky of the same hand. He pushed himself backwards obediently, and he immediately swiveled around in the same motion until he was precisely in front of his HP color laser printer. It was already producing and spitting out the suspect's likeness. Sean waited a few seconds for the copy, snatched it up and swiveled back around to hand it to Wade.

"Make three more of these, Sean. Give one to the chief, too."

"You got it."

"Debbie . . . Danni, join me in the next room."

The three stepped through a doorway. Wade flicked a light switch, and the place lit up like an operating room. There was a conference table in the center of the floor with a series of chairs positioned at its perimeter. Danni was gentlemanly, pulling a seat for Debbie, while the detective went to a cabinet with mugshot books stacked throughout. For the next 2 hours, Debbie, Wade and Danni reviewed photos of known offenders. They canvassed the books for every white face they could find.

"Fred Gordon here."

"Fred! Hi, this is Lou, from SuperStar TV . . ." After a brief conversation with the renowned magnate of *Black News and Affairs*, Lou arranged to meet for lunch in Manhattan. They discussed the case against Douglass and the facts relating to Moet's murder. Fred was inspired by the opportunity to break the story first. He enjoyed controversy and took such dives at every possible turn. Admired by millions for his tact and aggressive, investigative approach with the president, with ambassadors from around the world, and even during his exclusive with O.J., Fred's talent upstaged the heaviest of the heavyweights. Nowadays, his face was syndicated nightly in every state throughout the nation, known for the integrity that he brought to every story. Lou and Fred hardly touched their food through the first hour of their meeting. The waiter had to re-heat what they ordered, and they didn't mind; it gave them more time to discuss old times and their school days at the *Center for Media Arts.* In total agreement, Lou and Fred shook hands as though they'd completed a world-renowned Peace Accord. They parted company; Fred strutting towards his newfound mission at National Broadcast News, while Lou was only beginning to address his long list of friends. Next person to see was Oscar Sutton, president of the Black Syndicated Radio Networks on Park Avenue. It sure paid to know friends in high places.

While Lou continued to work magic with his old friends, Greg contacted his fraternity brothers and informed them of the dilemma in New York. Georgetown University may have been a distance from the big city, but the school produced an ocean of accomplished black journalists who were scattered all over the nation. Greg made it a practice to maintain contact with his 4 closest classmates. *The Fabulous Five* was their acclaimed title. They were campus celebrities, known for their witty investigative techniques, exposing facts and injustices on campus and off, forcing the most important issues to the forefront of administrative and political agendas. Aside from their tight skills, they were committed to one another. When a distress call went out, no questions were asked. *Roll call.* A week after Greg contacted his frat brothers, *The Fabulous Five* were together again, huddled in a suite at the Grand Hyatt Hotel on 42nd Street in Gotham.

The journalist superstars had a surefire formula to follow, one that Professor Hopkins taught them well. "*Treat every story as if it were your first and your last,*" he would say. "*Someone's life depends upon the impact of your words . . .*" He also warned them to "*use every means necessary, the news services, colleagues and foes, publishers and editors . . . mailroom clerks. Make yourself the longest list possible of avenues to expose your story and then double that effort. Leave no stone unturned.*"

Four years after their graduation, Jamal, Andrew, Reginald and Rick created a bi-coastal network of media saturation. Along with Greg, the group had columns, cover stories, editorials, content and consulting positions at major regional magazines, newspapers and websites in most major cities. When there was an issue that affected or *infected* the black community, these brothers joined forces to cause a unified consciousness throughout the country. The NAACP, CENTER FOR HUMAN RIGHTS, AMNESTY INTERNATIONAL, ACLU, and at least a handful of other organizations all kept a focus on the themes and issues that *The Fabulous Five* brought to the plate. If they were talking about it, it had to be important. And as they masterminded their latest strategy in the generous hotel room, dressed in sharp post-collegiate and corporate wear, the issues related to the "FREE GILMORE!" campaign were printed on yellow legal tablets and spread out on top of the queen-sized bed. The room was a bolt of lightning energy; a blur of suspenders, bowties and spectacles, and an extemporaneous collaboration of ideas, suggestions and opinions. It was almost time for action.

It was Brenda who suggested Manhattan Proper as the location where Wade, Debbie and Danni would join her. Some Tuesday night comedy to loosen things up; perhaps the raw, black humor would settle the sensitive nature of their planned discussion. Maybe the climate would even alleviate some stress from a long day's work.

After the show, close to midnight, Brenda guided the quartet for a 5-minute drive to the USA Diner on Merrick Boulevard. They warmed themselves with coffee and cocoa, and Debbie and Wade shared a chunky slice of strawberry shortcake.

This was all Brenda's idea: the meeting, the comedy and the dinner. Sure, Wade made the phone call . . . he needed her anyhow. But it was all on Brenda's terms. She was in a position to state demands, especially now that she knew what she knew. The justice, the rush to judgment, the misconceptions . . . and now the FREE GILMORE! campaign. *Ohhh, shit!* She almost blew her top. This was *her* story first. *Her* angle and *her* leads. How could this leak out without her involvement?

And all after she did her goddamned slave hours!

When Wade agreed to the meeting, Brenda felt better, but still unsatisfied. She needed to push herself back up front on this one. That *might* help to relieve her of some of that used feeling she was carrying around.

At the diner, far and away from Manhattan Proper's hysterical entertainment, Wade reintroduced Danni and Debbie, explaining how they came to meet. The information shared at the diner was actually confidential police business, but Brenda pressed Wade so well—as if she was his wife or something—that he was feeling behooved and beside himself with obedience. Besides, his intentions now (even if he was still an officer of the law) were somewhat personal. He had to admit to himself that he was sinking his teeth deep into this case. It had become an investment of time and energy that he intended to see through to completion. And he had close to 10 deputies at last count!

Wade knew that Brenda had some close interest in this investigation. He also recognized her position, talent, and resources to be limitless in value. So a 6-pack of apologies and a half dozen new responsibilities lured Brenda in. Now there were 11 deputies. But, by the time the 3 finished shooting off various elements of the story to Brenda, her body was whizzing with adrenaline. She was feeling like her favorite childhood characters: a sort of Nancy Drew concealed inside of Foxy Brown's body. Brenda added what she heard to what she learned from Ken Stevens and, BOOM. *She* indeed had just as much, *if not more* of the story than the FBI. After all, the FBI . . . or even Wade hadn't read into Ken's journal as she had. The slave hours were starting to pay off.

Dancers Unite!

Fool's Paradise could always boast about *"100 Dancers!"* The club could brag about being *"The Leader in Adult Entertainment!"* And tell your friends all about *"The biggest celebrities from sports, music and film!"* But the arrest and confinement of Douglass posed the most significant challenge to the industry leader. It was proof that all the money and success in the world could not buy a person's immunity. The reality is, if some local, state or federal authority wants to, they can swoop into an empire, take what they please, and make up their reasons later, after the damage has been done.

The injustice and charges with which brought all of these problems called for a response. It all called for a pool of political strength and the outcry of the people. The team behind FREE GILMORE! hatched the plan; and sure, they knew that there might be an uphill battle because of the stigma of *topless dancers and adult entertainment* as the backdrop to their dilemma. But, this was the world of the patriarch, in an age where sex and pornography ruled; shock-jock Howard Stern on the radio and television, coercing women (only) to strip and show their entire bodies; the biggest A-List actors, Tom Cruise and his wife (at the time), Nicole Kidman, starred in their own virtual butt-naked sex film, while A-List actress Halle Berry won her Oscar by also giving a good on-camera fuck; and then those mostly naked billboards standing 100 feet high on Times Square—how could anyone miss being brainwashed by it all? Anything but would be a state of denial!

But even if the circumstances surrounding Gilmore's tragedy called for a movement of conscious brothers and sisters, of political and community leaders to speak out against the agents and agencies behind it all; even if those who might otherwise come out in support were kept in the shadow due to the moral dilemma of issues in the so-called socially unpopular, politically-perilous world of sex, obscenity and adult entertainment ordinances, there were still others to turn to for help. It became evident that "Team Gilmore" had to recruit their own vigilantes and advocates, no matter who.

"That motherfucker ain't never done nothin' for me. *Let 'em rot,* for all I care!" Claudine, the forerunner of belligerence and deceit, was a cancerous element amongst a number of dancers who were no-shows. Some others had excuses like school and not having a babysitter. But Dino and Demetrius kept on pushing. They were able to convince more than 50 dancers to go along with their plan. Valerie rounded up 17 more herself. Most of all the top-shelf dancers were up for the challenge, as though they were intelligent enough to understand the depth of the dilemma and that Douglass was partially responsible for their bread and butter. Not that some of the girls *weren't* brilliant. Just that a few of them were naïve and only went along because of a friend.

Dino rented a schoolbus, and on a chilly Monday morning, everyone loaded up in front of the club. There were close to 70 dancers in all, including Valerie, Debbie and Mechelle. Mechellee was 7 months pregnant now, and more than ashamed of having left—either that, or it was just damned convenient to be amongst friends.

There were also 5 staff members who boarded the bus. Demetrius acted as chief of security and Dino drove. A boom box kept things lively with a DJ Envy mix tape, and Greg addressed the group with instructions and predictions for the occasion. Meanwhile, the bus was a blur of fur coats, leather outfits, calf-high boots and perfume. Valerie acted as resident waitress, passing out cups of hot coffee and crumpets from Dunkin' Donuts. Dino and Demetrius chatted about the best directions to Passaic County Jail, as the bus continued on its pilgrimage to FREE GILMORE!

In New Jersey, a block away from the jail, Dino paid a gas station attendant twenty bucks to create a parking space on his property as the dancers engaged in their last-minute preparations; pushing up their vinyl halter tops or adjusting their skin-tight pants. One girl might be pulling her hair back into a purposeful ponytail, while another was adjusting a wig. Someone else was retouching her makeup. Finally, one by one, dark and light shades of brown-skinned women descended the steps of the big yellow school bus. The women were voluptuous, colorful and wide awake. They carried big signs and banners that proclaimed "FREE GILMORE!" "JERSEY INJUSTICE LIVES!" "LONG LIVE SLAVERY!" "PASSAIC'S TOBACCO GAS CHAMBER!" "MANDATORY SMOKING-OPTIONAL JUSTICE!" "FALSE IMPRISONMENT + FALSE ARREST = TRUE CRIME!" The banners and signs said it all, while being held and waved by a casting call for the world's biggest outdoor strip show.

An audience was inevitable. But instead of the area being bombarded by a stream of exotic entertainment, onlookers were surprised by revolt and protest towards law enforcement, the judicial system and the torture inside the jail. Never was a picket line so attractive! So alluring! Such a contradiction! Darryl had his video camera rolling, as he maneuvered to obtain exclusive footage for the special broadcast he was arranging with some local news stations back in New York. He was plotting to reach 8 million homes with the story.

All the while, the dancers kept with the plan and followed instructions, walking in line formation, stepping to the leadership of Cinnamon. She initiated the vocal rap.

> *"Let Douglass Gilmore Go—*
> *He Didn't Murder, No!*
> *You Had No Right To Take Our Man*
> *You'd Better Let 'Em Go!"*

Even the gas station attendant was unfocused, following the dancers with his eyes, and already pumping $18.00 worth of unleaded fuel for a $5 purchase.

By the time the curvaceous cavalry of calves assembled in front of the Passaic County Jail, the area was raining with bystanders. It was still a bit chilly, but the dancers kept warm with loud chants and a determined march in an endless, elongated oval. Darryl weaved through the onlookers to catch their expressions on camera, and also captured the excitement of uniformed corrections officers who stood outside of the jail's entrance. Within an hour, the bright light of the sun created brilliant setting for the live UPN9 news broadcast that reached an estimated 12 million homes. Reporters appeared one after another, from talk radio and newspapers—all part of Greg's plan. His four Georgetown buddies were also present with pads in hand, following the marchers and recording statements. They helped to turn up the volume on the event, pulling cellphones out at various opportunities, pretending as if they were doing some instant reporting to a higher authority. During the next hour, vans showed up from 2 New York networks (*another* 15 million homes that would be exposed to the conflict). Eventually, the street was closed off and Danni couldn't help but to enjoy the chemistry of it all. And now, one idea was not only affecting the hundreds of people who congregated in the streets, but also tens of millions of viewers, readers and listeners who might be at work or home.

One of the dancers pumped the volume on the boom box, and Jay-Z's *"Hard Knock Life"* banged through the speakers, boosting the energy of the march. Dozens of voices were now screeching with the hook in the jam, lil-orphan-Annie-style, bopping along with signs floating up and down in the air. They all shouted in chorus:

> *". . . I flow for chicks wishin'*
> *they din' have to strip to pay tuition,*
> *I see yo' vision, Mama!"*

Police presence increased, but the demonstration continued for an hour or so until 1PM. The movement was noisy enough to affect the morning rush hour and the afternoon lunch hour. Mission accomplished.

When the bus returned to New York, Greg had a buffet waiting at Fool's Paradise for the troops. In addition to the food, there were pads of differing stationary and pens ready for a post-picket letter writing campaign. In the rear of the club, while the enterprise continued to bustle with music and exposed tah-tahs, Greg addressed the ladies once again.

"Thank you once again for your time and energy today. There's one more quick task I need to ask of you. In your own words, write a *Dear Judge* letter. Let the judge know your association to Douglass Gilmore, what you know about him and even Moet. If you know more, then write more. If not, speak with my colleagues standing here in blazers and ties—the *reporters* who approached you in New Jersey . . ."

A few chuckles erupted.

"If you're angry about what's going on, then spill your guts. The only way this issue will become *really* big is if we make it so." After a few questions and answers, and a full plate of food, the dancers got kicking. They jotted down their feelings, concerns about Douglass, the conditions at the jail, and they questioned why the case was dragging on for so long. The efforts in the rear of the club drew more and more attraction from the crowd of regular customers. Many of them even totally ignored the action on stage until there was no more stage show. Soon, everyone in the club, including customers and staff, became engrossed in the letter writing. For some dancers, it was back to English 101, as in some cases customers leaned over and assisted them with spelling and syntax. For others, it was a frenzy, having not written a letter in months or years.

Gil was busy himself, in the office with the door locked and Claudine's head bobbing up and down between his legs.

A Firm Go

Brenda was quite bold, inspired by desperation. It was more than a month since her last episode with Ken; or for that matter, with *anyone*. She felt that she had put a "down payment" on a relationship and that she "invested" quality time. She expected something more out of it, if even an explanation as to why Ken hadn't returned her calls. There were 2 returned phone calls from Ken to Brenda's 10 messages. Both of his calls (and she was certain that he calculated the timing) came when she was on the air.

To keep her mind off of Ken (if that was possible), Brenda practically found things to do at her place; and if not that, she watched news footage of the various baseball games that Ken pitched in—videos that she got from the sports desk at work. Nonetheless, she still anticipated their next tryst. And one more thing on her mind:

I still owe him one more slave hour.

Inevitably, the distance encouraged the naughtiness in her; a good enough excuse for her to act on her instincts. She grew balls since being with Ken Stevens—enough to find herself across the street from his building in the Village. It was just another night for her. The broadcast was the usual scatter of grief and theory for awestruck viewers to absorb appreciatively or apprehensively. Either way, Brenda knew, they had to eat it up regardless.

Brenda sat quietly in her platinum Lex, munching on golden honey apple chips, watching vehicles cruise into and up out of the garage in Ken's building. It was nearing midnight.

She subconsciously timed the raising and lowering of the garage door, suddenly wondering if her idea would work.

Brenda poked at her cell phone, expecting again to hear Ken's answering machine. When his voice sounded in that same ole digital tone she hung up and waited for the right time to strike. When the opportunity afforded itself, Brenda followed another car down into the garage—using that access as her own. It was something Brenda recalled Ken doing when he had first brought her home. And now, those minor details were making things so much easier. Those little tidbits of information were turning this into somewhat of an adventure, and so far her plan was working smoothly. She peeled off from behind the leading vehicle into the direction of Ken's parking space. The idea was to be impulsive; to surprise him as he had her the morning she read his journal. And the further she moved along, the more confident she grew about her plan.

Okay, so maybe she did see something like this before, an idea she ripped off from the movie *Boomerang* (with Eddie Murphy and Robin Givens), when she surprised him with that sexy teddy under her overcoat. Brenda smiled, knowing that Robin's character had *nothing* on the baseball outfit that Brenda had in store; how she aimed to shed every thread of clothing she had on, and to surprise Ken when he came home. She hoped he would be returning soon, but as she made the bend and looked for his parking space, his black Navigator was already parked. The engine was cold.

Funny, she thought. *I just called him less than a half an hour ago.* Brenda pouted, and in her own deep thought, she contemplated some alternatives.

Again with the impulsive behavior, and remembering the dynamics that were required to operate the elevator, Brenda waited a few more moments for the resident to lift up and away before she stepped up to press the button herself. The car eventually returned to the basement and Brenda executed the actions of her "master," Ken. Up she went, deeper than ever into her surprise attack, expecting to blow Ken's mind. Even before the elevator reached the second and third levels, Brenda took the leap of faith and began to shed her clothes. She began with her top, then she stepped out of her slacks. By the fourth and fifth floors she deliberated about her bra and panties, asking herself if Ken was worthy. Thoughts of his celebrity, fame and fortune encouraged her further and before the elevator finally stopped she squinted, concentrating on how far she and Ken had gone and the taboos that she'd turned in his bed. Brenda paused for a few beats, the elevator moving upward with every passing second.

Hell, you've already seen everything, she determined. And that's when she told herself, *fuck it*. Brenda anticipated Ken's wide eyes and hungry manhood as she dropped her head, looking down at her naked, proud nipples. Her nostrils flared with heavy anticipation, and she deviled her eyebrows in that fiendish, satisfied expression. Her mind was eventually consumed with a playful mischief, as the car came to a halt at the penthouse. Brenda rolled the tip of her tongue along the surface of her teeth, as though she had her own slam dunk to execute. She carefully pulled the strap, separating the horizontal doors of the elevator. The atmosphere was as dark and cavernous as when she first visited.

He's sleeping; no need for him to activate the alarm, she reckoned. Then, with the doors still fully opened, and the elevator's light lending subtle visibility, Brenda gathered her clothes, tossed them to the floor inside the loft, and she gently closed the doors behind her. With the room pitch black again, Brenda sidestepped the welcome mat and used the moon's glow to guide her to the hallway. There were pin lights along the edges of the carpet, leading towards the back, right side of the loft. There were also pin lights leading up the stairway in the dining room. She climbed cautiously, wanting to take Ken by complete surprise. She wanted to amaze Ken with her own creative spontaneity. But as Brenda rounded the corner to Ken's fairytale bedroom, she was consumed by the scent of sex, flickering candlelight and a mellow volume of Roy Ayers' *Everybody Loves The Sunshine*.

Brenda took a deep breath as she tiptoed closer, with her eyelids fluttering, enough to get caught up in her own amazement. She couldn't believe her eyes. Ken was voraciously billowing on top of a young, submissive, hairless Latin boy. He couldn't have been more than 17 or 18 years old at most. And there was Ken, piling into the boy's asshole as if he was a human jackhammer. The youth was arched over with his face buried into a few pillows, his ass elevated and his reaction muffled.

Umphs and arghs.

Brenda's reaction on the other hand *wasn't* muffled, just stiffed. Her presence was unfelt. The bedroom activity was so intense, so aggressive, that Brenda almost wanted to applaud. For a few seconds of measuring Ken's audacity, listening to the profanities and watching his smelly, raunchy pummelling, Brenda stood in awkward amusement. She folded her arms. Then she shifted her position, her stance, and switched her hands to rest on her naked hips. She almost became *jealous!* When Brenda saw how much Ken was perspiring, that took the cake. She busted out laughing, sincerely tickled that Ken was putting in so much effort. Her explosive scorn was, of course, loud enough for Ken to hear. And the action stopped completely. Brenda threw her open fist to her lips too late. Dizzy with the shock of it all, and realizing that she'd been discovered, she went on giggling at the absurdity, then she pivoted and went quickly to retrieve her clothes at the entrance to the loft. Still a little delirious, Brenda wondered aloud, "How did I ever miss *this* in his journal."

She descended the stairs and headed for her clothes in a determined stride. She could hear Ken calling out to her, hurrying to catch up to her. Real quickly, she turned to see his bathrobe flying open in the rush. And just as Brenda was crouching down to pick up her clothes, Ken grasped her elbow and spun her around.

"What are you *doing* here?" Ken was irate. But Brenda was questioning his nerve. The whole revelation was a gas. Ken Stevens the jock. The 64-million dollar man. The slave master. The fucking **homo!** Brenda was shouting with her mind, and all the while still caught up in sheer disbelief. She observed his slightly glistening limp dick between the folds of the robe that he had hastily tied.

"Ahem!" Brenda drew her head back an inch and looked down, challenging Ken's hand on her elbow. Ken immediately released her. She went back to collect her clothes, stepping and reaching into them.

"Mr. Stevens. We can talk about this another time. I wouldn't want to disturb your moment with the batboy. By the way, is that boy of age?" Brenda paused for a moment, then she went back to finish fastening and buttoning. "As a matter of fact, *you know what?* Never mind. I don't wanna know . . ."

Now a tear in her eye. Ken just stood there speechless.

". . . just tell me something . . ." Brenda was now finished with her clothes, just enough time to finally inhale. She gathered her thoughts. "Was our thing . . . was that *serious*, or were you just *using* me?" she hissed. Ken began to speak through trembling lips. But again, Brenda cut him off. "*And don't you fuckin' lie to me!*" She had her forefinger in his face.

"I . . . I *do* . . . care about you." Ken's hesitation made her furious. All she needed was a 2-foot reach, and she used that reach to smack him hard across his face. Then, Brenda turned to open the elevator doors. But they didn't give in her haste. She spun to address Ken with that raised brow.

All she had to say was, "*Now!*" Brenda contracted the muscles in her face, more frightening than a cobra, willing him to act. Defeated, Ken moved to help her and she left.

CHAPTER EIGHTEEN

Behind the Scenes

The first early morning demonstration outside of Passaic County Jail was so effective that the team set it up for a second go at it. The dancers all agreed, even if just for kicks. Naturally, when they became aware of all the publicity and television news coverage, the outfits were embellished *just a tad bit*. Sequined bras. Glittering, shimmering, bright, skin-tight skirts and plenty of fishnet stockings. Not to mention all of those fabulous hairstyles. Sum it up to the girls all going beyond the call of duty to look their best, as if they were looking for that golden Hollywood opportunity. They certainly fulfilled the objective, attracting a small legion of followers. Even men that worked at the jail and in the vicinity became addicts and voyeurs of the voluptuous demonstrators; establishing conversations, some even taking the 40-minute trip down I-95 to see more of their flesh after work. You had to love it when a plan came together.

* * *

Fred Gordon left an indelible impression on his viewers, detailing the issues relating to Douglass's arrest and the case in general, while blasting the FBI and the U.S. Attorney's office for mishandling many of the various elements. The young man was in jail for over 7 months without the setting of a trial date, or without the benefit of knowing what evidence he was facing. Hell, those weren't *benefits*, but his legal rights as a citizen protected under the U.S. law. Fred also focused on the horrid conditions at the county jail and the stream of incidents that endlessly branded the facility as *the worst of the worst*. Moreover, Fred kept the intensity with a follow-up story after the dancers demonstrated the second time.

The Fabulous Five filled in the various pockets of regional and national press outfits with stories and subjects that ranged from "THE TRAGIC LIFE OF A DANCER," to "MURDER WITHOUT A SUSPECT." Their editorials and columns were strategically placed in all major publications, newspapers and just about every well known black magazine. But not only was the country *familiar* with the Gilmore case and the FREE GILMORE! campaign, Douglass was suddenly becoming a household name along with his various accomplishments, contributions to the community, and the unusual circumstances that put him in the cleft of purgatory. If there were any negative marks on his life's blueprint, they were far outweighed by the good he'd spread. Funny how the press can turn anything they wanted into a newsworthy feature.

Brenda Feather quickly defeated her thoughts of feeling used, because now it was *all* about her J—O—B. After she caught Ken red-handed . . . after she went out of her way to creep up into his loft, lifting the big elevator doors and all . . . trespassing nonetheless . . . just so that she could surprise him with her naked body! She went through all of that only to find him fucking one of the Yankee batboys in the ass!! It was enough to make her scream! She *still* couldn't believe it! The motherfucker had her thinking that he was the biggest gigolo, laying that big dick on her like he did . . . and come to find out that he was really nothing more than a downlow brotha! **JESUS!**

Brenda was both enraged and worried; enraged for all of the obvious reasons; unable to reach him . . . him not returning her calls . . . the whole *Mission: Impossible* move she pulled to get up into his home unnoticed. Bigger than all of that, *all the shit they did together!* She *surrendered* herself to him! She TRUSTED HIM! And now? All she could say was Fuck! FUCK! FUCK FUCK **FUCK!** She spent almost 24 hours claiming and exclaiming that men were **all** fucking assholes. But not Ken! No, Ken was a fuckin' asshole **and** a flaming, freakin' faggot! Brenda laughed like a hyena as she stood by her answering machine listening to message after unanswered message. Ken had transformed into a mass of fright. Not only had Ken envoked Brenda's most vindictive conclusions, but she also possessed a critical key to his closest of secrets. *New York's star pitcher has a gay lover?*

"**Huh!** *The relationship with a stripper. All this slave-hour shit. Wow.*" Brenda was talking to her inanimate, unthinking, unfeeling answering machine. "It was all a *front!* But, Jesus, Joseph and Mary, am I ever the *last* woman that you wanted to piss off! Ohhhh, you were *brilliant* at first. Had me twisted with guilt and shame. Had me caught up in your utterly large, flamboyant lifestyle. But who's *the man* now? Things *change!*" And now Brenda was determined to break the complete story without *aaay*-nother waiting moment. She felt that the "*license to ill*" was now hers to exercise. So what if Ken was with a stripper, a batboy or two hundred other women around the country. *And?*

"*And life goes—the—fuck—on, you BASTARD!*" Brenda was verbally hot. And there was no stopping her flames. *He's not gonna lose a penny of that sixty-four mil. A tarnished image? If the public **really** knew better, they'd find them a new hero.*

That very next day, Brenda re-ignited the Ken Stevens engine, with all previous reports blending into part one of her own exclusive 4-part story. Her delivery was greatly anticipated, having been promoted heavily on the network itself, on its affiliate radio stations and in the metro section of the newspaper. After hearing the full story straight from the horse's mouth, Brenda's production supervisors gave her the go-ahead on the exclusive, fully supporting her no-limits approach.

They knew what to expect from their top anchorwoman—nothing but high-powered resources. Still, most everyone was led to wonder about what it was that Brenda knew different from all else that had been reported. *What was her hook?*

Ken was rarely pinned to the television like he was that evening of Brenda's first report. He obviously had a stake in the broadcast . . . a concern for his future. Already nervous from having surrendered all secrets to Brenda, Ken sat at the edge of his bed with the giant screen in vertical position, awaiting her wrath. Ken was already waving his head at instant replay-speed, stuck on the revelation that Brenda's exclusive was announced as the *top story*.

Ernie Anastos segued with the introduction and Brenda began to spew her story head-first. Ken could see it in her eyes. He was about to be buried. The question was, how thick was she about to make the mortar?

"*. . . During my 8-week investigation of this story, I have come to one dramatic conclusion: this case is being mishandled in all of its extreme elements . . . from the U.S. Attorney's office in New Jersey, the strategies behind this pursuit, to the FBI, the pawns and minutemen who have not only botched and bungled the investigation, but who have redesigned this murder case to suit their own fictional beliefs . . .*" Brenda served her information, established her seniority in the players' circle, and she delivered chasing blows all within one sweeping, 5-minute outline. She lengthened the anticipation by leaving the viewers in suspense. Brenda didn't reveal names *yet*, but she promised to name names in the later segments of her series. She titled her series "The Botched Bronx Murder Case," and all the television graphics supported her bold position.

At Passaic County Jail, inmates were pumped up, buzzing and electrified about the visual impact of the news broadcast and how it brought the world (so to speak) to their doorstep. Because there was no exposure to the outside, through windows or otherwise, prisoners didn't experience the instant impact of the voluptuous, picketing dancers. They had no way of knowing *what was* going on outdoors. Visits were denied for the time being, and correctional officers were ordered to maintain a *code of silence* for security purposes. But when UPN9 happened to catch tits and ass images on the TV, the evening news suddenly became the most important show on the tube. Men quickly congregated near the monitors, gesturing to one another to "*shhhh*" as they listened and watched attentively. The name *Gilmore* was mentioned numerous times, along with the words *murder, topless* and *FBI-organized crime task force*. All the buzzwords and images solidified Douglass as (once again) the big fish in a small pond. Instant celebrity overcame the 4B dorm. Douglass had already won over the most whimsical of the motley crew. But now, the universal language of tits and ass capsized the inmates with emotion and restlessness. Douglass was almost immediately inundated with questions and small talk. If ever there was a kingpin, Douglass sure earned that status now. All sizes and makes of men, regardless of the inhibitions or falsities which had previously prevented communication with Douglass (regardless of Spanish, Haitian, Caribbean and other nationalities) dropped their protective walls if only to say hi. It was instantly a cinch to *create* subjects and reasons to approach Douglass. And justly, he felt the popularity and the adrenaline pumping through his body. However, with no other means of release; with no way to personally celebrate the excitement, Douglass simply drowned in it all, soaking up the euphoria around him, answering questions about dancers, the topless business and about the bullshit charges that put him in jail in the first place. Despite his incarceration and related hardships, Douglass was now able to experience that whirlpool of inner joy and appreciation, despite the challenges he faced.

CHAPTER NINETEEN

The Great Awakening

It was a lazy autumn Saturday morning in New Rochelle, quiet like a bed of roses welcoming the sun, with the clouds giving way to a Godly light. Underneath it all, tucked deep inside the Gilmore home, four exhausted, tuckered-out, overly satisfied lovers laid spent and spread in various positions across Douglass's mammoth water bed. They could have been four heaps of clay, except for their legs and arms, hands and feet, layered and buried under one another like a motionless puzzle of anatomy. At once and without warning, Douglass was the beneficiary of one incredible evening of sex. Thanks to the Everglo liquor and its clever mix of tequila, vodka, caffeine and ginseng, all of it filling their systems with unbridled energy, the marathon seemed to go on for hours . . . and it *did*. From mid-afternoon when the girls came home from shopping, and then beyond the nap and fruits that they ate off one another. The entire ordeal was one giant, unextinguishable fire. But there was a price for such pleasure and satisfaction. And now, in the wee hours of the morning, they would wake up to see *exactly* what that was.

Mechelle was the first to rise. She was feeling slimy, and soaking in her own pool. Wet and fidgeting. But even before Mechelle opened her eyes, her baby was shifting uncomfortably, now snug against Mechelle's insides. The sex had to be to blame; how they celebrated Douglass's homecoming . . . engaging in one wild orgy that inevitably induced the process of labor. In other words, Mechelle's water broke, and all four of them—Mechelle, Douglass, Valerie and Debbie—were all laying in it! *Yuuuuck!*

A Visit from Murphy

On Thursday there was the turmoil at the jail. Friday brought the courtroom melodrama. And Friday night entertained that blitz of sexual activity that would test the stretches of even an overzealous imagination. Naturally, since Douglass seemed to already be on a roll, there was more drama in the forecast.

The next 40 minutes were a blur; although Mechelle had been packed and ready for a trip to the hospital, a trip that would presumably take place in at least ten more days (or so she thought), Murphy and his laws brought about different plans. Phone calls to 911 emergency and to Mechelle's physician didn't seem to get the instant response they'd hoped for. So, paranoia ensued, slowing the second hand and simultaneously thrusting all else into hyperspeed. No one was prepared for, nor were they expecting, this moment. Debbie was even *less* prepared than that, dashing to a closet for towels and dousing them under hot water. *For what?* They were useless now that the bed had soaked up that gooey fluid; and still useless for Mechelle, who was on the phone, beeping the physician mercilessly. Even if Mechelle's doctor *did* return the call, it'd be pretty difficult for him to get through with the phone in constant use and no Call Waiting. Meanwhile, Douglass was also on a phone with the emergency room at New Rochelle Hospital . . . taking careful direction, waving Debbie away with the wet towels and stretching the phone's cord to its limit. By the time the operator cut into the connection, informing Douglass to terminate his call to receive an incoming emergency call, there was a **rat-ta-tat** from the front door knocker.

The ambulance, a shiny white and red vehicle, was parked just outside the entrance with the motor humming. Meanwhile, in the paranoia, the bedroom and bathroom was still a rush of naked bodies, except for Mechelle. And Demetrius, who was home . . . *somewhere*. Then, it seemed, out of nowhere, ambulance workers were stepping through the home. There was some order now, everyone almost all covered up, and it became evident that Demetrius had dashed to the front door to admit the paramedics.

"Well, I heard Mechelle's scream . . . and then you were yellin'," said D in answer to Douglass's inquiry. "So I knew it *had* to be the baby was coming." Demetrius explained how he had come home from a long, busy night at the club, and he didn't bother to look anywhere but at the shower and the bed.

"And it's a good thing you didn't," Douglass told him. "You woulda had *anotha* kind of sermon to preach if you saw me with them three!"

"*Lawd*, have mercy on this man. Can't leave you alone for a minute, huh? I thought I heard somethin' funny at five in the morning. *Blasphemous!* You're all goin' straight to hell. Don't worry, though . . . I'mma pray for y'all."

* * *

While the 3 EMS workers scurried through the house, eventually administering things, executing their initial evaluation on Mechelle, Debbie had already hurried into the previous day's jeans, and Douglass did the same. At the same time, Valerie was in the bathroom dressing, taking a few extra moments to pick up bras, towels, panties and inedible portions of strawberries . . . spraying disinfectant. She didn't get to the bedroom in time enough to zap *that* musty air; the odors of sex and caramel.

Once the ambulance swept Mechelle and Douglass away, Demetrius eventually followed, bringing Valerie and Debbie along until, eventually, everyone landed in Mechelle's maternity room. Tests had been done and everything looked okay by the time visitors were permitted. Mechelle was now dilated by 2 centimeters. So the wait might be hours. While in the room, standing over Mechelle's bed, across from one another, Douglass glanced up at Debbie, Debbie at Valerie and Demetrius at them all, knowing full well that there was lingering guilt in the room. There was an urgency for laughter but it was withheld in the presence of Mechelle's recurring labor pains. She eventually showed a desire for a bit of privacy with Douglass, and Demetrius left with the others. They did return an hour later to drop off a few bouquets of fresh-cut orchids and such, and the presence of flowers was highly appreciated.

They changed the room's look tremendously, bringing color and fragrance that soothed and delighted, despite the slight headache that was troubling her.

Back at the house, Valerie and Debbie imitated a kind of command center, informing a few close friends and family members of Douglass's return. Greg inevitably helped them, immediately racing from his home in nearby Mt. Vernon to join the fever. Together they worked to put together a welcome-home bash to be thrown at Fool's Paradise. Perhaps they didn't have their heads screwed on tight, thinking that Douglass would show up for the party with a newborn bundle in his arms. But they proceeded, despite their CSD (common sense deficiency), and a party was set for Saturday evening. Ultimately, they only wanted Douglass to come and show his face.

Danni came in from Queens, and Dino from his apartment

in the Bronx. The team was together once again, all of them arranging balloons, streamers, party favors and other decorations. There was a big WELCOME HOME sign, a buffet, and a cake big enough for an army. The phone lines at the office were buzzing with inquiries from catering firms, party stores and the local restaurant supply, all of them rushing to gather the orders. Valerie and Debbie contacted their phone lists as well. Everything, it seemed, was coming together nicely.

By 4 PM, Mechelle was 3 centimeters wide, ever deeper into the delivery of the new baby, while organizers were on ladders, balancing on bar stools, taping and stapling, hanging and tacking. Gil waited and watched in the foreground, usually wide awake over his styrofoam cup of Guinness Stout beer. He was happy about the homecoming and impressed by the support that was shown for his son, approving all requests in preparation for the party.

Additional dancers, perhaps as many as 30 or so (uncommon for an early Saturday evening), crowded the dressing rooms and the stages, all a part of the growing anticipation for the night. From experience and word of mouth, women knew that a big party at Fool's Paradise meant big money for them as well. Yes, many of the dancers were appreciative that Gil's son was home free; after all, they *did* join the demonstration on those chilly mornings in New Jersey. Not only that; the promise of some extra money on a Saturday night was convenient. It meant rent payments, grocery shopping and the cell phone bill that had been sitting unaddressed for weeks. Pay dirt.

As usual, the dancers contacted their best tippers, inviting them to the "*big homecoming party.*" Anything for a theme . . . any excuse to make money.

By 6PM, and about six centimeters into Mechelle's labor pains, the club was more than half-full, and yet the party was in full swing. The synchronized activities of the hospital room and the excitement, the sensation at Fool's Paradise were nearly one and the same. Almost poetic synchronicity. On one hand, there were the energies and sensations that lured Mechelle to the pit (to the club) in the first place—the music and the vibrations at the club that stimulated her imagination;

her imagination and energies were personified through the sensual performance and movements of her body. And her body . . . her energy called and desired Douglass's own. The relationship was retroactive; the club acting as the glue which kept them as one and subsidized and supported the conception of a child. And while the music (*Break For Love, Din-Da-Da, Set It Off*) continued pumping in the usual fashion, accommodating the showcase of tits and ass, the bottom line was clear: the enterprise that Douglass helped to build . . . the idea that transformed an auto-car garage into a multi-million dollar establishment, the money that poured in only to be dished out at a faster ratio . . . all of it was now transcended by something most incredible. The creation of another human being. And all of that was only the reality if—big IF—the baby did in fact belong to Douglass.

By midnight, the club housed and hosted a massive amount of customers. Sadie was most vibrant, attracting attention to the stage with her slick, black thong that was sprinkled with mahogany brown leopard spots. The spots blended perfectly with her bare limbs and captivating facial expressions, almost as though there were holes in her outfit that reached deep into her soul. Sadie liked to dance barefoot, like those good, determined, loose African dancers. She was just as aggressive as they were, pumping her juicy ass to the booming bass of house music. Then things turned serious, as hip hop took over. Chuck Chillout was up in the deejay booth, blasting everyone's ears off with KRS-ONE'S *"Emcees Act Like They Don't Know,"* starting a fire that Sadie was damned sure to add gas to, pumping out her plentiful bust. Then simultaneously pulling it back in while pushing out her pelvis and hips. Bust. Pelvis. In and out, just like that, the motions were jerky, fast and determined. Both hands were on her hips. Then one flipped to the back of her head, with another on her ass. Then they switched with the next jut of her pelvis. Everything in sync, and purposeful. Every pump and shuffle across the stage was uniquely Sadie. Her signature. Snap and pop. Her hand moves to grip her waist, and she's doing a lil' Hawaiian wiggle. Now, the other hand is grabbing a breast, with her ass winding in the musky air. All the while, patrons eyes were affixed . . .

mesmerized. Eventually, Sadie submits to the anxieties of her audience, peeling the material from her breasts, untying the supportive string from around her neck. The outfit slithers down to her waist and she toys with the idea of total nudity, affording a glance here and there. The mystique of it all is enough to bring customers to the edge of the stage with $10 and $20 tips.

Back at the hospital, Mechelle fought through tumultuous times. Almost fully dilated, she breathed heavy with that horrified expression on her face as the fetal monitor cranked up to a faster beat. Her heart's activity was amplified by the speakers on the device. The intensity was building, something like the *dum-dum, dum-dum. . . . . dum-dum, dum-dum . . .* music score from a *Jaws* movie. Mechelle braced herself, grabbing the side bars of the bed, the sheets, her hair . . . *anything*. She shook as if she felt a quake inside her body. Certainly there was. Then she slowly calmed, murmurs and moaning escaping her lips. Reactions from the pain in her uterus. And to think, the nurse said this was a *mild* contraction.

"The baby's coming, but you've got to push." The nurse sounded factual while feeling at Mechelle's wrist and looking at her own to measure the pulse. A couple of minutes passed until Mechelle began to wiggle again. Moaning. Heavy breathing. *Faster*. She strained her neck and braced herself with her fingers entwined with Douglass's. Her eyelids expanded so wide, afraid for her life. Then with her teeth gritting, cheeks and chin and brow contorting, Mechelle shivered again until the eruption returned. The nurse reaffirmed the "*push*" directive. Douglass braced his ass and jaws almost as deliberately as Mechelle. The look in his eye questioned if the sex was really worth all of this. Mechelle blew three times and held the fourth to push—recalling her prenatal classes. She did it again and tried to catch the contraction, adding to her pain. The nurse seemed displaced, as though she wasn't *really* a part of this, calmly checking the EKG and the intra-uterine pressure. So calm was the nurse that it threatened to make Douglass spitting sick.

"A heavy contraction . . . *good*," said the nurse, most unimpressed. Unfazed. Douglass inhaled, afraid that if *this* was "good," what the hell was "*great*" like. Mechelle deflated again and collapsed in numbing pain and a state of exhaustion.

* * *

"China up!" Gil barked over the microphone as usual. Uncouth. Abrasive. The captain of the ship.

China was tall. But there was so much more going for her: her "chinky" eyes, her stunning shape, that copper-toned tan, and the long, black hair, all added to her absolute beauty. The contact lenses which she wore were unnecessary, since she was "a natural," riding the median between an Afrocentric, ghetto-girl (with her sassy street-smart dialect) and the exotic, Oriental princess (the posture, the sensuality, the attitude). It was a blend so unique that she didn't need to do a make-over before she came to work. China woke into the characteristics of exquisite beauty, culture and sexuality, and it was that way for every waking moment, until she put her head back down to rest.

On stage, China stepped and moved and wiggled in the most provocative, erotic way. Every gesture she threw was effortless. Each swerve was intentional and by design. She was pleasing and delightful to the eye; not overdone or exaggerated.

The Method Man and Mary J joint was thumpin' with that deep, grungy groove: *"All I Need,"* but China was that smooth coffee ice cream, melting . . . oozing over hot apple-hip hop beats and rhymes. A contradiction that could've tasted *oh-h-h so good.* In stiletto heels, China stepped proudly across the stage with her arms draping casually along, commanding all attention in the room with luscious, exotic poise. She'd lay eyes on individuals, making them feel exclusive. When she shifted her lure to address the next man, the previous one never even noticed her widespread appeal—China was suave like that; to make you think it was all about you. Then, in the quickest transition, she parted her lips wantonly, becoming the salacious bitch that men want in the bedroom. She would lean up against that wall of mirrors, with her ass beaming for all the voyeurs, jiggling her cheeks up and down repeatedly. She pushed herself away from the reflection some, bent over, and with one hand still against the mirror, the other delivered an arousing, self-inflicted spanking. *Bad girl.* China didn't have to remove her top to maintain a customer's imagination. His, his . . . and even *his* imagination as well as the wildest dreams of that guy over there were hers to squander.

CHAPTER TWENTY

Done Deal

Heading back towards New York, from the New Jersey Turnpike and then onto I-95, Douglass couldn't help thinking that the meeting wasn't long at all. A half hour at best. And it wasn't as difficult as he thought it might be to convince an investor that his was the greatest, most profitable proposal of all time. All he could think to do was smile to himself to match the joy that he felt inside. Valerie was with him, an ornament for anyone checking, yet fortunate just to be there; to experience it all.

Swing, the leader, organizer and producer of the popular R&B group JAYCI, had just agreed to back Douglass for the full $500,000 investment needed to take over the club from his father. Swing was impressed with the idea that he could make money, be part-owner in a spot where he, his group and his celebrity friends could congregate, fraternize with the dancers and feel at home; and he could do all that without the headaches of operating a nightclub. Douglass promised him all of the above, knowing that a 19-year-old who'd been responsible for over 15 million records sold didn't want much more than to be loved, to feel accomplished and to have his ego stroked. Sadie could handle that task *all* by herself. And if she was busy, there was China; and behind her, there'd be someone else in line right behind her. Valerie wasn't as impressed as Douglass was by Swing's home, but in Douglass's deeper evaluation he could see the whims of young wealth here. Here was an entertainer who already came through the club time and time again, and now he wanted a piece of the action. It was only right.

While Douglass and Valerie waited in a living room with furnishings that were still wrapped, or still in the boxes, Swing was down in the basement, cutting some tracks in his million-dollar recording studio with another group, a girl group that he had conceived. In the meantime, there was no mistaking new money. This was quite a large house; maybe 13,000 square feet. There were no curtains yet; stereo equipment was fresh out of the box, barely touched, with the various components scattered in a corner of the living room. Styrofoam pieces that protected the equipment were also on the floor with empty boxes. The fireplace was unused, without a speck of dust. A giant screen TV still sat in its box unopened. Douglass felt as though he'd interrupted a major shopping spree. The fixtures in the bathrooms were shiny enough to use as mirrors, they were so new. Cordless phones were everywhere, some cellular, some residential.

What all of this meant was, Swing and his group of singers were getting dough. And it all made Douglass that much more secure about the business of entertainment and the musical genius he had come to know well. Even *that* was convenient, not necessarily because Douglass was a 12-year veteran in the entertainment business, but because Swing, his group JAYCI and many of his colleagues and associates who were also young, successful entertainers, simply made Fool's Paradise a second home. Since their interest was already established, Douglass knew for sure that this would be the deal of a lifetime.

"Ain't no problem," said Swing. "If you got a deal with your father and he'll sell the club for five hundred, I'll put up the dough . . . I'll also put up the dough for the refurbishing you wanna do . . . and you and I can split profits until we're buried in the ground."

"Bet," said Douglass. And the two shook hands.

Now that Douglass had his major investor, he needed to get the club out of his father's hands. He had to get him to agree to the terms of his deal before things got bad . . . before the staff robbed Gilmore's blind, or worse, before the State Liquor Authority recalled the club's liquor license due to the prostitution, and other such inappropriate behaviors that were thriving within. Douglass was about to approach his father with a proposal that would knock his socks off. For Swing, the only thing left to do was sign wherever and make out a check. That meant, maybe, one less Ferrari that the singer, songwriter and producer would buy this quarter.

By the time that Douglass stepped into his dad's office, content that all was about to be said and done, Gil had already done some research. Douglass had told his dad of his intentions, and with whom he intended to do business with. So, that afternoon Gil was skeptical enough to ask questions and to come up with his own opinions.

"I don't wanna be no partners with no *rap* group." Gil twisted his mouth as if to admonish that genre of music.

"What are you talkin' about, rap group? JAYCI isn't a *rap* group. They're a *singing* group . . . and they make *songs*."

"Well, they have a rap image and I don't want to turn this into no rap club." Douglass, on one hand, felt he had to defend rap music; something that he was certain his father knew *nothing* about. On the other hand, buying the club from his father had nothing whatsoever to do with rap music as much as it had to do with keeping the family business afloat. He felt his father was guessing, or at most, pigeonholing the individuals based on what he heard.

"Well, I have news for you, Dad. We play their music in the club all the time. Not only that, if you're so much against rap . . . the fact is that more than sixty to seventy percent of the selections that play over the speakers here are *rap* songs. So what's your point?"

"Look, I'll tell you what the *point* is . . ." Douglass saw his father grimace like he used to do before he popped him upside the head as a youngster at the family grocery store. ". . . This club is running just fine without your ideas, your rap friends and their money . . ."

"Rap friends? These are *investors*. What's the difference? Money is money. You said you'd sell for a million, with five hundred down. So I got the five hundred."

"And what about the rest? What am I suppose to do after I get the money? You end up messing up the cash flow— changing everything . . . *then what*? Plus . . . the girls here aren't gonna work for *you*. Look at your attitude. Nobody's gonna wanna work for you." Douglass huffed through his grin, almost anticipating his father's insults.

"Of course the dancers aren't gonna be working for me, because they're *not* gonna be working here at *all*. Half of the girls you got here are lousy looking or lousy money makers. Others are questionable prostitutes. The staff is nothing but a bunch of lechers and thieves. They've been rippin' you off left and right . . . rippin' you off means they're rippin' me off."

"Well, I say, if it ain't broke don't fix it. And as far as I'm concerned, the deal's off."

"I don't think you wanted to sell in the *first* place. You were right to ask '*What am I gonna do after I sell it to you*,' because this is your life. If you could eat, sleep and live here, you would . . . and you've been running this club like you run your car, your house, other people, and even your *family*. You've *abused it all*. You've made one big mess of business, of other people's lives and of *your* life. Stepped on everybody you could, just to get your way. You've chased everybody away; your wife, your daughters and now *me*. I'm the only one you had left . . . and not for nothing, *Dad*, but if it wasn't for this club and this business, I really wouldn't have been around you *either*. We *never* really **had** a relationship. I was just there for you to use. I thought it was my *gift* to be able to operate the cash register at the grocery store and to be able to sell liquor next door *simultaneously* . . . I thought it was a *gift* to be able to do that at ten years old. But the truth is, you were just saving money on salaries. Using me for cheap child labor . . . like a slave!"

"Hey, you wait a minute . . ."

"No-no, you're not gonna out-talk me, because the fact is that any hopes I had for a well-financed college education were diminished when you used the scholarship money that my *mother's* parents . . . *my* grandparents put away for me!" Douglass was full of adrenaline. He knew that he was dropping a bomb, and there was no stopping him now. "You've screwed up your credit, my credit, my *mother's* credit, my mother's *brother's* credit . . . use-use-use, that's all you know how to do is **use** people to have things *your* way. That's the **only way you know!**" Douglass was choked up, suddenly realizing that he went all the way off. He verbally pummeled his father. But he didn't want to let up. He *had* to get it out. He knew that this was his last stand.

"For your information, since the beginning of time . . . fathers don't **charge** their sons big unobtainable sums of cash to take over the family business . . . once their sons have proven themselves, they pass it on and live off of their good fortunes. They **teach** their offsprings how to run it and guide them along proudly. A million dollars?! Ha-ha . . . you think this club is worth a million dollars? You stay in this office, screw who you want, with the door closed . . . locked. And your staff . . . *your* staff is out front at the register, at the front and back door, in the bathroom . . . screwing *you*! And you expect me to stand by and watch all of this? I put my sweat and tears into this place. I went to my friends and their contacts to get licenses and clearances for the club. Even with a million dollars you couldn't have opened this club without the right resources . . . *my* resources. And something else . . ."

—Tears were welling in Douglass's eyes now—

". . . I promoted the biggest, most successful night this club ever experienced *or* profited from . . . residuals are *still* coming in from that promotion a year or so later. . . . and this is how I'm treated? Listen, as far as I'm concerned you can **have** the club, the house, the car, *and* the money and you can *shove it! It's* not worth it. *You're* not worth it!" Douglass walked out of the office, not slamming the door behind him, and simultaneously brushed the tears away while dashing towards the exit. Blood was rushing to his head and he was even a bit dazed from the emptying of his soul. But the bottom line was that he felt liberated. Alone and scared for the instant, *yes.* But, more importantly, he was free. Leaving from under his father's wing.

With his first breath of fresh air outside of the club, he could envision the staff inside, behind him, grinning and satisfied as though their ears were pinned to the door and walls. They must've sensed the severance and even *wished* for it to happen, for their own job security.

Swing eventually got word of the hostility in the Gilmore family, and pulled out. He was discouraged by the lack of unity. And Douglass couldn't blame him, thinking that maybe he should have shut his mouth and played along until his father had no choice but to hand the business over to *somebody.* After all, his dad was in his 60s. But the tension was obviously too great to bear. Because, for Douglass to sit and watch the mischief and his crumbling dream was more torture than the prize was worth.

Easy Living

Living arrangements for Valerie, Mechelle and Debbie grew to be much more than just "acceptable." They were convenient, beyond compare. They all worked and lived and cared for

Destiny; all of them accepting Douglass's brand-new baby girl as their own. And they also made money together as a team.

All three women became heavyweight commodities in the adult entertainment industry, with more work at the high-class gentlemen's clubs in the city, and higher paying gigs like bachelor parties, business functions, and even team celebrations. The three once put a show on (and took their clothes off) for a real-estate tycoon—a 50-year-old—who got so excited his heart began to beat irregularly until he fell over in his chair. The hotel where the anniversary was held had a doctor in the house. Apparently, it wasn't as bad as it seemed. More like a cramp than a heart attack or a stroke. His friends and family immediately broke out of their anguish and tears, erupting into hysterical laughter. On another occasion, there was a mechanic who was getting married. So the girls arrived as planned, waiting for the guy to come back from lunch. He had been working on a particular vehicle before he left, so impulsively, the dancers plotted their scheme. Valerie was stretched out in a blazing thong on the back seat of the car. Debbie was in a similar outfit on the front seat. Mechelle was propped on the trunk of the car. Upon his return from lunch, the shock on the mechanic's face was like an alien encounter. He looked around for his boss and coworkers, unaware that the joke was on him. Eventually, his colleagues were barricading the entrance and exits to the garage with the bachelor now cornered by the vixens. The mechanic climbed various walls, like a tarantula frightened out of his wits, as if he was trying to escape an inferno. His face dripped with perspiration, his eyes were wide open like an opera singer's, and he even pissed himself, evident by the tiny wet spot near his zipper. The girls had never seen anything like *this* before. Generally, a man calmed down and went along with the teasing after a couple of minutes, realizing that there'd be more joy than pain. But this husband-to-be was ridiculous. He went on (half screaming like a bitch) climbing on top of the car hoods in the dingy garage, pulling down fan belts, tools and such, escaping the threat of the erotic dancers for more than 20 minutes. When they finally caught up with him, he sat obediently against a set of old, oily tires, biting his nails to the cuticles as the triple-threat team made a puppet out of him.

The threesome had an even bigger adventure on a trip they took overseas. The one and only Sultan of Brunei hired the threesome for a yacht trip. He sent a 747 (complete with stewardesses and a full flight crew) to get the women in New York, and they flew to Brunei, where they were to put on an exclusive show for the Sultan. When they arrived in Brunei, they were pampered and chauffeured for a grand tour of the Royal Palace. It was a monster, made of marble, brass and gilded domes, with more than 1,700 rooms. The 2-hour tour got them all wound up for the big party set for that evening. From the palace yard, a brilliant, white helicopter lifted them up and over the spectacular, sprawling dynasty and above the Pacific Ocean until they descended towards a sharp, white, 152-foot yacht labeled "TITS."

"A little bold, isn't he?" Valerie mentioned. And she had to show the others what she meant, pointing down from the helicopter so they all could see the name of the yacht.

"If ya got it, why not flaunt it," said Debbie. And she and Mechelle shared in a high five. From the aircraft, the girls could also see that the super yacht had two pools, a miniature golf course and a second helicopter. There were some other people looking to the direction of the landing pad, with glasses in hand, as the helicopter made its landing.

Aboard the boat, the girls were treated like trophies, introduced to more Mohameds, Abduls, Hakeems and Hajjis than they could bear to stomach; all of them with so many fanciful, identical smiles and all. Lots and lots of teeth. There were so many Princes and Chancellors and Prime Ministers that it could make a girl dizzy. And the celebrity list was one for the history books, including moguls of fashion, magnates of business and icons of song. Finally, they were escorted to meet the 44-year-old playboy himself. Downstairs at the restaurant, the girls were seated at a corner table designated for the Sultan. When he arrived, he had all manner of assistants and hangers-on surrounding him. Debbie was particularly engaged in the jewels about his wrists and fingers, while Valerie concentrated on his eyes.

"He's just a man," Valerie repeated to herself.

Later, after dinner and some one-on-one private dancing in the on-board disco, the 4 retreated to the Sultan's lair. The dancers prepared for their customary private showing, and one by one emerged from the bathroom in sexy garments. During the performance, the Sultan tried to get fresh, slipping a finger beneath Mechelle's thong, touching the folds of her sweaty flesh. She quickly snapped out of the Arabian Princess-role and smacked him hard enough for his turban to jump off his head. The Sultan smiled devilishly like that was something he was accustomed to and all three girls left the room supportively, also laughing at his Royal Highness and his pressing erection.

Mechelle, Debbie and Valerie inevitably left the boat within an hour, and in solidarity, they cheered about their $300,000, a fee that had already been wired to their U.S. bank account.

Notwithstanding the peculiarities or the eventful experiences, these were exciting times and adventures for three young women who came from different worlds; all of them with their life's challenges and with their skeletons in the closet. They didn't think money, but they certainly worked like money machines. And Douglass was blessed enough to be their unofficial treasurer. They didn't even much care about the *how-much* and the *what-to-do* part of the money. Because, as a team, they simply immersed themselves in the fun and frolic of it all. With all that financial freedom, Douglass lived like a king, and his daughter, Destiny, like a pampered princess. There was lobster, crab legs and salmon for dinner two and three nights a week thanks to Valerie, who was the cook in the group. And Douglass's eighty-thousand-dollar wardrobe was just as complete as any one of his lovers', even with their vast array of dresses, outfits and shoes. You name the maker, they had it. From the Jimmy Choo shoes, to the Gucci and Prada handbags; from the full line of Baby Phat wardrobes, to the Tiffany jewelry to the high-end perfumes—they had it all! Meanwhile, the atmosphere was stressless, and the living and loving, abundant. Altogether, their savings neared $600,000, most of it thanks to the Sultan's binge. Now, since they experienced big, they got into the practice of *earning* big. So accordingly, they wanted to live big, too. First things first, the girls had to leave the Gilmore home. They were all too close to Douglass's pop, who was as nosy as he was desperate to know how they were

achieving all of their success. However, to them, he was merely
a landlord now. They paid him a monthly rent to stay at the
house, but other than that, there was no communication. They
hardly saw each other. They no longer worked at Fool's Paradise, and Douglass was too busy handling their affairs to give
a damn. It was an unfriendly atmosphere at times, to see the
father and son bicker over petty shit, and so it was inevitable
that they all find a better place to be. They hung on for as long
as they dared, until they located a large townhouse closer to
the shore. The want for 100% liberation compelled Douglass
to hurry the move. But he also wanted to separate the business
and family life. Following the move and stabilization of Douglass's entertainment enterprises, there were plans to take a
much-needed and well-deserved vacation to Florida.

Within days of their commitment, the North Avenue dwelling was emptied until it was hollow. The furniture was trans-
ported to the townhouse and the business equipment went to
the new office on Main Street. The last string to sever was the
car. Instead of the Toyota Camry that Fool's Paradise financed,
Douglass picked up a new Lincoln Navigator. Black, sleek and
luxurious, the vehicle was a popular catch. He needed it to
transport, protect and impress his women, as well as it was
indicative of his rise to success.

After the move and just before the trip to Florida, Douglass
sat alone in the townhouse, looking out through the sliding
glass doors. In the distance, past the back porch, was the Long
Island Sound. It was a brisk winter's evening with the moon
glowing . . . illuminating against the water. Douglass was cozy,
with a hand-knitted blanket to comfort him. In one hand was
the manifesto and plans that he'd conceived while in jail. After
a while, he set down the papers and affixed his focus out towards the horizon, as though Destiny was there. Meanwhile,
Destiny (now 2 months old) was cuddled and sleeping like a
warm, lil munchkin beside him. He couldn't help but imagine
his little girl and the future that awaited her, knowing how
much of it might be predicted; as though he could see the future. He wanted things to be easy for Destiny, or at least *easier*. Not the trials and unnecessary struggles that he had to go
through, many of which he managed to overcome. It was

time for a firm decision. No guessing or playing it by ear. Douglass thought about the various directions that he was going and where he had come from. Who was with him. It was like reviewing a film in quick time, only now he *was* in total control. He *could* see his ultimate destiny as if it was the clearest image in his mind. All he'd have to do was press ENTER.

All in the Family

"See, Sal . . . We got dis here problem in the Bronx."

"I know a little bit about da Bronx." Sal was the spittin' image of Edward G. Robinson, with the *"you dirty rat"* voice and all. He was being facetious about knowing a little about the Bronx, having been born and raised there.

"I know you do, Sal. Dat's why I'm speakin' wit' you how I got issues." The two mobsters sat adjacent to one another as they popped half-dollar tokens into the noisy slot machines of Bally's in Atlantic City. The dinging and ringing sounds were constant in the air around them, although their surroundings already dazzled the eyes with mirrors, lights and colors that were dizzying to look at. The voices humming and the clanging of change might be a slight bit deafening for the average person, and perhaps that's why so many elderly folks didn't mind it. But not Sal, a capo with the Tocci family of New York, or Fat Jimmy, the porky capo from the Bianco family of New Jersey. They were accustomed to the life, the sights and sounds of the casinos. It was comfortable for them, and besides, the noise helped to conceal most any conversation.

At any casino along the boardwalk, history had been made as the mafia elite played judge and jury. Hits and executions were ordered, hostile takeovers and extortion schemes were set up, and kidnappings and hijacks were common calls. And sure, Sal and Fat Jimmy (the two experienced "goodfellas;" the next generation of AC's mafia families) were aware of the cameras high above, or hidden behind 2-way mirrors. Hell, they were responsible for quarterbacking the contracts to install the security system! *Why wouldn't they know!?* However, this meet wouldn't be of extreme importance to the Feds. It didn't matter if Feds, or any other Atlantic City law enforcement, was hawking, so they decided. It was just a convenient spot to talk about, well . . . *simple* favors.

"There's a spot that your people got up there. Like an auto body shop . . . but some moolies moved in and made it a strip joint . . ."

Fat Jimmy pulled his lever.

"Oh . . . I know the one—I *definitely* know the one. My people can't believe we slept that fuckin' goddamned goldmine opportunity. Then a bunch of fuckin' niggers move in, *boom-bam-zip-bop-boom*, they drop some change in there and *badda-bing-badda-boom*—they make millions."

"Yeah, well . . . dat's water under da bridge, see? They're in there now. And see, we got sumpthin' special happenin' just across the street."

"Oh *yeah*, it's like dat?" Sal was scooping out 20 dollars in coins that he won. He didn't give the winnings a second thought.

"Oh yeah. A little sumpthin', ya know. Anyways, we need you guys to bring some pressure. *Any* kinda pressure. Just do what you gotta do." Fat Jimmy popped 2 more coins.

"It's not that easy like dat, Jimmy. They got a lease for a thousand fuckin' years. It's fuckin' signed, sealed and delivered, too." Sal pulled his leaver.

"Well, then, there's gotta be sumpthin' *else* we can do."

"What's in it for us?" Fat Jimmy ignored the 50 coins that fell and squinted as he turned to face Sal for the first time in nearly 5 minutes.

"Sal . . . you know what's in it for you? *Peace of mind's* in it for you—that's what . . ." Fat Jimmy raised a serious eyebrow.

". . . How much interest you suppose your people have over here in A.C.? A hundred a year? Two hundred?"

"Probably sumpthin' like dat."

"Well, you just remember that next time, before you ask what's in it for you's guys. We don't ask you's no questions like dat concernin' Bianco interests at da fish market or wit the construction . . . so . . ."

"Hey, easy, Jimmy . . . alright. I gotta talk to my guys. You talk to yours. No more sit-downs from here. This could become serious. Anything we do, we go through the usual way . . . *kapish*?"

"Uh—kapish." A 7-foot wrestler-type was posted near the slot machines, waiting on his boss with another eye on Fat Jimmy and *his* escort as they headed out of the casino. Outside of the entrance as the limo pulled up, Fat Jimmy poked at his cell phone, looking like he had luggage . . . a pillow, under his shirt and in the seat of his pants.

"Hey, Tony. I want you's guys to stay focused on the Pretty Girl. Faggetabout about Fool's Paradise from now on—understood?" No sooner did Jimmy get an answer before he snapped the cell phone closed and stuffed it in his blazer pocket. Sal was already being chauffeured back to the heliport, where a chopper would be waiting to cut through the sky towards his warehouse in Jersey City.

"Jay . . . do we have any guys at the SLA in New York?" Sal was sitting next to the wrestler-type, but raising his voice, wanting to be heard over the puck-puck sounds of the helicopter propellers.

"I believe I have a buddy who's with their investigative unit—I could call him." Jay didn't carry the vocal dialect that was typical of the Guido mafioso-type. He was well read and didn't hesitate to say he *loathed the stigma that preceded such imbeciles*. Whatever that meant.

"Alright-then. Arrange a meeting. Work something out with them." As the aircraft swerved towards the New York skyline, Sal considered the stakes of the Biancos building a strip joint in Tocci territory. Without a second thought, he opened his Nextel and punched in a number to *his* boss.

Tony the Crow hung up the phone, finished his burger, and yelled for the next candidate.

"*Next!*" A slinky, white girl in a one-piece bathing suit came strutting out from the dressing room. Clicking her heels across a wood floor that was complete with sawdust and debris, she stepped up to the stage that was enclosed by a circular bar. Her hair was dirty blond and she was piled with red lipstick, blushed cheeks and rose-scented perfume that tainted the air about her. Mixed with the smell of fresh sawdust and sweaty construction workers, the aroma in this club was nauseating.

"Okay. Music!" Tony barked as he wiped the ketchup off of his lips and fingers. The pale, colorless dancer began to warm into a sway with her arms and body. Her legs were scrawny and her smile was artificial; and she was very focused on Tony as if she was trying real hard to sell something. She batted her heavily enhanced eyelashes at him and executed a cute half turn, holding onto a pole with one hand and pulling at her butt cheek with the other. She bent over as if to show him more assets, but it was no use. The candidate was not only flat-chested, she had no ass.

"Okay, okay. NEXT!" Tony seemed unsatisfied with his cheek in his palm. He took a deep, helpless breath and rolled his eyes, wondering if this was the best that the booking agency could send in. There was less than a month left until the inspectors were to sign off on things, and then there was that week before Christmas Eve; the grand opening. The club was coming close to the finishing touches. A million dollars' worth.

Let's Go

Wade had never taken a vacation in all of his years on the force. Even when his partner was cut down, he remained loyal to the job, mainly to find his partners' killer. And indeed, finding his partner's killer was therapy in itself. But what kind of therapy was there for *not* finding the killer? Wade decided that he *would* finally take his vacation time, before the craziness of the holidays set in. The department owed him a year, plus he had little more than a year left before his retirement. So the opportunity was perfect. In all of his years on the force, he'd seen all of the lifestyles that a man could imagine; even that of a cavewoman (considering his meeting Juicy). He'd rubbed elbows with the rich and famous; the poverty stricken and the homeless. He'd experiences a career full of stories and pain, with very little joy and pleasure. And now, Wade decided that it was due time that he pursued pleasure and joy for himself. It was indeed the moment of truth, and these heavy concerns weighed on his mind as he cleared his desk and filled his box with the awards from the wall. He couldn't help but to spin through the memories of each memento. Meanwhile, the office was sluggish and unusually quiet today. It was disheartening to see another good man leave—like losing an arm. There was also an overcast of dissatisfaction because of the unresolved matter of the past year. Still, the office gave Wade a standing ovation as he proceeded out of the squad room; a box under one arm and shaking hands with his free hand. His vacation was approved, but everyone knew what his plans were—hell, he cleared his *desk* out. His life as a detective was over. Wade stepped into Chief Washington's office for a quick so-long.

"I didn't know if you wanted this now." Wade reached into his belt for the service revolver.

"Nahh . . . keep it till you come and see me after vacation."

"What for, Chief? You know I keep two others on me."

"Yeah, well . . . I don't feel like doing the paperwork right now. Keep it with you . . . and that's an *order!*" The chief was being jovial with his tone of voice. Then he turned friendly again.

"Where you goin' for your vacation? . . . I mean, it's none of my business, but just in case a *certain* killer shows up and wants to surrender to you in person." Wade couldn't help smiling and shrugged in response.

"Well, just be careful. After the force, we're still friends, alright? And I want my friends all in one piece." Wade and Washington exchanged a bear hug and abruptly parted, heads swiveling to the left and right in case anyone was questioning their masculinity. Not a chance. The entire office was under surveillance as the layers of eyeballs in the squad room were focused on the two and their compassion for one another.

"Can I treat you to a drink, good buddy?" asked a rookie cop.

Wade declined. He already had plans for the evening with Brenda, who agreed to an evening at the Blue Note jazz club down in the village. Brenda sort of shuddered when Wade mentioned "*the Village*" on the phone. He made a mental note to ask her about that later. The two entered the club side by side, suddenly feeling as if they'd walked into a warm closet space, just not *quite* as small. Everyone in the 200-plus seats in the house was offered an intimate, unhampered view of the stage where a 4-piece band's instruments sat alone and waiting. Most of the food service and intimate conversation that took place before the show was underway and the couple waisted no time, each diving into separate orders of shrimp scampi and a "Rachelle Ferrell Daiquiri." The room filled up quickly, with energy so busy and snug that celebrities went almost unnoticed. *Almost.* Even Wade could see Nancy Wilson at a corner table with a few friends to keep her company. And any novice would be able to recognize Carmen Bradford sitting with a friend on a tier with the very best view in the house. There was a knowing amongst the audience that no jazz lover or music aficionado could be in a more desirable place at a more appropriate time.

Besides having that shoulder-to-shoulder closeness, the Blue Note could also boast about featuring the most notable performing artists and song stylists in the world, and accordingly the band of three men marched towards the stage to begin tuning and adjusting. A moment later, an announcement commenced, requiring *no smoking or flash cameras* and then a warm welcome . . .

". . . *Give a warm Blue Note to Rachelle Ferrell!*" The band began the opening bars to Rachelle's signature song "*Welcome To My Love,*" while she did her best to smiling fans. Rachelle eventually grabbed the microphone and serenaded the crowd, suspending everyone's belief with her incredible voice. Brenda and Wade were 2 tables from the stage, in the center of the club, basking in the melodies and swaying in song. It was a test to focus on one another with such an attraction soaring free on the stage; however, they did connect with a few glances here and there. Partway into the performance, Rachelle melted into her song "*I'm Still Waiting,*" and the lyrics seemed to penetrate the couple. Wade reached for Brenda's hand across the table while they shared in the sensation. Brenda's heart fluttered with each high note. The songstress provoked them more, standing at center stage, delivering a strong bridge in her song.

> *You'll be my knight in armor,*
> *I'll be your queen.*
> *We'll be together at last*
> *We'll shaa-re our dream,*
> *Nothing's gonna stop us now,*

Come, let's begin . . .
Right awaaay . . .
Why not todaaaaay!!!

Rachelle's voice was a heavenly calling, floating through the misty, blue room . . . gently caressing the minds of everyone with her sopranic, melodious blessing of loving song. Her high notes flirted through the atmosphere like a loose sparrow, while her low tenor notes were sensual and riveting. The presentation was provocative of passion, and softened Wade to recognize the beauty before him. He had messages in his eyes, and instantly, Brenda could feel it. Their legs tangled under the table, and the feelings crept back up into their eyes. The magic in the music made this a magical, intimate moment, causing each to question how they arrived at that point of love and devotion.

Brenda's tendency, on the other hand, was one of addiction; she wanted to jump across the small table at Wade until they both toppled over onto the others seated directly behind them. She came to know herself and that sex was indeed a big passion in her life. However, she was wise about it and wanted to experience it wisely. She was tired of false assurances. Wade, she was certain, was as real as a man could be and her intuition told her that he in turn needed someone like her; someone caring and compassionate. But what she wasn't sure of was the timing of their coming together. Her mind kept saying, *"If I do this now, what will he say?"* or *"Would I be going too far?"* For sure, Wade had her twisted upstairs . . . deliver *that* news, Miss TV Anchor!

But this was quite an emotional day for Wade, too. Enough to surrender to whatever Brenda decided was right. Inevitably, Brenda had Wade take her home. She issued him a promising, loose kiss and then dashed out of his vehicle into the foyer of her midtown address. After Brenda disappeared past the doorman and through the lobby of the building, Wade found himself caught up and mystified. He felt the warmth of Brenda's presence when she was there, and empty once she left. That ole familiar sensation was back again. There was a knock on his car window. He jolted from his dreamy state of mind. Eyes wide.

"Sir . . . is everything alright, sir?" the doorman.

"Oh . . . sure." Wade flashed an assuring smile. He took his hand off his revolver and pulled off as if to escape the emotions consuming him.

South Beach

The girls felt like they were part of a traveling dance troupe of a sort. There were 7 of them in all. And baby made 8. Four men. Three women. The crazy thing about it all was that Debbie, Mechelle and Valerie, while having 4 good, strong, able men with them, the women were devoted, in love with and giving love to only one of them; lucky Douglass. And there wasn't so much as a hint of jealousy among the others. Greg was smiling all the while on the JetBlue flight to Florida. Whether it was back in New York or now, here in South Beach, the setup was simply novel to him. Somehow (he knew) being by Douglass's side would bring him similar good fortune. Demetrius was still murmuring, *"Blasphemy!"* and *"Y'all are going straight to hell."* However he always smiled when he said that; like he thought this was all cute. Danni was here in Florida as well, and he was content; now in his mid-40's, all he knew was how to roll with the show. He'd been there, done that, if you heard him tell it. And no, he had no interest in any part of Douglass's world—not *that* world, anyway—although he was still very protective of Debbie, keeping his vow to look out for her. So, Danni coming to work for Douglass fit just right. And, speaking of which, Douglass was half past the point of no return, watching over Destiny, fanning the infant, certain not to let the warm Florida climate aggravate her. He was beyond happy these days; he was a free man, with the loves of his life, and he had all the luxury one man could dream up. This was the world according to him. A portrait that *he* painted, and, by and large, the paint would harden just as he intended.

The trip down here was specifically for the vacation, although the dancers couldn't help but venture out to various clubs to compare the action to what they were accustomed to. The bigger plan here was Douglass's announcement regarding the future of his family.

The group stayed at the Fountain Blue Hotel in 2 double-room suites. Demetrius was alone in one room with Destiny. Danni and Greg shared the adjoining room. Next door, Valerie and Mechelle shared a water bed in that adjoining room, while Douglass was in the master bed. Debbie paired with Douglass for the first night after winning a coin toss. Sex was like that for these three—nothing new to anyone else—and they were all content, with everything else so damned convenient. Mutual love and respect between them all. Any spats that surfaced were immediately squashed thanks to Douglass's iron-clad commitment to unity. And, of course, with all the money floating around, who had time to argue?

All the while, for the past 3 months, the most satisfying, selfless sexual encounters were exercised whenever time permitted. A lot of fun, a lot of experimenting, and a lot of soiled towels. Naturally, there were interferences like work, keeping the townhouse in order, and caring for the baby. But this Florida vacation was no reason for the sex routine to change. After Debbie came Valerie, and after Valerie was Mechelle. It was like this for the first 3 days. And in between the romps at night, Douglass took time to plan out his address to the group.

It was near sundown when Greg was going over the plans with Douglass in his suite. He popped a surprise on him at what he considered to be the right moment.

"Who?" Douglass asked in response to Greg's surprise.

"Some . . . *friends* from New York." Greg was evasive, a little leery and uncertain as to whether he'd done the right thing.

"Okay, Greg . . . *come on*. No time to beat around the bush. Everyone is supposed to meet out on the beach in an hour or so."

"Ahh . . . . I sort of invited them."

"On *my* bill?"

"No—of course not. They paid their own way. That is . . . Brenda *and* Walter did. They wanted to surprise you."

"Brenda Feather . . . Walter Wade? Together? Here in Florida?"

"Uh-huh."

"Why?"

"I'll let *them* share that with you . . . nothing serious, though. Nothing about Moet or *that* whole mess."

"Alright . . . this oughtta be good. They're coming down later, too?"

"If it's okay with you."

Douglass huffed and wagged his head. "This was supposed to be just a family thing, Greg. But, whatever . . . Wade was helpful with springing me from the bang; so he's a friend in my book. Now, we need to get back to the business at hand."

Greg was looking like Don Chi-Chi, with a cell phone to his ear, a short-sleeved, colorful Hawaiian shirt and yellow swim trunks. Douglass was just ahead of him, with the blue trunks and a white t-shirt on. The two were on the ground level of the hotel, walking out onto the patio, around the in-ground pool and lounge chairs into the warm evening air. Just beyond a line of palm trees, with multi-colored lanterns strung between each, Demetrius, Danni, Valerie, Debbie and Mechelle were relaxing quietly in lounge chairs facing the ocean. Destiny was awake, gulping at a bottle of milk in Demetrius' arms. Demetrius, the nanny. There was a small flaming campfire on the ground next to them, sending a pleasant aroma of pine into the air and providing a glow under the darkening sky. Now, as the group formed a perimeter outside of the fire, Wade and Brenda were seen strolling up the beach like lovers. Douglass looked at Greg.

Greg shrugged a "*don't ask me.*"

Danni was the first to speak. "Hey, Wade."

"Wade. What's up?" Demetrius was just as surprised.

"What's up, guys . . . you all know Brenda Feather." Everyone acknowledged her, while the group made room for the couple to join them. They remained standing like targets.

"So, Wade . . . what brings you to Florida . . . South Beach, Florida . . . The Fountain Blue—*in* South Beach, Florida." Douglass was making a big deal of the coincidence, looking again at Greg, and then back towards Wade, still curious nonetheless. Wade smiled and Brenda chuckled under her breath. The two embraced each other, side by side. Danni looked at Demetrius with that "*ooh-brother*" drawl.

"We just came for the fresh air, of course. To, uhh . . . to escape the cold weather and the rat race in New York . . . *aaaand* to announce that we're getting married." Wade unveiled their secret casually, pulling a blushing Brenda closer still.

"*Wooow*," Danni said, having gotten to know Wade pretty good.

"Well . . . do we have the glasses and Dom P to celebrate, *Greg*?" Greg took a second to whisper to Douglass, reminding him of their agenda.

"Oh right . . . right. Okay, very well, Mr. Wade and Miss Feather—or shall I say Mr. and Mrs. Walter Wade, we'll toast in a moment. You may be seated." Douglass was being jovial, recalling his days in court.

"I *also* have an announcement to make. Sorry, I don't have a drum roll for all of these fabulous announcements . . . we will be opening our own nightclub. A new, state-of-the-art, topless club . . ." The ladies brightened with excitement. ". . . the club will be called Gilmore's, Black Beauty. I intend to raise 2 million dollars over the next 90 days and to have the club opened for business by next spring."

All in attendance were happy about the announcement. Brenda was still glowing and googly-eyed from Wade's announcement. Greg was standing just behind Douglass. Proud. The dancers were already into their own conversation about the club, wondering this and wondering that.

"There's more . . . we're gonna give a big presentation; we expect . . . no, scratch that . . . we *will* have the investment dollars necessary to go on with the project. When that happens . . . I'll let Greg share this part with you."

"Once the investment has been affirmed, all of us will be off again; this time on a recruitment crusade. I think Chicago. We figure that if there are more fine women like Debbie in Chi-town, they can *definitely* come and work for us. We'll be scouting for forty dancers . . ."

Debbie twisted her lips, wondering how realistic he was being.

"We'll put out a big ad campaign and we'll have a video presentation. We're gonna be professional, like this was a big ole movie casting day. We'll have hundreds of girls, and we'll get to pick the cream of the crop. In New York, we're going to put the dancers up in houses. Ten to a house. They'll have fitness regimens, good diets and routine health and dental services. Five day, eight-hour work weeks. Equal salaries, investment incentives. G and I have worked out a compensation plan that can beat any other . . ."

"Now there's more—" Douglass cut in. "But those are the basics. Greg and I will hammer out and fine-tune, but you should get the idea. The ball is rolling. Ads have been placed in the *Sun Times* and *Tribune*, and we'll be doing some radio ads in about a week. We've sketched out responsibilities for everyone, and I'd like to toss those at you tonight . . ."

The most compelling words to come out of Douglass's speech that night were: ". . . We don't ever want a tragedy like what happened with Moet." He was adamant about his intents and the group felt it. He took suggestions, concerns and critique as genuine, while keeping an eye on his prize. They popped the bubbly amidst the moon's glow, the crackling fire, the water and the waves, the seagulls in the air, all of it setting an incredible atmosphere for the unveiling of this ultimate dream.

CHAPTER TWENTY-ONE

Ascension

Meetings of this sort were made for warehouses. Meager light from hanging bulbs. Cavernous. High windows; a lot of them. Crates. Wooden platforms. Lots of cement surface, enough for an execution, a dismemberment or a top-secret meeting. The Tocci family used this particular warehouse for all of the above—and for hijack storage as well. Being just off of busy Rockaway Boulevard and minutes from JFK Airport, the Queens location was also a convenient one. Inside, to the rear, at a classy wooden banquet table that was a remnant of a hijacking from years past, Jay and a crew of henchmen looked on as Sal listened to the onslaught of spitting invectives.

". . . what do these ginnies think we're running here, a fuckin' boarding house, where's they can come and go as they please without payin' dues? Then they's got the nerve to threaten us . . . what was dat you told me, Sal?"

"Peace of mind, boss."

"*Ohhh!* So the BIANCOS are gonna let the TOCCIS have peace of *mind,* huh?!" The Don was red hot, and his pound of graying hair shook out of place like swaying grass in the ocean deep. Sal seldom witnessed the Don get angry. Tense, yes. Aggravated, *indeed.* But angry . . . that meant a body would be floatin' in Sheepshead Bay within hours. And all things considered, he was close to the edge right about now.

"This is the highest form of disrespect. To come to OUR territory without so much as a whisper . . . that's SHIFTY! And DAMNED DISRESPECTFUL! And to top it off with a threat? **AAARRRGH!**" The Don was foaming at the mouth now. This tantrum had already gone into an hour. Long enough. And Sal just stood there, content that he wasn't to blame. He'd personally witnessed the Don pull a weed-whacker out of nowhere one night and slice a henchmen's head clean off. So this was a *good* night. Now everything seemed to move in slow motion. Sal was watching and listening, but the arms waving and the mouth moving in front of him were a hazy vignette of slow motions and deep, growing echoes. Sal turned to look at Jay, the tyranny reflected in his eyes as well. Jay returned the glance and they both leveled their eyes back at the big man. The word "*respect*" drilled into both of them. Then, before Sal could blink, the Don pulled his forefinger from under one earlobe, across his neck towards his opposite ear. That was the gesture. Terror unleashed.

Even When You Win, You Lose

"Look, Ma. No hands!"

Gil was headed down a steep hill on a bicycle with no breaks. The mob wanted him out so that they could build and grow with no competition. He had virtually chased his son away, and gave his staff all access. He became negligent with the lease option on the New Rochelle home—six months in arrears, to be exact. The club payments were a few months behind, giving the property owners the wherewithal to void the contract and raise the rent.

And just so, since Gil wasn't holding up his end, the property owners *did* indeed raise the lease payments to $10,000 a month. **TEN THOUSAND!** And poor Gil had no choice but to pay it. Blood money. Everything he had accomplished though the years, the peanuts he had gathered and the money he had invested was tied up in Fool's Paradise. To add fuel to the fire, representatives from S.L.A. came and launched an investigation relating to sexual propositions made by a few dancers.

"It's Dino, Gil . . . pick up." Dino was speaking to Douglass's answering machine at the Main Street office in New Rochelle. He was so accustomed to calling him by his father's nickname. It was late in the evening, otherwise Sharon, his secretary, would be in to take the call. There was a beep, but Douglass caught the call just in time.

"Hey . . . just got back about two hours ago. You comin' over? There's a lot to talk about," said Douglass.

"Gil. They closed your father. The S.L.A. came in . . . some undercover shit. I didn't even recognize them." Dino was hyper. Demetrius was wide-eyed as he listened to the speakerphone voice.

"So, what happened?" Douglass was casual, not a nervous bone in his body.

"They made some propositions to a few of the girls—everyone turned them down; *cop* was written all over them."

"So who . . ."

"*Claudine.*" Douglass smirked at the mention, as if he should have known.

"Never fails. You lay with 'em, you live with 'em. Funny, my father used to say if *it ain't broke don't fix it.*"

"Gil . . . the shit is broken *now.* They locked your pop *and* Claudine up overnight. Let 'em out the next day. But they padlocked the club . . . sledge-hammered a hole in the wall; sawed a hole in the door and wrapped a big ole *thick*-assed chain through there. They weren't *playin'.*"

"Dino, I hear you talkin', but I told you this would happen a long time ago."

"I know. I know. I think Gilmore's is over, Gil. For good."

"Where you at now?"

"Yo, man, I'm on the job. I begged my boss to give me extra hours. The closing fucked up a lot of people, man. Gil even lost his house. Everybody's out looking for jobs. A few are auditioning at the new club across the street . . ."

"Across the street?"

"Yeah. *The Pretty Girl.* They're not open yet, but it looks like mob money all the way. Listen—I'll get with you Saturday."

"Dino, we gotta talk."

"Okay, I promise, Saturday." Douglass hit the speakerphone button and the connection went dead.

"I knew something was up across the street, Doug. Some of the girls have been tellin' me about it. Some Italian named Tony is at the wheel. They say he doesn't know what he's doin'." Demetrius seemed to be right on top of things, not at all thinking about the job he just lost.

"Yeah? Well, let 'em go. They can't touch what we're about to do. It's always been that way, ever since I was a youngster there were copycats. But they could never quite match my juice. Now come on, let's go over some more of the details for Sunday."

The day was fast approaching. Douglass titled the event "*Investor's Day.*" The ad in the papers boasted a 50% return on investment within one year. The sell was designed to provoke action.

And did it ever.

Greg handled the particulars, reserving a small ballroom at the Ramada Inn Hotel, picking the best dancers to be hostesses, making copies of the business plan, arranging for the refreshments and organizing the schedule for the day. He called a few of his Georgetown alumni, "The Fabulous Five," to assist with the publicity on the Investor's Day event in New Rochelle, and also the Black Beauty Day in Chicago. The guys would handle most of the work remotely, but Greg assured them that they *could* be physically present for Black Beauty Day in Chicago. That got them excited and working even harder. Finally, Greg devoted $2,200 to a meager publicity stunt which the Fabulous Five perfected. He hired 13 stretch limousines from a local company, and directed them to show up at 11:30AM—the presentation was scheduled to begin at noon. While investors straggled into the hotel, they couldn't help but to be impressed by the blitz of stretch limos which virtually reached around the perimeter of the hotel. The cars added prestige and significance to the event, so much so that men who happened to be rooming at the hotel—diplomats and businessmen alike—came to the event. By 12:30, the hard work, clever tactics and precise planning paid off. Close to 100 investors or their representatives were in attendance. Some came in their own limousines or at least a high-priced foreign car. There were ladies in business outfits, men in suits and even lawyers. Some attendees brought attache cases, many were taking and making cell phone calls, while others were empty-handed and skeptical. The welcome committee made the visitors feel comfortable. There was soft jazz music and bunches of red and black balloons floating high above each round table. Chairs filled rather quickly and the anticipation was on high. There was a sense of modesty amongst the staff, yet somehow they all knew that this presentation would have to swim or sink. And because there was only a sprinkle of women amongst the sea of male investors, the dancers on hand felt most comfortable, knowing what they knew about men and how most of that first impression was but a facade. They were pros at seeing through men and their smoke and mirror games.

Douglass strolled affirmatively in a back hallway, peeking though a window now and then to get a feel. In moments he'd have to face them all and put it down. He'd have to motivate that money until it wiggled out of their pockets and purses, right into his hands. His attitude was determined, and he was convinced that every one of those individuals in the ballroom were born educated and successful for the sole purpose of investing in his new club, *Gilmore's Black Beauty*. Douglass was committed to making it happen.

Through a portal window in the swinging door, Douglass thought he'd recognized some faces in the crowd.

"Should we keep it on steady record or use the voice-activated mode?" Hammer and Walsh were in the ballroom, trying their best to be undercover. Walsh had an uncharacteristic pair of horn-rimmed glasses on, a pair of jeans and a V-neck velour pullover sweater. Hammer wore a pair of blue and white Nike sweats with matching kicks. He was fiddling with a miniature tape recorder, a fresh cassette tape. He operated as though he was racing to beat out a deadline.

"Keep it on steady, Hammer. We don't want to miss anything . . . hey—there he is." Walsh nodded towards the extreme left of the room.

The ballroom was diverse with many white, black and Arab men and women sprinkled throughout. One or two Asians stood out, obviously outnumbered. Greg expected this and was prepared. Hostesses gave special attention to those members of the audience who seemed out of place. One particular table had a team of darker black men, dressed in distinguishing African fashions, head wraps and all. At first sight it looked so obvious that it could have been a gag—costumed men that arrived at the wrong event. But as Douglass stepped out into the ballroom, ignoring the theme of eyes that evaluated him, he realized that his eyes did not deceive him. He circled to the "African" table and approached the rear of the room with a warm smile.

"Fumi."

Old Friends, Long Money

"Mista G'more." Douglass was at a sudden loss for words. He had not seen the Nigerian since he was draped in torn army threads back at Passaic County Jail and they barely got to say goodbye when the feds snatched Douglass up out of there. And then there was that damned statement about the *universe* bringing them together . . . to think that *actually worked!* Fumi suddenly looked shorter with his generous, squinting, smiling eyes and his humble, wide grin. Yet he appeared more powerful now with the support of his entourage of other Nigerian men behind him. Within seconds the two were in the hallway outside of the ballroom, summaries about their trials and tribulations, post-Passaic. Fumi's team of Africans (6 in all), stood nearby, posting like soldiers in all-black corduroy, safari outfits. It was now 12 noon and Douglass could see Greg vying for his attention. To the side of Greg, Demetrius, Dino and Danni waited and wondered what was going on.

"G'more . . . you know you have shown me your plan long ago . . . and I would not be surprised if you have improved and fine-tuned it to the best of your ability. But, now that I have been called here, regardless of the ad in the *Wall Street Journal,* I recognize my purpose, my friend . . ."

—Fumi placed his hand up on Douglass's shoulder—

". . . You have my support. I'm looking forward to investing in your project. But, more than that, I am more interested in investing in *you.* I want to *help* you." Douglass was hearing, but not truly listening. His eyes were on his own team of soldiers standing by.

". . . Okay, I've got to go and do this presenta—*what?*" Douglass was so busy with his thoughts that Fumi's commitment was almost ignored.

"I said . . . I will invest in your project. I have already seen indications of your resilience, Douglass. And that is all I need to see—and I want to be first to commit. How much did you say you would need?"

"Oh . . . uh . . . t-two million." Douglass was falling apart inside, and the emotion rose into a stutter, but he held out from collapsing there in the lobby.

"Okay, Douglass. Consider it done. And there is much more where dat came from." Douglass was seduced by Fumi's soft, affirmative tone—the voice he spent months with in jail. Fumi inspired his confidence there on the inside; and now, he was doing it again on the outside. Fumi's expression didn't crack in the least. He was intent and sincere as though it was not to be questioned. He stood a foot or so shorter than Douglass, but his affirmations were as tall as any monument. Douglass curled his forefinger at Greg. Greg rushed over with Demetrius, who was steadfastly awaiting directions, while Dino remained still, keeping an eye on the actions of everyone. He found it hard to trust anyone.

"Greg . . . run with it," said Douglass.

"Okay. You ready?"

"Greg . . . take a deep breath. You know my presentation

back to front. We've rehearsed it together in Florida and here in New York. Handle it for me."

"What's wrong, why aren't . . ."

"Greg—" Douglass cut him off. "—Think about it this way . . . the only reason that we're going through with this presentation—?"

Douglass looked at his friend Fumi.

"—is so we don't get sued for wasting people's time."

"Why? What's wrong?" Greg held a frazzled expression. Douglass put both hands tightly on Greg's shoulders and smiled.

"Because we already *have* the money, Greg. Greg, meet Fumi. Fumi, meet Greg, my right-hand man." Now, Dino and Demetrius were shaking hands with Fumi's men and everyone was getting all buddy-buddy. The group of black men had swollen to a dozen, and just about everyone in the room was looking in their direction.

Greg was ever more charged with excitement, ready to begin the presentation before the curious audience. He pivoted and stepped past Demetrius and Dino.

"Fellas?" Douglass didn't say any more (and a slight tilt of his head), and the two immediately followed Greg towards the platform at the front of the ballroom.

"Please . . . come wi' me, Mista G'more." Fumi and his ever-distinguishable Nigerian dialect and smooth gestures were infectious, almost controlling Douglass's senses as would a puppet-master.

"Danni, I'll be a minute." And now Danni stepped away.

While Greg called the audience to attention, Douglass was escorted into one of two hotel elevators. They rose one level and exited through the rear entrance of the building. As they proceeded through the glass doors, the men converged on a trio of shiny, black Navigators. Douglass was thinking how everybody must like these trucks as he followed Fumi into the rear door of the center vehicle. The door was closed behind them and remaining soldiers paired off into the front seats of each Navigator. Fumi mentioned a few words in his native

Yoruban tongue and the driver picked up his 2-way radio mic from a tray between the seats to repeat the directives to the driver in the lead truck. Douglass nearly melted into the soft leather seat, no choice but to face the televisions in the headrests and other generous electronics in the trunk. The back of the jeep, the walls, the panel overhead, and the console that divided the two back-seat passengers, were loaded with luxuries. Temperature controls, stereo with CD changer, the global satellite hook-up, 3 separate mobile phones, a fax machine and a laptop computer that could swivel from a back panel of the driver's seat.

"How did you expect us to travel, by camel?" Fumi was replying to Douglass's amazement as the younger of the two had to rub his eyes, wondering what the hell he just got himself into. *Is Fumi a CIA operative or some shit?* Douglass now craved to know the truth.

". . . So to answer your question, no. I'm not with the CIA and I'm not an Ambassador. I am an African prince. One of thirteen hundred grandsons. We are all Princes working towards becoming king of the Yoruban Tribe. Our accomplishments, contributions to our land, to our people and our determination is what separates a prince by birthright from a prince in power. I *too* am working towards becoming King." Douglass allowed his eyes to wander dramatically.

"Well, you're doing a pretty good job, if I do say so myself." Fumi extended a generous smile as the caravan headed south on Route 1.

"By your standards here in America, this may all seem like accomplishment. But this is not new to my people. Our family has treasures and wealth untold. Much of it is buried and protected from the outside forces of the world; forces that are planning and plotting to rape our land. Some of it has been awarded to us by elders who want to see us do good in the world and to build on our family's accomplishments. We are a truly powerful people, Douglass." Fumi held a discerning gaze. Again, his confidence glimmered like the spark in his eye. "I'm simply an African man who has come to the states for prize investments. The only reason this government trapped me was because of red flags I must have raised during my spending spree . . ."

"*Spending* spree?"

"Yes, Douglass . . . it's called our Buy America campaign. I'll tell you more about that later. But you must at once know that my efforts in this country are all admirable. I've paid sales tax and property tax on all of our purchases. I've invested millions into sound businesses with respectable terms, yet certain adversaries . . . and we'd like to recognize them as *jealous* men . . . have been misleading to the courts. I am not a criminal. I am a man of honor. However, I believe that if you have dark skin in America, you cannot escape the hatred that is still deep in the soul you are born with. You are presumed guilty, and you must work your way up from there. However, to see true criminals, all one needs to do is to look at the history of this country. They have killed tens of millions of my people . . . your people . . . the very first people on this earth, just in order to fulfill their own wrath. They've slaughtered us. Suffocated us. We have been severely punished. Before the white man came to Africa, we were the world's superpower, with the wealth of human resources and the wealth of spiritual resources. Today, they have left us scrambling . . . killing one another for our own natural resources. They've massacred many millions of our people, leaving our natural resources, our human resources and our spirits in shambles . . . and they still smile in our faces. The culture and the unity that was once our sacred formula is now what keeps us apart. My land is breaking apart because of an internationally sanctioned rape and a lingering condition of dementia. The world owes Africa a *tremendous* debt." Douglass felt a tightening in his chest and some guilt for his complacent American dreams.

The lead Navigator turned right off of Route 1, only a few miles from the Ramada, and headed past a sign. "THE POINT. NO TRESPASSING." The vehicles weaved down a two-lane drive, approaching a giant iron gate with a small shed set out front on the median. As the short line of trucks got closer, the watchman inside of the shed stood up and investigated the procession through his pane-glass window. The guard's demeanor swiftly adjusted from inquiry to humility once he'd recognized who was coming through. Accordingly, he activated the gate to electronically open so that it wouldn't slow the progress of Prince Fumi. He waved, half salute, and the convoy of vehicles glided past in as-usual fashion. Once the vehicle reached a clearing, breezing out from under the marvelous canopy of oak trees to the left and right of the road, the bright daylight swept the entourage into a breathtaking panorama. Expertly landscaped, the road was lined with foot-high rose bushes. The bulbs were tiny and a thrill to see in full blossom. Outside of that, the road was surrounded by the Long Island Sound, making it seem as though they were sliding across the water's surface. The tract of land stretched out to a cape where a large home was positioned at the end of the road on a small island. The closer they came, the larger it grew. From a quarter-mile away, the house reflected the sun and created the image of a round, symmetrical diamond, surrounded by a pristine blanket of grass, a gallery of colorful flowers and the calm waters of the Long Island Sound. The group rolled up a circular driveway and stopped just short of the entryway to the residence.

"Welcome to The Point, Douglass." Fumi's eyes shined in a knowing way. And Douglass bought into the feeling, with no choice but to smile at it all. He could see evidence of New Rochelle in the distance. There was Hudson Park, Glen Island and a theme of private beaches spaced between the public ones. Further back, up on a crest, was the Wildcliff Historical Arts Center. Many boats were docked or covered, out of season. Although the attractions were a couple of miles of water away, the difference between where he lived and where he stood now (outside from distance) was the same separation of studio thinking versus the mansion mind. The home itself was a marvel to look at, something like a habitat of rustic, cultural flavor, pleasantly trapped inside of a crisp and nearly transparent architectural masterpiece. Yes, it was fanciful like a castle, but in a post-millennium sort of way. Douglass guessed that there were close to 15 acres of island or better. The architecture was its centerpiece, like a jewel set on top of a green velour pillow, yet composed of glass and steel, sweeping rooftops projecting the notion of a circular fortress. The men left their vehicles and flowed towards the pavilion which shaded an open, arched underpass. The passage was like a short tunnel, aligned with fern trees, and the walk was layered with the authenticity of cobblestone. After passing through, Douglass realized that the

walk-through led into an open courtyard. In the center was a
pond with an active fountain at its core. Inside of that, elevated
on a hill of stones, there was a glistening, black-iron, oversized
statue of an African woman balancing a basket on her head.
Fumi could see that the masterpiece captured the attention of
his guest.

"That represents the burden of all the black women. They
carried before slavery, during slavery and still today, after slavery is said to be abolished."

The house with its various sections enclosed the courtyard
and the pond with floor-to-ceiling picture windows, two levels
of them. Circling the pond and the centerpiece, the group
moved towards the far end of the courtyard and an entrance
distinguished by two massive doors. They were black and
looked heavy on sight; perhaps balance precisely, these were
the kind of doors you could fit a grand piano through without
dissembling it. As they approached, the doors were opened as
if calculated by someone within; a man in white safari cordu-
roys.

"Good day, sir." Douglass recognized the vibrating voice,
the respect and personality as a constant amongst his fellow
Africans.

"Thank you, Chuckuma." And they proceeded on a grand
tour. The estate was indeed roomy, bursting with high ceilings, beams, skylights and windows galore. The halls were
marble, and when they weren't, there was absorbent carpet
that slowed each footstep. There was dramatic accent lighting
at every turn, and also directed towards limestone lifelike
statues near each doorway, as though each open room had its
own gothic security. White walls were adorned with endearing paintings of African Kings. There must've been a hundred
of them positioned at various ascents and balconies. The home
was cleverly modern . . . almost cosmopolitan, but with gratuitous amounts of indoor palms, plants and wild flowers. A
horticultural free spirit ran wild through every hallway and
balcony.

Douglass was captivated by a soft rumble of drums that
streamed throughout the house. *Radical!* And cultural, too, just
like the colors of deep brown couches, black throw pillows,
black sofas and ivory chairs. Kente references draped about.

Interior and exterior views were unobstructed. Incense was mild and reminiscent of herbs and wildlife. There were even gardens indoors along the hallway floors, with floodlights plotted close to the replanted, towering trees which reached towards the ceilings. And then, to virtually create endless withdrawal from the outside world, the home was sophisticated. While it was simple, lofty, comfortable and quiet, with every bit of furniture sculptured and relevant to the motherland, the residence also had its neat hooks. There was a large breakfast room at the east side of the home, offering a view of an endless sound. There were a few winding stairways; one was the larger in the entrance hall, complete with a spectacular gallery of legendary jazz singers to entertain the climb. Finally, the gardens, the underground game room, tennis and basketball courts, indoor/outdoor swimming pool and a pool house with sauna and jacuzzi left little to the imagination, isolating and insulating everything from the jaws of the outside world. And still there was more.

A private movie viewing room was created according to Fumi's specific tastes. A giant 100-inch screen, framed by red velvet curtains. Harlem Renaissance-style woodwork with gold-emblazoned trim. The plush, black carpet ran wall-to-wall. In the corner of the theater room was a concession stand, just like the big theaters, stocked with *Now-or-Laters, Juicy Fruit, Doublemint* and *Big Red* gum, *Hershey's Kisses, Jolly Ranchers*, and *Sugar Daddy* caramel pops. In an adjacent corner sat an old-fashioned popcorn machine. A music system was wired for each room in the house. In the master bedroom, filled with panoramic water views, there were three 5-foot panel displays, situated in a semi-oval across from the king-sized bed. Other audio-video components were inset behind a sliding glass panel in the wall. They included a high-end, digital satellite music system, a digital video disc player, a satellite system, and a voice-operated personal computer. Commands to the PC were picked up by microphones in the headboard and deciphered by voice recognition software, to be viewed on any of the 3 monitors. Besides access to the Internet, voice commands also controlled air heating and cooling systems, security, video phone and a telecommunications network. Every instant that Douglass blinked seemed to bring forth another amenity to tell of. He wanted to explode when Fumi told him the price was *only* 20 million.

Only?

However, in their ensuing conversation, as the men all reclined in the sunken living room with a fire blazing near to them, Douglass soon realized who he was associating with. Fumi made it all too clear; living, breathing and now speaking up to the status as one of Africa's most aspiring diamond mine owners. Now, Douglass could see that the home in all of its magnificence befitted, but barely caught up to, a man in his 40's who had already amassed profits of three hundred million in the past year alone, with various investments in the United States. Moreover, Fumi had recently purchased 187 fast food restaurants, several exclusive sports cars, and 4 Gulf Stream jets.

"O-h-h-h . . . I see. And now you want to add a *topless* club to your list of toys?" Douglass's jaw was still lowered, in awe of all he'd heard and seen in just one hour.

"Actually . . . Please, Chuckuma . . ." Chuckuma came over to refill Douglass's glass of orange juice. "I am spearheading the *Buy America* campaign. As you are aware, there are billions and billions of dollars in Africa not being put to good use. *Buried.* Perhaps I am ignorant to even mention amounts, because the reality is that *nobody* knows the extent of wealth in the motherland. If it's not diamonds it's iron ore, if it's not gold, it's cocoa, and if it's not agricultural resources, then it's oil or gases. Africa is the world's mightiest land of wealth. *Still.* The land is limitless in terms of valuation. The lineage of my tribe . . . the Yoruba tribe, is the most powerful tribe in all of Africa. One of substance. We mean more than this itty-bitty President. More than this nation's so-called Fortune 500, and beyond meaning when it comes to spiritual, or cultural heritage and roots. They have uprooted some of us, but not all. I have come here to the United States not only to invest and to make *more* money with our money, but I have also come to rescue some of my people who are cowardly, ignorant or either naive to the wealth of life that awaits them in their native homeland." Douglass wanted to smack himself, feeling that this must be a big dream.

"So . . . no. It's not the topless part that impresses me. In my homeland I see topless everyday. It's natural, and I would never have to pay admission . . ." Fumi looked to his soldiers and they smiled in kind. "I'm really investing in *you*, Douglass. Even if you thought owning and operating a football or basketball team was profitable or important, I'd support and finance the purchase. It is not the investment, Douglass. It's you." Douglass took a long, methodic breath, as if it was his last exhale of headaches and misery . . . as if it was his very first inhale of wealth untold and a lifetime of plenty. His mind was busy with expenditures as he began to satisfy his imagination with images and intents.

"Chuckuma . . . ola edo." Fumi mentioned something in the Ebu language. Chuckuma proceeded forthwith, quickly returning with an attache case. It was thin like a paperback dictionary. Fumi laid the attache on the glossy, black coffee table which separated them. He popped the tiny latches and retrieved 2 small, leather pouches from inside. From one pouch he poured a small pile of stones—obviously diamonds. They sparkled like solid formations of spring water. The prisms and definitions were see-through and yet reflective of any evident light. From the other pouch, Fumi poured a separate pile, a larger pile of rocks. They were larger, less defined and quite yellowish. Not as brilliant as the other pile but a greater mass.

"Diamond class one-oh-one, Douglass. What pile would you prefer if you had your choice? This pile? Or *this* pile?"

"*Uuuhh* . . . I guess, this one." Douglass was unsure what Fumi was getting at, but predictable nonetheless. He pointed to the brilliant diamonds.

"Bad choice."

"Well, Fumi . . . to tell you the truth, any choice is better than no choice at all." Douglass laughed to himself.

"Yes, I see . . . well, what these are," indicating the larger pile, "are unfinished, uncut diamonds." Fumi picked up one and let Douglass review it closer. "See, this diamond that you're holding now has the finished value of this entire pile of polished diamonds over here. It's a little uglier, but with some finishing and cutting and polishing, it's worth probably three hundred and seventy thousand dollars." Douglass suddenly looked harder at the stone, *real* careful with it now. He quickly realized that the pile which it came from had about 20 others that were just like it.

"Now, in villages and jungles and on shores in our land, these uncut stones are laying out in the open; they may be a foot below the earth's surface, or maybe one hundred feet down. But those that walk over them everyday have no need for them. They don't place a value on diamonds as they do food and clothing, or shoes."

"You mean, an African would prefer a pair of Jordans over a stone that could buy them two thousand pairs of Jordans?"

"Yes, but they have no way of using diamonds, as they do . . . Jordans. Just think about walking down a dangerous street in New York and you are held up at gunpoint just because the man wants your Jordans. You'd give him the Jordans I hope, because at that point in time, your life is more of a priority than some silly sneakers. Well, that is the same issue in our land. The same mentality and priority. Circumstance has a gun to the heads of our people. We are forced to sacrifice the full value of our Jordans—our diamonds—for the mere priority of survival."

Boston Post Road: Part One

Like a nightmare pulled out of a fantasy, Douglass shook from his drowsy state of mind, with two of Fumi's soldiers waking him, looking around from their seats in the front of the Jeep. He'd fallen asleep on the ride back from The Point and was now in the parked Navigator in the hotel parking lot. When his eyes cleared of film and his mind of haziness, Douglass could see familiar faces leaving the hotel with folders and proposals in hand, discussing details as they headed back to their own parked vehicles.

"Are you okay, Mista G'more?" One of the escorts was genuinely cordial.

"Yes, of . . . of course. Thank you." Douglass leaped to exit the Navigator.

"Mista G'more. You're forgetting something." Douglass looked intuitively back towards the seat and grabbed the small leather pouch. Now he suddenly became lost in time, recalling the details of the mirage. He was to use the uncut diamonds to acquire a construction loan. The rough stones were worth 3 and a half million dollars. At least. The funding source, wherever he went, would give him 3 million with the diamonds as collateral. But he was to use the money in trenches of $250,000 and provide Fumi with detailed reports of his progress. There was a simple handshake that bound their agreement. Fumi merely wanted the principle back, plus whatever percentage Douglass felt was amicable over and above current interest rates. That's probably the straw that broke the camel's back; knocked Douglass out cold as soon as the motorcade drove him away from The Point. The rest was up to him. He felt like he needed Fumi's soldiers when he remembered that the small sack in his possession was worth over 3 million dollars. But he reconciled and asked himself, *"Who the hell would think that this pouch was worth 3 million?!"*

Inside the hotel and down in the lobby outside of the ballroom, Douglass could see that his staff was already reviewing fond memories. The scene was nothing short of the exhaustion that resulted from a busy night at Fool's Paradise. Glasses and balloons scattered about, tables dissembled and chairs everywhere. All at once the family that loved and supported him rose to greet him. That's when he told himself, *If they only knew.*

Sunday night was as tragic as well as it was eventful. While Douglass and his followers celebrated the rest of the evening at Emily's Restaurant in Harlem, spending enough to invest in the future of that establishment, trouble was brewing in the Bronx. Tony was asleep, snoring on an office couch, with a thin Versace-shaped damsel waking from under him; stressing for breathing room. He'd promised her a job. She couldn't dance worth a shit, but with a favor provided he'd take her on. Now that the favor was done, she really need to get out from under this pot-bellied fool. A lil' suck and fuck meant nothing to her; she'd been here before. Now it was time for a shower.

"Shit! It's like one in the morning."

"Where ya goin', Sally?"

"Home to shower, *man*." Sally revived the chewing gum that was stale between her cheek and gums. Tony yawned, his thick, cruddy exhale nearly hitting her in her face as she pulled on the street clothes over her nude, frail frame. Tony turned over after watching her one last time and mumbled into the couch.

"Gimme a call. And use the back door. Make sure you shut it, woman." Sally didn't bother responding, and after gathering her things she shot out of the rear door—expecting to catch the very next subway to leave Dyre Avenue—and she slammed the door behind her. It was partway down the driveway when she was suddenly pushed up against the side of the building.

"Who are you?" a muffled voice demanded.

"S . . . Sally . . . I—I'm a—a dancer."

"Dancer," a voice told another.

"Let 'er go." Another voice ruled above all. "And don't you dare turn around. *Git*."

Another voice said, "And don't even bother coming back. Kapish?"

Sally feared for her life and balance her stilettos along the graveled driveway until she disappeared down the sidewalk. The crew of arsonists continued their strike, hulking back towards the gas cans they'd put down, back to dousing the perimeter of *The Pretty Girl*. The fumes were already strong, but the gangsters didn't care. All six of them were milling about, going for more cans in the pickup truck, completing their orders. Gas was poured and splashed along the base of the building, at every exit and corner. The men kept it up until they could see the drenched walls glistening under the moonlight. Seconds later . . .

WHOOSH!

By two in the morning, the group of celebrants was laughing and filing out of Emily's, headed for the curb where the jeep stood alone. Angus locked the door behind them, ending a night for the Gilmores to remember; a night of good food and fond memories of their struggle. Snow was beginning to trickle down, just encouraging the whole *gotta-go* attitude. Valerie, Mechelle, Debbie, Dino, Demetrius, Greg, Douglass—all of them filed into the jeep, while Danni got behind the wheel. There was a calm in the vehicle as the ride home inspired deep thought, wide open eyes basking in the amazement of their instant success. Everyone's mind was on Chicago and the task ahead of them.

Along I-95, minutes from New Rochelle, Danni recognized a glow in the air. Upon a more focused examination, he realized that this *wasn't* a giant candle. A fire was blazing. He woke the others and Douglass insisted that Danni take the exit to investigate.

As they approached Boston Road, and the intersection near to where Fool's Paradise once thrived, they fixed their eyes on the events about 100 feet from the intersection.

The Pretty Girl! Ohmigod!

There was a police blockade erected to block traffic from turning right towards the activity. A fire truck had apparently just arrived, with men now jetting back and forth around the emergency vehicles in the vicinity. Police were posted about, making use of themselves, while traffic cops stood at various intervals, directing the early morning traffic into U-turns or alternative routes. Meanwhile, the Pretty Girl was blazing like a sky-high birthday candle under the early morning snowfall. While firemen searched for a working hydrant, police stood by and watched the building go up in flames.

"What are the details, Sam?" Chief Washington was on the scene, all too aware of the infamous popularity of this particular intersection. Fool's Paradise over there . . . The Dunkin' Donuts shop over there . . . and so on.

"Likely an arson, Chief. There's one gas can in the rear, abandoned just feet from the building. The business isn't open yet, so there's no reason for anyone to be inside. Nobody has contact numbers for the owners or any caretakers. So far, unless somebody left the coffeemaker on inside, it looks like an outside job . . . close as I can see to arson."

"Any witnesses?"

"Nadda one." The chief went to his vehicle to contact headquarters.

"Patch me through to . . ." Chief Washington made the emergency call to Wade.

Wade reached for his ringing phone. "Wade speaking."

"Sorry. I just needed your opinion on something. How's the vacation?"

"Just groovy so far."

"By the way, I'm missing my favorite news anchor lately . . . you know, the one from my favorite evening news program. Any ideas where she might be?"

"Huhmph . . . ," Wade laughed under his breath, ". . . no idea, Chief. Okay . . . now I'm awake. What's up?"

"It's a fire. Down here on Boston Post Road."

"Don't tell me. Fool's Paradise?" Brenda rolled over with her eyes closed in a satisfied warmth, putting her hand to Wade's bare chest. Snuggling.

"No. That's been closed for a couple weeks now."

"Yeah?"

"Yeah . . . S.L.A.'s call. Lost their license. No, this is a spot within view of Fool's Paradise. On the other side of the intersection. They were building a club here called The Pretty Girl . . ."

"I know the spot."

"Well, it's nearly destroyed now. Looks like arson. Any ideas?"

"I'll sleep on it and get back to you." Wade hung up his cell and nestled with Brenda's head in his embrace. His eyes were open, thinking about Douglass's plans for the new club. The new club was planned for a huge warehouse on the same block, except across the street from where The Pretty Girl was being developed. *So much activity in one area.* Wade could see why the Chief called him. All he'd have to do was place a call. Not now. Too comfortable with Brenda nude against his body in a South Beach hotel. Tomorrow was another day.

Douglass breathed a sigh of relief, now confident that the fire was not interfering with his plans for Black Beauty. It was a strange coincidence that it was just across the street from where Black Beauty construction would begin the following week, but he didn't think much of it.

Danni made a U-turn to avoid the police activity and they headed back towards I-95. He passed a limousine that sat at the curb, close to the 24-hour Dunkin' Donuts.

Inside the limousine, Fat Jimmy was feasting on a half-dozen bag of donuts, washing it down hastily with hot coffee.

For Fat Jimmy, this was like watching a movie, complete

with being visibly nervous, sweating from his receding hair-line. He kept the tinted, Plexiglas partition raised so that Bruno wouldn't detect his hysteria. But Fat Jimmy was caught between a rock and a hard place. He had a meeting set with Tony at 1 AM, but the place was now an orange glow of light. *My money. The family's investment, going up in smoke.* Jimmy was shaking ridiculously, and secretly wondering if Tony might be inside. He phoned the club helplessly. Busy signal. He just knew Tony was inside. Incinerated. *I just know it!* And now, he wasn't even concerned with Tony's body as much as he was with facing his boss . . . Anthony, the son of mob boss Chucky Bianco.

The Black Beauty auditions were about to commence. Every string was pulled and every resource accessed so that this event would blow the roof off the mother. Douglass involved everyone except for Dino, who was all about the construc-tion. It was necessary for Dino to oversee the contractors so that the Black Beauty Manifesto was followed down to the XYZ. Moreover, if there were issues that he couldn't address, Douglass was a cell phone call away. Included in the Chicago event were Greg's comrades from Georgetown U.

All the while, for a week and a half at least, the Fabulous Five had pumped the volume on the audition for aspiring eth-nic models and dancers. There was a poster that called for all ages and a website that was constructed as the key ingredient. For $5 (a substantially low photography fee), women and girls would show up in their best outfits. Those over age 18 would take swimsuit and lingerie shots. The best of those in atten-dance would be placed on the website with creative graphics and their biographies for about a year, until the next audition came around. Essentially, the website would serve as a black model's gallery where fashion photographers, video producers and even film directors could review images for selection and potential work. Those that were not selected would receive a set of photos from their audition and a note of appreciation. Meanwhile, everybody would be happy. Black Beauty Interna-tional would be the catalyst and also have first pick of those future candidates who might be interested in dancing at the new Black Beauty. There were brochures made to match the posters and distributed to beauty salons throughout the area. Radio interviews were conducted, and Valerie, Debbie and Mechelle filled in as spokeswomen for the search. The hotel Marriot posted the Black Beauty Search on their marquee and news coverage was arranged for the big day.

On Wednesday morning, the 8:30 flight from New York arrived with the entire entourage at O'Hare Airport in Chicago. All twelve members zipped through the terminal, and after a quick stop at baggage claim, they headed straight for a mini-van that stood outside in the passenger pick-up zone. A hired driver took the group down the expressway towards downtown Chicago to the Center City Marriot. As the bus approached, everyone admired the tall buildings and ritzy atmosphere. Basketball was in the air, an energy that Chicago thrived on. But no time for that since bigger and more personal agendas were in store for the event organizers. There was one day until a city's worth of black beauties would converge on Center City, into the waiting arms of one hungry, well-financed entrepreneur.

CHAPTER TWENTY-TWO

Chi-Town: Part 2

"I have a funny feeling about tomorrow, Greg."

"Good or bad?"

"Let's just say a good problem. I expect that we will get just what we asked for. Maybe a thousand bodies. Maybe two." Douglass and Greg were alone, watching the glow move from one number to the next, as their elevator car rose upward. The hotel manager had just briefed the two about the excitement which the Black Beauty Day campaign generated. Phone calls. Visits. More visits. Some women showed up on the day they *heard* the announcement instead of waiting for the date that was advertised. One parent was so irate, she phoned the Better Business Bureau and they in turn phoned the hotel for more details about the who, the what, the where and the why. Always gonna be a mom who's a wannabe, Douglass thought.

"We can handle it. Our team is smooth. Remember . . . *Team Gilmore!*" Greg was being facetious, but Douglass was seriously tightlipped. "Besides . . . you've done bigger events by yourself."

"I guess . . . just last minute jitters. The biggest entertainers have told me the same thing. Even though they've performed in front of thousands, every experience is a new one . . . with new, nervous energy. Still, we need to be on our P's and Q's."

The elevator was moving past the 20th floor now.

"By the way, what floor are we headed to?" Greg had made all of the preparations with the hotel and it made Douglass feel like a third wheel, ever since Greg became more of a fixture by his side.

"We're all staying on the twenty-eighth floor. I got you the double room that you asked for. The same hook-up like in South Beach. Everybody else is doubling up. Demetrius is watching Destiny at night. As for the auditions . . . that's all going on in the penthouse. The top floor. We're gettin' classy, with hors d'oeuvres, wine and cheese . . ."

"For the older—"

"Of course, Doug. Only for the afternoon session. It's fruits, veggie snacks and Kool Aid in the morning for the children. In the afternoon, after the hotel staff freshens up the rooms, it's age eighteen and over. That's when we pour it on heavy. I'll show you the layout of the penthouse later . . . it's not too far from all of our discussions. Just turned up a notch. As for now, we'll need the rest. The setup will most likely be all night. There will be a couple of hours for rest, then we're up and at 'em, like at six AM tomorrow."

"Do I get the feeling that you're starting to like this more than me?" Greg smiled back and cut the conversation by stepping out of the open elevator doors first, searching for their assigned rooms. The rest of the staff was close by, if not just behind them, toting the various equipment, registration forms and other accessories for the presentations. While resting in his hotel room, with eyes half drowsy and half awake, Douglass considered the turbulence of activity that was taking place all because of his ideas. The hotel was already flagging dozens of callers inquiring about Black Beauty day. Douglass was familiar with the frenzy, not unlike his days while handling

"TALENT WANTED" responses with his ex-girlfriend. Some naive, some meticulously curious, but everyone hungry for more information. Hotel receptionist had to be somewhere caught between lack of patience and utter frustration, while straining for the event organizers to show up. When they did, they did, and the hotel staff just couldn't wait to redirect the inquiries. In fact, as Douglass was swiping his room's key card through the digital reader on the door for the first time, the phone was already buzzing. And there it was again, with the girls busily putting their feminine touch on the room and juggling responses while in motion.

A Swarm of Black Beauties

Thursday, December 5th

Darryl maneuvered as inconspicuously as he could with a broadcast video camera balance on his shoulder, recording all night long as the various rooms on the top floor were organized and prepared for the expected crowd. Balloons and orchids were the pink and canary accents that brought fresh color and fragrance to the atmosphere. Tables and chairs and velvet ropes were arranged in the lobby and foyers to create a reception area and to control the movement of applicants so that they'd be directed to the banquet halls. Inside, a VCR and five TV monitors were positioned for optimal view. Come 6AM, the staff was rested and hungry. After one last, quick run-through (as if the night before wasn't already filled with exhaustive rehearsals), the staff sat together for a 45-minute breakfast. The 4-course, catered meal was a particular large one for the hungry, anxious staff. They savored the eggs that were cooked to order, and the orange juice that was freshly squeezed, all right before their eyes. A bulky, Oriental chef moved quickly, with a flair about him—you knew he did this every day. Just about everyone dug into the modest heaps of fresh pastries and drowned themselves in coffee. Everyone, that is, except for muscled men one and two—Demetrius and Danni—on the job throughout the trip to Chicago, during the setup, and now on the morning of the event. They maintained communication like pros, with earphones and miniature microphones attached to the lapels of their sporty blazers. They were disciplined and poised enough to be Secret Service agents.

As the 8AM hour neared, Demetrius greeted mothers and their daughters as they stepped off of the elevators and up to the registration tables. Mechelle orchestrated the operation in the lobby, making sure that applications were completed and that registrants were provided with a questionnaire. After registration, it was into the banquet hall where the presentation was about to begin. Surprisingly, those who responded to the advertisement adhered (for the most part) to the scheduling—*youngsters only* in the morning. By 9AM, the presentation began with a sea of eager faces as attentive as could be. Debbie and Valerie kicked the day off with an introduction and Greg followed them, offering the "Opportunity Of A Lifetime." There were scores of females looking on; either older, with responsibilities on their minds, or younger, with stars in their eyes and not a care in the world. Some dads were also in attendance when no mother was available to accompany their child. And in very few instances, both parents were there in support. Greg covered the various areas of the Internet gallery, using a laser pointer and diagrams projected onto a large screen. The diagrams were complete with graphics, photos and descriptions that explained how the program worked. Greg then ventured into the possibilities of being chosen for *Face Of The Month*, where a $100 prize was to be awarded to the winner of a monthly vote by website visitors. Finally, he segued into a video presentation that had a commercial appeal and which drove home the bottom line so that the adults, young women and girls alike were compelled to take advantage of the one opportunity that required the least experience; a way to get into Black Beauty International's "**Black Beauty Gallery**."

When the video ended, Debbie and Valerie stepped up to the platform again to introduce the program founder. Douglass made it short and sweet, basically welcoming all into the BBI family. That was his job, to close the sale and to provoke the next step—if it hadn't been done already. For the next 4 hours, the event staff processed and photographed more than 350 candidates for the website. A lot of the young mothers (quiet as it was kept) also signed up and got in on the action. By 1 o'clock, before the first shift of registrants were even completed, the second group had begun to fill up the adjacent ballroom. These women were 18 and over, trickling in, spilling in, and finally pouring into the penthouse ballroom. The large space reached capacity within 30 minutes, and a partitioning wall had to be opened to accommodate another 300 registrants. With the hotel staff scurrying to clean up the more obvious debris, the transition turned into one big juggling act for the Black Beauty Day staff. But it went along considerably well. The subsequent presentation commenced for a standing-room-only crowd.

By 2PM, the entire penthouse floor was wall to wall pussy. The kids were gone. In with the weaves and perms, clogs and stilettos, skirts, ponytails and makeup. Perfumes of varying fruits, flowers and other illusions penetrated all common sense. And the perky titties and tight asses were in outrageous abundance. The floor was consumed with an all-adult crowd of 2,100 applicants, with presentations happening simultaneously in separate wings. In another room, snapshots were being taken and downloaded to a computer hard drive. Greg and his journalist comrades were helpful (to say the least), very absorbed in orchestrating and navigating the women between dressing rooms, photo rooms and bathrooms. Demetrius was steadfast, with groups of women gloating over his physical perfections. Meanwhile, Douglass charged through completed questionnaires, red flagging hot picks and pointing out those women whom he wanted to speak to. His confidence was swollen something like shopping with an unlimited credit line at a market that sold only the juiciest fruits. Doe-eyed dolls didn't hesitate to respond when Douglass curled his finger at them, or when in passing, he simply said to *"Come with me."* He was the man to watch as he searched for 40 new dancers, 40 bright personalities, with beautiful bodies and (of course) that ever-alluring smile.

His objective wasn't hard to match, browsing through those endless lures for his attention. There were short ones and tall ones, thick boned and frail. There were females who thought they were pretty and others who underestimated their own impact. The damned penthouse had to be shut down, for God sakes, with candidates still downstairs in the lobby grieving for access to the top. However, Douglass put a stop to any more participants, asking the hotel management to block access from the elevator. Now, the only way to the floor was via the roof.

By 10PM, Douglass had spoken directly to more than 100 women whom he hand-picked according to their question-naire and (what he recognized as) their vibe. The key factor that brought him to say yea or nay was if a candidate was ready to pick up and go. After all, what good was a lollipop if you couldn't suck it? It was a long event and Douglass knew that the women and his staff were edgy from being on the floor all day. So he surprised everybody, having the hotel staff cater dinner for everyone. Before a lamb could shake its tail, there was a massive banquet going down. A long table was set out front on the platform, and dozens of round tables were ar-ranged all throughout the hall. Douglass presided over the feast as a king would his kingdom and he smirked. It was in-teresting to see his own girlfriends react to the room full of competition. They had been exercising their given authority all day long, but suddenly their faces expressed humility, per-haps realizing that any number of these top picks in the room (the top 100 respectively) might replace them. Sometime later he pulled them to the side.

"Listen, I've been watching you . . . and I *know* you've been watching me . . . oh *yeah!* You've been watching me . . ." Doug-lass made a face that was humorous enough to break the ten-sion in the small circle. "But seriously, girls . . . *ladies* . . ." he put his open palm to Debbie's cheeks, "I'm not leaving you." Now he held Valerie's hand. "I just wanted to make that clear. I'm-not-leaving-you. Do you understand? We are family. I know it's cliché, but it's so real. And the more that we believe in family and *practice* family, then the more faith we'll have in one another. The more faith you have in me, the more I'll grow. *Got it?*" They all nodded, in some cases, a bit silly with tears in their eyes. "*Good.*" The group returned to the banquet.

Halfway into the meal, Douglass leaned into Greg to bring focus to a few hot spots in the room. It was evident that none of the staff had ever seen so much raw, black beauty in one place. So many shades of brown; even white girls with black features, and other nationalities that embraced the concept of black. Greg's colleagues were undergoing their own conversations about who was the hottest. After the meal, the waiter poured champagne for everyone and Douglass led in a grand toast for the hundred or so persons in the room.

"To Black Beauties!"

"***To Black Beauties!!***" the women echoed and lifted their glasses also.

"To Black Beauties!!" Douglass repeated. And they answered him. "Ladies, you are truly the world's most beautiful women. We've photographed you. We've interviewed you, and we've wined and dined you . . . I feel like I'm on one big ole massive first date!" The crowd chuckled. "But now, we're gonna hire you." There was a hush, and an obvious energy embraced the room. "Everyone knows by now that I've built an adult entertainment complex in New York. And you also know that we're looking for a legion of dancers for the club. We've reserved this decision for late in the day so that there would be a mood. You see out that window? The darkness outside right now? That indicates money to me. Ours is an *evening* business. So guess what . . . every time the sun goes down . . . what happens? Exactly. That's when we make money. I make money and you make money. Like a nocturnal money machine . . .

"On the questionnaire you filled out, the questions were designed so we could get a full understanding of your situations at home, school, your jobs, et cetera. Overall, everyone here is sick and tired of their jobs, you're childless and you're ready to make it big in New York. Have I got that right?"

"Yes." The crowd answered in unison.

"The fact is that we'll only be selecting forty of you tonight . . ." The voices and whispers hummed and buzzed. "That doesn't mean that you *won't* be involved with us, the website, or other plans that we have. We may someday open a second club and come back to get all of you . . ." He smiled assuringly. ". . . But just so you know, we'll be keeping your information on file and every one of you is guaranteed to at least be part of the Black Beauty Gallery on the Internet. So give yourselves a round of applause for *that* accomplishment . . ."

The room applauded. The staff added to the applause.

". . . But again. Forty girls." Douglass amused himself, pretending a drumroll. "Now, let me ask you this once and for all. Is there anyone in the room that *isn't* ready to go. Don't be shy.

Raise your hand if you're not ready." Nobody spoke up, but there were a few heads that were uncertain, as though everyone would be boarding a bus immediately. "Excuse me . . . in the leather jacket. Y-e-s, you. Tell me what's on your mind."

"I . . . uhm . . . I have a dog at home. He . . . well, I don't know what to do with him if I have to leave tonight." The young woman must have been 21 years old at best. Douglass smiled to console her, letting her know that her problem was not really a problem at all.

"Don't worry, honey. We're not body snatchers, throwing you all on a bus tonight."

Giggles in the room.

"But seriously, girls, we're not a kennel, either. No dogs. No babies. None of that. You'll have to decide to choose this million-dollar lifestyle over the one that's been tying you down. You'll have to decide what your *true* priority in life is. Now, our staff may be able to help you troubleshoot with certain issues . . . if you're selected . . . and the bus to New York won't be leaving Chicago until about week or so . . ."

The heads throughout the room seemed to rise all at once, as though there was one deep sigh of relief. "So . . . without further ado, Darryl, the gentleman you've seen roaming and crawling around the banquet hall with a video camera, has put together this twenty-minute video for you to watch. It's a little more in-depth, about what to expect from us, what we'll expect from you, and how our program works. Going to New York might seem exciting, but please keep in mind that this is a business. A multi-million dollar business. Greg." Demetrius acted on cue, cutting the lights off, while Greg started the video. As waiters milled about, collecting emptied plates and silverware, the black monitors came to life with the image of a Gulf Stream jet soaring through the sky, descending towards a landing strip. The sound of the engines, a hollow, winded, whiffing noise, and the *Miami Vice* theme music were effects which underscored the narrative: "Black Beauty International presents . . . Your Million-Dollar Lifestyle . . ." The music bounced on as the jet landed. The graphics transposed over the moving aircraft, affirming the narrator's words with fancy, platinum lettering. As planned, while the video worked its magic, Debbie, Mechelle and Valerie stepped away from the table, their eyes working a little harder to see in the darkened room.

"Excuse me . . ." A timid voice and hand reached out for Debbie's attention. Debbie almost brushed it off with a perfunctory, *gotta-go* response until she looked a little harder.

"Hi . . . oh—*hi!!!* What's *happenin'*?" Debbie spoke excitedly, but at a low, respectful volume. She led Trina, an old acquaintance, to the rear of the room, out of the way from the presentation. They traded brief updates about one another before Debbie had to run and get back to business. It seemed that Trina didn't expect Debbie to remember her, a neighbor from her block. And, indeed, Debbie had become so . . . so . . . worldly.

"Hey, Trina, I've gotta go do something. I'll be back—we can chat later. Go watch the video. It's good. And I'm in it!" Debbie smiled proudly and dashed towards the foyer where Mechelle and Valerie disappeared. On the monitors, the jet plane was parked and Valerie descended from its open hatch, down the steps, to the pavement. The music faded out and the narrator supported the the sights and sounds on the video: "*And now, here's your hostess, Valerie . . .* " The video showed Valerie strutting across the blacktop to where a waiting chauffeur and a shiny, white limousine stood. She carried a shoulder bag fancy-freely, with the camera capturing a full body view of her. "*Welcome to the world of Black Beauty. I'm Valerie and I'll be your tour guide on this preview of what we call your Million-Dollar Lifestyle . . .* " Valerie was now nestled inside of the limo. "*As you know, we're conducting a search for the most beautiful women of color. Those who are selected will be on their way to a most successful career in show business . . .* " A close-up showed Valerie's upper body. She was snug while reaching out to accept a martini that was conveniently handed to her. She sipped and continued her dialogue.

"*Whether it's your dream to model, to dance, to appear in videos and movies, or to be seen in magazines or in our calender . . . Black Beauty is your ticket to a world of desires fulfilled.*" The images on the monitors reflected snippets of a model's photo shoot, an active photographer, as well as there was a syncopated rhythm of hip hop beats. Then the images showed exotic dancers while the camera panned from left to right. More sensual displays, a few dancers with provocative moves. The blitz was classy and surely tested the edge. There was Valerie, back in the spotlight, still in the limo. Now she had magazines and photo calendars in her hands. The hip-hop beats faded out.

"This is an idea whose time has come . . . and the opportunity is now available to women of color who are age 18 or older . . ." Valerie put the items down at her side, picked up her bag, and the video cut to a view of the limo progressing around a circular driveway, until it parked in front of the entrance to a mansion. Valerie got out of the limo and walked through the front door which was simultaneously opened by a butler. The butler welcomed Valerie with a smile and a bow before she took a strut down a hallway, as if to walk straight though the mansion. Seconds later she emerged out back, approaching an in-ground pool, buxom as ever in a strapless 2-piece bikini. At the pool's edge, she went on to say, *"So what are you waiting for? Join me . . . dive in!!"* Valerie took the dive into the pool and classical music accompanied her underwater image. The camera maintained focus on the distorted, watery view of her figure until she reached the opposite end of the pool to come up for air. Except now, the underwater image that appeared to be Valerie was actually Debbie, who came up for air as if by magic. At the pool's edge, Debbie picked up where Valerie left off.

"Hi . . . I'm Debbie . . ." And from there, the video depicted the man behind the plan, using his growth in the entertainment industry as leverage to further captivate viewers. Then there were images of construction workers laboring and building, and eventually the hard labor images were transcended by an artist rendition of the finished complex. Darryl smiled at his work as the video projected living conditions of comfort and luxury accommodations. Vacations, jewelry, celebrity events as well as other gifts and bonuses were projected as incentives. There were opportunities such as swimsuit videos, magazine layouts, modeling for TV and dancing in music videos. There were 8-hour work schedules, training, orientation and a fitness program to keep dancers in shape.

There were also medical benefits and educational quarters for girls who maintained stability and growth as assets to the enterprise. Finally, aside from the weekly salary, there was a profit-sharing program that was available for all participants. All of these elements were detailed briefly; however, enough to paint a picture of organization and structure. At the end of the presentation, once the monitors went dark, the lights were turned up to a dim, gloomy level, and a strobe light was switched on and a multi-colored laserlight show began shooting streams and rays of color towards the platform. The horns and trumpets which introduced Cheryl Lynn's *"Got To Be Real"* sounded off and the bass carried the electric vocals, turning the room into an instant club scene. One at a time, for about 3 intense moments a piece, Valerie, Mechelle and then Debbie came to life on stage for the all-female audience. The dancers seduced onlookers as they would a male audience, and it excited them even more to perform for their own sex. Leather and lace, chiffon and silk outfits wrapped in one way or another about their bodies, the girls advertised it, made their pitch and sold the exclusive exotic dance for inevitable applause. And that was the cherry on top. The presentation was over. The lights went back to full blast; Greg ended things by letting everyone know that decisions would be announced momentarily.

The room filled with high anxiety, with everyone wondering who would be chosen. At 11PM, conversations and murmurs carried on as the all day affair had reached its climax. The staff congregated in a semi circle, discussing selections and their whereabouts in the room.

Meanwhile, amidst the settling and adjusting, Debbie indicated to her homegirl Trina that she should meet her in the rear. Trina had her eyes on Debbie all the while, beckoning for her inside help, never missing a blink.

"So what's it like?"

"Girl, if you only knew. I'm living large. And it keeps gettin' larger by the day. For real, I feel like Cinderella. That's how I'm livin'."

"Wow . . . and that's your man?"

"You could say that . . . but this thing ain't like Chicago

livin'. You know, like livin' for yo man and all. I have a *family* now. A real-live, stick-by-my-side, extended family. And there's not an empty spot in my soul."

"Woo-woo-*woooo* . . ." Trina stared at Debbie like a movie star.

"Debbie, do you think they picked me?"

"I'll just let you wait and see." Debbie hid her grin and gave Trina a warm hug. Then she returned to Douglass's side.

Hot as Hell

Friday, December 6th

Agents Walsh and Hammer took the information from Chief Washington and ran with it. Otherwise, they were getting nowhere. Having attended the Investor's Day event got them nothing but a business plan and an eyeful of exotic dancers. They couldn't figure out where Douglass disappeared to, but hung in there for the presentation anyway.

And now things were getting serious again. Another body. Tony the Crow was blackened to a crisp inside of The Pretty Girl and investigators were certain that it was arson. Almost a week after the fire and a tedious morning at the building department, the agents found the rightful owners of The Pretty Girl.

"Babe, could you please get that?" Pauly was down in the basement, fixing the hot water heater and shouting once he heard the doorbell a second time.

"Alright . . . alright already!" Mrs. Givanni was wrapped in a bathrobe, waking out of her lazy slumber. Her hair was wrapped in rollers and a freshly lit cigarette hung from her lips. She pulled the door open, already cringing in anticipation of the winter climate.

"Mrs. Givanni? This is Agent Olgenhiemer and I'm Agent Walsh [they both raised their slim wallets with credentials showing] with the FBI. We'd like to speak with your husband."

"But moy husband already served his toyme . . ." The missus had a thick accent; like Popeye's Olive Oil.

"Sorry, ma'am, this is unrelated to any past encounters.

May we see your husband, please?" Walsh was direct, while Hammer kept a sharp eye inside the house. She let them in and showed them into the living room. Seconds later, the agents could hear arguing coming from the basement. Meanwhile, they couldn't help but to notice the lacquered furnishings, mirrors, chandelier, and crystal. The carpet was plush and the couch was inviting. Certainly not the life of a criminal reformed. When the arguing from below subsided footsteps could be heard climbing from the basement. More mumbling. Hammer swore he heard a male voice demand, "Just keep your mouth shut!"

"Oh—hi.. What's new?"

"Sir, this is Agent Olgen . . ."

"Hammer. Just call me Hammer."

"And I'm Agent Walsh. We'd like to have a few words with you. Alone, if at all possible." Pauly got the message and whispered to his wife. She begrudgingly went on her way, now puffing furiously at her cigarette.

Saturday, December 7th

Chucky Bianco was just 3 years into a lifetime bid. The B.O.P. had him buried in Marion, Indiana, under 23-hour-a-day maximum security lockdown. While the elder Bianco anticipated his appeal meeting with a favorable decision, his son Anthony, a headstrong bodybuilder, assumed his father's role as the head of the family. Mob boss.

It was evening again, not necessarily the required setting for any such power meeting; it just so happened to work out this way. And also, this wasn't just power. A man was killed; a Bianco solider. There were indications of a territorial violation behind this . . . a man down and a 900 G's investment, all gone up in smoke.

A few earners stood by while, one by one, 4 weighted-down Lincoln town cars and two limos swooshed through the entrance, parking at various degrees in the open area of the warehouse. A plane could be heard taking off overhead since Newark Airport wasn't far away. And that was a great edge for the big shipping business that the Biancos operated here.

A ballet of activity ensued; car doors opening and closing.

Large and small suited men in dark colors and sunglasses decended on one particular area, the center of the warehouse. One of the men escorted a slinky white girl to the forefront.

"This is her, boss. Sally." Sally looked a slight bit apprehensive standing more under the light than anyone else.

"Sally, we need to know exactly what happened . . ." Sally started slow, but eventually spilled it all; her evening of pleasuring Tony and the men she ran into in the dark driveway.

"Are you sure you heard somebody say *kapish*?"

"Yes," she said, frightened.

Fat Jimmy wagged his head, and Bruno took Sally and put her in the back of a car.

"That does it. It's definitely the Toccis . . ."

"How do you know, boss?"

"Because *nobody* uses 'kapish' any fuckin' more. That's Salvatore's funny ways. Besides, Jimmy, didn't you tell me that he had an issue about us being in New York?"

"Yep."

"Well, now we got issues wit dem. Mikey . . . you take that girl somewheres. Keep her at your house if you have to. I don't want her talking. I don't want a word of this to reach the street. We got work to do. Now my pop always taught me, *an eye for a fuckin' eye!* So, we're gonna fight fire with fire. Those fuckin' Toccis are gonna roast—Jimmy."

"Yeah, boss. . . ."

"You sure that Black Beauty club is *their* thing?"

"Gotta be, boss. It makes sense. What kind of coincidence is it for our spot to catch fire out of nowhere and all of the sudden a brand-new club opens across the street. Across the fuckin' *street!* It's like they're burnin' us out and then pissin' on our grave. I want revenge. And I want it now!!"

"Calm down, Jimmy. I call the shots here. *I* want revenge. And *I* want it now!!" Anthony had spoken.

"Cipriani."

"Sir, we've got news . . . I think you should set up the three-way."

"Okay. But I hope you're not cryin' wolf." Cipriani put Walsh on hold and buzzed his boss, Bobby Zeal. Hammer was on an extension in the same office with Walsh.

"Okay, Walsh, Cipriani says this is urgent. Talk to me."

"Sir, I've been keeping Mr. Cipriani updated all along about our movement on the Bianco-Gilmore associations. Recently there was a fire in the Bronx. It was a club called The Pretty Girl. We did some investigating and found that the owner was just a front. His name is Pauly Givanni, an ex-con who had done eight years up at Allenwood Penitentiary for embezzlement. We visited him and pressed him. He spilled the beans— told us about money laundering that he was carrying out for the mob and some other things. He's laying sweet, up in a Scarsdale home . . . doesn't want to go back to prison and agreed to testify against Anthony Bianco."

"*Theee* Anthony Bianco?" Nobody could see it, but that buzz word made Bobby Zeal's eyes light up. Bobby's former boss, the U.S. Attorney whom he'd succeeded, was responsible for putting Chucky Bianco away. Now, Bobby could get the son! The next generation of mob bosses would be his before he even got his feet wet!

"Yessir! I believe we can meet the standards for racketeering, tax evasion, money laundering, wire fraud and extortion."

"Well . . . now we're finally getting somewhere. What about this Gilmore character? And the murder in the Bronx?"

"Sir, quite honestly we don't see how that ties in. I'd like to say we made a mistake, as much as I don't want to say it, but there's still the issue about the dead dancer. It's hitting too close to home. Too close to this case."

"Well, I'll think this over. You all keep an eye on things and I'll see if we can get us a few warrants."

Sunday, December 8th
It was almost cold enough to see spit freeze in mid air. The 1AM darkness seemed to make it that much colder. There was a gusty wind that changed directions and a sprinkle of snow was just beginning.

"There she is . . . let's see if'n we can't make 'er blacker than she is already."

There were two town cars and a limo tailing them. All windows of the vehicles were tinted, but this was the same ole likely scene of a mob hit. There were 5 soldiers that got out of the town cars, easing the suspensions for the vehicles. All of the men were in black overcoats. Anyone who didn't have a wool cap was a fool. They knew that Fat Jimmy was in the limo behind them and wondered if the boss was in the vehicle also. The team of mobsters were at the side of the building, on an off street from Boston Post Road. They faced the massive wall that was the side of the club. It was high enough to be 4 stories and wide enough to fill a half-city block. The men hadn't been out of their vehicles for a minute when a fuel tanker snailed around the corner. Suddenly, it looked larger up close then it did traveling down the expressway. The driver was one of *them*, and seeing him brought on a smile or two—meaning the hijack went smoothly. The truck pulled up just towards the middle of the building, in the center of the street and ahead of the limos in audience on the adjacent curb.

The goal was simple . . . they would hose the building down and one match would send it into the depths of hell. The boss wanted a body, yes. But this was a start. And they might even get lucky.

"Alright, let's do this fast," Vinny announced.

"Pull that hose out," Sergio added.

"Which hose?" asked Joey.

"Any . . . both of 'em!" Everyone seemed to be giving orders. Nobody knew how to work the valves, or that they were fucking with over 8,000 gallons of fuel. The truck carried 5,000 gallons of diesel and 3,000 gallons of gasoline. Angelo was one of the cocky ones who liked to throw his weight around. But all he had was fat surrounding his intestines, and besides that, ants probably got in and ate his brain cells.

Angelo pushed past Felix, who was holding one hose, and also Joey, who held the other. While Felix was careful to hold his hose in the direction of the building, Joey wasn't embracing the nozzle tight enough. He was just pointing it at the ground, waiting for a disaster. Angelo was pressing buttons now, not sure which was which. He started to turn the lever, a steering wheel of a smaller kind. He turned it all the way—full blast—but nothing happened. He began pushing buttons again. Without a hose in his hand and with virtually nothing else to do, Sergio stood back, nearly a car length away, and lit up a cigarette.

Out of the corner of his eye (still pushing buttons all the while), Angelo caught the spark of light that flickered from Sergio's match.

"PUT THAT SHIT AWAY, YOU FUCKING MORON!" Angelo yelled at Sergio like a football coach on the opposite end of the field, but his voice had scared Joey into seeing what Sergio was up to. When Joey turned, the hose also turned, and it was pointing in Sergio's direction. It was just then that fuel jumped out of the hose all of a sudden. In a split second, fuel shot alongside of the tanker, out of the hose and onto Sergio's overcoat.

The fuel splashed all over him.

The match he had tossed ignited the fluid.

Sergio lit up like a narrow flame.

He turned paranoid and ran to the left.

To the right, then left again.

While all of the gombada were amazed at the sensation of seeing Sergio blow up like a torch, they didn't realize that the fire now spread along the ground. Joey had turned into a flame-thrower. He stood still with his bulbous eyes turned to mirrors of fear. In that split second, Joey also became a moving torch as the flames engulfed him. He began to spin around like a bumper car shooting liquid flames in every direction. Now the flames caught Felix, whose hose was also spraying fuel, until all five men were on fire with hoses shooting flames everywhere. The fuel's direction was as erratic as the screams and hollers that pierced the air. It shot out towards the limo and showered the cars with flames and a thin blanket of fuel. Bruno revved up the engine for a quick getaway. But before he could think, there was an eruption. The tank ignited and there was an explosion that could challenge a volcano blast. The tanker flipped, and all hell let loose at its rear. The long tube essentially took flight, rocketing through the air to hundreds of feet aboveground, until it fell and exploded a second time on the median of I-95. Every last animate or inanimate object in the wake of the explosion was caught in a furnace of fury, incinerated and left in ashes.

* * *

"Man, you can't do with it . . . can't do without it. This I-95 might be our bread and butter, but there's not a week that goes by without a major backup." The staff was returning from their Chicago promotion having just flown into LaGuardia, and they were looking forward to getting back to the townhouse. In the jeep, Demetrius drove, while Debbie, Mechelle, and Valerie were slumped against one another in the backseat. Darryl was in the far rear seats alongside of his video equipment, and Douglass was in the passenger's seat co-navigating. It was Demetrius who suggested that they turn off of the throughway and Douglass who chose the side streets to take. He was leading in the direction of the club. Anxious to drive past; to see how far it had come along. But snow was beginning to fall, and even Boston Post Road, which ran parallel to I-95, was backed up. It was 2 in the morning and they agreed that later in the day would be better. So they widened their maze, and maneuvered down local streets of the Bronx until they reached the tip of Westchester County and inevitably, the town of New Rochelle. Ironically, the traffic jam kept them so far back on I-95, they never realized that the reason for the backup was an attempt to destroy the club.

Boston Post Road: Part Two

Monday, December 9th

Chief Washington was called at once, and he wasted no time in getting to the scene on that Boston Post Road side street. This event was definitely FBI-level-shit, he considered.

"What the fuck is going on around here, Sam. These are within a week of each other . . . . tragedies . . . death. This area is like fucking Vietnam."

"Chief, this *could* be some kind of accident . . . a fuel truck exploded."

"Yeah, but this happened between one and two in the morning. Bodies are laying out like charcoal in the snow. Then you've got three bodies over in that limo laying on its side. That's eight bodies. Call the feds in, Sam."

By 8 AM, construction workers showed up to Black Beauty as usual. They were nearly a week into the job, yet they had finished so much. Where 10 or 15 workers might have worked on a nightclub contract, 134 were hired to expedite production. Dino was both diplomat and General in keeping pace and moving fast. His biggest concerns were the bar, the stages, the catwalks, the kitchen and the utilities. Everything else (he felt) would be simple, "usual" work. He also took photos as the work progressed. It started as one empty, cavernous building. Four walls, a roof and a cement floor. Big enough to be an airplane hanger, 10,000 square feet, in fact. But as the major construction took root, the venue developed some character. The centerpiece was similar to a giant hand with only three huge, extended fingers. At the base of the hand shape (where the palm might be), there was a massive attraction made of stones and artificial palm trees stretching up high into the air. Walking in the entrance of Black Beauty, the three fingers were actually three stages with services bars that ran along their perimeters. A brass pole was planted in each of three main stages. Elevated catwalks were everywhere in the complex; along the walls, across the center of the club and down the middle in the rear. Douglass envisioned a tropical atmosphere to emulate a reflection of paradise, something that the original Fool's Paradise never accomplished. Aside from the main stages, there were seven others. They were round, and seats were built around them for exclusive audiences. Two of those round showcases were actual jacuzzis with their own light shows.

A food bar and café was situated at the far left. Five of the round stages were situated at the rear right, while two others were either at the front right or left. Also at the front right of the club, couches enclosed one stage and a back room where videos and specialty items were sold. Adjacent to that area, on the left, red velvet ropes enclosed the other stage and a series of tall and short cocktail tables and chairs.

Second level entertainment would be available in three corner VIP areas. The fourth corner, in the rear, was reserved as the deejay booth. Finally, there was a kitchen, dressing rooms with showers, a lounge for staff, two offices, a storage room, a coat room, a box office, and a few restrooms. Dino certainly had his job cut out for him, and all of his years of hospital construction would now pay off for something more personal.

Once all of the major construction was completed, Dino figured to spend the last week installing the various electronics, TV monitors, touch screens, sound system, special lighting, video surveillance, glass and mirrors, more palm trees and plants, pool tables and the telephone system. Dino woke up every day with a hunger to do more and to do his best. For him, this was the job of a lifetime, where he couldn't wait to get to work.

On the morning after the tragic explosion, Dino arrived to find the side street blocked off by police and roadblocks. First, he figured that the block was being checked for some kind of oil or gas leak. But closer investigation told him a horror-filled tale. The NYPD was there in force. The FBI agents were obvious in suits and ties. Outside of law enforcement, there was a tremendous black spot and black residue all over the street, the sidewalks, and the side of the building. Strewn about were bodies covered by white sheets. There were other areas with white chalk outlines that were illuminated brightly against the charred pavement. Across the street from the building were three overturned, blackened vehicles. Dino noticed that one was longer than the others, turned on its side. It looked like a bomb had exploded and left no survivors. Instantly concerned with what was happening inside, Dino raced into the entrance of the club. But it was business as usual. Contractors busy and on schedule.

"I'll tell you what, Hammer. The bodies on the street are burnt to a crisp. But the bodies that were in the car are merely blackened. I've seen the photos on the wall back at the office day after day and week after week. I can ID those three like I can ID my own children. Bruno drives his boss around in the limo. The boss was Fat Jimmy and with them . . . Anthony Bianco."

"You mean *theee* Anthony Bianco? The mob boss?"

"Yup. And Bobby-boy ain't gonna like this—I promise you. He'd rather win a trial . . . a conviction. Put his ass in jail like his father. But he won't get points for this."

"What do you think happened, Walsh?" The two deliberated and tried to act authoritatively with all of the municipal cops watching every move. Meanwhile, inside Black Beauty, Dino was on the phone with Douglass giving him the full update.

CHAPTER TWENTY-THREE

Reaquaintance

Friday, December 13th

A luxury bus is about to reach its destination. In one of the windows reads a handmade sign: NEW YORK OR BUST.

"Today's gonna be filled with good luck. Can't you see it now? Panties hanging everywhere. Bras off. Women walking around butt naked all day long." Douglass looked at Debbie like her skin just melted off. He was never so amazed at her comical wit as he was with that statement. She sure knew how to liven up a moment.

"Debbie, I know the business is about tits and ass, but let's try and be diplomatic about it, shall we?" Douglass laughed at his own humorous try at "diplomacy" and made googly eyes at Mechelle and Valerie simultaneously. They were standing outside of a factory building in downtown New Rochelle. The property was a catch, discovered by Greg, advertised as a loft. When the group went to see it and saw how convenient it was for the housing for the dancers, they almost wanted to move in themselves. Finished wood floors. High ceilings. Walls were white-painted brick. Large picture windows. Beams and rafters and storage spaces that were indicative of city living; but all of this was located smack-dab in suburbia.

"There they are." All eyes were directed towards the high end of Webster Avenue, the block where the bus rumbled down and pulled up to a slow stop. Valerie stepped out to welcome the group; the first image the girls would see . . . and recognize. Douglass wanted that. He wanted the institution of his operation to be an all-women affair. Valerie welcomed the bus full of women to New Rochelle and indicated what their first day might be like. But the bottom line was confusion.

"All weekend, Debbie, Mechelle and myself will be helping you all get settled. Things like beds, blankets, pillows and room assignments will be worked out. We'll go over responsibilities, meal schedules, hygiene and laundry. Now, I know that you're dying to get off of this bus, so please take your time, grab your things and let's get busy."

For the next few days, all of the dancers got settled, and they began to buddy up and become familiar with each other's names. Name tags were issued and required to be worn under the collarbone during orientation. A sort of probation period. The staff felt it was important for everyone to feel a sense of belonging and that it was more feasible when everyone addressed each other by name. Most everybody had unique names, like LaKeesha, Tamara, Joy, Blossom, DaShawn and Kareema. There was a set of Kellys and three Lisas. There was one other Valerie. Douglass teased his girl once by suggesting that he might get confused between the two. That was an opportunity for Valerie to push him into an unused storage space of the loft, and while he stood over her, she showed him why he would *absolutely* not mistake her for any other woman. Case closed.

For the days to follow, a fitness instructor, a beautician, a nutritionist, and a cook made the dancers feel pampered. Some clever dance moves were taught, and they were warned about the unspoken rules of adult entertainment. Also, each employee was reminded of the policies, and of their agreement with Black Beauty. If they violated the rules—any of them— they would be terminated from the program. Dancers were also reminded that there were 60 other girls back in Chicago that would fill their shoes in a heartbeat. So the opportunity held its impact.

Saturday, December 21st

"Nice to have you back . . . in New York, at least."

"Thanks, Chief . . . gettin' married, you know."

"Is *that* a fact?"

"A shapely, celebrity-type."

"Is *that* a fact? So you went all this time without a steady . . . without a wife, just to catch you a famous piece of ass? I could've given you a complimentary ticket to the Soul Train Awards and let you take a squad car down to Hunts Point for some head."

"No, Chief. She just *happens* to be in the spotlight, and well . . . I still like the part about the piece of ass and some head. I'm getting older, you know."

"And wiser, I see. Listen, I wouldn't bother calling you, but . . . there was another incident on Boston Post Road."

"Oh really?"

"I thought you might know about it, marrying a newscaster and all . . ."

"How do you know about the newscaster?"

"*Uhm* . . . well, a little birdie told me."

"Well, supersleuth, for your information, I stayed in South Beach for three weeks. She had to leave after a week. Continuity at the TV station is a big issue there. So I do **not** know the details." Chief filled him in and Wade hung up, somewhat disturbed that he had let the case get on without him. According to the Chief, the FBI was leaving the case alone. The mob was literally massacred. Their Pretty Girl business was burned to the ground. But there was still the question of Moet's murder. And apparently, that wasn't important enough for them. It wasn't embezzlement, or laundering or racketeering. She was just another body left dead in the Bronx. It wasn't like it was D.C., or Boston.

But the murder was important to Wade. Unfinished business, indeed. His commitment to Brenda liberated him. His 3 weeks in Florida eased his mind. And with all this death and tragedy having come to his own backyard of the Bronx, he felt re-ignited and was eager to complete his mission. Being back in his apartment with that ole familiar scent of the single life (or was that the dogs?), Wade was hungry again. Something had been bothering him all this time. Somehow, some way, the killer knew Moet; or at least, he knew *of* Moet. Wade realized that the killer was a *he* and that *he* was a white man with dark hair. *Or was it blond?* One witness said dark, one said blond. No matter. That wasn't as important as the "*who*" in the puzzle. Wade continued to stare at the composite from the police artist and also the one that Debbie described. He had all the prime players, dancers, staff, and lovers laid out on his bed. How was it that nobody else saw this guy, except for Ken and Debbie? Wade thought out the possibilities. Maybe the killer was a hired hit man. If that was the case, what was the motive and who would or who *could* pay for such a job? Was someone lying to Wade? Between Debbie and Ken, Ken was obviously able to afford that kind of service. But why would Ken do this . . . threaten his career. He had loads of money and fame.

Wade had to look beyond that, however. He watched too much *Columbo* to let that *I-have-money* myth slide by without further scrutiny. Wade made a mental note. National gun registry. Ballistics. Wade returned to the videotapes; going through each one, from start to finish. It was less exciting this time, and more detail stood out, since Wade focused this time.

Despite that focus, after two tapes, Wade fell asleep.

Monday, December 30th

Wade's apartment was set up like a command post. No squad room. No phone calls. No Feds. No nothing. He did manage to get out once or twice. There was a date with his fiancé and a visit to Black Beauty. When he stopped by only days ago, the club was almost complete. They were moving some pool tables in and checking the sound system. Wade was following up on Douglass's offer for head of security. But he didn't know what he was truly getting into until he actually stood inside the place. It was *huge* and left very little to the imagination. He gave some pointers to Dino about the electronic surveillance and warned Douglass about the safety of the dancers once they left the club. But ultimately, he didn't want to begin duty until after the new year. If nothing surfaced, at least he would have given it his best shot. As for now, he felt like he was racing the clock. Just two days until New Year's Day, and he was reviewing videos. Having seen them all twice, he recalled that there was one other tape. One that was still lodged in the video camera when he visited Moet's home a second time. When Wade realized that the tape would not fit in his tape player, he was forced to shoot over to the major electronics store to purchase an adapter that would enable him to see the video conventionally. He was anxious to return home to see the tape, and once he popped it in the player it was as if he was seated at a premiere—the way he felt when he saw any of Moet's tapes for the first time. On his large screen, the tape began with total darkness and then some fuzz. It was at its end. He rewound it until images lit up the screen. He even had to tilt his head to get a level view. Apparently, the videocamera was laying on its side, running non-stop, and Moet didn't know that it was recording. There was a man's voice. Then two different female voices.

". . . So please keep him company till I come out of the shower."

"Sure. So what's your name?"

"Bobby."

"How do you know Moet?"

"The club . . . and private parties."

"Oh . . . okay. That's cool."

"You work at the club? I haven't seen you."

"Uh-huh."

"You do parties, too?"

"Yeah . . . but you're Moet's client so . . ."

"I pay reeally good . . ."

"Like how 'reeally good?'"

"Maybe four hundred for a party."

" And you think that's worth my time? You're kiddin'."

"Okay . . . okay . . . eight hundred."

"Now you're talkin', big boy." Wade could only see from the couch on down, and the voices were coming over hollow and tin-canned. Apparently (and Wade couldn't see this either) the girl gave Bobby her number. *"My name is right there. Don't wear it out . . . and please put it away. Moet is not to know about this. Am I clear? Otherwise I'll yell rape during the private party . . . So don't fuck me—or I'll surely fuck you. Got it?"*

"Oh yeah—okay." Wade still had his head tilted and his poodles (who usually weren't the slightest bit interested in what was showing on the boob tube) were begining to mimick him. Bones already had a cramp in his neck from watching with Wade for the past few moments.

Wade wasn't sure about the accent and had to call Brenda for help.

"That's Caribbean, silly. The girl's probably from Barbados."

"Valerie."

"Who?"

"Never mind. Gotta go. Thanks, love. Bye."

Wade pushed the receiver and poked again at his residential phone. He needed to speak with Douglass directly.

"Yo."

"Gil?"

"No. Greg. He transferred the calls to me. He's big-time now, you know. Who's this?"

"Wade. I need to talk to him. Do you know where he is?"

"He's probably getting fitted for a tux. You know the whole New Year's Grand Opening." Greg was at the club.

"What about Valerie?" Wade ricocheted the follow-up question.

"The girls are probably with him. He's extremely busy with all . . ." Many voices were humming busily behind Greg.

"Listen to me, Greg. I have reason to believe that Valerie, and maybe Gil are in danger. It may be a long shot but then again I may be right."

"I can try to reach him. The house. The loft. The car. I'll try. But last I heard he was having a private thing. Ya know——he and his girls. He told me to look for him at the Grand Opening." Wade thanked Greg and took a deep breath once he hung up the receiver. *Damn, the party's tomorrow and I don't even have a tux*. Wade thought fast and eventually dialed Brenda again.

Douglass's Words

I was in Cos Cobb, heading back from a long night of fun at the Norwalk Motel in Connecticut. Our small family threw a mini-picnic on the floor in our room where we enjoyed watching Destiny crawl about. I, for one, was thrilled. But it was total glory to see Valerie and Debbie with as much pride in my child's movements as Mechelle and I. I could have frozen that image in time; and it meant so much more than any business venture, celebrity associations, or even all the adventures we've had in bed. And, trust me, we had some crazy-wild times.

But it was these moments that mattered the most. The promise that I see in my baby replaces everything. Destiny is the foundation of everything I've done. A living breathing reflection.

And just to think, there was a question of whether Destiny was even mine or not. I still get the chills when I think about what Mechelle went through. The shit she told me about . . . North Carolina. Had me trippin'; like, I wanted to take my squad down there and find those redneck fools. In my dreams I kept telling myself, *"In and out. That's all we gotta do. Get in there . . . shoot shit up, and jet."*

But I can't lie. Shit is so nice nowadays with the money, the sex, and the new club . . . then, all of a sudden I got like forty other women I'm responsible for? Nah . . . I can't fuck this up. I've come too far.

As we glided down I-95, back to New York to prepare for the big party, no more glory could be packed into my truck. It was party time. And on some ole *whatever* state of mind, we stopped over in Greenwich to do some last-minute shopping before I decided to open up communications once again with the outside world, resurfacing from my little seclusion in the next state over. The first person I called was Dino.

Douglass

"Wade called. He said something about you and Valerie being in great danger." Dino was rushing the conversation.

"So he's on the job already, huh? Does that mean I'll see him tonight?" Douglass remembered Wade's extended vacation.

"He said he'll be by with Brenda. He's been calling all day today asking for you . . . concerned about security tonight . . . trying to work this problem out with the metal detector . . ." Dino had a phone in one hand, a Coke in the other.

"Problem?" Douglass asked, lowering the music in the jeep.

"Gil, the walk-through isn't operating properly . . . the mercury that came with it—to maintain the balance and sensitivity—wasn't in the box, or misplaced or something. We're still here tryin' to get it working now. Wade suggested a wand . . ."

"No wands, Dino. I've got the *world* coming down tonight and I don't want to be disrespectin' people on our first night. I know you guys are gonna know the celebrities, but there's so many *more* important people coming that you *won't* know. But fuck it . . . *everyone* is important. Besides, this is invite only. So we should know . . . or we're *supposed* to know everyone who's coming."

"True."

"Who's there now?"

"Brent, Walter, David and Bruce . . . Greg's college buddies, Demetrius is here with me, keepin' things on lock; most of the dancers are here . . . I think there's one more group of girls on the way over from the loft."

"That's it?"

"Gil, it's only six. This is New Year's Eve . . . people generally come out from eight o'clock on. Oh . . . Foxy's people are here. They're back in the staff lounge. Adina's manager called . . . said they were running late, but we could count on them for showtime."

"You see that, Dino . . . we should have had another large act—somebody to keep these young performers in check. If they knew their spot on stage was being jeopardized, they'd get off that C.P. time."

"Gil, when do you guys expect to get here?"

"A couple hours . . ."

"Well, just do me a favor. Be careful. This is a big night, *your* big night. I want to see everything go smoothly."

"It's cool, Dino . . . just tell Wade that me and the girls are fine. And make sure those dancers blow up every one of those balloons; when the clock strikes twelve tonight I want to see it rain in gold, black and green."

"You got it."

What was Wade selling him? Douglass had witnessed danger first hand, and as far as *he* was concerned, he'd faced death . . . if not, he was damned close to it. What could possibly hurt him now? He was *untouchable!* Beauty at his fingertips, sex at his beck and call, money stacked as high as Jack's beanstalk. This wasn't hard to do. *Sure* . . . it was rough. But after rough comes fine, and after fine, it's polished. Life was good . . . and about to get better.

On the night of the party, it was Douglass's idea to dress down in black and gold tuxedos. Even the ladies. Walking into the club with all the faces, all the excitement and music welcoming him; it was something he lived for, as well as they were perks that came along with the territory. The dream that he had been sleeping with. So the black and gold would be appropriate. Black was their essence, their depth and their soulful confidence, while gold was the success, the substance and the prosperity of generations.

Janice was doing a wonderful job babysitting Destiny,

pampering her, answering her whims and sniffs. Burps and bottles and beckons. Janice was like a nanny—*no mon*— Jamaican with that rich accent (if you were privileged enough to hear it). She said little, minded her business, and was sharp as a needle when it came to attending needs. And she was also waiting at the townhouse, to get her responsibility back—her little bundle of joy—when the family returned from Connecticut. She had been left back to give them some privacy, and was filling the void by preparing the outfits, corsages and a light meal to hold them till the buffet at Black Beauty was within arm's reach.

Always appearing as though they'd been on a significant trip, the family of four trekked up the walkway, noticing the waiting limo at the curb, bags on their shoulders and in their hands, Destiny snug and bundled in Debbie's arms. They hurried inside as a sudden wind would, and took on various tasks, caught up in the excitement of the big night. Janice took Destiny in her arms and stepped immediately into her duties. Finally with the door shut, the indoor warmth secured them until an hour or so later, when they would emerge once again. Everything was proceeding so perfectly, just like the dream. But now, it wasn't just Douglass's dream, or Valerie's, or Debbie's or Mechelle's. Now, it was everyone's dream.

There was a bystander looking on. Waiting. Plotting. Anticipating the perfect opportunity to strike again. He was at a good distance from the townhouse, in his same ole worn-down Chevy. He was watching enough to be sick with jealousy . . . consumed by his own angry heart. He was building confidence enough to destroy and to turn one man's dream into his own demented triumph.

Mechelle's Words

My body feels like it's taken a roller coaster ride in the last few months. I don't feel sick or anything, but almost as if someone . . . maybe God, picked me up like I was a small toy, he wound me up as much as he could, and then put me back down to march around like an overexcited toy soldier . . . I'm starting to wonder if I can take all of this excitement, considering I just had a baby. I *know* it's like close to a year now . . . well, 8 months, two days and 16 hours, to be exact . . . but who's counting? It's just that everything is in hyper-speed. I've never had it like this . . . living in the lap of luxury, being around so much money, so much sex, and . . . well . . . other women? Two years ago, I would have never imagined all the changes I've gone through. I remember I wanted to kill myself after . . . after . . . *man*, I can't even go *there* anymore. Just thinking about it makes me shiver with hate. I'm so glad my sister was around 'cuz, I mean, I didn't even see a *doctor*! What the *hell* was *I* thinking?! Aaaahhh . . . exhale, Mechelle . . . That's right, girl. Shoop-shoop it, baby. *Maaaan* . . . if I didn't talk to myself (like the psych I longed for), Lord knows where I'd be right now. Probably nailed in the coffin or something. *Anyway* . . . I've got nothin' against Debbie and Valerie. I mean . . . I do *feel* something for them both. How can I help it with all the crazy shit we did together. I mean, we must know each other's bodies like we know our own. Thing is, I know they want children. I *know* that's what they were saying with their eyes, back in Connecticut. I may *play* stupid, but a girl did have some college—*hello*. I ain't no Buckwheat. I just know that this is a good thing. All of it. I don't feel empty anymore. I have love. I have Destiny. I have a *real* man, with *real* money and big dreams. And he's livin' this shit for *real*. I could have never dreamed this stuff up in 10 lifetimes. It's like, every time he says something it gets done. *Oh no, baby . . . I know you said you're not leavin' me; but me? I'm **definitely** not leaving you!*

"Hey, Valerie, don't think 'cause you sittin' next to the man means you the one gettin' dick tonight." *There I go . . . startin' some shit again. Hope she knows I'm kidding.*

"No," said Debbie, gettin' all in my business. "Actually, she's just sitting next to him because *she* knows that *I'm* getting it later and . . . I *do* appreciate you reminding her for me, Mechelle." Debbie was doing her very best to hide her smile, looking in a hand mirror, checking her makeup with the help of the light on the door panel of the limousine.

"I have news for all of you nymphos . . . after that session back in Norwalk, you know . . . the one with the triple-decker move we did? I can't see myself with a dime's worth of energy for any of you . . ." Douglass was truthful at best and sarcastic at least. He immediately put his ear and attention back into the cell phone, still trying to get a grip on the scene at the club, I guess. Meanwhile, the girls and I carried on about splitting that dime's worth of energy between us; and how we were gonna force-feed Douglass that new drink, Everglo—the one that's green and has ginseng and tequila in it. That'd get him up all night!

While we're drivin', Douglass put the speakerphone on so we could hear what was going on in the club. Demetrius spoke up and over the loud music behind him. Demetrius said, "O-h-h . . . I see. You guys are up to your shenanigans again. *Blasphemous*." It was clear that Douglass *wanted* Demetrius to overhear how we were carrying on in the limo; and maybe he was still intrigued about D's interactions with Heather the porn princess. He even expected the response and almost lip-synched Demetrius's response word for word. Douglass smiled at his own cleverness. What a life.

Mechelle

Demetrius's Words

I used one of the many telephones in the club to take Douglass's call; I immediately knew I needed to be somewhere quiet, with "*Hey, Mr. Deejay*" thumpin' all loud like it was; or at least too loud for *me* to hear much of anything. I wanted more silence and decided to head for the office.

"Doug, hold on. It's real loud in here, and I gotta work my way through this crowd." After I put the receiver on hold, I made my way up the stairway to the right side of the room.

"Gentlemen, please step in, away from the entrance if you would. We have to keep this area open." I had to play traffic cop up in there, with my arms extended wide, directing a small group of men away from the path immediately inside of the club's entrance. Maintaining order in a club and still managing to keep a courteous demeanor, I continued on, with my eyes acting as guides, navigating the way through the many personalities who were invited, sharing assurance and appreciation as I passed. In a way, as close as Doug and I are, this feels like my project, too. I may not get paid as much as he does, but I'm doin' good.

I trotted up the steps and followed the catwalk to the very rear of the club. There's a brilliant, gold-painted star on the DJ's door. *Bop . . . B-bop-bop* is the code that would tell Terry who it was.

We gotta get a buzz-in lock for this door, I told myself. But Terry opened it and gave me a nod as he stepped out of my way.

"Good job, Kid." I lightly tapped Kid Capri's shoulder, careful not to interrupt him as I passed. Then I used a key to unlock the back door to the executive office, a passageway that Douglass had Dino put in, in the event he'd wanna speak with the DJ in person. Huh . . . plus he plays a record or two himself sometimes. That old itch gettin' back at him I guess; like when he used to play at the old Fool's Paradise. And don't get me wrong, cuz this is all still real blasphemous to me. But I can't help thinkin' that *those were the days*.

Demetrius

Demetrius was headed for that same panoramic view of the club that was also available from the large and spacious office, complete with the luxuries and excess. A big desk with an English leather chair was situated in the corner, close to the passage to the DJ booth. There was a massive video surveillance system with 8 small monitors and a larger one for entertainment purposes. Aside of the surveillance and sandwiched between a rack of stereo equipment and a giant screen television was a visibly soft white couch. There was a conference table (oakwood with 12 seats positioned around it) nearby the 6-foot picture window offering a towering view of the entire establishment. And that's just about where Demetrius stood as he picked up the receiver from the telephone on the conference table. The glass was tinted so that Demetrius wouldn't even be noticed by the blanket of bodies down there. Heads were bobbing with the music, bartenders pouring endless drinks while dozens of attractive dancers lured audiences at various areas of the club. All of this, the fun and laughter, the conversations and the music was muted by the soundproof obscurity of the office.

"You must be in the office now," Douglass guessed.

"Yeah. Where are you?"

"About ten minutes from you."

"Well . . . this is it, Dee. The club is *packed*. People are everywhere, and there's still a long line outside."

"Is the outside orderly?"

"Pretty much. Dino is on the door with Danni. All the girls are here, fifteen-minute schedules for each stage just like you asked. It's all going smoothly. *And they look good, man!* The outfits are catchin' everyone's attention. That's all people are talking about. The outfits, the colors and the club. It's like they don't even recognize the dancers *themselves* . . . oh . . . they've been asking for you, too."

"Sounds good. Metal detection still not working?"

"No. Dino is using heavy discretion out front. If they aren't on the guest list, or they don't have an invitation they ain't gettin' in."

"Good. We'll get that thing fixed by tomorrow. Or the next day, anyway. What's up with Foxy and Adina?"

"They're all here. The show will be on time for ten. Wade's here too—with Brenda."

"Sounds like a good time is waiting for us."

"Let 'em in." Demetrius spoke into the mic on the lapel of his tux, making a decisin regarding the front door.

"Huh?"

"No, Doug . . . I was talkin' to Danni—told him to let Ken Stevens in . . ."

"Okay, see you in a few."

"No. Dee. Wait . . .

". . . Dee, this may sound silly, but I've lived in the same house with you—for a few years now—and we hardly get to talk . . ."

"So what's up?"

"Douglass, I'm looking down on one incredible sight right now. I'm not talking about the *girls*, I'm talking about the whole thing. Just to think, you dreamed this up in jail. You planned it out down to the letter and now . . . your manifesto has manifested itself. Blasphemous as it may be, it's givin' hundreds of people jobs, keepin' girls off the street . . . givin' some type of hope. You're makin' money and you're not even *here*! My point is that the good Lord has blessed you, friend, and I'm proud to be working with you. I'm proud . . . *real* proud to be your friend." Demetrius was scanning the crowd as he spoke aggressively.

"Thanks, Demetrius, I'll put that in the bank. Just tell me one thing, would you?"

"What's that?"

"Are you positively sure that you're not fuckin' Heather?"

Demetrius answered the jab sincerely and then hung up. He checked his watch and decided to be out front when Douglass arrived. He left the executive office and strolled through the manager's office until he was exposed to club music once again. He strolled down the catwalk and descended the steps to the opposite side of the club. He stopped a moment to take in one last look before he went to the entrance. Wade was standing by the bar with Brenda seated just next to him. She was wearing tinted shades that certainly protected her eyes from the laser lights, but probably more so to protect her identity. Demetrius smiled to himself, knowing that the attempt would attract more attention than not. *She's a little paranoid*, he thought. At that instant, Demetrius recognized Ken Stevens walking through the entrance. He had a shorter, white man with him. *Probably his agent*, he thought. Demetrius crossed the front of the venue, weaving through teams of suited men. He greeted Ken briefly and indicated for a waitress to accommodate him before stepping outside.

Greg's Words

Standing outside of the entrance, looking at a crowd of ass-hungry men, felt Godlike. And there I was holding the keys to Heaven's gate. Now, all of a sudden, everyone wanted to be my friend. The publicity more than paid off, but if I had let any more people in there, Black Beauty would've exploded. *Wow.*

What a splash. So much preparation with the balloons, the decorations . . . the singles. Yeah, singles. We had to literally buy *thousands* of singles, 'cause that's how the dancers get tipped. To top that off, Douglass wanted black and gold balloons held up near the ceiling by a net. It took us a daggone week to find that net; and even then, we bought it from a circus owner who had gone out of business. Finally, with all of the woman-power I could gather, we blew up the balloons and got them up in a net. Dino had to do some high-wire artist-type moves, but we got it done. Do you know that Douglass had us put like a thousand singles up there with those balloons?! Everybody seemed to be lookin' up at the ceiling all night, thinking "*Look at all that money.*" And then, I'll bet any amount of money they were thinking about paying their bills with that same money. I had to get a giant bucket, I had to make sure there was enough staff on hand, and of course beer and liquor companies were on the last-minute tip. We had cases of champagne stacked up to *here.* The front entrance was a whole 'notha thing. A riot! Those guys that were on the list tried to be fashionably late, and those who were *not* on the guest list (but who had every opportunity to call in advance) decided to show up anyway. The funniest thing I ever saw was that rapper-wannabe, Puff Daddy, show up with ten of his goons. They double-parked their vehicles and stepped up to the roped-off area as if they owned the joint. I didn't even bother to address the situation. Instead, when Dino looked over at me for the green light, I gave him a thumbs-down. To see Puffy turned down like a dope fiend in need of a hit made me feel like a hater. But I worked hard to put that event together; the red carpet outside, the big Hollywood search lights swinging through the sky. And out of the blue, sir-Hollyhood comes up without warning, basically disrespectin' *our* shit. Oh, well, this was one video that he wouldn't be showing his face in. Just when Hollyhood rolled out, Douglass arrived. He was in *style*, man. The *real* Hollywood tonight. It was at that precise second that I was never more proud to work for him. The money, the women, the status . . . I know there's more to life, but . . . can you blame a twenty-four-year-old? Maybe when I get older I can think deeper thoughts.

When Douglass got out of the limo and approached the entrance, with Valerie leading the way like a hood ornament, and Debbie and Mechelle on his arms, I almost wanted to bust with envy. My skin began itching from the goosebumps. They looked so sharp, all wearing tuxedoes and derbies. Once they walked in the door and settled in the VIP area upstairs, it seemed like nothing else mattered. To me, the bottom line was anybody who was in the club was supposed to be and anyone who wasn't, *fuck 'em*. I told Dino to hang a SOLD OUT sign and lock the door at 10PM.

Greg

Walter's Words

"Ken . . . buddy, how ya doin'?" I *meant* to catch Ken off guard, in the event he was thinking about ducking me.

"Detective? Is that . . . *hey*! Detective Wade! Funny seeing you here."

"Actually, Ken . . . as of tomorrow, I'm retired from the police department and I'll be working here at Gilmore's Black Beauty," Wade advertised. "Head of security."

"This is a jewel of a club," said Ken. "I've been to a lot of . . . huh?" It looked like Ken almost pissed himself when the woman next to me casually took off her glasses.

"You alright, Ken? Oh . . . I'm sorry. Brenda . . . Ken Stevens. Ken, this is my fiance, Brenda Feather. Have you two met?"

"Why of course, honey. I've interviewed him before . . . hi, Ken, how are you?" Brenda reached her hand out to shake Ken's like some subtle peace offering, but at the same time she gave him the once-over with her eyes. That's when I thought something funny was going on. Ken looked a little naked when she did that, and as if to avert her spell he introduced Max.

". . . I call him the Max-man. He's responsible for getting me all my big money deals."

"Tell me, Ken . . . what kinds of things do you buy with all of that money?" asked Brenda.

I couldn't believe Brenda asked that question. She hit the nail on the head. But I didn't share my thoughts with her. I didn't tell her that I had Ken as a main suspect. Perhaps it was coincidence . . . I don't know. He didn't seem fazed by the spontaneity of her being all nosy and stuff. She can be so crass sometimes. But I guess it comes with the package. Now that I had Ken's attention, I was sure to keep an eye on his every move. I found it pretty peculiar how the metal detector wasn't working and that he was here. I was thinking that his motive might be jealousy; that Moet told him about her altercation with Douglass. Ken may have taken his frustration out on her . . . then, maybe he just went killing people all over the place. There was one other thing . . . I checked the national firearms registry. Every state has to comply and every gun owner is listed. Ken purchased a piece less than 2 weeks before Moet was killed. I also had Star check ballistics to see what kind of gun the bullet came from. It was most likely a .45, which is what Ken had. I couldn't help thinking: *he was the one all along.*

So there were plenty of good reasons for me to go to the big New Year's bash at Gilmore's. Plus, Brenda wanted to see where I'd be working. I think she wanted to see what kind of girls she was up against, and how I would react in that type of environment. If she only knew. I also believe that she was intrigued to experience the topless environment for herself. She did say that she'd never stepped into such a place before. *I'm always looking for motives!* Ken, on the other hand, was all over the club when I expected him to hang tight in the VIP area. He must be freakier than I thought. His roaming was enough to keep my attention off that Adina chick. Talkin' about how *she's a freak in the morning, freak in the evening.* And that Foxy rapper gal. I was absolutely appalled with her talkin' about "*ain't no nigga*" . . . and her "*ill na na,*" as if we couldn't see that she was referring to her vagina. Those girls needed to have their mouths washed out. I may be gettin' too old for this stuff, but it seems to me that the young people are taking the next generation straight to hell. They're exploiting all we worked for, all we got beaten for, and all we got lynched for preserving. Now that we have most of our human rights, what do they do? They threaten scores of sacrifices and sufferings, with whimsical, four-minute songs. Whether it's singin', rappin' or the spoken word, these youngsters will go to any limit to record their voices and to fabricate a core of like-minded, weak-minded followers. I suppose that's freedom of speech for ya. Besides, Gilmore wouldn't be selling it, or hiring me, if men weren't buying it. So I guess *I'm* even caught up in this self-perpetuating, round-robin of unscrupulous behavior.

Walter Wade

Oh? *That's a new trick* . . . Wade was as close as could be to Brenda, maintaining her confidence, sharing her cranberry juice. Blowing his mind was a dancer who was holding onto the brass pole and stretching her bare leg and foot out over the bar. The customer just next to Wade had his tongue almost hanging out of his mouth, eyes red and singles flashing. A bartender followed the dancer's wishes, placing a champagne glass before the patron and subsequently handing the dancer a bottle of Alizé. With her toes hovering over the glass, inches away from the man's nose, the dancer reached down as far as she could with the bottle and began pouring the champagne against her calf and then her knee and then her thigh, until the bubbly trickled down her leg, enough to fill the glass. Wade couldn't help wondering if . . . and then the man answered Wade's question, drinking every drop of the champagne and savoring it with a glow in his puffy-red cheeks. Brenda kept her eye on the man to whom she pledged her love, closely monitoring his reactions. Wade knew he was being held under the microscope, so he took the opportunity to head for the men's room. By his leave, that same dancer bent over towards Brenda and asked for her autograph.

In the bathroom, looking at the mirror over the sink, Wade threw some cold water on his cheeks, wanting desperately to revive his complexion and thinking of how he'd have to witness these activities as a requirement of his new job. He didn't mind. What man wouldn't? He just didn't want Brenda to know he didn't mind.

Debbie's Words

I have to say that, next to our trip to see the Sultan, this party ranks pretty damned close. Isn't that Patrick what's-his-face, and that Oakley guy from the New York Knicks? And I know I've seen those dancers before, grinding in some BET videos. I may not have been born in New York, but I wasn't born yesterday, either. *This party is the bomb!* The lights are shootin' everywhere. There's so many dancers that I stopped counting, and everywhere I turn there's a television monitor facing me. I haven't been to too many other clubs, but I have been to a few . . . and those two jacuzzis looked a little extra to me. I mean, they definitely work. Guys are standin' all around them like the jacuzzis are actually stages. *Stages!* And more stages! There's like ten stages in here, with spotlights lighting up the dancers . . . and there's even more girls dancing on the cat-walks. I swear, if I didn't have a tuxedo on, stickin' by Douglass and all, *boy, I'd be out there turning it on right now.*

Debbie

"Did you say something, Debbie?"

"Valerie, I feel like I'm in a dream, and if I wake up I'll . . . I'll be dizzy. Is this shit in-cre-di-ble or what?"

"Or what! Are you diggin' Kid Capri? He's like . . . given me a fuckin' orgasm with this music. The whole club is an orgasm!"

"I believe it, I be-lieve it." Back and forth, the girls traded opinions, leaning into their conversation across the front of Douglass's chest. Meanwhile, he reclined on the couch in the VIP area. He was bubbling with joy inside, basking in the dream he'd originally put to paper . . . living the reality that he put in motion.

Adina and Foxy put on incredible shows. They were about as provocative as some of the topless dancers themselves, almost naked up there on the stage. Douglass was thinking that he might offer them a job if their music careers ever fell off. And they *would* fall off. *Eventually.*

At 15 minutes to twelve, the excitement took another step forward as the club full of pleasure fell deeper into anticipation. Demetrius was just behind Douglass, keeping an eye on everything. He held his middle finger to his earpiece, wanting to be clear about what he heard.

"Hold on, Danni . . ." Demetrius moved in close enough to whisper.

"Danni says Fumi's outside. He has six with him."

"Oh! Most *definitely!*! Let him in **now**. Tell Danni to have Dino escort them directly to VIP." Just then, Wade was approaching. He snatched a nearby chair, and in one swift motion, he sat it immediately facing the couch, blocking a part of Douglass's view.

"We've gotta talk."

"What's up, Wade?"

"Gil, I believe I'm right on the tail of . . . " Wade was even having trouble uttering . . . totally believing his speculations on the case. . . . "I think there's some trouble lurking. For you . . . and for you Valerie." Wade pivoted his gaze from Douglass to Valerie. He wanted them to see the sincerity in his eyes and that he meant business.

"Okay . . . I'm hearing you. But the thing is," Douglass took deep breath, "that I'm not surrendering to fear. Me and my people are being protected by the best in the business. Aren't you the best detective in New York? That's what they *tell* me. And look at Demetrius behind me." Douglass didn't even have to look behind him to know that his good friend was posting like one of those Salam-malakim-dudes that watched Farrakhan's back. "He's one of my closest friends. He lives with me for God sakes, Wade. I feel like I have my own exclusive guardian angel who doubles as a bona-fide ninja. And after Demetrius, there's Danni and then Dino. I've taken precautions because I realize that I'm an endangered species. What else can I do?" Wade was listening to Douglass, but his eyes easily wandered to a far corner of the VIP area. Ken Stevens stood tall over 2 dancers while his agent had eyes glued on the abundant breasts before him.

"I guess everything's okay then . . ." Wade looked up at Demetrius, indicating that he should keep an eye on Ken. Wade had already alerted Danni and Demetrius as to his suspicions and theories. Even they felt that he was far fetched, but agreed to keep it tight anyhow. Fumi and his men were approaching now. So, Wade respected their privacy and stepped out of the way, taking the chair with him. He looked down, almost 100 feet away, and saw that Brenda was talking with the bartender, expecting that the conversation was nothing but cordial. His eyes instantly captured a shot of the entire club, highlighted by a giant neon sign that hung high above. It was a loud orange:

GILMORE'S
BLACK BEAUTY

"May I speak with Valerie for a minute?" Wade started his question before he even turned to address it. Douglass sent a confident expression her way.

"Alright. But she's been a warm bookend next to me. Don't keep her for long." Douglass flashed a quick smile. Valerie got up while Douglass made some more room for Fumi to sit comfortably. They shook hands and both took a seat.

Ten, Nine, Eight, Seven . . .

"My friend . . . I expected nothing less from you." Fumi maintained his warm smile, while his eyes canvassed wide and far. His comrades were shaking hands with Demetrius, directing their focus on the events down below.

"I don't know who you're foolin', Fumi . . . I couldn't have done this without you . . ."

"That's not so, G'more. You had a plan, and yes, we met some time ago. But you stayed with your dream and you were relentless enough to perfect it. Maybe ninety percent of the human race doesn't take it that far. You probably did not know where you would get the money . . . but you *did* know that you would get it *somehow*. Every resource you've ever needed was with you all of the time; in jail, at home . . . here," Fumi stretched his palms out like a birds wings, "at Gilmore's Black Beauty. Your every resource that I speak of is right here." Fumi pointed to Douglass's forehead. It was a gesture that felt forceful, just a pointed finger; but somehow it had a grip on his soul.

"Listen, G'more . . . I want to stay and enjoy all of this with you, but I cannot. I must go . . ."

"So soon? Come on, Fumi . . . it's almost twelve . . . the New Year . . ."

"G'more. I have a trying situation to face at home . . ."

"At The Point?"

"No. At *my* home. Nigeria. There is a new President that has been voted into leadership. He is a lifelong friend. He was once a General in the Nigerian Army, and even one day saved my life . . . to make this short and sweet for you; a brother of mine has taken the post of General in the Army and there is talk of rebellion. There is a discussion of a coup. Our people have struggled long for democracy, like your people here have struggled and died for human rights. I must step forth and persuade my brother from his dissension. If I don't, the new President will crush him and there would be massive bloodshed in the interim. My family has called upon me and I have no choice but to heed to the call."

"What about the investment, the club . . . the . . ."

"G'more . . . I shall return. And even while I'm away, I shall always be with you. As well, I will keep you in my thoughts . . . Sefu?" Fumi called to one of his men. He handed a small box to Douglass. Douglass took little notice and passed the box to Debbie. He was more concerned that his friend had to leave. "Now I must go to catch my flight." Fumi stood up. Douglass had to shake out of the sudden shock, finally standing himself. They hugged as men do.

"G'more . . . remember something. If we stand tall it is because we stand on the backs of those who came before us."

Suddenly, there was a bell that sounded. The one minute bell. Douglass watched Fumi lead his men out of the club, leaving the New Year's celebration behind. Waitresses had been on standby all along with trays of freshly poured champagne. Foxy and Adina were nearby and Ken Stevens also grabbed a glass with 40 seconds left till midnight. Ken stepped closer to Douglass. Demetrius observed, unexpected.

"Congratulations! I saw your proposal. My agent came to

your Investor's Day presentation. Wish I could have invested."
Ken was feeding into the growing energy.

"Thanks. Maybe one day we can do something."

"Cheers!" Ken lifted his glass.

"Cheers!" Douglass lifted his to meet Ken's.

"THIRTY SECONDS TILL THE NEW YEAR!"

Douglass kissed Debbie, then Mechelle before he signaled
for Valerie; and then he kissed her. As Valerie left Wade's side,
Wade was reminded that Brenda was not with him. He noticed
that she was already climbing the steps towards the VIP area.
Douglass finished with Valerie and hugged his two performing
guests. A photographer's flash was bursting with blinding light
all the while.

"FIFTEEN SECONDS TILL THE NEW YEAR!"

Almost spilling the champagne, Douglass held his glass up
high.

"HIP-HIP—"

"HOORAAY!"

"HIP-HIP—"

"HOORAAAY!!"

"WHOSE HOUSE?"

"GILMORE'S HOUSE!"

"I SAID, **WHOSE HOUSE?**"

"GILMORE'S HOUSE!!!" And at ten seconds till midnight the crowd of 50 in the VIP room led their own count-
down, while the thousand-plus below roared simultaneously.
Wade captured the moment before it actually arrived, grabbing
Brenda.

"Happy New Year, darling."

"Happy New Year to you, lover." They embraced and drowned
each other in saliva.

"HAPPY NEW YEAR!!!" Douglass gave the thumbs-up to
Dino, who was standing on the catwalk with 4 buxom dancers
at his sides. They all held on to the rope which reached up
high where a latch controlled the net. They all tugged the rope
at the same time and the black and gold balloons, along with a
thousand one-dollar bills, were released. The mass of gold,
black, and green fell whiskfully towards the audience below.
The money fluttered back and forth indecisively, swaying and
cascading through the atmosphere, down-down-down, to-

wards reaching, erratic revelers. The release of the attraction above also served as a cue for the deejay to let the record play. Douglass was tired of *that ole lang syne* and played God, replacing the old dusty standard with Mary J. Blige's *Be Happy*. The bass was appropriate for the moment, and it seemed to perfectly kick-off an emotional high in the club. The dancers screamed in response. Some men danced around in circles and out of rhythm, others sang the words to the song in unison. All the while dancers on various stages either wiggled and gyrated to their heart's content, or they kissed and hugged one another wishing in the New Year. Kid Capri hadn't yet begun to put on his show.

> *"Let's take this back to the old school*
> *Let's take this back to Union Square!*
> *Let's take this back to the LQ*
> *And party like we just don't care!"*

Kid Capri's voice dominated the audience and the dancers went ballistic as he shuffled records, moods and the climate (as if by design) with his precise selections.

> *"The bridge is over*
> *The bridge is over*
> *Biddy bye-bye*
> *The bridge is over*
> *The bridge is over, hey hey . . ."*

After Kid Capri dropped the KRS-ONE classic, he stung everybody's emotions with "*The Big Beat*," and seconds later he switched to "*Roxanne*" with terrorizing sounds crashing through the club's powerful sound system. But the deejay didn't know how to stop, fusing old-school hip-hop with old school soul; droppin' big-beat-blastin' jams and mixing them with the latest hits.

Douglass was so high in the moment, receiving a king's procession of kisses and congratulations, that he lost all sense of time and space. This was his utopia and nothin' else mattered at all. Just when the nirvana seemed to lull, at 3AM, Douglass's pre-arranged private-dancer session blasted off.

Valerie was the one who picked the 5 hottest bodies in the legion for an exclusive hour in the VIP area. Half that exclusive crowd was celebrities from the worlds of basketball, baseball and tennis. *Big names.* There was a famed boxer, some hip hop artists and also some radio personalities. Brenda was long gone; took a cab home at about 2 in the morning. Ken Stevens and his agent had their own lil corner locked down, with dancers stepping in his mini-playing field one by one. Wade was still standing by, frustrated but also glad that his theory wasn't coming to life. Mechelle and Debbie simply remained fixtures at Douglass's side, pointing out various faces in the club.

Wade did get around to speaking with Valerie again once Brenda left.

Valerie's Words

I was shaken when Detective Wade asked me about Bobby. I didn't think anyone knew about him. Heck, I didn't even know what happened to him until Wade told me that he was murdered, and that someone sabotaged his jeep. I think our last party was the night before he died, too. I told Detective Wade what I knew, how I met him at Moet's house, and that I did some private parties for him. He was a kinky man too, wantin' to wear panties . . . *a woman's* panties and bra while I danced for him. It was pretty hilarious at first. I couldn't stop laughing. But I think it was the fourth time when being around him was starting to make me sick. And then the detective started asking me about David and more questions about Moet and myself. I felt like a criminal or something, the way he was drilling me. But he says that these people were involved with *me*, and that may be why they're dead now. And I made it clear that "*No, I did not fuck David or especially that queer Bobby.*" He also asked me about Ken Stevens, but I honestly never met him till New Years. I don't even *watch* baseball . . . *bor-ing!* Finally already, he showed me this police drawing. It looked a little like a customer . . . I think, or maybe someone I once knew. But nothing came to mind right away. So he wants me to call him if I can remember. *Oh brother!*

* * *

"Douglass, are you gonna open this?" I asked him and handed him this little box sitting on the couch. With all the action, he must have forgotten it.

"Oh . . . that's Fumi's gift. We'll open it at home."

"What's this . . . out of sight, out of mind? Come on, I get all wet when it comes to gifts," I said, more excited about the gift than he was.

"Thanks for that bit of helpful information. Alright . . . how come you're always tellin' me what to do . . . ? Stop tryin' to be my *mother!*" Douglass was being jovial. Valerie leaned in to reply in his ear.

"I can't be your mother, baby . . . but you can be my daddy *anytime.*" Douglass mashed Valerie's face (playfully) with his open palm and opened the gift. A question mark overcame his face, there was a set of keys and a phone number.

"O-kay. I guess I'm suppose to know what this is. Let me guess . . . it's the key to life!" Debbie was sitting in Douglass's lap now, Mechelle had just returned from tinkling and the private dancers were shaking up a storm for the dozens in the VIP area.

"Call the phone number, silly!"

"Are you in my business, woman?"

"No . . . but it's like—*duh* . . . common sense, dude." Debbie went valley girl on him.

"Demetrius, lemme have your cell phone." Demetrius handed him the slim digital wonder from his shirt pocket and Douglass dialed forthwith.

"Good morning." The voice alerted Douglass to check his watch. It was 3 AM.

"Oh, I'm sorry . . . this number was left with me . . ."

"I'm to inform you that the key you are holding is now your own, sir . . . Prince Fumi has left his house for you."

Douglass almost dropped the phone as his body stiffened. He thought he had heard what he heard, but he wasn't sure if he heard what he thought he heard.

The Point

"You comin'?" Ken wanted to pop Max upside the back of his head, but the twerp would probably sue him.

"Ken . . . just this one day, man. Can't I have some fun, huh? It's a holiday . . . *officially*, man!" Max was rocking back and forth on the outer soles of his feet, within a scent of the thongs wiggling in front of him. He was OD'ing on the dancers.

"Max, we've been invited to breakfast with Gilmore."

"You go . . . it's good publicity. I'm gettin' *laid* tonight. These girls ain't no fan club poultry, man . . . this that *good* chicken."

"Do me a favor, Max . . ." Ken slipped a folded 100 bill in Max's pocket. ". . . Take a cab home. You can't drive like this." Max squinted his face when he calculated Ken's insinuation. But Ken was gone now, so Max went right back to drooling.

"Max can't come, but I'm game," said Ken.

"Cool. My Jeep is out back . . . a black Navigator . . . pull up behind and follow us."

"You too? I'm driving a Navigator, too . . . black."

"Another Lincoln fan, huh? A man after my own heart. Okay, luxury-man. Meet us outside." Douglass also had a slight buzz goin' on, after 4 glasses of bubbly. The ladies were helpful, escorting him down the steps. The party on the main floor seemed as lively as ever . . . even with just 300 people left in the club. Longtime *Gilmore's* customers congratulated him as he passed by—all smiles. It was only when Ken and Douglass tossed those acknowledgments to one another that Wade and Demetrius realized Douglass had invited Ken to breakfast. And now, as Ken peeled off of the entourage, Douglass headed towards the back entrance.

Outside the club, the twilight hours were looming and a line of taxis were stretched from the entrance of Black Beauty into the next block. Drivers were standing outside of their vehicles soliciting every last partygoer to leave the complex. Across the street, that same dark Chevy was parked with the window opened. Moet's killer now sat wide awake with binoculars zeroed-in on the entrance, and on Ken, who was now emerging from within. During the past five hours, he couldn't help but to doze off. However, there were images on his mind that all climaxed to one big jolt that shook his body. It was as if he'd just woken while driving in 55 mile per hour traffic . . . a nightmare. Now, Ken was turning the corner at the right side of the club and crossing the street, over to where his truck was parked. Ken turned his alarm off and got in. He turned over the ignition, lowered his window and rolled the jeep closer to the rear of the club, across from a fleet of vehicles that were idle in the back lot. Ken let his seat back a little, reclined himself and rewound the images of the evening.

"Say . . . aren't you that baseball star, Steven something or other?" Ken was startled, but it was nothing that he hadn't experienced before.

"Sure . . . Ken Stevens."

"Can I have your autograph for my son, Bobby? He really loves you, and he's got your baseball cards on his mirror, too."

"O . . . okay . . ." Ken reached to his glove compartment where he kept his 5X7 photos.

"Say . . . it's kinda cold out here. Do you mind?" The stranger indicated the passenger seat and put on a shiver to dramatize.

"Why not. Come on around." Ken popped the passenger lock, feeling spirited with the holiday climate and all. While the man circled the vehicle, Ken got a closer look through his windshield. Baseball cap. Overcoat. Jeans. That's all he picked up, aside from the guy's vitality and that he was a white dude with dark hair spilling from under the hat. Ken shrugged it off. Nothing extraordinary about this—just another baseball fan; sort of. Meanwhile, the man jumped in and recited what he wanted written in the photo.

"To Billy . . .

"I thought you said Bobby?" Ken had just pulled the top off of his marker when he gave a second look at his passenger.

"Yeah . . . Bill, Bobby, Buddy. Same difference. Put on there, '*Thanks for your love and support . . . Ken Stevens.*'"

Ken shrugged off the incongruity and simply rushed to get it over with. *Comes with the territory*, he considered.

"Nice *jeep!* You guys must get these things free . . . like *what do they call 'em*, perks? Just like the sneakers and stuff . . ." Ken already had the photo extended, hoping the guy would *get 'n go*. "You baseball players get it all, don't you? Money . . . fame . . . pussy."

Now, Ken caught a bad vibe. Suddenly, the friendly father of a fan sounded like a demented wrestling fan. An altogether different situation.

"I wonder if you can sign something *else* for me . . ." That's when the man reached into his overcoat and pulled out a black-barreled .45-caliber pistol. He kept it in his lap with his free hand cradling it. "Now don't get excited, Mr. Baseball. I just need your assistance."

"Listen . . . if you're here to rob me, just take my . . ."

"Uh-uhh! Just don't move those hands there, buddy. Put 'em up on the wheel. Gowon."

"Please, just take my wallet and go. You want the jeep?"

"This ain't about no **jeep!** . . . Or your money. Just sit quiet . . . I wanna wait here with you and see what's in store. You celebs always have the key to the city. So, now I got the key to the man *with* the key."

It wasn't more than a few minutes later when a group spilled out of the back door of Black Beauty. There was Valerie, Debbie, Mechelle, Douglass, Demetrius and Wade. Douglass waved for Ken's acknowledgent from across the street.

"Wave back—go ahead." The gun wiggled as incentive, and Ken gave a quick wave and a blank expression. Douglass and friends piled into one of 5 identical trucks. "Looks like we're going for a little ride, aren't we."

"You're that guy that killed Moet. The one I saw that day at her house."

"You know, for a jock you're not as dumb as I thought you'd be. So now that you have all the answers . . . **DRIVE!** And **SHUT THE FUCK UP!**"

Ken's perspiration was showing now. He was shivering, and his heartbeat was thumping like a drumroll. The two jeeps made their way down the side streets and onto the main road until they reached the throughway. It was a short drive up I-95, to the exit close to The Point. Ken kept one car length behind the leader all the way to The Point. The security guard stopped the lead car and promptly let him pass after a call to the house. Ken had clearance as well. The stretch of road took the jeeps to the oval driveway in front of the home, a quicker arrival than Ken would have liked. Somehow, Ken saw this fool getting stupid and he had no reason why . . . except that he was a killer. There was no questioning his credentials. Demetrius pulled up to the right side of the driveway, just before the walk-through. Ken parked one car length behind him. All six disembarked from the truck.

"Tell 'em you'll be right in . . . reach out and tell 'em."

"Hey . . . go on. Give me a minute, I'll be right in." The stranger in Ken's truck hunched down, remaining out of sight, until he was certain that everyone was turned and heading into the home. And just before Ken could fully adjust his head back in the window of the jeep to face his captor, *whop!* The man thrust the barrel of his pistol into the back of Ken's skull. Ken didn't quite black out from the strike, so he hit him again. Out like a light. With a gash and some blood to go with it.

"W-o-o-o-ow . . . I can't believe this place."

"Are you serious? Fumi left this for you? For *us*?"

"It seems that way. Chuckuma just ran down a few particulars for me . . . but it looks like this is the gift of gifts." Even Wade was caught up in the atmosphere, giving special attention to the jazz legends that were exhibited along the stairway.

The ladies eventually broke off into their own direction, checking out the mostly stainless steel and tile kitchen with ultra-modern appliances. Douglass was guiding Demetrius through some of the finer luxuries of the 30-room home. Now, they were in the home theater while Chuckuma was upstairs preparing an early breakfast for 7. Wade found himself upstairs, looking down from one of the balconies. He could see out towards the front. Ken was not in his jeep and Wade sprung awkwardly back toward the staircase.

"Douglass. Douglass . . . *Demetrius!*" No answer. The house was so big and the two men were in the basement, next to a massive game room. Now, the ladies were out on a patio that was set off from the kitchen and dining room.

"Mechelle, do you believe this view?"

"I'm lovin' this. Look at the flowers, the shrubbery, the Long Island Sound. They must go out boating from that dock."

"They probably have a yacht, Debbie."

"They . . . *they??* Girls, this is *Gilmore's house!* I mean, for real, we keep saying *they,* and they is really *us!* We can have our *own* yacht trips. Big house parties with all of the girls . . ."

Gilmore's House

"You know, back in Chicago, they make a big deal about *Playboy,* Hugh Hefner and the Playboy Mansion . . . *but for real?* This house makes the Playboy mansion look like a doll house!"

The girls eventually headed back indoors.

With the patio door opened, Valerie saw Wade first.

"*Ladies!*" The girls almost jumped out of their skin, Wade was so abrupt, like the drill sergeant he never was.

"Where's Douglass? Demetrius?? Has anyone seen Ken?" Wade was hyper, eyes swinging all over the place. "I want you guys to stick by me. *I MEAN IT!*" Wade only startled them at first, but once he shouted, they all jumped in unison. At the same time they moved towards Wade, he looked past them where a figure suddenly rushed into the dining room through the open patio door. He had his arm extended and his .45 pointed—specifically at Wade.

"Don't try me, sir. I'm a very good shot. *Very* . . . good."

Debbie appealed, "Oh my *God.*"

Mechelle grabbed Wade for support and gasped.

Valerie simply stood there, amazed, with her mouth hollow and dry . . .

"*Richard?*"

"That's right, Valerie, it's me. I'm here to rescue you."

"Rescue *me*? What happened to *you*? What are you *doing* here? What—is—going—on?!" Wade could see Valerie's fear was dripping with her tears. At the same time, he had Mechelle in one arm and Debbie in his other. He saw that Richard was more focused on Valerie, even though his gun was pointed at Wade's head. Wade's body felt like an ironing board, with hot irons at his waist, at the small of his back, and on his calf. His firearms were calling him, only the ladies were a *big* problem right now.

"Oh . . . I gained a little weight . . . changed my hair some . . . almost overdosed . . . you know, the basic **GIRL LEAVES BOY SHIT!**"

The eyes in Richard's face were on the verge of rupturing as he released his rage. Wade had his arm away from Mechelle's shoulder now, reaching towards his back. He was moving them further away at the same time.

"You must have taken me for a fool, Valerie. You just thought you could use my love up for so long and just up and leave WITHOUT ANY EXPLANATION!"

Wade felt the need to act. He'd have to push the girls to the floor first, and then shoot. If he aimed and shot first, he might be jeopardizing a life. Better he took all the risk.

"But I'm over that now, Valerie . . . it's been a while . . . you know? I think I'm healed . . . now that I'm here with you. Here to rescue you. Uh-uh-uh . . . don't try it, mister." Richard wasn't standing in place anymore. He reached for Valerie, but she was apprehensive. He shuffled closer until she was standing next to him. He put his arm around her neck and pulled her closer. A rough kiss. And his palm grabbed her breasts through the tuxedo. Valerie looked over at Wade and the girls, unable to give an explanation, but knowing that this was her fault in some way.

"Remember those lips, honey . . . these hands? Remember how **I LOVED YOU!?**" His voice was fading up and down again. He was obviously angry. And his last shout was Wade's cue.

He pushed the girls away from him and as he raised his arm, Richard beat him at his draw, busting off two shots. One caught Wade's upper arm. Another to his chest. Wade fell to the floor and lay there, eyes wide with pain. Richard stepped over and picked up Wade's piece. Then he patted other areas of his body.

"I know you cops keep another one somewhere." Richard pulled the velcro strap from Wade's calf, releasing the 9 millimeter from his ankle, complete with holster. Feeling more confident, Richard ordered the girls to a corner of the dining room and placed his own pistol on a counter. He strapped the holster haphazardly around his shoulder, looking like an adolescent Jesse James imitator. Now he had two pieces, one in each hand, as he motioned for the girls to move into the hallway.

"Come on, we've got others to find."

"Douglass! That sounded like gunshots."

"Gunshots? Are you sure?"

"I know a friggin' gunshot when I hear one, Doug—and those were gunshots."

"We've gotta get up and see what's happening. The girls . . . Wade . . . Chuckuma."

"Easy, Doug. Let me lead. Please. Stay back." The two eased out of the game room, creeping like in a *Scooby Doo* cartoon.

"Keep steppin', ladies . . . I have a surprise for you." With Wade bleeding on the floor behind them, Richard prodded the girls along. "Let's find a bedroom."

"Valerie, what's going on? Who is this guy?"

"A crazy bastard, that's who."

"Yeah, well . . . you were *fucking* this crazy bastard?" The girls whispered amongst themselves. They now stood in the main foyer, a gallery that was central in the house.

"Now, girls, I know who's here in the house with you, so the deal is . . . they either come on out and I don't shoot anyone. And if they don't, you guys are going one at a time . . . beginning with . . . *you!*" He pointed a gun at Debbie, and she screamed.

"What's your name, you pretty, caramel treat!" Debbie answered with her hair tight in his grip and her head bent back until her eyes met his. "Well, let me ask you" Richard spoke in her ear at a low volume, ". . . you like fucking girls, don't you? I said, **don't** you?" He pulled her hair tighter. She squealed and answered with fear in her voice.

"Yes! Yes! Ye-e-esss!" she cried aloud.

"Good . . . good answer. I'd say we're doing pretty good, wouldn't you, Valerie?" Valerie had her arms crossed now, coming to remember that this arrogant, obnoxious bastard once controlled her every move when she lived with him.

"**WOULDN'T** you, Valerie?" Richard pressed the nose of one gun to Debbie's neck, with the other gun and a whole bunch of Debbie's hair squeezed in his grip. He whispered into Debbie's ear and she cringed and whined in response. Then he put his mouth over hers and kissed her apprehensive grimace.

"Now, that didn't hurt a bit, did it? Kissing a **MAN**. Now, Valerie, call your **FUCKIN'** friends, or she gets it **RIGHT** here—**RIGHT** now."

"That won't be necessary. You want me? You got me. Now . . . please let her go." Douglass was calm about it, emerging from the basement.

"Good . . . good. Now where's your friend? The big guy."

"I'm here." Demetrius stepped out of the stairwell from behind Douglass. The two didn't seem to have a plan, or a clue as to who this guy was. They just knew they were facing two loaded guns.

"There's no need to hurt . . ."

"Listen to me, big man. I do the talkin' here—*understand*?"

"What we're gonna do now is go upstairs. Ladies with me . . . guys, you stay behind us." Pistols pointed everywhere, Richard was stepping backwards up the steps, with the jazz legends behind him. The girls were somewhat of a shield for him, with Demetrius and Douglass both tempted to lunge and grab the gun.

"Don't you try and be a hero, now . . . you know, we've already got one lying on the floor in the kitchen . . . so, I don't need to show you a *resume*, do I?"

Upstairs, Richard pulled down a gold decorative tassel from some velvet curtains. He tossed it to Douglass.

"So we finally meet. The playboy himself. So how does it feel to have so many luxuries . . . so much money . . . so many women at your feet?" Douglass was speechless behind Demetrius as they continued following the man with the power. The man with the guns.

"I bet you didn't know about me, *did* you? You didn't know that *I* was fucking Valerie **FIRST**, did you? Well, for your information player, this one is **TAKEN**!"

"I am not taken," Valerie said with an attitude.

"You *are*! And shut up. This is *my* game. Do what you're told."

"I'm not doin' **SHIT**. And *don't* get me twisted with the girl you *used* to know . . ."

"But Valerie . . ."

"Don't '*But Valerie*' me, you sick, demented, obnoxious pig. We never had nothing then. We don't have nothing now, and we never will have nothing in the future. And . . . you wanna know *something else*? I'm pregnant now, you impotent bastard. So there!"

Everybody's face froze on account of *that* news flash.

Richard seemed to be disarmed by Valerie's demanding tone. And then she shocked everybody again when she walked back down the steps. Richard was standing at the top of the staircase, looking over the balcony. Mechelle and Debbie were behind him now, out of harm's way.

Someone Richard had overlooked; Chuckuma appeared out of nowhere. He was in the bathroom just inside of the gallery on the main floor. He darted across. Richard shook from his own hysteria and shot twice at the moving target. He missed. But Chuckuma was just a diversion.

"Put it down!" Wade was to the left, posted behind a life-sized statue of limestone. Wade's tux opened up and the vest he wore was loosened and visible. He hadn't been hurt bad. Richard went to him with both guns firing. Wade had been here before . . . nothing new. Meanwhile, Demetrius went to grab Valerie and they crouched down at the bottom of the staircase.

Then, from the right of the entry hall, a shot rang out. It hit Richard in the arm . . . spinning him in that direction. Then another shot hit him in the chest. And he fell back against the wall where a Billie Holiday portrait was positioned. Richard lifted his gun to shoot again.

It was the guy he swung on at Moet's house!

I knew I shoulda slugged that dude when I had the chance!

Richard was laughing all the while. Unfocused enough for Wade to take the chance and cap him in the leg. The first shot missed. The second *pop* hit, and Richard stumbled and rolled down the stairs until he hit the marble floor, head first. Blood began to seep from under him in a growing pool.

Douglass ran to get Debbie and Mechelle upstairs, while Demetrius rushed Valerie away from the lifeless body. Wade came out of hiding, standing over the body. He looked in Ken's direction. Ken, with his .45 down by his side, showing some remorse. Wade closed his eyes slow and thoughtfully, happy that Ken was around yet ashamed for his own misjudgments.

"I guess everything ain't always what it seems," said Wade.

"I tend to believe you," Ken replied. And he used his hand to brush off Wade's tuxedo as well as his own. They were standing in front of a walled mirror, both of them checking out one another's reflection.

"And just to think . . . you picked a murder suspect to be your best man."

"It was only for the season tickets, son . . . purely for the perks." The two laughed heartily as they took one last deep breath and one last look at their reflections. The groom and his best man, with all of their personal challenges, triumphs and imperfections.

"You ready to do this?"

"I'm de-finitely ready to do this."

They opened the dressing room door and stepped out through a foyer until they were recognized by the crowd outside. Demetrius cued Greg by their Secret Service-type communications, and Greg signaled the vocalist. The piano blended with the sound of seagulls flying overhead. The melody was as fluid and undeniable as the clear, spring sky over the calm and endless waters of the Long Island Sound.

And then Rachelle Ferrell's voice made it all seem valid; the wedding outdoors at The Point; Douglass, hosting and financing the wedding and the reception; and over 50 beautiful women standing like flowers around the yard where Brenda awaited her husband for life.

"Long as . . . I'm living . . .
I'm loving . . . loving You . . .
Long as . . . I'm dreaming . . .
I'm dreaming . . . dreaming of you
Long as . . . I'm singing . . .
I'm singing to you
Long as . . . I'm breathing . . .
I'm not leaving, leaving you."

Rachelle captured the hearts of every last soul who witnessed the groom walk down the lawn to meet with his bride. After the vows, the ring and the kiss, the vocalist took everyone to church with her jubilations of song. Douglass was positioned on an outdoor couch with a team of women standing behind him and a few sitting at each side. Photographers seemed to be popping flashes at him more so than at the rest of the wedding attendees. Brenda's co-anchor Ernie, Ken's agent, and a brigade of celebrities joined half the police force, filling the property to capacity.

There was dancing, networking and plenty of food during an afternoon-long reception.

"Do you think that will ever be us?"

"Now . . . this is so beautiful. All the white, the yellow . . . the dresses and flowers. Why would you wanna break up the mood?"

"Maybe we could have a wedding for four?" The girls all laughed through their joyful tears. They were the head bridesmaids for Brenda and this was all making them sick with happiness. Douglass was close enough to overhear the conversation. They did not detect his presence.

"To tell you the truth, girls . . . marriage isn't gonna make me happier than I am. I've got a beautiful little boy and he brings more joy to my face than I could ever imagine feeling in one day. Plus . . . I have Destiny," said Valerie. "I mean, I feel like she's my daughter, too. Look at her running around, so pretty like a princess."

And only now did Douglass feel like he was missing something. Like he should be reaching for some higher heights. Because, after all, what more was there for a man to do in life if already he had everything he'd ever dreamed of?